HAUNTING OF A WITCH

THE SAVANNAH COVEN SERIES

SUZA KATES

ICASM PRESS
SAVANNAH

Published by Icasm Publishing LLC
5710 Ogechee Rd. Suite 200 #278, Savannah, GA 31405
www.icasmpress.com

Library of Congress Cataloging-in-Publication Data

Kates, Suza
Haunting of a Witch / Suza Kates
    p. cm.

ISBN-13:978-0-9849030-5-4
ISBN-13:978-0-9849030-6-1 (ebook)
I. Title

Printed and bound in the United States of America

10 9 8 7 6 5 4 3 2 1

For my mother,
because she always believed

THE COVEN

Anna St. Germaine
Hair: Long, straight, sable brown
Eyes: Sapphire blue
Color: Sapphire blue
Cat: "Ivy" gray female with lime green eyes

Anna sees visions of past, present, and future. She is the coven's head witch and is a descendant of the three women who originally banished the demon Bastraal three centuries ago. Her ancestral home is on an island off the coast of Savannah, Georgia and now serves as coven central.

Claudia Grant
Hair: Straight, long, flaming red
Eyes: River green
Color: Coral
Cat: "Rowan Von Ashbi" coloring of an American Wirehair with yellow eyes

Claudia is a history professor who only needs to touch an object to sense its past and previous surroundings.

Hayden Wells
Hair: Brownish red "caramel"
Eyes: Golden brown
Color: Pale pink
Cat: "Daisy" black tortoiseshell with yellow eyes

Hayden is a medium from San Francisco who sees and talks to spirits/ghosts.

Kylie Worthington
Hair: Long, wavy golden-blonde
Eyes: Hazel
Color: Yellow
Cat: Sassafras "Sassy" also a long-haired blonde but with bright yellow eyes

Kylie is a college student who's "on a break" to do her part for the coven and is able to control electricity in any form.

Lucia Ruiz
Hair: Long, wavy deep brown
Eyes: Brown
Color: Red
Cat: "Iris" black Persian with blue eyes

Lucia was born to privileged wealth in Spain and has the ability to find anything that is lost. She is an adventurer, world-traveler, and renowned relic-hunter.

Paige Reilley
Hair: Shoulder-length, white-blonde with ragged bangs
Eyes: Turquoise blue
Color: Turquoise
Cat: Tiger Lily "Tiger" brown and gray with white chest and belly, bright green eyes

Recently discharged from the military, Paige is a soldier in every way with the added abilities of super-strength and speed.

Shauni Miller
Hair: Long, straight, black
Eyes: Emerald green
Color: Green
Cat: "Cuileann" black short-hair with green eyes

Shauni is a nature-loving biologist from Colorado and communicates with animals telepathically.

Viv Sakurai
Hair: Shoulder-length, black, angled bangs
Eyes: Gray
Color: Purple
Cat: Kikoku "Kiko" orange tabby with yellow-green eyes and a grumpy disposition.

Relocated from Chicago, Viv is a physicist searching for an explanation for her own special power of telekinesis.

Willyn Brousseau
Hair: Wavy, shoulder-length, light blonde
Eyes: Pale blue
Color: White/cream
Cat: "Snowball" pure white with golden eyes

Willyn is a nurse, a mother, and a Christian. Raised in Alabama, she uses her healing powers to help those in need. She came to Savannah with an additional package, her young son, Tadd.

1

The woman stumbled and fell on the rain-slick cobblestones, a distressed cry of pain jarring from her on impact. Tall, brick buildings hovered on each side of her, allowing a narrow view of the Savannah River at night.

Given the late hour and the dying storm, few people were out, especially here on the far end of River Street. All was quiet but for a faraway blow of a ship's horn. The alleys were dark and empty.

Just as the killer wanted.

The woman gave a quick, jerky glance over her shoulder as he moved closer. Her sable hair was damp and frizzy from the lingering humidity. Her eyes were huge brown coins, wide with fear.

She scrambled to her feet on the uneven street, black as onyx and shiny with moisture. The stones had lapped up the cleansing rains, and now, after her tumble, they tasted his victim's blood as well.

He smiled as she struggled to stand in her high heels and wondered why any female would wear such things on the hazardous downtown roads. But they did show off her lovely, long legs.

Sudden and raucous laughter shattered the silence. Smokers

braving the misty air on a balcony high above. The woman jolted, and when she thrust her face up and to the side, the killer saw she was about to scream.

With a squeeze he discharged the device in his hand. Twin lines shot through the air and struck her lower back as the Taser pulsed its disabling energy into her body. She spasmed with a long, keening moan and collapsed. Her knees went first, then her waist, as she folded into herself and crumpled. Shivers racked her form as she lay helpless.

Swift and agile, like the athlete he was, the killer moved to her slumped position on the ground and lifted her over his shoulder. He was tall and muscular, so her weight didn't faze him as he glided into the shadows.

Instead of heading straight to the river, he veered left, toward a tunnel behind the towering, brick structure. The building's bottom floor had previously housed a night club, but now the boarded-up space was empty. No prying ears or eyes.

The killer left the woman on the cement as he quickly disabled two of the light bulbs in the underpass then listened to ensure he was alone with his victim.

Only the low static of distant traffic floated to his straining ears, and he knew the time was right.

The woman was groaning now, one hand clenched in her brown tresses as if she was trying to force her mind to clear. Drawing a syringe from his pocket, the killer removed its plastic cap before jabbing the needle into her arm. The drug would keep her quiet and weak.

His intent was to take her life, but he didn't want her dead yet. First...there were things to be done.

He put the spent syringe back in his long, black coat—leather to leave no fibers—and removed a knife instead.

With one ripping slice, he cut through his victim's skirt. The soft, blue fabric slipped to the sides with a *whisp*. He performed the same action with her shirt, leaving her only in panties and bra.

The lacy lingerie was black, and he smiled. Perfect.

Leaving her bra intact, he flicked the tip of his blade through one side of her panties then positioned himself between her thighs. He fumbled with his own clothing but stopped long enough to withdraw a small vial of black ink from another pocket.

He was here for more than one purpose.

A hideous rush of power coursed through him as he reveled in what he planned to take for himself, not only now but in the future.

The poor, fragile woman beneath him didn't know the role she played. She couldn't fathom the sacrifice to come.

But he could, and the idea had him throbbing with need. With hands that shook, the killer opened the vial and dipped his small finger into the black liquid. Then he took a steadying breath before drawing a symbol on his prey's pale, flat stomach.

One side of his mouth lifted as he noticed the mark's similarity to a ribbon. Like the kind all of the so-called benevolent causes in America liked to claim with their own color. They put the cheery yet still sad ribbons on clothing, on their cars.

Stupid sheep. Let's see how they like what he had to say.

Once his chosen symbol was in place, the killer quickly put away the vial and gripped the woman's hips tighter. She whimpered and tried to flutter her eyes open in response to his cruel fingers digging into her flesh.

Holding his mouth near her ear, he said, "Now I'll have what I want." With a shudder of pleasure, he inhaled. Her brown curls still smelled like flowers, despite the dirty, wet ground she lay on.

Resisting the urge to bite her skin, the killer lifted his head in the murky darkness.

And thrust.

~

The problem with ghosts was how quietly they moved.

Though the intruding spirit hadn't spoken or made a sound, hadn't jostled any leaves on the surrounding plants, Hayden knew it was there just the same. Those who had not fully passed tended to give off a distinctive energy, kind of a sparkly tingle, like the static from laundry straight out of the dryer.

So while they might be able to get close, they could never truly sneak up on her. And most didn't try.

Hayden wasn't only a medium. She was a witch. One who'd recently participated in a ritual with some very old, very powerful dirt that had turned up the volume on her mystical powers. The burial ground soil, infused with both light and dark magic, had been discovered by her friend and sister witch, Viv.

All of the women in her coven had received a boost in strength from the ceremony, and Hayden was still harnessing the full extent of her ability.

She needed her yoga and the balance it provided more than ever.

Keeping her eyes closed, she tried to maintain focus. Most ghosts respected her boundaries and knew when to leave her alone.

They were usually very polite, as that only served their ultimate purpose. What they wanted might vary, but some part of them needed closure before they could move on to the next existence.

This ghost, however, was pushing the boundaries of etiquette. She was hovering, and the tingle had become quite invasive.

"Please move back, and I will be with you shortly," Hayden whispered. "After I'm finished." Sparing a quick glance for her visitor, she recognized the form as female before she faced forward again and expelled a long, slow breath.

Seated in the lotus position, legs crossed and hands resting on her knees, Hayden looked at her limp fingers. Her nails were painted a pearly golden-pink, much like the leading edge of the dawn that had just broken over the island and the surrounding seas.

She'd watched the rising sun through the solarium windows. February had slunk in without any warning of the actual cold it would bring with it, even to the warm climate of coastal Georgia.

So Hayden's morning yoga ritual had been relocated to the high-ceilinged greenhouse with its wealth of lush foliage and glass panes. With a good view of the outdoors, it was as close as she could get to nature.

The hardwood trees were bare, with gray and spindly branches reaching for the sky. The starkness of the surrounding forest was broken by the occasional fuzzy green of a pine tree. Birds still flitted from shrubs to the cold, dead grass, as if they didn't realize winter had come.

Light was creeping over the land now, but only a few of Hayden's housemates would be up and moving. The women of her coven all lived in the island mansion, though the estate was owned by Anna, their leader, and her brother, Quinn. The two of them were sleeping but would probably stir before too long.

The only ones who ever saw the dawn with Hayden were Paige, the soldier who still hit the day early and hard, even though she was no longer in the Army, and Viv, the physicist who needed fewer than six hours sleep to be at full charge.

Then Willyn would be up, her six-year-old son, Tadd, bouncing around the huge house and pulling his mother along with him.

Just as breakfast was beginning to scent the mansion, Claudia might stroll down the mahogany stairs with some sort of history book in hand, followed by Shauni and her boyfriend Michael.

That left the two members of the coven who still managed to sleep late, even with the threat of demons and various other black-magic creatures knocking at the door.

Lucia only rose early when out looking for the next long-lost relic, and Kylie-the-coed...well, she was only living up to her title.

Fully intending to get her yoga in, Hayden kept her spine straight and tall, allowing her life force to flow freely through her body. She breathed deeply again, letting the calm ride in with the oxygen her muscles would need for her routine.

Meditation always came first, to prepare her mind and spirit for the day's challenges. Yoga had been a central part of the lifestyle change she'd adapted years ago, a way to maintain serenity in a world that was anything but peaceful.

She breathed again and let her mind melt away to a safe, warm place. Tranquility was essential to her. She needed the quiet. The composure.

Hayden was the least demonstrative woman in her coven, and she knew her sisters believed her to be the quintessential mellow San Franciscan.

She'd heard that saying about still waters, but sometimes, that stillness only covered what raged beneath.

"Are you almost done?" The voice sounded too close to Hayden's ear, and she yelped in response.

A black and yellow blur flew from a nearby wooden bench. Startled by the sudden noise, Hayden's cat, Daisy, had jumped a foot before rushing deep into the plants. They rustled now as the feline ran for cover. Daisy was a sweet, little tortoiseshell, though a bit flighty and neurotic.

Poor thing probably wondered why her human was always talking to empty space.

Huffing out a breath that was far from peaceful, Hayden

raised her eyes to the ghost. The woman was mostly transparent, as spirits were wont to be, but her brown eyes were bright beneath a crinkled brow. She was bent down in an effort to meet Hayden's gaze, and evidently, to make sure she was being paid attention.

"I guess I am finished, since you're determined to interrupt." Hayden rolled out of her seated position and stood. "But for future notice, my mornings are sacred. It's the only time I take completely for myself. Business shutters are closed."

Daisy made a cooing sound from the greenery, as if she seconded the opinion.

"I'm sorry," the woman said. "I've been looking for you for so long, and it's an emergency."

Stretching her arms high above her head with palms pressed together, Hayden offered the ghost a small but sincere smile. "You'll get used to your new state of being, at least until it's time for you to move on."

The woman shook her head wildly, swinging brown hair back and forth. "It's not that. I know I'm…" She swallowed and Hayden wondered, as she often did, if the actions of the dead were necessary or simply force of habit. The ghost squared her shoulders. "I know I'm dead. That's not the problem."

Hayden let her hands slide down and studied the woman more intently. Her eyes were full of confusion, which was fairly normal for the newly dead, but they were also wide with fear. With panic. Something rarely seen in souls who had nothing but time to fill.

Unless they were re-living a scene from their previous life, as this spirit obviously wasn't. The woman spoke clearly and acted as if she knew who Hayden was, or rather *what* she was. She was apparently in the here and now.

"What day is it?" the woman asked, making Hayden pause to reassess.

"Tuesday."

The woman looked pained. "I knew it had taken me a while to find you, but three days?" She ran a hand through her hair, though her fingers slipped through the tresses like water. Motion was smoother for ghosts. No friction.

Hayden held out her hands to soothe her visitor. "Why don't we start with your name? Then you can tell me what you need."

The sun broke through at that moment to shine in Hayden's eyes. The rays lit up the spirit in front of her until only a shimmering outline was visible. Hayden shifted to the left, and the form reappeared.

"Ronnie," the woman said. "It's short for Veronica. Veronica Laine Miller. You'll need to know my full name. And more. For when you go to the police."

Ahh. Now pieces were clicking into place, and the ghost's sense...no...*Ronnie's* sense of urgency was more understandable. Her death had been recent, most likely three days ago, and had evidently come at the hands of another person.

"Ronnie," Hayden began in a gentle tone, "do you remember how you died?"

"Remember? Not only do I remember, but I go through it every night at the same time. I'm trapped in the most horrible moment of my life. I never thought death was supposed to be this way!" She hugged herself as her face crumpled with tears.

And Hayden felt like an uber-bitch for having made the ghost wait one single second. She pressed her eyes closed to hide her shame.

Then Ronnie's words hit. What she'd described was *not* what death was supposed to be like, at least not the ones Hayden dealt with. Most people who were gone but not-quite-gone-all-the-way were stuck for their own reasons, usually some sort of unfinished business or trauma they couldn't get past.

But she'd never heard of a ghost being stuck on replay.

In a smooth efficient voice meant to get Ronnie calmed down, Hayden asked, "What do you mean you've been looking for me?

Others have told me it's easy to find mediums. That we have a particular glow only spirits can see." She moved to take a seat on the bench, giving Ronnie plenty of room to pace.

Though they couldn't exactly bump into each other.

The spirit was still agitated, wringing her wispy hands as she walked... no, *floated* over the stone floor. "Yes, yes. I've seen them, but you're the one I need. They guided me to you."

An ice cube seemed to roll down Hayden's spine. "Who did?"

Ronnie threw up her hands. "I don't know. Voices. They want to help, and they sort of burrow inside my head. I don't know how to explain it, but they pushed me around in the fog until I found you." She covered her face with her hands. "I can't believe it's been three days. I'm so tired, and I don't know how long I can keep this up."

Tired? Hayden had never heard of a ghost getting tired. And where were these voices coming from?

Hayden pressed her hands harder against the bench. She didn't want to upset Ronnie any further by showing her own mounting distress. But whatever was happening with this spirit was way out of bounds.

Even in the world of the dead there were standards and customs. There were rules. And someone or something was seriously breaking them.

Staring straight into Ronnie's frightened eyes, Hayden asked, "You don't think you can keep what up?"

If ghosts could shiver, Ronnie did. And in a voice as hollow as a void, she said, "Hiding."

2

The house echoed with silence as Hayden eased down the wide staircase. Her bedroom was on the third floor, on the level overlooking the great room, but now the gathering place with multiple seating areas and a large-screened television was empty.

The rich aroma of coffee drifted to her nose and a fire crackled in the hearth, so she knew others were roaming about.

She would just have to find them and gather them up. There were very few secrets in the coven, since any new developments had the potential to affect them all.

Each of the women had come to Savannah to discover that their lifelong abilities weren't due to luck or genetics alone. The unusual *gifts* were simply side effects of their inherent witchiness.

Oh, and that it was their destiny to defeat an encroaching demon who wanted to take over the world. Just a slight detour in the lives they had each been leading before they'd been summoned.

So whether her visit from the ghost was a sign that her trial had come or not, Hayden needed to fill her friends in on what she planned to do.

Yes, she had a duty to her coven and the prophecy they'd

all inherited, but there were still others who relied on her. For whatever reason she'd been chosen to help lost spirits, and her latest visitor was in dire need.

First she strode toward the kitchen and peeked in. A fire blazed in the hearth here as well, under the old-fashioned oven that had been built long, long…long ago. The gray and brown stonework made the modern kitchen feel cozy and historic.

At the large island of granite, a lone figure sat reading a book. Willyn lifted her head and smiled, her blue eyes lifting at the edges with warmth. "Morning," she said. "Mrs. Attinger isn't feeling well today, so it's every witch for herself."

The island and its castle-style home weren't the only things passed down to Anna and Quinn from their parents. Mr. and Mrs. Attinger had looked after the St. Germaine home and its children for decades.

Hayden made a note to herself to check on Mrs. Attinger later in the day. She hated hearing the spry, older woman was ill, especially since she'd taken them all on as honorary daughters.

And as each of the women who'd passed their tests so far had also found love, a few honorary sons had been thrown in as a bonus.

Speaking of which. "Where is Dare?" Hayden asked, gliding over to the cabinet to retrieve a self-contained cup of tea. She popped it into the machine and hit the brew button after placing a white mug underneath the tiny silver spout.

Willyn brushed her golden hair back with both hands and held it in a makeshift ponytail as her eyes went dreamy. "He's taken Tadd out to explore and do, you know, male things."

Hayden's heart filled with warmth then released with a sigh. It was good to see her friend so happy. So content.

And it was a double blessing that Dare, Willyn's new husband, was also a wonderful father to little Tadd. A witch in the making. Savannah Coven Two-Point-O.

Taking her cup and blowing the steam away from the hot tea, Hayden did her best to appear calm and unconcerned. "How about the girls? Anyone else around?" She sipped, cringed at the minor scalding of tongue, and added, "I sort of need to talk to you guys."

Willyn's eyes popped into rounds. "Uh-oh. Did something happen?"

Hayden recognized the seemingly innocuous question for what it was. Her sister was really asking, *Is it your turn?* "Something's happened all right, but I'm not sure it has anything to do with the coven, or if it's just my work life hunting me down. Guess I can't even hide in a warded mansion." She tried for a smile but it felt flimsy.

"Claudia, Anna, and Viv are in the library," Willyn said. "And I think I heard Paige come in from her run." She stood and managed a real smile, soothing and healing, as was her way. "I'll go get her and we'll join you and the others. Do you want me to wake up the sleepyheads?"

"No, what I have to say doesn't require a full-on assembly. I just wanted to let you guys know what's going on." Hayden didn't elaborate.

And Willyn didn't push. Instead she walked backwards toward the door and twirled her finger around to indicate the expansive room. "I don't see any pink flowers, so that's a good sign."

"True," Hayden said with a sigh. Then she patted the amulet that rested on her skin, just above the V-neck of her ivory sweater. The center stone was pale pink and surrounded by a swirling pattern of silver, with eight smaller gems of various hues rimming the edges. Eight colors to represent her eight sisters.

And so far, only three of them had seen their colors all around the home in floral arrangements. The flowers were Mrs. Attinger's way of showing her support for whoever was facing their individual test. For the witch that had been chosen for a turn at the wheel and a chance to steer the prophecy in the right direction.

No pink flowers. Hayden wasn't sure how she felt about that.

It would almost be a relief to get on with her trial. And to be done with it. Each time one of them had her turn the stakes went up and the danger increased.

Now that she and the other women had been infused with residual power from three ancient witches and had been touched by the demon the three had destroyed, who knew how bad things were going to get?

Her flats made a soft, scuffing noise as she walked across the slate flooring toward the library.

She opened the massive door to find Claudia and Viv at separate desks with their noses buried in books. Anna was at the base of a rolling ladder, pointing up to a particular book she wanted Kylie to retrieve.

Hayden did a double-take. Yep. That was Kylie up on the ladder. "Hey," she said with a grin for the college girl. "What's our little ray of sunshine doing out of bed at..." she checked an imaginary watch, "well before noon?"

Kylie was about to respond, but Paige grumbled from the hallway and beat her to it. "What do you mean? I'm always up early."

Hayden choked on a laugh. Paige? Ray of sunshine? The humor was not lost.

"I'm here, so let's get the party started," the lean and mean soldier said as she dropped into a comfortably over-sized, leather chair. Her hair was still damp from her shower, but the ends were already drying to a white-blonde. Angel hair on a deadly woman. But one whose heart was in the right place.

Hayden glanced around. "Where's Shauni? I was hoping to tell as many of you as I could."

Anna clutched at her chest when Kylie jumped down to the

floor, but after a shake of her head at the younger woman, she said, "Shauni drove back with Michael to the mainland. His vet tech called in sick, so she's going to fill in."

"Perfect job for someone who can talk to animals," Kylie said. "I'm surprised she isn't working there full-time yet." She went over to Paige and squeezed in with her in the huge chair. Paige moved over and tried to look annoyed, but the lift of one side of her mouth gave her away.

Willyn walked in and perched on the side of the desk where Claudia sat and focused her attention on Hayden. "This is all of us. I didn't wake Lucia. She has morning sickness."

Anna spewed the coffee she'd just picked up to sip. "Waaa?"

Willyn laughed and waved both hands. "Sorry. Not that. She's got it's-too-early-in-the-morning sickness."

Anna shook a finger. "I think Dare's having an adverse effect on you."

Willyn simply wiggled her brows. "Something like that." Then she sat up tall and motioned to Hayden. "Okay. I'm paying attention now. Promise."

Claudia had her red hair in a bun, looking the part of history professor. She stretched and turned in her seat to face Hayden just as Viv stood and walked closer. The no-nonsense scientist got straight to the point. "Tell us." Her gray eyes flooded with worry.

Viv had been tasked with the most recent trial and had located the demon's burial ground. She'd also suffered from her contact with the monster's remains and knew exactly how bad his evil tasted.

Hayden rushed to assure her friends. "No worries. I don't think I've been called to trial, but I do have to take care of something. You guys just need to know."

When all faces grew serious and all eyes landed on her, she told them, "I've been visited by a spirit."

Kylie pulled her knees up and wrapped her arms around

them in the chair she shared with Paige. "Isn't that fairly normal? For you, I mean." Her hazel eyes lifted at the corners with a bit of a grin.

"Yes and no. Obviously the seeing ghosts part is routine, but the situation this particular woman is experiencing is very different. She needs my help, as most of them do, but she's also suffering, and I just can't put her off."

"Of course not," Anna said, her face softening. "How is she suffering?"

Edging farther into the room, Hayden meshed her hands together. "She says she's reliving her death every night. Her murder."

"Murder?" Claudia asked on a gasp.

"Yes. Apparently she was attacked a few nights ago and has been looking for me ever since. She said she wants me to help find her killer, so she can leave." Hayden shook her head. "It's all very odd. Almost nothing about her lingering is like the others I've dealt with."

Anna pursed her lips. "Her lingering?"

"It's my own term for what happens to the ones stuck between life and the afterlife. Somehow it feels friendlier than other words I've heard used, less frightening and less permanent." Hayden lifted her cup and tasted her tea, a much more comfortable level of warm now and sweetened with honey.

Claudia tapped her pen on the desk. "You said she was looking for you? How did she know to do that?"

"That's the other strange part. Voices have been communicating with her, somehow instilling her with information. They guided her to me and are also the ones who've made her believe she's still in danger."

"From what? Exorcism?" Paige made the offhand remark but immediately squinched her eyes together in regret. "Sorry. That didn't come out right." She caught Kylie's hand in a lightning-fast move when that one tried to swat Paige's thigh.

"So what's she afraid of, this ghost?"

"Ronnie," Hayden supplied. "She isn't sure, but knows she has to keep moving, changing locations." Hayden swallowed against a dry throat, despite the tea. "She's hiding from something, but even she's not sure who or what. She just kept saying that I had to help find her murderer, so she could be free."

Hayden shuddered as dread crawled up her neck. "I've never talked to a spirit who was so aware of reality, fully accepting the fact she's dead but still existing in fear. Most of those who suffer do so by being trapped in memories of their lives. It's as if Ronnie's trapped in her own horror movie, one that keeps being played over and over."

Hayden dropped a hand to her side. "So you see why I have to help her. Besides, things are still pretty quiet on the prophetic front."

"Huh?" Kylie asked, and the older women laughed. The sunny-blonde coed made a face before saying, "Oh. That must have been one of those older-person references you guys are always making."

Still in no mood for games, Viv stood with legs at shoulder-width and put her hands on her hips. "Are you sure this isn't the start of your trial?" Then the Asian woman glanced to Anna, their seer. "Any visions or nudges? You always seem to know when it's somebody's time."

Anna shook her head and shrugged. "Nothing."

Hayden caught Viv's worried gaze. "No magical hummingbirds, glowing skin, or electric books so far. I haven't seen anything out of the ordinary."

"But your ghost has," Paige said then added with a smile. "Ronnie has."

"Yes." Hayden had known her sisters would understand, but the support was always nice to have. "So you see why I need to get started. And if it is my challenge, so much the better.

At least I've got an established goal." She drained her tea and said, "So when the boat gets back, I'll be on my way to the mainland."

"What are you going to do?" Willyn asked.

With a sour look on her face, Hayden heaved a heavy breath. "One of my least favorite requirements of the job." She tossed back her caramel-colored hair. "I've got to go talk to the cops."

~

Joe Jr. found his parents in their favorite spot, the living room. Though technically the name on the deed said St. Germaine, the elegant, yellow home on the mainland belonged to his family. In all the ways that mattered.

In their usual positions, his mother and father sat at the far end of the room with tall, white bookshelves behind them. Claire sat in her armchair of beige with large, coral blooms for a burst of warmth. She was reading a book, and from the looks of it, history. His mother had a secret fetish for peculiar and offbeat segments of the past.

His father was currently absorbed in his Sudoku puzzles and was stretched out in his leather recliner. The one piece of décor Joe had insisted on picking had been that chair. A solid and serious green. No stripes, flowers, or even, as his father called them, curly-Qs of any sort.

Living up to a very American tradition, Joe held his recliner in high esteem. It was practically sacred.

Joe Jr. smiled as he studied the two people he loved most in the world. All was as it should be.

He hated to disrupt their well-deserved respite, especially with the subject he intended to bring up, but he could no longer put it off.

A fiery itch had begun growing in his thoughts some months ago, and for whatever reason, the feeling had finally erupted in a blaze, hot enough to scorch his unsettled mind. He'd only found relief after coming to a decision.

There was something he had to take care of. And deep in his gut, he knew the time was now.

"You two taking it easy?" he asked, gliding into the room with his hands resting easily in the pockets of his jeans.

Claire looked up. "That's the plan, though these rites of manhood in the Amazonian basin I'm reading about are trying to make my skin crawl." She folded the book and set it on the table between her and his father. "What's troubling you?" He never could get anything past his mother.

Joe also put aside his puzzle book to give his full attention to his son.

No backing out now.

Pulling up the matching foot rest, Joe Jr. positioned himself near Claire's chair and sat. He searched for the peace the room always inspired with its arched windows framing a view of the bay. Tropical plants in huge, exotic pots almost brushed the ceiling with their thick fronds, and the buttercream walls made him think of his mother's cooking.

But despite the familiar surroundings, Joe Jr. couldn't find the calm.

"I don't want to keep any secrets from you," he said, causing Claire's relaxed expression to firm into one of concern. His father raised his chair into a sitting position and leaned forward. Joe Jr. shifted and took a deep breath before continuing. "The night Jen was taken and killed has stayed with me, as it has all of us, but not for the obvious reason. I still feel for Nick and Viv, but that's not what I'm talking about."

His mother pressed her mouth into a tight line, and he was sure she knew what he was about to say. And she didn't like it. The windows rattled from a burst of cold winter wind rolling off the ocean. "I've been thinking about Regina," he said. "And Sylvia."

"You mean Sylvie," Claire corrected, her jaw tensing visibly.

His father reached over to place a hand on Claire's, providing both restraint and comfort. Joe was a man who usually knew what was needed, especially where his sweetheart was concerned. And right now the three of them all knew what Claire was thinking. Her baby boy was talking about trouble. Big black-hearted, trouble.

Mama was not happy.

"We have to do something," Joe Jr. said. "We have to try to help her." He sat up straighter. "At least, I do."

"No." Claire's voice was like an ice-encrusted whip. "The only thing you need to do is stay far away from that girl and her evil friends." She dropped her brown eyes to her hands where they clenched in her lap. "You let Anna and the girls worry about the Amara."

Then she lifted her eyes back to his and drilled a stare into her son. "And Sylvie is one of the Amara."

"She's also Regina's daughter," Joe Jr. said, unwilling to give up his stance. He'd known to expect a battle, but this was one argument he was going to win with his mother. Even though that occasion was a rare thing. "Regina was your best friend, Mama, and I know you loved her. You still do."

"Of course I do. She was a good woman and you're right, we were close, as close as any two women can be outside of sisterhood." Claire put her fingers to her temple and rubbed in a circle. "Her death put a hole in me, that's for sure, as I know it did her baby girl."

She dropped her hand then and scowled. "But we all suffer one way or another, and that's no excuse for turning to the things Sylvie has. She's made her choice. A foolish one. And I don't want you doing the same thing."

Joe Jr. tilted his head but held her gaze. "That's exactly what I'm trying to avoid. Something's in me, Mama, speaking to me. Nudging me into action."

When Claire turned away, he looked to his father. Joe gave his son an encouraging nod, slow and deliberate. Joe Jr. chose to push on, assured that with his father's support, his mother's would be close behind.

"Mama. You always taught me that doing nothing in the face of evil was as bad as performing the act yourself."

Claire whipped her head back around to face him. "I never wanted you to run into a fire to save the person who'd set it! Sylvie's turned to them time and again. She helped hurt some of the girls, your own friends, and would have done more if given the chance."

In a soft voice, Joe Jr. met her fury with cool, clear, compassion. "She's lost, Mama. That's all. She let her pain steer her, and that's her mistake, but how would Regina feel if she knew we stood by and did nothing?"

He took his mother's free hand and shook it. "Would you tell her we were too afraid to try at least once, now that we know her girl is in trouble?"

His father spoke up then, startling both Joe Jr. and Claire with the unwavering strength in his voice. "What would Regina have done if things were different? If Joe Jr. were caught up in bad dealings, you think she would just leave him to it?"

"Lord, no." Claire gave a tiny laugh though her eyes were still grim. "Regina had spunk. She would have snatched you up by your hair and beat some sense into you." Claire stifled a sob as it tried to pour from her chest, but Joe Jr. heard it anyway.

"I know you're worried, but I promise to be careful. I wanted to tell you and Dad, but honestly, I'm doing something either way. With or without your blessing."

Claire sat silent for a moment then sighed. "You feel that strongly about it." It wasn't a question.

Joe Jr. nodded. "I do. But I'd rather have your support."

His father patted Claire on the shoulder and stood. "Well, you've got mine." He started to walk away. "Anyone for a cup of Joe?" He smiled at his wife and son after making his favorite joke.

Wiping her eye and sniffling, Claire said, "Absolutely. And make mine Irish."

"Mama," Joe Jr. said with surprise.

"If I'm going to sign off on my boy running after trouble with a pretty face—and don't think I didn't know that girl would grow up gorgeous—then I'm going to have a cup of fortitude if I feel like it."

Joe Jr. scoffed and told himself he hadn't noticed how Sylvia looked, but his mouth twisted in annoyance when her brown-sugar eyes flashed in his mind. He cleared his throat. "Uh, dad, there's one other thing before you go."

Joe stopped midway across the room and turned.

"You know I've always been proud to have your name, but I was thinking, since you go by Joe…"

His father held up a hand. "Son, I've been waiting for this day, and I absolutely agree." He lifted dark brows. "You were the one who insisted on being called Joe Jr. when you were small. Just like my dad, you'd say." Joe laughed. "It's been confusing a time or two over the years, so I think using our full name would be a nice change."

Relief swelled inside of Joe Jr. He'd been afraid he would hurt his father's feelings, but he should have known better. His dad was always one step ahead of him. "Thanks." It was all he could muster around the huge frog in his throat.

His father tipped an imaginary hat. "Don't mention it." He winked and added, "Joseph."

Swiveling where he still sat, Joe Jr., now Joseph, looked to his mother for her opinion. She reached for him and captured his cheeks in her hands, just as she'd done for as long as he could remember. "Joseph," she whispered. "It's a fine name for a fine man. Just promise you won't forget," she kissed him on the forehead, "that you'll always be my baby."

3

Hayden clutched the front of her brown peacoat together as a damp, frigid breeze gushed down Ogelthorpe Avenue. Even the gigantic oaks spaced along the stretch of the median seemed to shiver, and Hayden was glad she'd brought some heavier clothing with her when she'd abruptly re-located to the South.

Of course, she would only need the garments for the four or five weeks that Savannah could actually be described as *cold*, but on this gray and dreary day, the jeans and coat served her well.

On the drive in, she'd noticed the yellow grasses of the marshlands and the wet, sticky fog that hovered among the sickly looking reeds. An odd and none too pleasant smell of seafood gone bad had wafted into the car, and she'd tried to dissuade herself from taking that as a bad sign.

Despite her gifts and her profession as a demon-fighting-witch, she wasn't particularly superstitious. She knew why her day was shrouded in trepidation, and it had nothing to do with the sorry weather or her ghostly visit from that morning. The source of her disquiet was her intended destination.

And it looked like she'd finally arrived.

With a tight ball of dread in her throat, she scanned up three stories of aged brick. Inside was one of the city's police departments, and she had it on good authority that homicide detectives worked here, in what was the oldest continually operative police headquarters in the nation. It was called The Barracks.

Lucky her.

In her experience, cops tended to come in two types, cookie cutter shapes with little to no variation. Hard-shelled and soft on the inside. Or hard-shelled...and even harder on the inside. The latter being the kind she tried to avoid, since they usually just blew her off straightaway or used what little time they spared her for hurling insults.

Nutcase. Quack. Grifter. Con. Wack-job. If there was a nasty description for a person who spoke of the paranormal, she'd been called it.

Dredging up the courage she relied on to get her through these types of visits, she inched forward and watched as a couple of broad-shouldered and loudly laughing men veered toward the building before entering through the glass door.

Hayden sighed. She hoped she got a good cookie cop today. All chewy and gooey on the inside. What a nice surprise that would be.

As she started toward the blue awning and cement steps, an all-too-familiar sight caught her eye. Was that an above-ground tomb? Yep. Just her luck. On the back side of the towering police station was a sprawling and ancient graveyard.

She wasn't all that surprised, really, since cemeteries and memorials could be found all over the city, often right in the middle of shopping districts or historic neighborhoods. It was kind of Savannah's thing.

Shrugging her coat up around her neck, she dismissed all her doubts and marched ahead. Ronnie needed her.

Hayden wouldn't let a little stinky fog and bruiser policemen scare her away. She'd been given a gift, and she would use it the best way she knew how.

She'd learned long ago that running from reality could be far more dangerous than simply embracing who or what you were.

And more reckless.

The hallway she entered was empty, but two men and a woman were standing in an open room to the left. Given the podium and lines of chairs, Hayden imagined this was a briefing room.

The woman lifted her brows in question, prompting Hayden to say, "I'm looking for homicide. I have information." Brief and direct was always the best way to be when it came to the police. The woman told her to stay straight until the elevator then take it to the third floor.

"Thanks," Hayden said, then followed the scratched gray and white tiles until she found the elevator. *Not too bad. So far.*

A brief journey up and the doors opened with a *ding!* Here the floor was covered by a steel-blue carpet, and the work area was open with multiple sets of desks grouped together in pairs. Partner set-ups.

Hayden immediately walked to the woman sitting near the front by herself. She wore a striking purple dress and high, high heels. Since no detectives would wear shoes like that, Hayden knew the woman was office personnel. "Excuse me. I need to speak with the detectives handling the Veronica Miller case. The woman found near River Street this week."

Apparently used to dealing with the odd happenings that always surrounded murder cases and homicide cops, the woman flashed a bright smile and pointed toward a long line of windows. "Detective Lonergan is right over there, sugar. He'll be happy to help you out."

"Oh...that was fast. Thanks." Hayden wasn't sure what to think of the congenial attitude. She knew the South was known for hospitality, but she'd never gotten in to see a San Francisco cop this easily.

The temperature inside the station seemed suddenly warmer, so she slipped out of her coat and draped it over her arm. As a makeshift shield, it would do, at least in a psychological capacity. She headed straight for the dark-haired man who was studying papers on his desk.

As she drew closer, he reached for a blue bowl and took some rainbow-colored pieces of candy and popped them in his mouth. Hayden swallowed to clear her throat before speaking. "Detective Lonergan?"

"Hmm?" he murmured, not looking up.

"You're working Veronica Miller's case, correct?" Either her clipped tone or the use of a murder victim's name got his attention, because he jerked his head up and stared at her. He gulped down the candy.

Then his mouth broke into a welcoming grin, but not an overly-enthusiastic one. For all he knew she could be a friend or family member inquiring about the progress on their loved-one's case. "I am, yes." His voice held a touch of accent, though Hayden couldn't say if it was Irish or Scottish. Maybe Welsh?

He said no more, so she took advantage of the silent invitation. "My name is Hayden Wells, and I need to speak with you about Ms. Miller's murder."

She cast her eyes around the open room as he continued to look at her, an odd expression on his face. "Is there somewhere more private, perhaps?"

As if jolted from a stupor, Detective Lonergan snapped his fingers and pointed at her. "Hayden Wells. You're not from California, are you?"

Uh-oh. Please, oh please, don't kick me out until you hear what I have to say.

Then, to Hayden's great surprise, he smiled even wider. "I can't believe it. You helped find those kids that time in Los Gatos, right?"

Hayden nodded, clutching her coat and holding her breath.

"I'll be damned." He slapped his hand on the open file and stood, reaching for her hand to shake. "I had just made Detective then and was assigned to a smaller investigation, but I remember you, or your name at least." He shook his head slowly and gave her a lop-sided grin. "You sure shook those boys up."

"And you took them straight to that underground room." His smile faded as his face grew serious. "You saved the lives of those children and taught a lot of cops a lesson in the process. One I never forgot."

He gathered up the papers and closed them into the file folder before grabbing a legal pad and indicating with a jerk of his head that she follow him down the hall. "So if you're here to offer help, I'm going to listen."

As the last bubble of worry burst in her chest to spread sweet relief, Hayden trailed after him. She couldn't believe her luck.

Not only had she slipped right in, but she'd found a cop who knew her, what she did, and was glad of it. He was open-minded, and if the smile was any indication, he was a nice guy.

Perfect.

And there was no denying the other thoughts running through her mind like a light-up marquee. She and the women in her coven had all come to accept the fact that romance tended to be a part of the fatalistic mix they were caught up in.

Well, most of them accepted it, but Paige was still holding out. She claimed there was no way she was running off that cliff.

Shauni, Willyn, and Viv hadn't appreciated it when the coven's warrior had added, "Like a bunch of damn lemmings," but they'd squabbled it out like friends do. Like sisters do.

Then they'd all made brownies.

Hayden smiled a secret smile as Detective Lonergan held a door open for her and joined her at the table inside the large conference room. He had the most gorgeous eyes, sort of a grayish-green. Light in color. Unique. And they were really set off by his dark, brown hair. He wore it short enough for the job but long enough to reveal a hint of curl. Just enough to give him a rakish look.

All in all, the man was a heartthrob, but not the chiseled and fine-boned, model type. His features were strong, reminding her of a Scottish warlord who'd gone a few rounds.

Wide shoulders on a fighter's physique completed the fantasy. And that cleft in his chin? Hayden blew slowly through her lips. Too sexy.

If it turned out that this was the start of her trial and Detective Lonergan was her meant-to-be? Then all she could say was—Yay, fate!

"Do you mind if I record this?" he asked, jarring her from her daydreams.

Hayden flushed with guilt, recalling the reason for her visit. How could she be noticing a man at a time like this? "No. Please go ahead."

She noticed now that he'd brought her to a very nice room. Maybe there weren't any smaller spaces available, but she had the suspicion he was trying hard to treat her like a valued guest.

If he did remember what her reception had been like in Los Gatos, then he was determined not to repeat it. The long, glossy table had a crystal bowl in the center with faux magnolias and green glass beads for color. A tray sat between them with two bottles of the best bottled water, chilled, and glasses for serving.

Detective Lonergan gestured to the drinks, but Hayden shook her head. He then pressed a button and stated the date, time, and both of their names. Trying to ignore the recording device, Hayden began to relay what she knew.

"I was visited by the spirit of Veronica Miller this morning, but she likes to be called Ronnie, so I'll do so from here on."

Hayden knew little details like that would slowly ingratiate themselves into the minds of those who were skeptical. It was a trick she'd harnessed over the years, particularly helpful when she needed to convince the doubters.

And there were always doubters.

"She asked me to help find the man who raped and murdered her Saturday night, so I've come to share what little information she was able to tell me." She stopped when it looked like Lonergan wanted to ask a question, but he waved for her to continue.

"She can't really describe him, because he was wearing a dark coat with a hood pulled up over his head." Hayden chose to leave out the part about the killer's glowing eyes, as Ronnie had described. She knew a report from a ghost was enough for most people to swallow. "But she wanted me to tell you she'd just come down from Bay Street and that she vaguely remembers being dragged into a tunnel behind an abandoned building. In case some sort of evidence was left behind there."

Hayden winced. "Ronnie didn't know whether or not her... body had been moved. After."

Slowly and after a great heave of breath, the detective said, "No. That sounds like where she was discovered." He narrowed his eyes with speculation. "Where had she been and where was she going? She lived alone and has no family nearby, so we're still trying to paint the whole picture."

"She'd just come from her apartment downtown and was headed to River Street to meet some friends at a restaurant." Hayden gave him the name of the place and he wrote it down on his pad.

Hayden hadn't realized her fingers were clenched white around the edges of her chair until she relaxed, and the blood flow tingled back into them.

She had to ask for a favor in return and hoped the detective would be willing to share. Quid pro quo. That is, if he felt

Hayden had given him anything useful.

Deciding she could use that water after all, she reached for a bottle and poured some into the short glass. The cool wetness felt good in her palm.

After a drink, she said, "Detective Lonergan, I need to ask you something as well."

"I'll answer if I'm able," he told her. "And please, call me Cole."

Cole Lonergan. It had a nice ring.

Focus. Hayden gave herself an internal slap. "The murderer painted something on Ronnie's body." She could tell she'd hit a nerve when his face tightened. He was trying not to show any response, but Hayden had caught just enough. "It's important I know what it was. It could help."

The detective maintained a stony expression before finally lifting one brow. "Help how?"

Time to lay all her cards out and see if her playing partner stayed in the game or leaped cursing from the table. "I'm a medium, as you know, and I'm grateful you accept that." She took another sip of cold, quenching water. "I've recently discovered that there are even more fantastic things in the world, and I believe there's more to what this man does to his victims than is apparent at first glance."

"How so?" he asked, still giving her no clue about what he was thinking.

"Ronnie says she can't move on because of this man and what he did to her. She says we have to find him before she can be released. That she feels *tethered* to this plane of existence."

Hayden held Detective Lonergan's gaze. "If I knew what he'd painted on her, it might tell me more about what was done to her."

"Done to her..." He brought both brows down abruptly. "We're not talking about something physical here are we?"

Hayden shook her head and waited.

"I hope I don't regret this," he grumbled. "Because as much as I trust in what you can do, there are others who won't. And some of those others outrank me."

He scribbled something onto a corner of the yellow legal pad then ripped it off to hand to her. "Swallow that when you're done," he said. And Hayden wasn't sure he was joking.

She studied the figure he'd drawn. It looked like two diamonds strung together but with half of one cut away. She turned it and looked from the side angle. Now it resembled a "Support Our Troops" ribbon. That was the best way she could think to describe it, only it wasn't yellow, of course, and had nothing written on it.

She glanced up to find his scrutinizing stare on the paper. "I really appreciate this, Detective, I mean...Cole," she said with a small smile. "I promise to help in any way I can."

His light eyes softened at the edges as he smiled back.

The door slammed open then and Hayden jumped in her seat. She jerked her head to see who had burst in on them so rudely.

A tall, angry-looking man stood glowering at them. Then his piercing blue eyes landed on the piece of paper in front of her and the symbol Cole had drawn.

Damn. She hadn't been fast enough to hide it.

He had deep blonde hair, cut with military precision but slightly longer on top, and his stance clearly conveyed annoyance. His jaw clenched tight as he looked back and forth between her and Cole.

He stepped in and closed the door soundly before barking out, "What the hell's going on?"

Despite his brutish behavior and obvious displeasure, all Hayden really noticed were those eyes. Like blue flames.

And even with the gravity of the situation, the fact she was here to help catch a killer, and the unfortunate reality that she and Cole were good and busted, only one thing flitted into her befuddled mind.

Blessed Buddha. It's Bachelor Number Two.

4

As soon as she let herself come to her senses, Hayden realized just how upset this unannounced intruder was. His voice seemed to thunder right through her bones, even though he wasn't speaking that loudly. "You want to tell me who this is and why she's holding a piece of confidential information?" he asked Cole.

Glancing across the table, she saw the detective staring back at the man. Cole appeared to be calm and unruffled. "Of course I will, but since you just got back, I haven't really had a chance to fill you in, now have I?"

Crossing his arms over a chest that made his white button down look far too appealing, the stranger remained standing and glared at Cole. "I'm here now. So fill me in."

Sighing as if dealing with a petulant child, Cole held his hand out, palm up, and gestured to Hayden then the stranger. "Ms. Hayden Wells, this is my bad-mannered partner, Detective Roch." He pronounced it like *rock*.

Then Cole held Hayden's stare for a moment as if telling her to buckle up. This was going be a bumpy ride.

He cleared his throat and told Detective Roch, "Ms. Wells has brought us some information on the Miller case."

"Then why didn't you call me? You knew I was in the

building." Finally Detective Roch shifted his heated blue eyes to her, and she would swear she felt the floor tilt beneath her. "What sort of information?" he asked.

Hayden opened her mouth, but Cole spoke quickly, cutting her off. "I've worked with Ms. Wells before, and I can vouch for her credibility."

Holding out his hand, Detective Roch stopped his partner from saying anything more. Then he ran a hand through his tawny hair and groaned. "Lonergan..."

"Just hear me out. I know how you feel about mediums."

"I've heard enough," Detective Roch said before snatching the yellow scrap of paper from Hayden's hand. "I can't believe you gave a publicity-seeking con-artist a crucial piece of evidence. What if she goes to the media and gives away what may very well be part of the signature? Every freak in the county will start using this symbol."

Fury bubbled in Hayden's chest. She'd been insulted before, sure, but never so thoroughly or so quickly. She started to speak, but Cole stood abruptly and beat her to it again. His eyes were flashing now, too, and his tone was just as angry as Detective Roch's.

If she weren't so ticked off, she would enjoy the two admirable male specimens before her. Two rams getting ready to clash.

And these guys were partners?

"If you'd cool your head for a minute, I could tell you she already knew our victim had something painted on her skin. Maybe I shouldn't have told her exactly what the symbol was, but I trust her and believe she can help."

Cole put his hands on his hips and blew out a harsh breath. "Now. Since I've already spilled the beans, according to you, do you want to hear what she knows that we don't, or are you going to just keep growling at us?"

"Fine." Throwing out both arms, Detective Roch moved to lean against the wall, still clearly distancing himself from

Hayden and her *con-artist* self. "Dazzle me."

Hayden decided she'd didn't care much for this guy. Round one definitely went to Detective Cole Lonergan. She preferred nice guys. That much she was sure of.

"She's provided our victim's whereabouts before the murder, what our killer was wearing, and where the victim was headed when she was attacked." Cole said his piece then sat down.

"Supposedly," Detective Roch said. "I assume this is all second-hand knowledge, right?" He raised skeptical brows at Hayden. "Details from a ghost? Hardly concrete."

"Her name is Ronnie," Hayden ground out. She was stunned by how hard she was clenching her teeth together. Forcing herself to take in some deep, cleansing air, she relaxed the muscles in her neck and repeated. "Her name is Ronnie."

"Sure. Great." He looked to Cole again. "Is that all? Can we get back to doing some real police work?" He lifted a shoulder. "No offense to the queen of hoo-ha."

Hayden felt her eyes go wide and a tickle of what felt suspiciously like laughter form in the bottom of her belly. "I'm sorry. The queen of what?"

Detective Roch waved a dismissive hand. "Hoo-hoo. Hoo-ha. Whatever you want to call it."

A line from one of Hayden's favorite movies popped into her head, and before she could stop herself, she said in an accent. "I do not think it means what you think it means."

Across from her, Cole burst out laughing.

Detective Roch just glared at the two of them as if they'd lost their minds.

Laughing now herself, Hayden told him, "I think you meant to say woo-woo. And while that's still a derogatory term, I'd much rather be the queen of woo-woo..." she clutched a hand to her stomach as it began to ache, " than of..."

"Hoo-ha," Cole finished for her as they both hooted until tears came to Hayden's eyes. Maybe it was all the tension in the room, but irritable Detective Roch and his misuse of terms was the funniest thing she'd heard in days.

After she and Cole regained their composure, Detective Roch looked coolly at them and asked, "Finished?"

"Yes," Hayden said, sipping her water for good measure.

"Hayden," Cole said, bringing her gaze to his. There was a remnant of a smile left on his face, but she could tell he had returned to duty. "I'd like you to come with me to the crime scene. Maybe it will jar something."

"What?" Detective Roch pushed off the wall. "Jar something for the ghost? What's going on, Lonergan? You're talking crazy."

"Just give her a chance," Cole told his partner in an even and logical tone. "If she doesn't come up with something, we'll reassess."

Detective Roch narrowed his eyes and poked a hard finger at Cole. "One chance. And only because the scene's already been cleared anyway. And if she's," he jerked his head at Hayden but didn't look at her, "going to the crime scene," he crossed his arms back over his chest, "you can bet your ass I'm going, too."

~

The sun was pushing its way through the clouds by the time the three of them rolled up to the vacant brick building. It was located on the far end of River Street and saw little traffic, auto or pedestrian.

Trevor was still pissed and slammed the door of the unmarked car to show it. The killer had probably taken the unpopularity of the area into account, choosing the spot for its desolation.

As Trevor followed his naïve partner and the woman Cole had invited into their investigation, he decided he'd keep his mouth shut and hope she tripped over her own fabrications.

How she knew about the painting on the vic's body was a

question he wanted an answer to. As far as he was concerned, Ms. Hayden Wells was as suspect to him as she was welcomed by his partner.

As they veered to the back of the building toward the tunnel, Trevor noticed the large green dumpster was still there to receive trash from the building that was being gutted. The unmistakable rankness of rot assailed him as they passed, and once again he thought of the woman who'd been brutally slain in this dark and lonely place.

He hoped she hadn't smelled that stink in her final moments. There were other horrible things, he knew too well, but for some reason the presence of garbage was further insult.

No one should have to die the way she had.

Veronica Laine Miller. He knew her name and would probably never forget it. No matter what the medium with the weird hair color thought. He knew the victim's friends had called her Ronnie, and damn that intrusive woman for acting as if she had to *enlighten* him of that fact.

He might use the words victim or vic when he was working the case, but he knew her name.

He knew all of their names.

"I'm sorry you had to come, but I'm glad you knew we needed you," the medium suddenly said to the back side of the building. Nothing was there, but he had to believe she knew that. *Great. The freak show's already started.*

Hayden Wells. Sure didn't sound like the name of a fraud, but then again, sweetness and supposed compassion were what sold the tickets.

Well, she could flash those big, golden eyes at him all she wanted. He wasn't buying.

He put up his mental and physical barriers, crossing his arms over his chest and standing by. Waiting. Watching.

Hayden nodded before turning to speak to Cole and then to him, as if he cared. She pointed into the shadows. "Ronnie says we're on the wrong end of the tunnel. She wants us to go all the way down to where it started."

Leisurely Trevor crept along behind her and Cole, his shoes causing the slightest scrape against the cement. He had to hand it to Ms. Wells. She managed to talk to thin air without batting an eye. A true actress.

She could have easily come to the crime scene before and taken note of where the body had been found. She was going to have to do better than this. A whole lot better.

When they exited the tunnel on the far end and found themselves near the bottom of stone steps, the medium looked straight ahead, occasionally bobbing her head and murmuring, "Mm-hm. Yes." Then she turned to him, because he was standing right behind her.

He saw her tiny, feminine Adam's apple jump and knew she'd swallowed. *Making you nervous, little liar? Good. You're no match for me.*

Whirling away from him and making her brown coat flare out at the bottom, she spread her fingers and made a motion with both hands as if she was batting the air down. "Right here," she said. "This is where Ronnie fell. She remembers, because it was after she'd first realized someone was following her. She panicked and stumbled in her heels."

Trevor felt the weight of his own frown trying to form, but he froze his face into an unreadable mask, not wanting to give her the satisfaction of thinking he believed her.

He was, however, picturing the abrasions the ME had found on the victim's knees and palms. From where she'd fallen on the cobblestones.

Now how the hell would this lady know that? Could she have been there that night and seen it all happen, or was she just guessing?

He shook his head. No. He didn't trust the woman, but his gut told him there was no way she'd stand by while another female was harmed.

He didn't know where she was getting her information, but he'd find out. That new kid cleaning up at the morgue, maybe? Could he be leaking information?

Trevor looked at the medium again. If money didn't do the trick, she was definitely attractive enough to swing a horny, young man's morals in the wrong direction. He told himself he would talk to the ME later and subtly scope out the situation. Right now, though, he was going to listen to every word Ms. Hayden Wells uttered through her pretty lips.

And if she happened to miss a step, he'd be there to make sure she fell all the way down.

He caught Cole looking at him then, and he knew his partner was thinking about the scrapes on the body as well. His face was blank, as if he was holding back judgment. At least his partner, the California Scot, hadn't gone so far he couldn't be pulled back.

"He was still several yards away from Ronnie when something," Hayden opened and closed her palms as if searching for a word, "something caused her pain and she fell. She vaguely recalls being unable to move. She wasn't paralyzed, exactly."

Hayden stared again into the air. "But she was suddenly incapacitated. Uncoordinated, like her body wouldn't do what she told it to."

This time Trevor couldn't stop the frown. The medium was describing exactly what would happen to a person who'd been shot with a Taser gun.

And she'd better have a good reason for knowing as much as she did. More than a flimsy claim that she was able to talk to the dead.

"What else?" he heard himself ask, and after her startled glance to him then Cole, he wished he'd kept his tongue still. His tone had made it clear she was getting under his skin, and that would only fuel her intent. "We don't have all day," he added in way of explanation.

Cole just rolled his eyes.

The woman pressed her lips into a thin line until they paled. She must not like being barked at, so he'd have to remember that. And do it as much as possible until she gave up and went away.

He was a damned homicide detective, and what he'd said hadn't been all cover-up. He really didn't have all day to spend on this hoo-hoo shit.

Or whatever.

She puffed a disgusted little huff through her nostrils and stomped back into the tunnel. She brushed so close he thought she was going to bump into him. Boy, was she mad. Her cheeks were all pink with restrained fury.

"He picked her up and carried her here. Right here." She looked down at the rough cement then, and the three of them fell into a mutual silence.

The blood had been scrubbed away. The torn clothes removed. But the images of what had happened on the ground were with them all. That, at least, was the truth. Trevor could see it in the medium's sorrowful eyes and the hand she slipped over her trembling lips.

She stepped back and rubbed her mouth as if trying to still the signs of her surging emotions. "I'm sorry," she whispered. "Sometimes it just hits."

"Yeah. We know," Cole told her. "It doesn't matter how much you're exposed to or how often you hear the accounting of what one human being can do to another. You never get truly anesthetized to it all. And the day you do..."

"Is the day you stop," Trevor finished for him. "Because you're no longer doing anyone any good."

The medium lifted her eyes to his, and they shimmered like finished amber in the faint sunlight filtering into the tunnel.

He might say they shared a moment of communion.

He tore his gaze from hers. She would have to care to understand what he meant, and no one who gave a damn about a murder victim would attempt to use their death for personal gain. He would do well to remember that the next time Ms. Wells put on an Oscar-worthy performance.

His phone buzzed in the pocket of his black jacket then, and before he even pulled it out, he could hear Cole's going off, too. He and his partner gave each other flat stares. They both knew what they were about to hear.

As he listened to the report and memorized the address he was being given, Trevor flashed a glare at Ms. Wells. He wasn't sure what they would do with her now, but as far as he was concerned, she could catch a cab back to the station. Or to wherever she'd come from.

He watched the red box with the words *Call Ended* pop onto the screen then rolled his shoulders back as he waited for his partner to tell him the plan. The medium was his responsibility, after all.

Cole coughed and said, "Ms. Wells, I'm afraid we have to go, but we can drop you back at The Barracks or wherever you need to go. As long as it's nearby. We have to…get somewhere."

"There's been another murder," she said, pulling her coat tighter around her as if to ward off the cold. But the temperature hadn't changed and the wind hadn't picked up.

"We can talk later," Cole told her, but before he could say more, she started shaking her head.

"No. Oh, no." Her head whipped to the side before she took two stuttering steps out of the tunnel and toward the steps. "I'm so sorry."

"It's okay, Hayden. We just need to go." Cole held out a hand toward her. "You don't need to go with us."

She slid him a look that was half distress, half frustration. "You don't understand," she said.

"I do. I know you want to help, but we can't let you go. We don't know the extent of what happened, and regardless..." Cole trailed off.

Trevor decided to take the matter in hand. "We'll drop you at the station, and that's it. You don't want to go to a fresh crime scene." He actually felt a tiny amount of concern for the medium as her face drained of all color. "Really. You don't need to see the next victim."

Hayden put a hand to her chest and continued to stare at the base of the steps. "That's just it." She drew a ragged breath. "I already do."

5

Joseph flinched when bubbles floated to the top of the murky green water and burst in rapid succession. He tried not to react to the things around him, he really did, but the area he was in was creepy, and there was simply no better word for it.

Ahead of him the edge of the marsh oozed underneath monster-sized trees to make the ground soggy, and all around him shadows seemed to double in size. It was quieter in the shade, but that didn't necessarily mean there was less activity or presence. The things that lived here just knew to be silent.

He'd traveled by boat today, since the route by sea was more direct than driving the forty minutes south of the city going by car would have required.

The town of Sunbury was a special place, he'd always thought. It promised a taste of the land in all its glory, with only a short commute to downtown Savannah. He imagined he'd like to live here one day.

If the prophecy went the right way and he lived to make those kinds of choices.

He'd grown up knowing about the prediction passed down from the three St. Germaine witches who'd lived centuries before. So speaking frankly about the fact he might die by a demon's hand, that was nothing to blink at.

Now that the coven had gathered and he'd finally gotten to meet them all, he had more hope than ever. Nine braver women he'd never known, and none of them shirked their duty. Their role to fulfill.

So Joseph wouldn't either.

That was why he'd meandered up the Medway River until he'd had to dock the boat and use the red canoe he'd stashed on board that morning. He'd pushed on, through smaller and smaller creeks until the thin waterways had become unnavigable.

After pulling the canoe up on the bank, he tossed his paddles in and slipped through enormous tree trunks until he found the trail his mother had told him about.

She'd been out in these parts many times as a young girl, so she knew the lay of the land. Back when she and her friend Regina had owned the woods and mastered the creek beds, as only children do.

Those innocent days had been long before either of them had kids of their own. Before they'd known a woman's heartbreak or a mother's worry.

So Claire's directions for her son had been accurate, though that oddly shaped tree she'd told him about was a great deal wider than she'd described.

He curved around the huge oak and found the beaten path. With the creek behind him now, he knew to travel straight ahead, until the trail opened into a clearing.

Something crashed through the underbrush to his right, but he kept his footsteps solid and true. Whatever was jumping around out there was bigger than a bread box. But smaller than a gator.

Light dappled through the trees and created a pattern of pale yellow lace on the forest floor. He could see why the woman he sought chose to live way out here, so far from modern convenience and modern noise. Life here was beautiful, clean and pure.

He heard a loud *plop,* and now he did speed up. Because life here could also be perilous.

Before long he saw a break in the tree line, but the wide space wasn't what told him he'd found what he was looking for. The bottle tree did.

A smaller and slower growing tree, just the right height for reaching on your tiptoes, was covered with jewel-toned bottles. Perfect for catching any roaming spirits who might intend harm for the humans living nearby.

Thanks to his mother's love for strange history, Joseph knew the bottle legend went as far back as ancient Egypt and Mesopotamia, when wind had blown over glass bottles, causing them to moan and sing.

Of course, people then decided the sounds were being made by mystical beings, therefore, the containers were obviously able to hold spirits. Over time, folks started hanging them on trees as traps, so the morning sun would rise and cast the evil beings out for good.

Joseph found it amusing that a nice pre-fab bottle tree could even be purchased in local nurseries. How things changed yet stayed the same.

As he walked closer to the cabin sitting dead center of the clearing, he noticed that most of the bottles were blue. Haint blue to be precise, the color of ghosts or "haunts," and often used to prevent their passage into houses.

The faded brown of the cabin also sported the bright, blue color, as all of the windows and doors were trimmed with paint that reminded him of the Caribbean.

The woman who lived here practiced hoodoo, but it looked like she was fairly liberal with her superstitions. Covering all her bases, so to speak, but that was a good thing.

Because Joseph was going to need everything she had to offer.

The weathered wooden steps creaked as he traversed them, but as he raised his fist to knock, the door opened with a swift whirl of air. "'Bout time," the elderly woman said, putting one hand on a hip as if she'd reached the end of her patience. "Been expectin' you, son, and you sure took your time about it."

With a curl of her gnarled, brown finger, she invited him in. She was reed thin but strong, if the wiry muscles in her forearm were any indication. Her once-black hair had gone full-white and was pulled into a tight bun low on the back of her head. She smiled at him then and even with her advanced age, displayed a set of healthy, ivory teeth.

"I know you had to come when the coming was right, but I was about afraid I wouldn't live to see the day," she told him as she pulled off a faded yellow sweater and moved toward a round table that seemed to serve as a work space. Or a craft table. The closer he looked, the stranger the implements and jars appeared.

"Cat got your tongue?" she stilled and asked him.

Afraid he'd offended the older woman, Joseph shook off the mesmerizing affect she and her words had on him. "No, Ma'am. I apologize. I just wasn't aware you knew I was headed out here." His brow pulled into a wrinkle. "Did my mother call you?"

"Don't have a phone. Don't need one. And Claire only ever sends letters, as a proper lady should." The woman, he knew her as Mrs. Lee, started around to the far side of the table and fell silent as she worked on putting together...whatever it was she was putting together.

The home was small but well organized and spotlessly clean. The décor was similar to what you might expect in an old-fashioned cabin, but newer appliances were interspersed here and there. Like the yellow Frigidaire and ...was that a laptop? She must have electricity out here, and maybe even wireless services.

Pondering the quirks of the spry little woman, Joseph watched politely and quietly, waiting for her to tell him what to do.

She evidently knew he'd been coming to see her—he didn't want to know how—so he assumed she was about to share something useful with him.

He was surprised to hear that his mother still sent letters to Mrs. Lee, but then again, his mother and the old woman's daughter had once been good friends. The hoodoo priestess scurrying around the room had been Regina Lee's mother.

And that made her Sylvie's grandmother.

Sylvie of the Amara, who his mother had warned him to stay away from.

"She's got good in her still," Mrs. Lee said as if she'd heard his thoughts. Somehow he knew she was talking about Sylvie. "My sweet girl's still in there. I know it. I catch glimpses of the child I knew, the one who brought me wildflowers on a hot July day."

She stopped speaking then and returned to her task. She pulled a brown paper bag from a drawer of the antique chest behind her and proceeded to tear apart the bag. She worked at it until she had a perfect brown square.

Picking up a pen from the table, she clicked the end of it before scribbling something onto the square. With a crooked grin, she held the paper up for Joseph to read. *Sylvia Marie Lee.*

Joseph firmed his mouth and nodded. The name was far too pretty for his comfort and made his lungs feel funny. Like all the air in them had been replaced with carbonated water. The sensation wasn't unpleasant, and that made him worry.

Just doing the right thing. Nothing else going on here.

When Mrs. Lee took the paper and put it in her left shoe, he stared bemusedly, looking forward to what she might do next. When she spread her hands wide and started tapping that foot, he began to have second thoughts.

Her voice flowed into the room then, and he realized she was speaking to someone, but not him. She was speaking to her granddaughter. "Sylvia, my girl. I need to see you. Tomorrow night, we must talk." *Tap, tap, tap.* Her left shoe kept hitting the wooden floor as she talked to a person who wasn't there.

"None of it was your fault, baby girl. None of it. Don't let that evil man's seed stick to you. Wasn't none of it your fault." *Tap. Tap.* "Now you must do as I say."

Joseph shifted positions as the woman's words started to bother him. What hadn't been Sylvie's fault? Who was the evil man? Her step-father? As far as he knew, the biological father had never been in the picture, leaving a pregnant Regina to fend for herself.

Joseph also knew that Regina Lee had died young. She'd fallen overboard from a small fishing boat and had been lost to the sea. Though some whispered she might not have fallen all by herself.

If the man Regina had married had been willing to commit murder, what might he have done to the small girl left in his care? How long had he had Sylvie before she'd come to live with her grandmother?

Joe clenched his fists at the idea. A single night could have been one too many.

"Son. Son." Mrs. Lee snapped her fingers at Joseph. When his vision cleared and he met her deep brown eyes, she said, "It's done. And now you got to promise to be back here tomorrow night. Just after the sun sets."

"Um..all right. But why? What do I need to do?"

"Just show up, is all. The rest will happen as it's meant to happen." She opened a beaten up leather journal and handed him a pink envelope.

He took it, testing its thickness and weight. When he started to open it, the old woman held out a shaky hand.

"Wait. Not yet." She looked at him and added, "Hmph."

Feeling more out of his element than he knew what to do with, Joseph slipped the envelope into his back pocket. "When?" was all he asked.

With a level of speed and agility that caught him off guard, Mrs. Lee circled the old table and chucked him up under his chin in an affectionate way.

With a smile so full of mischief her eyes literally sparkled, she rocked back on her heels and cackled. "You'll know when, son. Don't worry. You sure will know."

6

The courtyard of the bed and breakfast was absolutely stunning, and it didn't even have the riot of full blooming flowers that would be popping out come spring. The shrubbery was deep green and well-trimmed, providing softness to an area that was otherwise filled with stonework.

Pavers covered the ground in a pallet of gray and brick tones. The squares were thick and rough, telling Hayden they'd been installed long ago, probably original work. The large home that now welcomed overnight guests was stately and painted a deep, elegant gray, built for a young, wealthy bride in the mid-eighteen hundreds.

Luxury had staked an unyielding claim here, and the perfection of the courtyard conjured an image of what the home must have been like in its glory days. Stained glass windows set in the doors, wrap-around, covered porches, and tall, wrought-iron gates were all part of the lovely picture.

But not the corpse that had been found beneath the pre-blooming azaleas.

After seeing the new ghost appear by Ronnie's side at the last crime scene, Hayden had insisted on coming with Detectives Lonergan and Roch to the bed and breakfast, where a very distraught owner was wringing her hands over how the discovery might affect her guests. And their willingness to stay for all the time they'd booked at her establishment.

Hayden was now positive something weird was going on. Two women had been killed by the same man, their ghosts had then come looking specifically for her, and they'd both claimed their attacker had glowing eyes. Hayden was beginning to suspect supernatural involvement of some kind.

Other than the fact that she was talking to spirits, of course.

Chloe was the young girl's name, the one who'd been murdered here sometime during the night, and the story she'd told about her death was eerily similar to Ronnie's.

The attack. The violation. And the painting on her body. She remembered the cold, slick feel of the killer's finger on her stomach, but she had no idea what he'd drawn.

Hayden needed to know if the symbol on Chloe's body was the same as the one the police had found on Ronnie. With that in mind, she edged closer to Cole. He was far more willing to work with her than his horrible partner. Detective Trevor Roch.

She was beginning to think the man was as much of a *rock* as his name made him sound. Hard, craggy, and extremely painful if accidently stepped on.

Hayden glanced at the two spirits hovering in the corner of the courtyard. The women had been strangers in life but were bound together in death. And both of them were depending on Hayden.

She'd never had a task laid before her like this one, and with each surprising new twist, she wondered again if she weren't being put to the test.

The test of providence. Each witch of her coven had to pass a trial, or the Amara would win and their demon would be set free.

Part of her wanted to know if her mystical lottery numbers had been called, but part of her didn't care.

She would do whatever she had to do to help these spirits, no matter the reason. They were suffering in the afterlife through no fault of their own.

Hayden assumed Chloe would be going through the ordeal every night like Ronnie. Neither of them had mentioned the nightly replay of rape and murder to the younger girl. They were both hoping she might be spared.

The potential torment was another reason Hayden had to see Chloe's body. Maybe the symbol painted on Ronnie had cursed her spirit somehow, causing her to live through her attack over and over.

If Chloe's symbol were different...well, there really was no good option as far as Hayden could tell, but she needed to get as much information as she could.

Then she would take the mystery to her coven. In the unlikely event all of this did turn out to be related to the prophecy, they would have to be told. The murderer's ritual was unlike any Hayden had ever seen, or even heard of, and she was beginning to suspect a dark influence.

Just what she needed. More black magic in Savannah. Weren't the Amara and their rising demon enough?

She tugged on the sleeve of Cole's dark gray jacket to get his attention. "I know you're busy," she began, "but I need you to do me a quick favor."

Casting those gray-green eyes at her, he nodded solemnly. "If you think it will help."

Sucking in the cold air for courage, she said. "I need to look at the body."

"Out of the question," a male voice said from behind her. Hayden didn't need to turn around to know who the deep timbre belonged to, but she did anyway.

"I need to see what he painted on her body," she said, hiking one disdainful brow as she shored up her defenses and stared down her nemesis. Describing him that way said a lot about how dislikable he was, considering the enemies she had in this city.

Right now, however, Detective Roch was the one giving her trouble.

From his considerable height he stared down at her, forehead furrowed and eyes cold. He did nothing to disguise his suspicion, and her normally cool temper was sparking. He was so overbearing.

Had she thought him attractive before? How could she have ever seen anything other than that angry expression he always had on his face? The one he seemed to wear especially for her.

His eyes were the color of a mid-summer sky, and she noticed the dark circles beginning to develop underneath. His short hair was mussed from his habit of raking a hand through it, and his jaw was darkened by stubble, a shade or two darker than the deep blonde on his head.

That was it, Hayden realized. No wonder he was so foul-acting. He obviously hadn't been sleeping well, an unfortunate part of life as a homicide detective.

Cole didn't seem to be affected the same way, but everyone was different. For example, Viv could go full-speed with only five hours of sleep, but Hayden was a bear if she got fewer than seven.

With a new sense of empathy and determination to cut the cop some slack, she plastered on a patient smile and said, "I understand if you don't want me to get close, forensics and all, so maybe you could help me instead."

The gurgling fountain in the center of the courtyard was the only sound. She tuned into the soft flow as Detective Roch simply glared at her. "Help you gather details you don't need in the first place? Give you information so you can improve your performance?"

He put his hands on his hips and leaned down, speaking in a low, dangerous voice beside her ear. "Lady, you should just be glad I haven't helped you into the back of a patrol car headed for The Barracks. You may have my partner snowed, but as far as I'm concerned, you've got some questions to answer."

Cold fear clamped down on Hayden, like a vise around her ribs, squeezing the air from her lungs. She couldn't get into the back of a police car. Not again. Never again.

Without realizing it, she slid a step backward until she bumped into Cole. His arm shot out to steady her as she tripped over his shoe.

Detective Roch rasped out a sound that could have been a laugh or a disgusted dismissal. Then he pivoted and walked away, stopping to talk to a technician who was bent over the bushes with a plastic bag in his hand.

A familiar and crushing wave of guilt washed over Hayden, and she pressed her eyes closed as she struggled to rise above the flood. *I haven't done anything wrong. I haven't done anything. I'm here to help.*

She felt a warm, strong arm slip around her shoulders. "You okay?" Cole asked, concern etched on his face.

Hayden steadied herself and clamped her hands together. Her eyes drilled a hole into Detective Roch's stubborn back as she told Cole, "I'm fine, thanks. I just needed to get a little perspective."

With that she marched over to Detective Roch and came to a stop behind him. She didn't give him the courtesy of a shoulder tap or excuse herself for interrupting the conversation he was having. Manners and timidity had gotten her nowhere with him.

"You can help me, or I'll find out for myself," she said in a voice as bitter as the wind sweeping through the iron gates. "I'd prefer to have a good working relationship with the authorities, but that requires a modicum of respect on both sides. From what I've seen, you have nothing to give me but contempt and harsh words. So that's fine. I can do the same."

She forced her arms to remain hanging at her sides. She

didn't want to cross them over her chest as the body language was too obvious. Plus, it was a move he pulled whenever he was irritated, and she didn't want to mimic him in any way. The more distance between them the better.

She'd just get what she wanted and go.

"So what's it going to be?" she asked finally. "Civil or hostile?"

"Lady, if you want hostile, you came to the right man." He reached out as if to take her wrist in his hand, but Cole was suddenly there between them. Physically there between them, and Hayden was shocked to admit that was probably a good thing.

If Detective Roch had grabbed her, she would have bucked. Then he'd have her on striking a police officer, or resisting, or some other such bull.

Hayden froze and considered her state of mind. What was going on with her, and why was she letting this arrogant, judgmental, stonewalling, ignorant, close-minded man fray her last nerve?

And whoa. Those were a lot of adjectives for someone she shouldn't even be worried about. Why did she care what he thought anyway?

After the surge of temper came a secondary feeling of embarrassment. Hayden prided herself on keeping her emotions in check. Calm. Serene. Patient. She strived to be a non-reactive person if possible, because she knew what could happen when feelings overrode good sense.

And she swore she'd never let it happen again.

Now here she was about to duke it out with a cop. At a crime scene.

Okay, breathe in the oxygen. Hayden inhaled a long draw of cool air. Slowly. *Breathe out the toxic waste and negativity.* She exhaled, focusing on balance and control.

Pranayama. The breathing techniques of yoga helped link body, mind, and spirit. The *prana* referred to life force and *yama* to discipline. The exercises she employed daily for meditation could also come in handy when dealing with stress or chaos.

As Hayden shifted her eyes back to Detective Roch, she knew she'd need all the Zen she could muster.

"I guess I have your answer then, Detective." She stepped past him, closer to the stretcher where Chloe's body was hidden by a starched, white sheet. She stopped herself beside the fountain, though, unwilling to breach the perimeter of the scene the technicians were working. She didn't want to give Roch any ammunition.

Ignoring the two men who'd moved to stand beside her, Cole on her left and Detective Roch on her right, Hayden spoke. "Ronnie, could you help me out? I need to see." The ghost had heard all of the conversations up until this point and knew what Hayden wanted.

"Chloe," Hayden said in a softer voice. "Maybe you should leave. Just for a while."

The younger girl shook her head, making soft, orange curls bounce around her shoulders. "I'm staying." The mutinous look on the spirit's face told Hayden there was more to the bizarrely dressed art student. She was stronger than the knee-length black dress and polka dot tights had made her first appear.

Ronnie and Chloe had almost nothing in common other than the fact they were female and had lived in Savannah. And had both been caught alone at night by the wrong person.

"I think it's time for your friend to leave," Detective Roch told Cole, but his eyes weren't on his partner. The fiery blue traced from Hayden to the stretcher then back again, as if he wasn't sure what was going to happen and didn't want to miss anything.

Ronnie moved so quickly Hayden barely registered how the ghost ended up standing beside the stretcher. With a nod followed by a quick flick of her hand, Ronnie pulled back the sheet to reveal the body from head to hips.

Despite her bravado, Chloe made a strangled sound, part whine, part gasp.

"What the hell?" Roch growled. He surged forward. "Cover that body!"

But Hayden had seen enough.

She'd had time to take a good long look at the bluish skin and the stark black paint jumping at her like a movie in 3-D. The same symbol Cole had shown her at the station was on the left, lower portion of Chloe's abdomen. The wicked-looking ribbon throbbed as if being kept alive by its own pulse.

The mark was infused with magic. She was sure of it.

And now she really had to get back to the island to tell her friends. She needed their help, and she needed to talk to Anna's brother. Quinn would know what to do.

"Holy shit," Cole uttered, lifting his hands up with a bemused expression on his handsome face. Now he ran a hand through his dark brown hair, though it was with confused fascination rather than Roch's ever-ready pissed-offedness.

Now why did she have to compare the nice and very attractive Cole Lonergan to his warden of a partner?

After a moment, Cole regained his composure, but his hand stroked his jaw as he said, "I guess you realize this is the same guy that killed the other vic—" He stilled then added, "That killed Ronnie."

"Not to sound cocky, but I knew that already." Now Hayden did cross her arms over her chest but only in an effort to fend off the chill that had settled into her bones. "They told me," she whispered.

Cole simply frowned. "Yeah. About that, I know Roch is giving you a hard time, but I'll talk to him. I was a believer before, but after what I just saw…"

Hayden worked up a smile. "Thanks." She jerked her head toward Roch. "I guess I don't have to ask which one of you plays bad cop."

Together they watched Roch as he lectured a poor young man on the importance of making sure evidence was secure and protected from the elements. Oops.

"Don't take it personally," Cole said. "Roch still thinks you're in it for some kind of payoff. Fame. Glory. Who knows?" He notched his chin up in the direction of his partner. "Trevor's not a bad guy. He just cares too much."

Hayden couldn't stop the disbelieving laugh that escaped. "Cares? Really?"

"More than you know," Cole told her, his tone more somber and a touch defensive. "He takes his job seriously and has a hard time staying objective. Don't get me wrong. He's a great detective." The dark-haired man met Hayden's eyes. "Trevor is a protector. A guardian. And to do that well, he has to keep a sharp edge."

Cole put a hand on her arm then and grinned. "But don't worry. I can tell you're winning him over."

Taking a fast peek to where Detective Roch stood with his legs in a wide, warrior's stance, Hayden found him staring at her. Hard. "Oh, yeah. I'm really getting on his good side."

She shook herself and sighed. "I really need to go, but thanks again for bringing me with you. I hope it doesn't cause any problems between you..." she made a face and made a little pointing gesture toward Roch, "and him."

"No worries. Trevor and me, we're good."

"I am worried, though," Hayden said. She saw Ronnie and Chloe on the outside of the tall black fence. Maybe Ronnie had talked the younger girl into leaving the place of her horrible death. How hard would it be to look at your own mutilated body?

"The murders have been pretty close together, don't you think?" she asked Cole. "I'm no expert, but it seems like this guy came out of nowhere and is working fast."

"You're right. Every serial killer, if that's what he turns out to be, tends to have their own unique...style, you could say, but few of them move at such a pace." Cole tilted his head and sighed. "Hopefully he'll burn himself out. Get sloppy and make a mistake."

"Before anyone else dies," Hayden said.

Cole stayed silent, and Hayden felt more than heard Detective Roch approaching. "That's it for now," he said to Cole, clearly ignoring Hayden's presence. "I hate to break up the party, but we've got work to do."

"They found something?" Cole asked.

Detective Roch shrugged his wide shoulders. "We won't know for a while, considering how many people pass through here each day. Let's just hope most of them don't go digging around in the bushes."

"Right." With an apology in his eyes, Cole looked to Hayden. "You sure you'll be all right from here?" He said to his partner, "Ms. Wells was heading out anyway."

Trevor's blue eyes fell on her and she felt her heart miss a beat. His gaze was still intense, but alongside the usual doubt, she saw something else. Intrigue? Uncertainty? Whatever it was, the difference was apparent. Detective Trevor Roch was reconsidering his assumptions about her.

His voice rumbled as he spoke over the sounds of the ambulance starting its engines in the back alley. "Whatever the hell's going on, the killer isn't wasting any time." He ran a hand through his hair. "It's like he's on some sort of mission."

Hayden's nape prickled as if some unknown force was trying to get her attention. She studied Roch's profile and knew he and Cole would work relentlessly to catch the man who'd done those horrible things to Ronnie and Chloe.

The thought was comforting, because she could use some backup on this one.

Speaking of which, it really was time for her to go home. There would be a gathering of witches in the grand hall tonight, because she had a feeling Roch had nailed it on the head. This killer with the glowing eyes?

He seemed to be on a mission.

7

The delicious aroma of baking bread enveloped Hayden when she entered the mansion. She took a long, lovely sniff and hung her coat in the closet.

The day had been brittle with a wet, cloying cold, and the warmth of food and family had never been more welcome than at this moment.

Ronnie and Chloe had left the crime scene when Hayden had, though she suspected the two ghosts would reappear when necessary. Now that they'd found her, there seemed to be a mystical thread stretched between her and the spirits, a lifeline to help them find their way back.

They also seemed to know exactly when to show up, so she suspected they'd be back when she revealed her day's discoveries to the rest of the coven.

But first she would eat. The detectives had skipped lunch, so Hayden had as well. Now she was famished and needed to recharge her shivering body.

She passed through the stylish foyer and grand hall, following the tempting smell, until she entered the kitchen to see who was cooking.

The lead chef in charge of the night's meal was apparently Kylie, since the vivacious blonde was stirring a large pot and directing Viv to remove a separate one from the stove. "We want it to be *al dente*," Kylie said in a staid voice. "To the tooth," she clarified for any of the others in the large kitchen who might not have already known.

"*Si,*" Lucia said as she scooted Viv and Kylie out of the way so she could open the oven door and pull out three loaves of bread. "We want to be able to feel it on our teeth when we chew. Not too...what's the word? Ah, yes. Mushy."

The Spanish woman who could just as easily be a dirt-covered explorer by day or exotic siren by night set the bread pans aside to cool. "I don't like mushy."

Hayden took in the bustling room and cloister of women. "Honeys, I'm home," she called out, announcing her arrival.

Anna raised a glass of red wine from where she sat at the island, a large slab of gray granite reminiscent of a crescent moon. "See? Right on time, like I said." The sable-haired woman who led their motley crew of witches turned her attention to Kylie. "I told you she wouldn't miss the fresh penne."

Anna was a prophetess or seer, psychic to some. However one wanted to describe her, she could see and sense things that weren't obvious to the physical eye. She must have employed that gift tonight to help time dinner.

"Thanks, Anna," Hayden told her with a shake of her head. "That was considerate of you." She slipped onto one of the high stools at the island, feeling like a queen, just as she did every time she sat on the red-velvet cushions. "And I could use some comfort food right about now."

"Rough day?" Shauni asked, tilting two bottles of wine toward Hayden in question.

She rarely drank alcohol, but tonight it sounded good. Shauni held two good winter choices, Merlot and Syrah, both rich enough to stand on their own against the meaty red sauce Kylie was ladling onto the plates of penne.

Tapping the Merlot on the side, Hayden said, "This one,

thanks. Well," she added, laying the beige linen napkin over her lap as a large bowl of salad and baskets of sliced bread were put in the center of the island, "what's the occasion?"

The seating was casual and intimate, and Hayden realized Mrs. Attinger was once again absent. She must still be sick.

But the gathering of her friends in the kitchen was nice. Cozy. Flames flickered in the fireplace and through the windows, a stark, winter moon shone white against the indigo sky.

"No occasion," Kylie said. "Not really. We don't think."

"Smooth," Paige told the coed from where she sat beside her. "Real smooth."

"Hmph. Like it wasn't going to come out anyway. Nine women in one place? No way anything stays a secret." Kylie grabbed a tub of *healthy* butter and began to paint a steaming piece of bread with an artist's precision. She lifted her eyes to Hayden's with a mix of grimness and fortitude. "A few of us think your time has begun."

"Can you at least wait until we're all seated before opening the floor for discussion?" Claudia asked, scooting into the only remaining stool between Willyn and Viv. Her long ponytail was a blaze of red and swung as she bumped her seat forward two times. When she finally moved into line with her sisters, a familiar hum settled over them all.

When the nine had first come together in any enclosed space, the vibration had been startling in its intensity. Since they'd become more comfortable living inside their constant magic, they'd learned to tamp the energy down, to control it, reserve it for later use. Like when they came across an Amara member ready to go for a kill.

So now as they sat around the island, all Hayden felt was a pleasant, low-level buzz right around the area of her solar plexus. She knew the spot below her sternum was also the chakra for one's power and will, so surely the connection she felt there was more than coincidence.

Holding the youngest witch's gaze, Hayden raised her wine glass and swirled the crimson liquid. "You may be onto something, Kylie. My trial may have started."

While a few of the women exchanged glances, Anna's face remained impassive. But Shauni, Willyn, and Viv sat stiff in their chairs, unable to hide the flickers of worry that passed over each of their expressions.

The three of them had already been through a trial. Only they could truly understand what that meant, and though they'd each come through unscathed for the most part, they'd each come close to losing their own lives or that of a loved one.

Hayden took a big drink of wine as she mentally corrected herself. Viv's trial hadn't suffered a near miss at all. Jen's death had been a direct blow.

Each of them would be tested in order to fulfill the prophecy laid out for them so long ago, and the emotional roller coaster that went along with it was not only expected by the remaining women, it was accepted. As fate.

"I'll tell you all about my day, which has been enlightening, to say the least," Hayden said. "But first." She took a dramatic pause before pointing with her free hand. "Someone's going to have to pass me that grated parmesan. I can tell it's fresh."

"Right away," Lucia said as if she was retrieving life-saving blood instead of a topping for pasta.

Hayden accepted the bowl and gave herself a generous pile of the cheese before stirring it into the penne and meat sauce. With the heat of it rising to meet her open lips, she took her first bite before making a sound of ecstasy. "Kylie, I don't know what you were majoring in, but you can always fall back on your cooking skills."

"Aw, thanks. It's my grandmother's recipe. She had a hot affair with an Italian man when she was young."

Viv nodded and looked to the younger woman. "Now why does that not surprise me?"

"What can I say?" A grin of pure mischief spread over Kylie's face. "The women in my family are true romantics."

Claudia lifted one red brow. "And all men are named Oh, Yes."

They all laughed at the inside joke and the secret Kylie's cat had once shared with Shauni. Hayden was beginning to feel a bit lighter, and was glad to be in the company of those who cared about her and liked having her around.

She'd had her fill of being an unwanted guest today. *Stupid detective.*

Surprised to find herself letting Trevor Roch into her mind where he could taint the lovely dinner she was sharing with her friends, Hayden took a piece of bread for herself and chose the bowl of honey-butter instead of the green tub that claimed to be heart-healthy. After weathering murky fog and an ill-tempered man, she was due a little bit of ambrosia.

And she would *not* picture vivid blue eyes over a clenched yet handsome jaw. Even if that jaw had been nicely shaded with the perfect amount of stubble.

Halfway through the meal and well into her second glass of wine, she decided she was fortified enough to replay the day's events for the others. They'd already known she was going to the cops with her information and listened quietly as she told them about the two detectives and how Lonergan had recognized her name from California circles.

"And this symbol," Viv interjected when Hayden got to the part about the yellow paper. "Can we see it? Do you know what it means?"

"No," Hayden said, brushing a lock of her dull brown hair away from her face, at least that's how she thought of it, though others said it looked like caramel. "I was hoping Quinn might recognize it, since he's so well-versed in magical languages."

She pulled out the crumpled paper she'd stuffed in the front pocket of her jeans. "Or you, Anna," she added, passing the scrap to the woman who led them down the path of all things witchy.

But Anna studied the drawing a mere second before shaking her head in the negative. "No. I don't know it. I'm afraid we'll have to wait for Quinn."

"He's not home?" Hayden asked and knew from the throats that were cleared and the gazes averted that she'd said something wrong.

"He's out with a friend tonight," Claudia explained, and by the way she shot a wary glance at Kylie, Hayden surmised the friend was female. Quinn was on a date.

And Kylie was a study of aloofness as she scooped up a bite of penne.

Though Kylie and Anna's younger brother definitely had a spark between them, the two were more often like territorial cats, hissing and spitting at each other if they got too close. Despite the way they kept their distance, Kylie's complete lack of response and flat expression told them just how much the topic bothered her.

Veering back to the original subject, Hayden said, "I guess it's time to tell you the bad news. While we were at the first crime scene..."

"The first?" Viv broke in to ask. "I take it that means there was a second?"

Hayden nodded, her stomach tightening in an unpleasant way. "Another ghost appeared, and she also knew to come find me. Her name is Chloe. I don't know why I saw her so much quicker than I did Ronnie, but I suspect the spirits are connected. By more than being killed by the same man."

Claudia's already pale skin turned ashen. "And she's probably hiding from whatever Ronnie is afraid of. She'll probably suffer the same way, too. Reliving her murder again tonight."

Silence hung over the women and dampened the cheerful

mood. Hayden had known her news would have this effect, but in the business she and her friends were in, denial and avoidance weren't options. She would handle this herself if she could, but she would not risk more innocent lives by being proud.

She needed the joined experiences and wisdom of her coven. Each woman had come from a unique background with her own special view of the world. Her own insight. And Hayden would need them all if she was going to stand through her test and catch a killer.

And there it was. Her answer. She was facing her trial after all.

There had been no clanging drum or sounding bugle to let her know her time had come, only her own intuition. She could feel a change inside, somewhere soft and dark, hidden from the rest of the world.

She was ever-amused by the mystical world and its oddities. Each of them had been chosen in a way that was suited to their character and personality.

How fitting that her inner spirit was the one she needed to listen to. The one who spoke only when the mind was clear of other distractions and stimuli.

The one she tuned in to every morning while performing her *asanas*.

"No more wondering," Hayden said to the others. "I know part of my challenge is to help these women cross over, to find their way to their intended afterlife. And if their murders and whatever is happening to them after they're killed is part of my trial," she steadied herself with a sip of wine and a deep breath, "then the Amara must be involved."

Anna nodded, and Hayden could see she was bothered by something. "You weren't sure either, were you?" she asked Anna. "That it was my turn."

"No, and even though I shouldn't be surprised, I can't help

feeling a little out of control." With her eyes of cobalt shaded by worry, Anna added, "I suspected things would change as we progressed, but I still let myself become too comfortable. It's as if the first three tests were the beginner's stages. No offense," she said to Shauni, Willyn, and Viv.

"None taken," Viv told her as the other two nodded. "I was touched by darkness and Willyn was beaten and almost died." The coven's scientist winked at Willyn to show her affection and how glad she was her sister had pulled through. "But I don't think either of us would have traded places with Shauni."

Flipping her long black braid over her shoulder, Shauni fastened piercing green eyes on Viv then Anna. "In retrospect, I did have it easy, compared to the tests that followed, but not knowing what to expect, that was the worst part."

"And yet things are still changing," Anna said softly. "We have a blueprint for the trials but the gods keep making adjustments."

Reaching a lean and well-toned arm out for another slice of bread, Paige spoke for the first time. "If things didn't change, we might get complacent and fall on our asses. Yes, every time it's harder and scarier, but you also have to look at the positive from that."

"There's a positive?" Lucia asked dryly.

"Yeah." Paige bit into her bread and swallowed before answering. "Each time we get stronger in return. It's the natural evolution of what we're doing, and if we hope to have a chance in hell of standing up to the big boy at the end, each time has to be tougher than the last."

Anna's face relaxed and renewed excitement shone in her eyes. "That's exactly right, Paige. Leave it to our military strategist to see so clearly when I couldn't."

In a rare show of emotion, Paige covered Anna's hand with her own. "That's why we're here. You don't have to do everything alone. You're not meant to."

Heaving a breath, Anna twisted her mouth to the side. "I know, but glitches in my foresight are a new experience. I guess I'll just have to get used to it."

"Get used to something new?" Kylie asked on a laugh. "Welcome to our world. At least you were raised knowing you were a witch and were meant to save the universe." She wiggled her brows. "Or at least the historic district."

Anna hiked a brow at the younger woman then nodded. "True. That's true."

"So the next thing we need to do is figure out what's happening to the ghosts and what they're afraid of," Claudia said suddenly. Then she added a deep in thought, "Hmm," before propping her chin in a hand. The faraway look meant she was running through the encyclopedias in her brain. Of which there were many.

"Right," Hayden said. "Neither of them know what they're hiding from exactly, but they keep referring to a woman. I'm sure it's one of the Amara, but who? Ronja seems the most likely candidate, as their leader and a powerful witch in her own right."

"Maybe," Anna mused, "but I've never known her to have any capabilities as a medium. Then again, if she once communed with the demon Bastraal, I guess it's possible she could talk to the dead. But that still doesn't explain why the ghosts would be afraid of her."

"Okay, let's run through the women of the Amara." Willyn slid out of her seat and retrieved a yellow notepad. "I'll write them down."

"We probably should have done this from the beginning," Anna said. "A family tree, if you will, of the Amara and their individual powers. I'm sorry I never thought of it."

As Willyn searched an open drawer for a pen, Lucia and Kylie cleared the dirty dishes. The three sat again, and Hayden, filled with purpose, decided to switch her drink to water. She'd enjoyed the relaxing hour of camaraderie, but now it was time to get back to business. She wanted both body and mind to be clear.

"How about we start at the beginning," Shauni suggested. "I had to deal with Sylvie first, the hoodoo priestess."

"That sounds funny every time you say it," Kylie said with a smile while Willyn scribbled the name and description down.

Shauni allowed a grin to flit across her lips before growing sedate again. "Then I met Ronja, and we all know who she is. Black-hearted witch from ancient times, still alive, regrettably, after more than a thousand years since she made a deal with a demon."

Willyn scratched away as the others stayed quiet, then she spoke of her own trial. "Scarlett came after me in the tunnels, another witch and Ronja's confidante. She drinks Ronja's blood to have some immortality for herself."

"And Beth," Lucia said in a serious voice, well aware how badly the young girl had hurt Willyn by turning against her. "The Amara want her for their eighth female, and she is a Mare, able to affect the dreams of others."

Once Willyn looked up for more, Viv recounted her own run-in with the demon-bound thugs. "The two women who helped R.J. attack me in the park were Carson and Jack. Carson is an Amazon and Jack has super-speed and strength." She notched her chin up then and met Paige's aqua-blue eyes. "But she's not as good as our super-baddie."

Paige blew on her fingernails then buffed them on her shirt, a deadly grin on her face. "What can I say?" She winked after making the joke then dropped all pretenses as her brows furrowed. She looked to Anna. "The only one left is that brunette. The prissy one who was at the last fight. But that's only seven, even with Beth."

Lucia tapped a long, red fingernail on the gray granite. "I think I heard someone call that brunette Valentina, but you're right, Paige. There were only seven women there that night. How can the Amara avert the seven sisters prediction now? Maybe they aren't going to lose one, and Beth was meant to be the seventh all along?"

Hayden chewed on her lip. Lucia was talking about a myth, seven sages whose wives had betrayed them. All but one.

Ronja had come across her own prophecy regarding her and the Amara females. If the seven sisters occurred again, with one of the women breaking rank, it could lead to Ronja's downfall and the Amara's defeat.

The coven had been sure Ronja had recruited Beth as a pawn. A sacrifice. That she had lured the girl to her side with the hope she'd betray the Amara. She was meant to be the lost one, the one who turned against them.

Since Beth meant nothing to Ronja, she could be killed without loss and there would still be seven women standing, a magical number that would ensure the Amara's continued strength.

If Hayden and her friends had done the math wrong...

"No," Anna said, the word like a nail being driven soundly and surely. "There are eight women in the Amara. I'm sure of it. Now that we've put them all together, I realize there is a blank spot. I can't get a good sense of her, but I know she's there."

"Then why haven't we seen her?" Hayden asked, uncomfortable with the idea that one of their enemies was cloaked against Anna's proverbial third eye.

"Maybe that's part of her power," Kylie said, but before anyone could respond the lights flickered over their heads. The triangles of ruby, yellow, and blue that added a touch of modern to the kitchen blinked and trembled before going dark.

The women looked at each other with only the golden luminescence of the fireplace filling the room and lighting their faces.

Hayden blew out a breath as a biting cold invaded her body. It jabbed into her chest then pulled back out like a razor-sharp tide.

The source of the cold was alien to her. Foreign. She'd never felt anything like it before but knew one thing with certainty. It felt *wrong*.

The lamps above them shot back to life, glowing with rich color once again. But Hayden felt sick. "Ronnie. Chloe," she whispered. "They're afraid. I heard...a scream." She pushed away from the island with an urgency she couldn't explain.

"They've left the house." The inexplicable dread was coming from her gut, from that place referred to as instinct. "But they didn't just leave. They *bolted*."

And like a shot she was headed toward the grand hall, her friends close behind if the cacophony of scraping stools and raised voices was any indication. The room was the heart of the mansion, expanding upward to the next floor and the walkway there that formed a perimeter. On the other side of the railing were doors to living quarters.

Shauni's room was on that level, and the sound of sharp, high barking had Hayden spinning abruptly to find the animal-whisperer's dog dancing in a circle. The almost fully-grown Skid was going crazy, snarling in between panicked barks that confirmed what Hayden already knew.

Something was in the house.

"Skid!" Shauni yelled to her dog, more in fear than out of command. With his black hide quivering, Skid started edging away from the door and toward the stairs where he could come down to his human. Despite his apparent confusion and anxiety, the canine protector didn't want to leave whatever was invading Shauni's room.

When the deep brown wood of the door started to morph, Skid sprang back into action, barking and growling furiously.

All hell broke loose as cats streamed into the grand hall,

up the stairs, and from open bedroom doors above, backs arched and tails puffed. Kylie's cat, Sassy, actually leaped from a higher floor in a flash of gold. She grasped the rail then scrambled over to join the fray, causing Kylie to slap a hand to her chest and cry out.

Caterwauling took on a new meaning as the felines let out horrible sounds, terrifying to hear, even for the women who loved them. Dog and cats formed a fearsome alliance as whatever was pushing through the door distorted the image of the wood.

Whatever was there acted like a prism, making the mahogany appear stretched and shimmery. Hayden wasn't sure if the door was actually changing or if the entity was somehow magnifying physical objects. She blinked to get a better look.

"What the hell are they hissing at?" Paige asked, the worry for her own Tiger-Lily stamped on her face.

Hayden shook herself and looked around to the others. "Can't you see it?" she asked no one in particular.

Anna clutched her arm. "See what?" She was especially concerned about whatever was here with them. The entire mansion, even the island to a certain degree, had been warded to the best of Anna's ability. Hers, Quinn's, and the coven's. The Amara should not be able to attack them here.

So what was happening?

Staring hard at the door, Hayden saw the shape begin to morph. A swirling black covered the center of the wood, shifting and growing as she watched. Soon she could make out a familiar shape. Familiar but not quite right.

Then with a huge sucking sound, it was all gone. The glimmering prism, the bulging wood, and the dark form. A few of the women put fingers or hands to their ears. They had heard the noise.

"It's gone," Hayden said, still staring at the door. One by one the animals stilled and calmed, though none of them backed away. Not yet.

Finally Skid gave one last angry bark before turning to run down the staircase and into the worried arms of Shauni. She snuggled and praised the black dog.

"I think I saw a face," Hayden told Anna, unsure how to describe the rest. She still wasn't sure what she'd seen. Illusion, physics, or plain old magic?

"Was it a ghost?" Lucia asked, coming to her side and looking up to the door.

Hayden shook her head. "I don't think so." She rubbed her stomach and noticed the cold sensation was completely gone now. It had retreated along with the...thing.

Kylie now had her Sassy in her arms, patting down the long, blonde hair and kissing the cat's silky head. All of them were on edge. Confused. And for the first time in a long time, they were truly scared.

"Then what did you see?" Viv asked, unable to mask the terror in her gray eyes.

Bending to pick Daisy up as her cat scooted over to rub against her legs, Hayden breathed through her tight throat and steadied her voice before she spoke.

She wanted to appear steady and calm, though she was anything but. "I have absolutely no idea."

8

Sylvie was not happy. Not at all. She was agitated for an unidentifiable reason but was doing her best to keep that to herself. If there was one thing she knew about her service to the Amara—and make no mistake, service was the right word—she knew not to offend the reigning queen.

Ronja had summoned the members of the Amara, so not only would they all show up, they would do so eagerly.

With a clan such as this, though, other attitudes were perfectly acceptable, so she wouldn't have to fake it too much. Horny, apathetic, even full-on pissy were allowed in the conference room, but resentment for being summoned? That was a one-way ticket to a timeout.

And those were usually taken in the dungeon. With Ronja.

A harsh sound escaped her mouth, drawing a curious stare from R.J., her partner in crime. And that wasn't a bad cliché but realism.

She lifted one shoulder and turned away. She didn't have to share everything with him, and she sure as hell wasn't about to tell him her opinion of the Amara mansion.

What a joke. Sylvie had a prominent and solid place in the main house of the old, southern plantation, but somehow, she didn't think any ancestor of hers would be proud. The decaying old home had been remodeled all right, but torture-chic wasn't exactly her style.

Though the Amara held their meetings at the long, wood table, they were actually in a multi-purpose dining room. Tall-backed chairs of crushed, peacock-blue velvet lined the table. Twelve in all, with Ronja always at the head near the fireplace, and either Tyr or Scarlett, Ronja's lovers, sitting at the opposite end in front of the rear window.

A chandelier of delicately sculpted bones hung over the center of the honeyed wood while the spindly shape of the light fixture was reflected in paintings of ancient, withered trees set on black canvas.

The grisly pictures contrasted against the walls of deep blood red, splotchy as if the paint had been applied haphazardly. Or with someone's head of hair.

Sylvie didn't think too long on that idea. Since it was entirely possible.

Feeling the jittery nerves starting to crawl again, she jerked her mouth to the side, deciding to go for pissed off as her disguise for the night.

She was often just a step away from irritation anyway, so the others would think nothing of it. She refused to let them see how agitated she really was. That a scratchy and skittering sense of impatience was running up under her creamy brown skin.

Like living amongst a den of ravenous animals, revealing anything akin to weakness could cause a feeding frenzy. And she didn't care to be the target.

She would get through the meeting then take her leave. As demanding as Ronja was, at least she didn't monitor every hour of their lives.

The next day was free and clear, and Sylvie was glad of it. Along with the edginess inside her, an image of her grandmother's face persisted. A picture of the old woman speaking to her in a commanding voice.

If it was one thing a hoodoo priestess knew better than to do, it was to ignore premonitions or vibes. And this vibe was practically shouting her granny's name.

Sylvie sighed with acceptance. She would go tomorrow. As the sun set. Yes, that's what she would do.

The resolution sat well on her stomach, and the relief from her decision was surprising. Maybe she could chill after all. Pick up the night's menu for how-we-raise-our-demon and be happily on her way. But just as she moved to take a seat next to R.J., a hooded figure glided through the door at the far end of the room.

Searenn. The main reason Sylvie detested the meetings.

The woman rarely spoke, but when she did, it was in an acid-scorched voice. At least that's how it sounded. Like a flame thrower had once been used on her vocal cords. When raspy words floated from the shadow of her ever-present hood, it seemed as if an evil spell were being cast.

And given Searenn's natural talent, Sylvie avoided holding a conversation with the woman if at all possible. Why chance it?

Even R.J. and Ross steered clear of that one if they could. She was weird and scary, and for anyone in this group to think so? That said a shitload.

As if she could hear her thoughts, the woman turned her head slightly. Slowly. The cold stare impaled Sylvie, though she couldn't even see Searenn's creepy eyes. One black as rot, the other an icy blue.

A trio of silver glints shone near the freaky woman's mouth, and Sylvie knew that would be her lip piercings reflecting the candlelight. The chick did have a thing for putting holes in her body.

And the tats. Once and only once had she ever seen Searenn without clothing covering her torso and face. Ink covered almost every available inch of her skin, so she looked dressed even when naked. The only place tattoos didn't cover her was her face, sporting only strange swirls and markings at the edge of the hairline.

Sylvie knew the tattoos were some sort of mystical language, supposedly passed down through Searenn's heritage. A bloodline that had almost died out in the last two centuries.

And Sylvie, a member of the Amara, was grateful for that, because even those who were knee-deep in black magic knew certain threats should be eliminated.

As a door at the far end of the room opened, Sylvie swallowed the taste of fear and turned to stare. In walked Ronja and the rest of the horde.

As predicted, Tyr, the Native American psychic and muscular brute, took the far chair, leaving Scarlett to slide in next to Ronja. The redhead was coifed to perfection, straight out of a 1940's fashion catalogue.

Carson dragged in with her wild mane of hair along with Valentina, who never seemed to do much of anything except look pretty. Ross, the shifter with pale blue eyes came in next, followed by Jack, a Joan Jett wannabe with a much more serious punch.

Finally the sleazy lawyer entered, dressed for a GQ shoot with his sleek suit and shiny silver hair. Dalton was all human and served as the face of the Amara in all business dealings. But he was up to his tailored knees in this wicked shit swamp, just like the rest of them.

Last and definitely considered least came Beth. The Mare who could control dreams and the fresh young face who'd been conned into joining their camp. As the highest person on the totem pole—since Tyr had explained that was actually the worst ranking spot—Beth slunk in and was forced to sit in the only empty chair.

Next to Searenn.

Beth looked like a scared rabbit. As well she should, considering she'd walked right into Ronja's snare. Stupid kid had no idea she'd even been caught.

When the girl pinned her with those big blue eyes, Sylvie felt a twinge at the base of her skull. She wouldn't call the emotion sympathy, not exactly, but it was a close relative.

Truth be told, regret was a better description. Looking at the young but extremely screwed up Beth reminded Sylvie of another kid. One who'd been lost, angry, and full of magic. Perfectly ripe for Ronja's picking.

With a bad-tempered growl, Sylvie moved to the window to stare out at the shadowy and unkempt back yard. The front and sides of the plantation were expertly manicured. Even royalty would have a hard time criticizing Ronja's taste.

But the back. That part was wild. Allowed to grow unchecked and untamed with plenty of places for danger to hide. Ronja got a kick out of the duality, because it was just like her. Gorgeous at a glance, but deadly to any fool who stepped too close.

Sylvie felt better with her face to the cold glass. She imagined she could smell the distant marshes, a scent that always reminded her of her grandmother. Of security and acceptance. A place she would always find love.

No matter what she'd done.

She had once been that lost and angry kid, despite her grandmother's attempts to save her. The days of honesty and encouragement hadn't quite salvaged her ruined soul. Neither had the nights of soothing hands or the prayers that had been there to help when a teenage Sylvie had woken from nightmares.

From memories of another set of hands and the unmentionable things they'd done.

It was no wonder she'd followed right along behind Ronja, not blindly but eagerly. Sylvie had wanted an outlet for her fury. She'd wanted to hurt as she'd been hurt. She'd longed to take some revenge on the city, the world that had abandoned her.

Now she was getting her due.

She'd siphoned power from Ronja, and with it had come a new kind of agony. Heart-pounding terror the first time she'd stood by and watched a man die at R.J.'s hands.

And later, despair, as she'd pictured her mother's face and remembered her grandmother's words.

She would never be a good girl again, even if she'd always managed to refrain from harming another person herself, she'd been party to plenty of barbarism. And that girl. The one from the bar that R.J. had sacrificed for more strength and magic.

Sylvie clenched her fist, hiding it behind her thigh so the others wouldn't see.

That girl. Jen. She wondered if she'd ever forget the sound of her screams and the way they'd changed as the Amara had... worked on her.

The coven of bitches was one thing, but Sylvie had known Jen from the pub. She'd liked her, because despite their differences in friends, she'd never treated Sylvie unkindly.

So she had volunteered to deliver the note. The others had thought her brave to enter the enemy camp by herself, but that hadn't been her motivation at all.

She hadn't wanted to help them take Jen, and she still wished she'd arrived to the marshes later than she had. That she'd stalled instead of rushing out to that lonely clearing in the woods and the altar waiting there.

Then she wouldn't have seen. She wouldn't have heard.

"Care to join us, Sylvie?" Scarlett asked in the soft, cultured voice she practiced often. Despite the sweet sound, her eyes flashed a warning.

Ronja had entered the room and was waiting to begin. None of them should have needed prodding, but Sylvie had allowed herself to get lost in the past.

She deserved a verbal slap, and Scarlett was all too happy to deliver.

"Of course. I was admiring the landscaping. The new pathways are lovely." Sylvie took her seat with a forced smile, playing the flattery card for Ronja. Their leader's ego was her greatest downfall, but none of them would dare point that out.

Ronja inclined her head but maintained the haughty look on her face. Tonight she wore her platinum hair in a twist and a black business suit with a high collar. Everything she wore somehow gave off the *queen* vibe. "I'm sure you all remember the plan that's been set into motion," she said, "and the man who's been recruited for the task."

Their ruler slid a look of praise toward Dalton, the recruiter who'd somehow located a killer and finessed him into working for the Amara.

The lawyer spent time in some very depraved social circles, but culling out a murderer for their own personal use was masterful. And Dalton wouldn't have to get his hands dirty.

Unless he wanted to.

"The first two have been branded, and a third will fall shortly," Dalton told the group, straightening the cuff of his suit as if the mere act of speaking to them was beneath him. The lawyer didn't come around often, by his own choice, and he was the only one of them who could get away with the affront.

Ronja valued him too much to risk his defection or to kill him herself outright.

His superiority rankled a few of the other members, and Tyr's patronizing tone was proof of that. "Branded, yes, but neither of them have been collected. Correct?" Leaning to the side on the arm of his chair, his inky hair pulled into a tight ponytail, Ronja's male lover added, "How do we even know the markings will work?"

"They work," a harsh voice said before Dalton could answer, though he was poised to do so with a smarmy look on his chiseled face. Searenn had spoken but still sat like a broody statue. "I shared a piece of my *ayjehr* with him. Do not question my blood again."

If her low but barbed-wire voice hadn't been threatening enough, the mention of the magic word finished the job. Tyr was at the top of this particular food chain, but Searenn was strong. And held in check by a very thin rope.

If the woman decided to go rogue, Ronja and Scarlett would eventually bring her down. But not before she caused casualties.

Tyr had been foolish to let Dalton's arrogance goad him into speaking rashly. Now he had no way out but to make amends. He clenched his jaw and lowered his eyes, but Sylvie could see the effort cost him dearly.

Tyr had been a warrior in his tribe centuries before and an esteemed seer. The two attributes were only part of what had made him so attractive to Ronja. He was full of pride and wrath, a fitting partner for the queen of death.

Now he was practically choking on that pride, but Searenn would expect an apology. She would demand it.

No one but the owner was ever to speak of the tattoos and the mysticism inherent in their writings. It was taboo. Tyr had insulted Searenn's *ayjehr*. A crime punishable by death in her world.

"Forgive me," the Native American man ground out. "I meant no offense to you and yours. I simply ask if the man is worthy."

Searenn's dark gray hood moved as she nodded almost imperceptibly. "Worthy enough," she said. "Considering the return."

Ronja stood then and the flames behind her burst a foot higher inside the hearth. "Searenn will be rewarded for her offering," she said, glaring at Tyr with her lips pursed. "As will we all. Our hired hand searches for the third as we speak, and once she is branded, the three will be collected." She glanced at the hooded woman who nodded her head in one hard slash.

Sylvie held her breath in the face of Ronja's anger. She didn't want to do anything to draw her notice. Not now.

"And once they are collected?" Tyr asked, his coal dark eyes clashing with Ronja's. He would either get violently laid before the night was out or have his skin peeled from choice, tender spots. Ronja's blood would heal him after, whichever way they decided to go.

Ronja lifted a French-manicured hand to the eerie and still-quiet figure inside the hood. "That's where Searenn takes over."

9

Trevor shoved his hands into the pockets of his pants and let his gaze drift past the tall black bars to the river beyond. Gulls cried as they swept over his head, and the sun did its best to warm the winter day. The soothing combo did little to improve his mood, so he scuffed his foot against the now non-functional electric streetcar tracks running down the middle of the cobblestone road.

A murderer was loose in Savannah and was taking women out faster than Trevor and his partner could keep up. A serial killer here was an oddity in itself, but this one was moving fast and with a ritualistic element that made the stomachs of seasoned detectives churn.

His need for a sensible starting point was the only reason he was meeting with the so-called medium. If she was a fraud, he'd know soon enough, and in the meantime, he'd take any usable information he could get. Even from her.

Hayden Wells had agreed to come back to River Street, though Trevor had heard the surprise and hesitancy in her voice when he'd called her. She had to be wondering why he'd been the one to contact her and not her new friend Cole.

She should be here soon, and he would tell her then. In fact, he would spell it out for her.

She might enjoy her pretend conversations and laugh in secret at those who bought into her con, but he had no time or patience for her. She was nothing more than a distraction. A pretty bit of fluff, and it was too damn bad an attractive woman like her stooped to such levels. She had no shame.

A trio of young girls laughed from somewhere down the street, and the light female sound only made him grit his teeth. *Women are dying, dammit.*

In his town. On his watch.

Standing in front of the empty building near the first crime scene, Trevor watched a hand-holding couple turn into an alley that would lead up to Bay Street, with its fancy hotels, restaurants, and pubs. And a night club whose cross-dressing owner had been made famous in a movie.

All breed of people mingled together in Savannah, and they all liked it that way. Strangers were bonded by the simple truth of location. Transplants and third-generations alike, there was just something about Savannah. And those who got it, those who breathed it in and felt the rush, they stayed, choosing to add their own bit of uniqueness to the wild and unexpected mix.

Farther down the river front things were jumping as the lunch crowds swarmed. Trevor was ready for a bite himself, but would have to settle for takeout. Maybe he'd grab a sub sandwich as he walked, or a gyro from the Greek restaurant a few blocks down.

Cole would be waiting at the far end of the street, giving Trevor plenty of time and distance to get through to Ms. Wells. Her interference wasn't appreciated, so she would just have to come around to his way of thinking. Or else.

He wasn't a detective for nothing, and he'd seen her reaction when he'd threatened to take her in.

Most people would have balked or argued, even pleaded or cried, but she had gone stone white, her gaze shifting to the squad car with a mix of fear and contrition. Trevor knew that look well.

The lady had a secret, and if he was any judge, she probably had a record to go along with whatever she was trying to hide. That's why he'd called up an old acquaintance in California—all right, an old girlfriend—to see what she could dig up on the woman who supposedly talked to ghosts.

Christ. The things he had to deal with just to work a case.

He was going to make sure he didn't have to deal with her much longer. A nuisance is what the woman was, a con artist, and if he had to shove the ugly truth in his partner's face then that's what he would do. Cole had been duped, but the lies would end today. As soon as she showed up...the interrogation of Hayden Wells would commence.

Trevor turned then and saw her coming up the walk.

And his heart seized.

A breeze was blowing all that glorious hair around her face, and he'd always had a thing for the windblown look. Today she wasn't wearing the long, burdensome coat from before. Snug and faded jeans hugged her curves, nicely displayed beneath a short jacket his mother would probably say was off-white. She wore it over a pale pink sweater, something soft and fuzzy. The dreamy color found inside a seashell.

Dreamy? Trevor crossed his arms over his chest and worked up his best scowl. What the hell kind of word was dreamy? Not guy speak. Not cop speak. And Trevor was both.

As Hayden drew near, though, all adjectives and self-recriminations fled from his mind. The only thing he could see was a set of troubled but beautiful golden eyes. And they were staring straight at him.

About five feet from him she stopped and glanced around, confusion playing over her delicate features. She'd just realized Cole wasn't with him and didn't appear to be pleased.

Her disappointment at his partner's absence hit Trevor like

an unexpected jab, an imaginary coldcock. She wanted to talk to Cole instead of him.

The notion made Trevor's inner animal growl low and mean.

He continued to stare at her, then lifted a taunting brow as if to say, *Are you coming or what?*

Pressing her lips into a sweet little bow, his pretty adversary barreled forward with steady but determined steps. She felt put out? Well, too bad. She was dealing with him now, and her wiles would do her no good.

She met him almost toe to toe and lifted her head up in defiance. At least he could be sure they understood each other, no false pretenses or etiquette required.

And so what if she didn't like him? Hell, he didn't like her.

Instead of analyzing his sudden and over-reactive anger, Trevor decided he would channel the resentment instead. Besides, his goal was to get rid of the woman once and for all.

Her and her damn dreamy pink sweater.

"I can tell you're upset to find I'm the only one here," Trevor said. Did his voice sound defensive? He cleared his throat but kept the glower on his face. "And that's what I expected, since you know I won't wrap around your finger as easily as Cole."

Tilting her head, Hayden let her bottom lip drop open. He'd clearly offended her. "Wrapped around my finger. Is that what you think? That's an insult to me and to Cole." She pulled her jacket closed against the cold. "I'd think you would know your partner better."

Trevor tensed. That was part of the problem and why he was having such a hard time accepting the very strange situation he now found himself in. He knew Cole very well, and while his partner might be better-humored than Trevor was, nicer, funnier, and generally more jovial, that didn't mean he was a fool. Far from it.

Cole was sharp and had impressive instincts when it came to people. Part of the reason he'd climbed to detective so quickly despite coming to law enforcement later in life than most. So why was he letting this woman manipulate him?

Trevor remembered the sheet over the second body and how it had flipped up, almost as if in response to Hayden's wishes. *No. No way. I'm not buying into that. One coincidence doesn't equal proof.*

"I can't help it if you're offended by the truth," he said, clipping off the words to show his impatience. "I don't know what you think to get out of all of this, but I won't let your scheming interfere with the job I have to do. You need to stay out of this and stay away from Cole." Had his voice just gotten gravelly? "I don't want you messing with his head." *Yeah. Sure. That's why.*

"Oh?" She lifted her ginger brows to make such an innocent face that he knew he was being mocked. "In that case, I guess you don't want to hear about what I discovered." She swirled and stomped back the way she'd come.

And Trevor let her go. Past the corner of the abandoned building in front of the first crime scene. Past the alley to her right that would lead up to higher level streets. And when she was far enough away, he knew he would have to call her on a well-executed bluff.

Or was it? Using the length of his stride to close the distance between them, he began to think she really did intend to walk away and leave him standing there with nothing more than a view of her retreating backside. "Ms. Wells," he called when he was close enough to not have to shout.

She ignored him and kept walking.

Not a man to be made a fool of, Trevor caught up with his quarry in front of a busy gift shop. A rack of colorful dresses and T-shirts stalled her for a moment, and the pause she took was all he needed.

Intentionally using a gentle touch, he reached forward to take her by the upper arm. "Fine," he ground out, knowing full well she would know what he meant.

If amber could be carved into sharp, cold, daggers, that's what her eyes were now. "I've had enough of your insults. Either keep your thoughts to yourself or fake some courtesy if you have to. Either way, I'm not dealing with you anymore if you're going to treat me like a criminal."

Faced with the harsh reality of having done exactly as she accused, he swallowed the ire that wanted to spring back at her and asked in a controlled voice, "What do you have to share with me? About the murders."

A calculating look crossed her face before she shook his grip loose and smiled. Like a cat who'd just figured out how to open the bird cage. "I'll be happy to tell you everything. As soon as we rejoin Detective Lonergan. I don't think he'll want to miss out."

Backed into a corner of his own making. Beautiful. "Of course." Trevor swept out a gallant arm, waves of sarcasm rolling off as he did so.

There was no love between the two of them, and they both knew it. He would just have to make the best of their time together.

And hope Cole's charm worked the way it usually did with the ladies.

Trevor had done a one-eighty in less than a minute. He'd gone from needing to rid himself of a bothersome female to grinding his teeth in frustration because she was holding something back.

And when it turned out to be some coded message from Casper, he could kick himself and remember why he never dealt with psychics.

Silently he led the way down River Street, nodding to a waitress as he passed the seafood restaurant where people on an overhead balcony enjoyed lunch in the fresh air. The woman's friendly smile caused a surge of guilt inside, and he wanted to quicken his steps. To reach his partner and find out what Hayden knew and if it was anything useful.

This was his town. These were his people. And they were being marked like cattle then slaughtered. Picked off one by one.

Laughter and music rolled from a pub as they passed, and Hayden paused long enough to glance inside. "How long have you been in Savannah?" Trevor asked her, recognizing the curious and delighted look of a tourist.

"Oh," she glanced at him skeptically. Looks like he wasn't the only suspicious one. "We came here last spring."

"We?" Did she have a man in her life? There wasn't a ring on her finger, but these days that didn't mean as much. He'd know more about her background soon anyway, and her marital status wasn't important.

"I...um...have friends here. Some of us live together." She pointed quickly at two river boats that were docked, white with red trim and royal blue flags snapping in the wind. "You can have dinner on the boats?" she asked, referring to a banner that listed scheduled dinner cruises. "I'll have to do that sometime."

Trevor's cop antennae almost buzzed off his head. She was being evasive. And was doing a horrible job of it. If she was such a good scam artist, why couldn't she duck a question with more subtlety? It had been a simple and benign query, and any good con should have a story in place for just such an occurrence.

The tiny speck of doubt in his mind sprouted another branch. He'd already witnessed the sheet incident, calling it coincidence due to lack of a better explanation. And now the woman he'd been sure was a professional fraud was getting rattled over simple inquiries.

The numbers were not adding up, and whenever that happened, he knew he needed to stop where he was and examine his line of reasoning. Because he was headed the wrong way.

The real kicker was that he couldn't cut her off until he got the answers he needed. Trevor clenched his jaw so hard his teeth hurt. He would just have to find a way to deal.

When the bright red awning came into view, he actually felt relieved. They'd reached their destination and the place his partner loved most in the city. The candy store.

He'd have to explain why Hayden was with him and why he hadn't told Cole he'd called her. Two people would be pissed off at him then. This day was getting better and better.

The scent of freshly-made pralines enveloped them as they walked up the mild incline and into a world of sugared fantasy. Nothing could describe the way the store smelled except to say every breath filled you with a sense of warm, mouthwatering bliss.

Trevor didn't buy the fudge and candies like his partner often did, but he enjoyed the atmosphere and never minded a pit stop.

With the job he and Cole did every day, it was always a nice change to see the kids here running around smiling, pointing at glass partitions as treats were crafted right in front of them.

Everybody was happy in the candy store, and he often wondered if Cole came here for more reasons than his sweet-toothed cravings. Perhaps a vacation from the dirty lies the two of them had to sift through on a daily basis.

Trevor let his gaze fall to Hayden, who must have forgotten she was supposed to be mad. Her cheeks bloomed with a joyful flush as she took a hot praline sample, fresh from behind the counter.

"I love this place," she said to him before moving farther into the store to peruse the cases of candy apples, divinity in large fluffy rounds, and every flavor of fudge imaginable. Coated pretzels, pecan clusters, and more, but as Hayden stopped to study a tray of cookies, Trevor noticed how much her hair matched the color of the caramel apples displayed right next to her.

If he didn't know better, he just might believe she was sweet, too.

"Hey, pretty lady. What brings you here?" a familiar male voice asked from the far side of the counter. Just as Cole posed the flirtatious question to Hayden, his pale green eyes shifted to Trevor. Then he looked back to Hayden, who was now giving Trevor a dirty look.

Soon Cole's frown matched hers. And...Trevor was busted.

"Are you two together?" Cole asked just as Hayden accused, "You didn't tell Cole you called me?"

Holding up both hands to stop the building revolt, Trevor moved toward Hayden as Cole came around the wide sales counter at the far end, backed by a black and white checkered wall.

He already had a brown bag in his hands. Good. Maybe the sugar would help soothe his temper.

"I called her down here," Trevor started before taking in both of their hot stares and choosing to get it over with. No more maneuvering, because not only was it the only chance to pull his ass out of the oven, it wasn't his style in the first place. "I wanted to tell her to back off. To stay away from you and our case."

He spoke to Cole, because his partner's trust was paramount. He'd been wrong to go behind his back, and all he could do now was tuck his tail and take the reprimand.

Cole's gray-green eyes lit up like sulfur. "So that's how it is now? We each make unilateral decisions? No need to keep our *partner* informed?" Here came the polar opposite of Cole's laid back and friendly side. He rarely got upset to the point of raised voices and clenched fists, but it was known to happen. Like now.

"Better watch it or you'll crush whatever's in there," Trevor said, pointing to the bag gripped in Cole's hand. "I don't want to have the fact that I made you ruin your dessert on my conscience, too." He held his partner's heated stare long enough to convey his very real regret. "I shouldn't have kept it from you, but I thought I was doing right."

"Yes," Hayden put in, and her arms were crossed so hard he was afraid she might break herself. "He wanted to protect you from the evil rip-off artist who apparently has you...how did he put it? Oh yeah, wrapped around her finger."

Cole deflated at her words but only out of embarrassment for Trevor. Not because he'd forgiven him just yet. "Trevor. You didn't say that." He shook his head and breathed deeply through his nose. "I don't know what's gotten into you."

But as soon as the statement floated into the candy-scented air between them, Cole's eyes narrowed shrewdly.

He glanced at Hayden before giving Trevor the onceover and making a *tsk* sound. With a heavy breath, he reached into his bag and pulled out a saltwater taffy.

Popping the candy into his mouth, Cole chewed slowly, as if he was mulling something over. And when one side of his mouth quirked up in a devilish grin, Trevor lowered his head marginally. Just enough for his friend to understand and hopefully heed the warning to let it go.

Cole simply grinned wider. He knew.

And he knew Trevor knew that he knew.

"Well," Cole started off with a drawl. "I have a feeling I know the problem."

Trevor held his breath and froze where he stood. Cole was like a damned bloodhound when it came to certain things, and picking up on chemistry between people was his specialty. Trevor should never have looked twice at Hayden Wells, even if it was just in passing.

A man ought to be able to admire a softly curved face or sexy set of lips without feeling like he was on a damned matchmaker show or something.

"This is all about you, Hayden," Cole said. He slipped his

arm through hers, telling her they were a team against big, bad Trevor Roch. He paused then, enjoying the blood pressure spike he was causing his partner. His friend.

And Trevor could swear he felt his temple throbbing. *Don't be an ass, Cole. Don't do it.*

Hayden looked between the two men as if confused by their silent language.

"He doesn't believe you are a true medium. He thinks you're a con and that you can't communicate with spirits." Cole winked at Trevor when Hayden wouldn't see.

That was it then. His partner was definitely going to be an ass.

"And I have a suggestion." Cole tugged on Hayden's arm now, making sure she stayed on his side and went along with the plan. Whatever it turned out to be.

"What's that?" she asked warily.

"Savannah is one of the most haunted cities in the country. Ghost tours on every corner."

"Now wait a minute," Trevor said but didn't add anything when Cole shut him down with a raised brow. His partner had more he could say if he wanted to, and he was letting Trevor know he should take the out and be grateful. After the stunt Trevor had pulled today, he owed him.

"I believe Hayden will be a valuable asset in solving this case, but she can't do that with you blocking her. You need to get your doubts and suspicions out of the way." He asked Hayden, "I know it will be a busman's holiday, but the walking ghost tour is gorgeous at night. Are you up for it?"

Pressing her lips together and staring pointedly at Trevor, she said, "I guess that's the only way to get through to him." As if he weren't standing right there. "And I'm tired of all the skepticism." She smiled at Cole. "So when do we go?"

"Uh-uh. Not me." He took his arm away and stepped back, leaving her and Trevor standing closer together. "I'm not the one who needs convincing."

Trevor put all the you'll-pay-for-this in his stare he could as he watched Cole ease back.

"You want me to go with him?" Hayden asked wide-eyed.

The horror in her voice was enough to have Trevor glancing aside and changing opinions just as fast as he had before. Another one-eighty. "So I'm right, and you can't do what you say. You're afraid you'll be found out." His own smile felt aggressive as he watched her skin go from flushed to pale and back to an angry pink.

The blush was way too flattering on her.

"Fine. Just get ready to swallow your words," she said, tossing a long lock of that fascinating hair over her shoulder.

"Here," Cole said, holding out a taffy to Trevor and grinning. "You can chase the humble pie down with this."

"Hmph. I seriously doubt I'll need it." He rubbed his chin and purposely avoided looking at Hayden. "Besides, you know I'm more of a hard candy guy."

"Shocking," Hayden uttered under her breath. "Hard as a *Roch*, right?"

The play on words wasn't lost on Trevor as he pulled his phone out of his pocket to call the visitor center for tour schedules.

But despite all the banter and his remaining suspicions, he suddenly had only one type of candy on his mind.

Caramel.

10

In the day's dying light, the small cabin and surrounding woods took on a more ominous quality. Though he couldn't see the horizon from where he stood, the golden-orange glow permeated everything around him. Cold air and barren trees were all that stood between this clandestine meeting spot and the marsh.

Though meeting was a kind word for what was actually going on. This was an ambush, plain and simple, and the unsuspecting victim wasn't going to come quietly.

In fact, Joseph was not ashamed to say he was glad to have a seventy-something-year-old woman backing him up. Grandmother or not, she was the only person in the world that would be able to keep Sylvie in line once she arrived to find him here.

And Mrs. Lee assured him her granddaughter would show. After all, she'd stomped on a piece of paper in her shoe. What more could he have asked for?

His sarcastic thoughts didn't ease his mind, because truth be told, he was as positive as the old lady. He'd been raised with magic. He knew its taste and smell. And the ball of lead in his stomach right now was all the proof he needed. His sixth sense, that Anna claimed everyone had, was rearing up and shouting to him.

Sylvie was close. And she was headed this way.

As if to confirm, the haint-blue door creaked open behind him, and Mrs. Lee stepped out. She let her arms fall blithely to her sides, but Joseph could see her resolve in the set of her jaw and the way she planted her feet hips-width apart. She seemed to be battle-hardening.

Which didn't make him feel any better.

It wasn't that he was afraid of the woman who was now making her way through the brush, her path given away by the telltale rattle of shrubs, but he did have a bundle of nerves mixed with oily trepidation to deal with. Since that's what the lead ball had turned into.

He was only accepting the truth. That no matter what was said or done, this confrontation was not going to be pleasant. For any of them. But talking to Sylvie today was an intervention of sorts, and he owed it to his mother.

Because whether she knew it or not, his mother owed it to her childhood friend, Regina. Sylvie's dead mother.

She cleared the forest then and her steps came to a sudden stop. The silence was overpowering, and for a moment, he was afraid Sylvie would turn and run.

Then he saw the fire of hatred light up her brown-sugar eyes, and he knew he had a fight on his hands. He just hoped he could talk to her before she put some ball-rotting curse on him.

"How dare you come here?" she yelled, her footsteps in a fast, hard clip now, and headed straight at him. Forget curses or hexes, judging by the lean of her posture, she planned to take him to the ground. "She has nothing to do with this! You leave her alone!"

Just as Joseph braced himself for impact, Mrs. Lee barreled down the steps and angled her way in front of him. "Hold on, girl," she called, waving her hands to slow Sylvie's dash.

Feeling his male pride starting to shrivel, Joseph moved around the older woman and up to the foreground. Having a granny at your back was one thing, but damned if he would cower behind that red cotton skirt.

"Take it easy," he said to Sylvie in a tone mothers reserved for rude children. "I'm not here to do your grandmother any harm."

When she slowed her roll in exchange for pacing back and forth, fists clenched and tapping on her thighs, he added, "I came to talk to you."

"You should have found me in town, then, but I guess you were too scared to try something like that. Right? To face me alone? You had to come sneaking around my family."

She stepped toward him, her hand held up in a twisted form. "Bad play, *Junior*," she said with particular derision and insult. "Because that's not going to save you."

"Sylvia Marie," Mrs. Lee snapped. "You drop that hand and mind your manners. That's no way to treat a guest."

If a person could choke on air, that's exactly what it looked like the hoodoo priestess was doing. Complete with a rough gasp and reddened cheeks. "A guest? You can't be serious."

She poked a finger at Joseph, and he had no doubt she'd prefer to be poking through the walls of his heart. "Don't you know who he is? He's one of them. Those witches who want to kill me! To kill us all!"

"Now, girl, that's an exaggeration, and you know it. Joseph doesn't mean you any harm." Mrs. Lee reached a hand out to her granddaughter, but Sylvie wrinkled her nose and looked at the open palm as if it were filled with hornets.

"Joseph?" she scoffed. "You mean baby boy Junior?"

High in the trees a crow cried, and it sounded like he was telling his friends to come gather round. To settle in and watch the show. Caw! Caw! *Fight! Fight!*

Joseph rolled his shoulders back and crossed his arms over

his chest. Why was Sylvie so hung up on his name? Making fun like a school yard bully.

And every time she said it in that tone, he felt his impatience hitch up another notch. *Baby boy?* He ground his upper teeth over the lower to channel some fury. He'd show her a boy, all right.

"We haven't killed anyone, especially innocent bystanders." Joseph moved closer and blocked the hand she shoved at him. He got up close, ignoring the scent of jasmine floating off her light brown skin. "Can you say the same thing? *Sylvia.*" He wasn't the only one who'd changed his name.

Behind him Mrs. Lee gasped. "Oh, baby girl. Tell me it's not true. Tell me."

Her sharp cheekbones lost all their color as Sylvie cast her eyes to her grandmother. It was as if Joseph no longer stood there, and for a second, he felt a flash of guilt for putting the distress on her sculpted face.

Because beauty on the outside was never an issue when it came to her. Only her insides were in question. Her values. Her soul.

"Gran, I never touched that girl. I promise. I...I don't do stuff like that." Her hands wrapped around Mrs. Lee's wrists, clutching like desperate claws. "I promise I didn't hurt her. And nobody else either."

"But you didn't do anything to stop it," Joseph ground out, unaware he had so much roiling anger bottled up for Sylvie.

He detested the whole lot of the evil thugs she ran with. All the Amara could go straight to hell as far as he was concerned. He despised them, without a doubt.

But what he felt about Sylvie was different, like she'd somehow betrayed him, his mother, and everyone who'd ever cared about her. Or might have if given the chance.

"What would your mother say about your lifestyle, Sylvie?" Wow. He'd thrown that thorny gauntlet down quick, but time was critical here. If he wanted to save the thick-skulled woman in front of him, he couldn't afford to play nice.

This wasn't demon-worshippers anonymous or something. Sit down and introduce yourself. Tell us all about how you just can't help the things you do.

And there was the bone stuck in his craw. She had come from better stock. Whatever she had gone through, there was no valid reason to turn to Ronja. To want to summon Bastraal, a demon who would feast on the flesh of babes if shown the open door.

No. Excuse.

"You leave my momma out of this." Sylvie was shivering... no, she was quaking where she stood. And were her eyes shiny with moisture? That would mean she was feeling some strong emotion, but whether it was rage or misery, Joseph couldn't guess.

"Why, girl? Why do you do it?" Mrs. Lee twisted her hands around so she was the one holding onto her granddaughter now. Firmly but lovingly. "This ain't no way to chase the pain out. It will only grow. Get stronger. Uglier. Baby girl...please, stop now while you still can."

"Stop? How am I supposed to stop? Do you have any idea what..." Sylvia trailed off and pushed the angst from her expression, allowing bitterness and a steel wall of stubborn to cover her features instead. "There's no way I can leave the Amara. And..." She swallowed and squared her shoulders as she looked into her grandmother's eyes. "I don't want to leave. I like what I've found. What she's given me."

Mrs. Lee slapped her hand down through empty space in a demonstration of her incense. "Poison! Poison is what she's given you, and her toxin will rot you out, girl. From the deepest part of you, where it takes hold and suffocates all the love and light. From there it will spread and metastasize, worse than any disease."

The older lady turned to flee toward her house, pain and sobs filling her voice as she yelled over her shoulder. "It will rot you out!"

Watching her departure, Joseph realized how hard it must be for the woman to lose her grandchild to evil. And evil didn't come much worse than the Amara. He knew however much he wanted to help Sylvie, her grandmother wanted it tenfold.

"Shame on you," he said into the cool, breeze flowing between him and Sylvie. "What you do on a daily basis is bad enough, but what you're doing to her," he jerked a thumb toward the shack, "to the one person who loves you most..."

Unable to find strong enough words, he stalled and shook his head. Then in a low voice, he said again, "Shame on you."

"Fuck you, Junior! You have no idea what I've been through." She leaned closer, and he could feel her furious breath as she berated him. "Where were you then, huh? And your saintly mother? Because I know she's the one that put you up to this."

She shook her fists near his face, as if she was barely keeping herself from hitting him. "Where was she then, huh? Huh?!"

Joseph let her vent and stood his ground. He was pissed as hell at the selfish person standing before him, the woman who'd chosen sin over goodness.

But the more upset she became, the more cracks started to show, splintering from the amazing brown eyes that didn't want to cry all the way to her chest and the broken heart that still beat within.

And through those cracks he could see the girl. The child who had been cast into hell with no one there to save her. At least not soon enough.

And that girl was still terrified. Still hurting. Beneath all the threats and bluster, she was still waiting to be saved.

Instead of saying anything more—no accusations, no promises, no warnings—Joseph simply held out his hand.

The world around them slowed until the twilight seemed

frozen. No movement or sound, only the echo of his own pulse as he watched a multitude of emotions play on her face. She was motionless as well as she stared at his hand, the second that had been offered to her today. Then she sucked in a deep, hard breath and broke the spell.

"No," she whispered and staggered backward. "No. Don't do that." With pure terror in her wide, brown eyes, Sylvie spun on her heels and ran like hellhounds were baying for her soul.

There had been no threat here. Only Joseph and an honest offer of forgiveness.

As her steps pounded into the dark forest, he realized he was losing his chance. One he might not get again. For reasons he didn't dare admit, Joseph desperately wanted her to hear him, to come back and listen. He clenched his fists and shouted her name.

11

Trevor and Hayden had both been unusually quiet since the candy shop when Cole had essentially shoved the two of them out the door and sent them on their way. She'd walked alongside the tall, broody cop as they'd traveled several blocks on foot to the ghost tour starting point.

Now they stood outside a weathered gray house with turquoise shutters. The historic building was lovely and creepy all at the same time, having been turned into a popular eatery, one that got its name from a dark and bloody past.

The place was called a pirate house for more reasons than the fancy sign out front. It was a huge attraction in Savannah, and the grisly stories about murders and kidnappings only made the restaurant more intriguing.

As she finished her last to-go hush puppy, Hayden gestured toward the gathering group of tourists. "Looks like it's almost time." She and Trevor had taken their food in bags to eat outside as the gloaming fell over the city, casting its lovely and magical light across the river.

She was surprised by the excitement tingling through her body. Though she and the detective were still at odds and were both trying very hard to make sure eating together felt in no way like a *date*, there was just enough warmth in the winter air and just enough gold in the twilight to fill her with a sense of adventure.

Buddha knew she had seen enough of ghosts and hauntings in her lifetime, but the thrill of a spooky sojourn through history-laden Savannah was something new. The other people in the tour were chatty and lively, and their eagerness was contagious, so she found herself looking forward to the tour. A slow stroll on a gorgeous night in an amazing city, one that could best be appreciated from a pedestrian's viewpoint.

And if she could knock Mr. Cocky Cop off his pedestal along the way, that would only serve as a bonus.

By the time the perky young tour guide had gathered her flock and outlined their route, a huge, white moon was rising against the navy sky. To kick off the tour, they were led back into the restaurant and allowed into an area that was normally chained off to customers.

Soon Hayden saw why, and she instantly grew queasy as the lingering stench of death and misery grabbed her like a hundred greedy arms.

She felt a sturdy hand on the small of her back as Trevor asked in a quiet voice, "You all right?"

Realizing she'd wavered on her feet, Hayden swallowed the bile that wanted to rise and nodded at him with a weak and watery smile. "Fine," she said, unwilling to admit the smallest defeat. "Hazard of the job."

With that she turned to listen to the guide as she told of poor citizens being taken in the night and dropped down the center of the spiraling, stone steps. Those that survived the plummet to the dirt floor of the rum cellar were then shanghaied off through the tunnel, one of many that ran beneath the Savannah streets, and taken out to a waiting pirate ship.

Their life after that must have been horrific. Slave, torture victim, or if they were lucky, a wicked pirate for the rest of their days.

After the spiel, the group was allowed to walk down the stairs and look around. To feel the rough rocks and gaze back up through the stairwell. To imagine the fall.

But Hayden was more interested in the large, wooden door blocking the tunnel's entrance. She was reminded of Willyn's brush with death and how her friend had literally run for her life through a similar underground system. She'd barely escaped from Scarlett and her putrid yet sparkly red magic.

Shauni had been the first of the coven to face evil. Willyn had gone next, locating the ancient witch's book from centuries before. And Viv had used that book to find the demon's burial ground, from which the coven had taken mystically infused soil to perform a ritual. One that had increased their gifts. Their powers.

Hayden chewed her bottom lip and pondered the really worrisome question. Why did they have to be stronger? If Paige was right and each trial was going to be more difficult than the last, what could Hayden really expect? More to the point, was she prepared?

Feeling the swarm of bodies moving around her, she jerked out of her thoughts to see everyone climbing the stairs. She fell in behind the pack and rejoined Trevor on the upper floor. He hadn't gone down into the cellar, but since he was a Savannah boy, he'd probably seen it before.

Once outside she took a cleansing breath and shook off the last coating of gloom that had covered her in the cellar. The tour was in full swing now, and she fell into a relaxed stride next to Trevor near the back of the crowd.

The young woman leading them was well informed and entertaining, but Hayden had her own personal tour guide. One who knew all the stories, even if he didn't believe them.

So she pulled up her big witch panties and prepared herself for a challenge. To convince the king of cynicism that ghosts not only existed, they interacted.

The night was clear and breezy, cool enough for the appropriate level of spookiness, yet pleasant and calming. A nice change from the dirty, basement floor that had seen so many deaths.

Every entity was different, and some left a very real smudge on the places they'd died, even if their tormented spirit had already passed over. She was happy for the reprieve, but given Savannah's reputation for hauntings, the tranquility probably wouldn't last long.

While it did, she would let herself enjoy the beauty around her. They crossed through a park on their way to the next stop. Smaller trees with smooth, silky bark graced the perimeter of the square, and flagstone pathways added a touch of elegance. Wooden benches were framed and supported by blocks in some sort of cement and seashell mixture.

Hayden stopped to stroke her fingers over the stone. "Lovely," she cooed before she could stop the awestruck and very feminine tone from escaping.

"It's called tabby," Trevor explained. "Made of lime, sand, and oyster shells. Pretty common around here. Also in St. Augustine, Florida and Beaufort, South Carolina."

Hayden grinned in the dark, noticing Trevor pronounced the last city as *bo-fort,* sounding like a true southerner, while she'd heard many people say *bee-yew-fort* instead.

She preferred Trevor's version and the way his accent had slipped out, slow and syrupy. For an instant the hardened detective had disappeared.

Jabbing both hands in his pant pockets, he added, "You still haven't told me what you found out about the symbol."

And he's back, Hayden thought, noting how his eyes had tightened at the corners again. A sign of his impatience. Actually, it was simpler to count the times he *wasn't* being pushy or demanding. So far she was up to one.

"I turned the drawing over to an acquaintance," she

answered, tossing her head back to enjoy the caressing wind. "An ancient language specialist." Wouldn't Quinn get a kick out of hearing himself described that way?

"So you don't actually have anything. Yet."

She could hear the accusation in that last word, laced with a heavy dose of what-did-I-really-expect-from-a-charlatan? As if on cue, her defensiveness bristled into place. "You had no reason to trick me the way you did earlier. You insinuated over the phone that I was coming to meet you and your partner." She shrugged her jacket closer together in front, a subconscious gesture of self-protection. "Where I come from we call that deception."

"Where you come from people are a lot more...*open-minded*." Trevor had wanted to say gullible, but he'd promised Cole he would be a gentleman, since he was serving as host tonight.

He was doing his best, but something about this woman made all his muscles bunch together. He felt like a tightly-coiled spring just ready to blast apart, and for all his supposed skills, he couldn't put his finger on the reason.

He suspected her of being a con, that much was established, but there was something else. An electricity that shot straight into him whenever she was close.

And he still wasn't sure if he liked it or not.

Her hair lifted as a quick gust of wind rushed by them, and her scent found him. It wrapped around him. She smelled herbal, for lack of a better word, as if she'd rolled in greenery and something sweeter, more floral.

"What perfume are you wearing?' he asked, then shifted his hand to his holster as if to remind himself he was a cop and not a damned spritzer girl at the mall. Why had he asked her that?

"Ah..." She laughed a little, evidently thinking the same thing he was, then added, "You probably smell the essential oil I sometimes use when I meditate. Today was myrrh." She glanced up at him as they slowed and gathered in the empty street with the tour guide waiting for everyone to settle in more closely.

Then Hayden leaned toward Trevor and whispered, "Orange blossom body spritzer, too."

His legs and torso went rigid, and this time he could definitely put a name to what he was experiencing. Lust. Wild and rampant and coursing through his veins. Why he'd be so turned on by the words *body spritzer,* he didn't know.

Unless of course it was because they'd ridden on a breathy sound from between two full, pink lips. And not just anyone's, but the woman who reminded him of spun sugar and a walk in the garden.

Hayden Wells, who Trevor truly believed was trying to pull a fast one on his partner and best friend.

Yet here he was on a moonlit stroll with her, thinking about the color of her hair and the fact that she used essential oils on her light, golden skin.

And *damn.* He had to stop envisioning what she did with them.

Shuffling forward and a step away from Hayden, Trevor soothed himself with one thing. At least he knew why he was responding to her this way. His body wanted to move in for the arrest, but his mind told him he'd been given bad information. That there were things yet to be uncovered about the apparently kind-hearted medium.

Since he was on a case, there could be no midway point between mind and body. No common ground. So he needed to tamp down the sexual energy. Fast.

He noticed Hayden studying the street beneath their feet, also made of the tabby mixture. Then she glanced up as the tour guide started telling them about the three-story, white house behind her. The one with windows that looked like they belonged in Amityville instead of Savannah.

But Hayden wasn't listening to what the guide had to say,

and by the stricken look on her face and the hand clamped to her abdomen, he guessed she didn't need to. She was staring at a window on the top floor.

The top floor. For a brief hitch in time Trevor completely and unaffectedly believed in her.

Then he scoffed at himself and moved to stand beside her, remembering that almost anyone could buy a guide book to learn the city's grisly tales. She'd probably just done her research.

Still, he'd play along. He rested a hand on her shoulder, and instead of flinching away, she surprised him by grasping his fingers instead. "That is one bad place," she said. "So many spirits in one area."

"Are you talking to a ghost right now?" he asked, trying to ignore the soft clench of her fingers on his.

But no need, since she brushed them aside and gave him a disgusted look. "Did you see my lips moving?"

She pointed with a subtle lift of one finger until his gaze followed the line to the third floor window. "He's an angry guy, and he especially hates it when people stop to stare."

Trevor chuckled. "So do the owners." Mimicking her earlier body language he leaned in and whispered, "I mean, the ones that are still breathing." He jerked his head toward the group that was wandering away. "Which is why we're moving out. If you don't come on, we'll get left behind."

Determined to stop letting the man make her feel foolish, Hayden took several long strides and caught up to him. "There was an exorcism performed in that house, wasn't there? It was a while ago, but it scorched the area with its failure. No wonder," she said, cutting off Trevor's response. "That spirit isn't going anywhere. He was furious and has been for a long time."

She snagged the black material of his jacket near his elbow, making sure he stopped walking when she did. And paid attention. "He was pointing down and doing so with a great deal of agitation."

"Who was?" Trevor asked, running a hand through his hair. Then he stepped back.

What was wrong with him? Hayden blew out through her nose and channeled some calm. Maybe he just didn't like the smell of myrrh. Fine. Then she'd use it every day until she was no longer dealing with Detective Trevor Roch.

"The ghost in that house. Why would he want me to look down below?"

His dark blonde brows winged up. "You mean you didn't read about the crypt they put the house on top of when they relocated it? The man who moved that home along with another was pretty well-known. There was even a movie made about him and the murder he committed."

If the dictionary didn't define smartass then the expression Trevor was giving her now would. "Oh. I see," Hayden told him in a voice as flat as the brick sidewalk they were standing on. "You think I looked all this up, so I could improve my performance." She drove a finger into his chest, and *who cares!* if he was a cop or not.

He was also making her churn with anger. An emotion she rarely allowed to take control, because rash and foolish behavior often resulted.

"And when was I supposed to have brushed up on my ghost stories, Detective? I've been with you since I found out I was taking this tour under duress." Instead of letting him give an answer, because she was sure he'd come up with one, Hayden marched off in pursuit of their group.

She heard Trevor's steps behind her but was too upset to give him heed. Nor did she feel like appreciating the old-fashioned style pharmacy they passed, with its narrow brick structure, black wrought-iron balcony, and painting that had been preserved in the 1800-style script that read *Prescription* on one side and *Drugs* on the other.

Their next stop was a graveyard, and *joy!* It was the one on Oglethorpe just behind The Barracks. Well, if Trevor wanted to arrest her, he wouldn't have to drag her far.

He sidled up next to her and even through the thick shield of her anger, she could sense the warmth of his body. Probably due to all that muscle mass. Viv had told her men naturally generated more heat because of it.

Hayden tucked her hair behind one ear and wished fervently that he would edge away from her. Because she wasn't budging.

She jumped when his deep voice rumbled near her ear. His breath both warm on her skin and minty clean. "See any ghosts around?" he asked.

"Plenty." She put her hands on her hips. "It's a cemetery." Saying nothing else, she drew near the tall, black bars of the fence and peered in.

A flash of color caught her eye, and she pressed her face against the cold metal for a better look. She'd seen something red and low to the ground, moving with furtive steps. A child out in a graveyard alone at night? Surely not.

But she was just as sure whatever she'd seen hadn't been a spirit. She hadn't lied when she told Trevor there were ghosts here. Wherever dead bodies amassed, spirits often gathered, whether they were buried in the vicinity or not. She'd always assumed it had to do with some sort of supernatural vibe, because whenever she'd asked a ghost about the behavior they'd simply told her they liked it. They were drawn to burial grounds.

Easing back from the bars, Hayden turned to find Trevor staring at her, but his burning gaze scared her more than any fleeing figure out in the dark. He wasn't looking at her with annoyance, distrust, or even confusion. She couldn't put an accurate name to what she saw in the moonlit blue, but it made the center of her chest burn and her heart stutter.

A long, deep pull of recognition unfurled in her belly, and all she could think was, *Oh, no.*

She practically darted past him now as the tour guide took advantage of the flashing white hand to lead her followers across Oglethorpe and down toward their next destination. She didn't think Trevor would let her continue on without him, she really didn't, but there was always hope.

She didn't want to acknowledge what had passed between them in that moment of locked stares.

He was a cop! A sworn officer of the law, and how much of a fate-slap-in-the-face was that? Funny, destiny, gods, goddesses or whoever. Ha ha. Funny.

"Hayden," she heard him call her name, so she shook her head and put a finger to her lips. She pretended to be listening to the guide tell them the story of Wright Square and why there was so little Spanish moss hanging in the huge, crooked oaks standing guard there.

Soon they were all in the middle of the square, looking up to the long, thick branches that curved their way through time and the cruel winter air. A woman had been hung there years ago, months after she'd seen her husband suffer the same fate. The woman had watched through the jail house bars, bearing out the rest of her pregnancy, until she too would be strung up and "hanged by the neck until dead."

Hayden was still in a panic about Trevor, and whenever she shot a glance to him, he just held her eyes. He looked hard again, impenetrable, tinged with a bit of mad at the edges.

When he rotated his head to the side and frowned, Hayden naturally assumed he was brushing her off.

Then she heard it. Crying. A woman was crying, and judging by Trevor's turning in a circle to search the area, he'd heard it, too.

"Someone thinks they're a comedian," he said, lashing out at Hayden with stormy blue eyes as if she was somehow responsible for the sound.

"It's not me," she said with just as much vehemence in her tone as he was raking over her with a look. The group had moved on, but this time they didn't go after them.

Hayden searched for the source of the sobs, because they were back again. Not only did she hear them loud and clear, but her spirit radar was beeping insanely. There might as well have been a flashing red dot near the middle of the square.

Right next to a bench, in fact, because that's where she saw the ghost.

"I don't hear it anymore," Trevor said, his voice full of question.

"I do, and she's over there. She's talking to the couple on that bench, pleading with them to help her." Hayden wrung her hands together. "But they can't help. They can't talk to her."

"But you think you can." He walked over to Hayden. Between the demand in his eyes and the tic in his pulsing temple, it was as if he wanted her to deny it. To finally admit she was a liar. He stared at her as if he was giving her one last chance to come clean.

Hayden stood tall and let her hands drop to her side. She was calm now. Serene. And no one could make her doubt who she was and what purpose she served in this crazy, painful world. Not ever again.

"I know I can help her. Whether you choose to stay is up to you, but understand this, Detective Roch. I don't have to prove anything to you."

As she pivoted, Hayden's gaze landed on the ghost, and now the woman was looking back. "Can you help me find my baby?" she asked, rushing forward in a long white nightgown. "Can you help me find my baby?"

"Your baby isn't here anymore. Your baby has passed on. If you..." Hayden broke off when the ghost veered away from her and ran to meet an older man who was walking his dog through the park. "Can you help me find my baby?" the spirit asked the man, but of course, he walked right through her.

Hayden felt her soul slump along with her shoulders. She couldn't save them all, this much she knew, but now was a terrible time to fail. Not only would she be worrying over this poor, pitiful spirit who'd been lost for so many years, but she'd have to wrestle with the fact that she hadn't been able to bring the woman's suffering to an end.

And she'd have to choke down all that pride she'd just dredged up. She'd admit defeat to Trevor. "She's not able to, I mean, I don't think…"

"She's insane," Trevor said with a meaningful tilt of his head. "At least, that's what they say about her. The woman who was hanged here after she gave birth."

"Yes. She's trapped in her old life and unwilling or unable to see that she's dead. Some spirits choose to walk the earth, fully aware that they don't belong here anymore. Others are mentally shattered and get stuck between realities." Hayden's eyes watered, catching her off guard, so she hurried away from Trevor to hide the sudden and overwhelming sadness.

She'd made it to the corner of the square near the base of a monstrous oak when he grabbed her arm and brought her to a stumbling halt. She lurched to the side as her momentum side-wheeled but felt herself being lifted off the ground by two strong arms.

Holding her close, Trevor eased her down to her feet and kept her wrapped up tight until she spoke against his arm. "I'm steady now." She closed her eyes and inhaled the fresh scent of whatever soap he used.

Oh. He smelled really good.

When he didn't let go she hazarded a glance up and saw the same look in his eyes that had frightened her before, but now she was in his arms, pressed against the firmness of his chest.

With nowhere to run.

In the shadows of the hulking tree, they stared at each other, energy pulsing between their joined bodies. Obscured from the city moving all around them, they stood locked together. And Hayden wondered if he was as conflicted as she was.

She couldn't deny the physical reaction she was having to Trevor, but her head still argued the idiocy of it all, reminding her how much she resented Detective Roch. Too bad they were one and the same.

His neck corded with tension, and Hayden got the impression he was struggling not to kiss her. When his eyes flickered down to her chest, exposed by her open coat, she thought his mind had taken a lurid turn.

He released her from his grip and ran one finger along the V of her pink sweater. Her breath caught in her throat and her heart felt five times too large for her chest.

Then he scooped up the chain hanging from her neck and pulled her amulet out from beneath the soft fabric. Studying the intricate silver piece, Trevor rubbed his thumb over the center stone. The clear, pink gem that was Hayden's magical color.

She felt as if he was stroking the very core of her being.

Just as it seemed her legs would melt from beneath her, Hayden caught another flash of red in the darkness. Far across the park she saw the same small figure from before in the cemetery. Only this time the thing was crouched near the ground.

And it was watching her.

"Trevor," she said, urgency cracking into her voice. "We need to leave. There's something here."

He looked around in confusion. "What do you mean? A ghost?"

"No. No. I'm not sure." She started backing away as the red figure crept in their direction, skimming over the grass without disturbing a blade.

Her instincts were raging, but she couldn't make sense of the way this being was affecting her. She could see it, but it wasn't human. It wasn't a spirit either, at least none she'd ever encountered. What *was* it?

Whatever the creature was, it was coming for her, and...it was growing.

The cool night air was no longer refreshing, and the smell of the river made her gag. Dirt from the streets seemed to clog her throat and her vision. Her eyes blurred. "I'm going to be sick," she croaked and started to bend forward.

Trevor didn't let her, instead he grabbed her shoulders and pushed her upright. "Hold onto it until we get out of here. Just hold on."

Hauling her out into the street, he called to a young girl resting atop her Pedi-cab. Trevor jumped in and guided Hayden into the seat beside him before barking an order to go.

The girl's long legs spun into motion as she veered the bicycle-powered chariot toward a side street. "Just keep driving," he told the young girl before he turned to Hayden and cradled her chin in his palm. "Better?" he asked.

Gulping in the cleaner smelling air, now that they were leaving the square and that *thing* behind, Hayden nodded. "Yes. I'm sorry. I don't know what happened."

"It's been a long day. You need to get some rest." Amazingly, Trevor kept his arm around her and let her rest against him as they rode through town.

And equally astonishing, Hayden stayed put. She craved the nearness of another person right now. She was cold to the bone and shaken to her very center.

She had no idea what she'd seen back there, but when it had realized Hayden could see it, rage had scorched the air. Hatred and violence had emanated from its transparent red form, and Hayden had been swamped by the sense of decay. Sickened.

She could thank the strange powers that be for Trevor and his quick actions. He'd gotten her out of there just in time and hadn't questioned her for a second.

He'd whisked her away, steadied her step, and held her close, just as he was still doing. He'd done it all without comment or judgment.

Without a single doubt.

12

Savannah weather didn't lend itself to very much rain, only the occasional burst that could be counted on to pour itself out rather quickly. But on a rare, dreary day it seemed the gods made up for the unreliable showers, and this was one of those times.

Rain pounded the earth, woods, and the coven's island home as mercilessly as a drunken step-father. As far as Hayden's eyes could see was a deep and gloomy gray.

The heavy weather suited her mood, and as she leaned against the silk-papered wall, she let the thrumming sound of water hitting stone shudder through her.

For the first time in a very long time, she had skipped her break-of-dawn yoga ritual. She was too nervous to find her balance. Too terrified to be calm.

Horrific and unknown creatures were stalking the nights, and somehow, some way, it was up to her to stop them.

Whatever the *them* were.

She had a real need for comfort now, not only because of the rain, but the topic she and the others were gathering to discuss. After telling them all what she'd seen in the park last night, Hayden had willingly taken the Mickey in her tea when Claudia suggested it.

She'd also listened as the history teacher told her of the original Mickey Finn, famed bartender who'd drugged his patrons before emptying their pockets and dumping them into a back alley.

But the story hadn't lulled her to sleep as much as the smooth, velvet voice of her friend.

Even now, as Dare stoked the fire in the hearth and Anna patted the empty seat on the couch for Hayden to take, love and undying loyalty streamed around the room and into her bones, which still felt like their marrow had turned to ice. She had yet to fully warm up after the foul and frigid cloud of evil that had swept over her last night.

But her sisters wouldn't stop trying to cheer her. They wouldn't give up.

The sound of subdued female voices filtered in from the foyer as the rest of the coven drew closer to the study. They trickled in in various manner of dress, from Shauni's cotton green pajamas, like Hayden still wore, only hers were yellow silk, to Claudia's modern-glam, her tall, shapely physique decked out in a beige dress with a thin, gold belt.

Paige was sporting gray scrub pants with a sleeveless Rosie the Riveter T-shirt. As close to pajamas as she was ever going to get.

Patting the metal-blue of the sofa again, Anna lifted her chin up in silent invitation. The leader of their coven was curled up on one end of the long, stately piece of furniture and was sipping coffee from a clear cobalt mug. Her luxurious brown hair was twisted into a knot, and her eyes, the same blue as her cup, were soft. Encouraging. "Sit now, Sister, as this too shall pass."

"Yes, Sister," Kylie sang out in an imitation of Shakespearean dialect. "Do sit and partake of the libations." The blonde with an affinity for lightning-style magic laughed at herself as she beat Paige to the leather chair closest to the fire.

Paige wasn't defeated yet and settled into a similar chair near the black, grand piano. Leisurely she crossed her legs into a lotus and grinned.

There were plenty of places to snuggle into in the large study, and the women each found a spot. Lucia and Viv dragged chairs closer in, though Nick stopped Viv halfway and took over. The amiable bar owner was surprisingly protective of his new love.

The study was meant for a variety of activities—reading, paperwork, music-making—and was large enough for several all at once, but there was no denying the relaxed and inviting feel of the space.

Just like the grand hall, the sizeable room was trimmed in a luxurious and rich mahogany. A mantle of the same wood was over the fireplace, and above it, age-old scenes were etched into panels. Shiny brass rimmed the hearth itself, shimmering now from the light of undulating flames.

Three large, arched windows gave a view of the storm outside, and rivulets of water running down the glass cast moving shadows on the intricate Bessarabian rug. With silk wallpaper of dark gray and gold, the room was both splendorous and cozy.

Perfect for a long, rainy-day discussion of monsters.

Hayden joined Anna on the couch and noticed the dark table in front of it had been cleaned off. Before, interesting knick-knacks like antique books and medical tools had graced the ebony wood. Now they were gone.

Someone had prepared the space for other materials. Like the books and research papers Quinn had been poring over all night long.

Hayden had always been amazed by the St. Germaine library and its expansive shelves, but when she'd been shown the section stocked with books on ancient cultures and lore, she'd actually felt sorry for Anna's younger brother. Quinn had insisted on perusing every page himself, since he knew what to look for.

He'd already been working feverishly, after the incident the other night and the black form pushing through Shauni's door. But with Hayden's additional experience in Wright Square, he had become fanatical, running on nothing but caffeine and finger foods.

So it was no surprise when he entered the room looking like he'd been worked over and hung out to dry. His bark-brown hair was mussed, and stubble was thick on his jaw. Despite his ruffled clothing and appearance, his eyes were alive with discovery.

Until they fell on Hayden. She caught the flash of sympathy before he winked at her and lifted a thick, ebony book. "Got it," he said, moving to the table in front of her and Anna where he laid the heavy tome and other papers and books he'd brought with him.

As if sensing her human's need for emotional support, Daisy sprung from beneath the table to settle into a black and yellow ball in Hayden's lap. She licked her hand three quick times then commenced purring.

Clamping down on the last bit of fear in her gut, Hayden ran a hand over Daisy's soft, satiny back then looked up to meet Quinn's intense blue stare. She nodded once and said, "I'm ready. Let's hear it."

Every one of the witches had convened in the study along with Viv's boyfriend, Nick, the pub owner who'd lost a good friend to the Amara during Viv's trial.

Jen had been the first true casualty of this covert and mystical war, and if the current serial murders were Amara related, she wouldn't be counted as the last.

Willyn's husband, Dare, was still there as well, a powerful witch in his own right, and knowledgeable. He stood behind Willyn's chair, a large hand on her delicate shoulder. The only one missing was Shauni's boyfriend, Michael, who was working in his veterinary clinic today.

"First," Quinn said, then stopped to take a mug of steaming black coffee from Mrs. Attinger as she ducked briefly into the room before retreating. "Thanks," he called after her, sipped, and grimaced at the scald. "The symbol is definitely related to what Hayden saw upstairs the other night and again in the park."

"So what did Hayden see?" Lucia asked, beating everyone to the question burning in their minds.

Holding up both palms, Quinn cast a look around the room, pleading for patience. "Let me start from the beginning. The ribbon-like symbol painted on those girls' stomachs is part of a very old and very powerful magic. Spelled with a –ck at the end, that is, when it was finally translated into English."

"That old, huh?" Anna sent her brother a bemused smile.

His lack of humor in response sent an explosion of dread inside Hayden. She steeled herself and asked, "Or is it that bad?"

Quinn nodded sagely. "Both. Old as dust and more evil than most are willing to deal with, even others who are gifted. In fact, I'm surprised the owner of this symbol is still alive. Not many of their kind are."

"The owner?" Paige moved to pick up the book from the table, but Quinn stopped her with a soft touch on her arm. "Wait. This needs to be taken in small bites."

"Now you're scaring me," Shauni said, tucking her feet up under her on the loveseat she shared with Lucia. "What do you mean by owner, and what is their kind?"

"Just bear with me, and I'll tell you everything." Quinn drew in a breath and walked to stand in front of the fireplace.

Lightning flashed and thunder boomed, jolting them all. Quinn's silhouette in front of the roaring fire made Hayden think of scary stories being told to a group of children.

Only the stories were real, and they weren't suited for kids.

"Some say the earth was in turmoil after the creation of humans. That there were other parties who didn't want mankind living among them. Battles were fought and alliances made, with very few surviving to tell the tale of what really happened. As it is with storytellers, though, myths and legends were passed down orally." Quinn sipped his coffee again then set it on the mantle.

"One of the unions in those days resulted in a clan called the Droehk, not long after fire was discovered." Now Quinn did smile. "The Droehk lived in the vicinity of what would later become known as Dacia. Near the Carpathian mountains."

"Transylvania," Claudia murmured, working her long, flaming hair into a twist to hang down the front of her shoulder. "Astonishing what truth is often found at the heart of a legend."

"Please don't tell me vampires really exist," Kylie said, hazel eyes huge in her young face. "I was doing pretty well with everything so far. I really was."

"No," Quinn smiled at her, a particularly warm smile. Then he cleared his throat and returned to the history lesson. "No vampires. But the clans had certain capabilities. They developed a language that was used to capture the dark powers still present on the earth, after humans had established a foothold but before the shadow world had been completely vanquished."

"And the symbol is part of that language," Hayden said, remembering the pulsation of the gruesome black mark on Chloe's skin.

"Exactly," Quinn said, swinging out his arm to point at her. "The Droehk were so strong after gaining control of the writings and using them for their own purposes that other clans came together for the sole purpose of destroying the Droehk and their foul magic. The language, the *ayjehr*, as it was called, became forbidden. Anyone writing the symbols down was immediately put to death."

"They were hunted to extinction," Dare said. "That's why you were surprised one of them is still alive."

"Yes, but some did survive, and they clung to their power. They kept the language alive without ever writing it down on animal skin, papyrus, or parchment again." Quinn rubbed his upper arm as he said, "They put it on themselves instead."

"Tattoos," Viv whispered. "How clever." She sent an apologetic look to Hayden. "Terribly greedy and selfish. But clever."

Anna nodded slowly as she ran a hand along her rosy, satin robe. "The perfect solution. They could keep it with them always, yet hide it in plain sight."

"And they became more cautious," Quinn added. "The survivors had learned from the mistakes of their people. Any dark works were done in a more private manner, but the power, the bloodline continued." Now his blue eyes darkened. "And we have one here in Savannah."

"But what is this person, this Droehk doing? Why the mark on Ronnie and Chloe before he killed them?" Hayden could feel herself getting worked up. All this talk of evil as old as the earth was stirring up the nausea again.

She was only the fourth witch to face her trial. If this was what she had to deal with, how much worse would the challenges be by the end?

And whoever the ninth woman to be called was, Hayden hoped she could stand to wait until then. That she would endure long enough. That she would be strong enough.

A hand clasped Hayden's, and she raised her eyes to find Anna looking at her. "You were chosen for this task, Hayden." She squeezed her hand. "There is purpose in that. Meaning. You were chosen to save these women for one reason."

"What?" Hayden asked and was horrified to hear how raspy her voice was. Terror had sucked her throat dry.

Anna held her stare and told her, "Because you can."

Air whooshed from her lungs as she clenched her eyes tight and held on to Anna's hand. If the most talented witch of them all had faith in her, then she could do no less in return. Her friends were counting on her. Hayden opened her eyes.

Ronnie and Chloe were counting on her.

Hayden balled her fingers into a fist but relaxed again after Daisy mewled with a sound of concern. She stroked her cat and met Quinn's gaze. "The symbol?"

This time it was Quinn who went to pick up the big, black book he'd carried in. He flipped to a marked page and turned it so Hayden could see. There was that awful mark, and she was afraid she'd never be able to look at a special cause ribbon again.

"Over time, the fear of the Droehk was forgotten, and portions of the language merged with others. The ribbon-symbol eventually became a rune. In the runic alphabet, this is called Othala. The connotation varies, but the general theme is one of property or possession. Of slavery. It designates something that is bound to a person."

Quinn pulled the book away and closed it with the *thud* specific to hundreds of pieces of paper smashing together. "It was used by the Droehk..." He stalled then spit the words out. "It was used as a brand."

"I don't understand," Willyn asked, her blonde brows furrowed. "What good would that do the killer, and what are the ghosts hiding from? Are you saying this man has marked them to make them his?"

"And I thought Ronnie and Chloe said they were afraid of a female," Paige added. "The murderer is a man."

"I don't know for sure that the man is the Droehk," Quinn said before asking Hayden. "The spirits of the women never mentioned the guy having any tattoos, did they?"

"No." Hayden shook her head. "I'll find out if I can the next time I see them. They haven't been back since they fled the other night."

"Right. When that thing scared them off and freaked out all the animals," Kylie said, shooting Quinn a pointed look that said she was tired of waiting for the big bang. "So again. What are the things Hayden's been seeing?"

Quinn groaned and stood, dropping the book on the table to pace back to the fire. "As far as I can tell, the symbol was infused with magic then put on the women as a sort of tracking device. Their physical bodies weren't branded, but their souls were." He spun away from the hearth to face them again. "Ronnie and Chloe were marked so they could be found again after they died."

"Found by those things I saw." Hayden snapped it all together in her head. "That's why they left the house when that black form appeared. That's what they've been hiding from." She made an exasperated noise in her throat. "But who is the woman they're always talking about?"

"I can't be sure," Quinn told her, reaching for his coffee again as if it were laced with whiskey. "But she is probably a Droehk, and the symbol belongs to her. The magic belongs to her." He blew a breath out through clenched teeth. "And the dark power conjured by the inscriptions? The *ayjehr*? They are used for a specific purpose."

Hayden could hear her blood rushing as she waited for what he was about to reveal.

"The Droehk can summon and communicate with certain entities." Quinn looked directly to Hayden, standing with his legs wide and his arms crossed over his chest. Ready to deliver the bang. "They can control demons."

13

"Your hair really does look great," Anna told Hayden as she entered the private suite she'd reserved upstairs at the day spa as a treat for Hayden and any of the women who wanted to take part in a well-deserved day of pampering and relaxation.

Only Kylie, Claudia, and Lucia had accepted, since Shauni, Viv, and Willyn were spending time with their men.

And Paige, well, her exact comment had been, "Nobody's pulling out any follicle that God saw fit to put on my body."

Hayden smiled as she remembered the declaration and tilted her glass of water back for a sip. Laced with mint and garnished with a lime, the drink was cleansing and refreshing. She could use a little of both.

The first part of Anna's try-not-to-freak-out-because-we've-got-demons day had included a trip to the beauty salon. The male stylist there had forbidden Hayden to color or highlight her hair, which she hadn't intended to do anyway, and had suggested a little shaping up followed by a blowout.

She had no problem with her natural waves, but the straight do was an edgy and cool new look for her. The sharp layers around her face made her feel like she should be wearing black leather and carrying a sword, as any self-respecting demon hunter would.

Yet here she sat instead, lying around in a plush white robe and admiring her tropical punch mani-pedi.

What was she supposed to do if she came across a demon in the first place? Toss holy water toward its semi-transparent body?

The coven didn't know how to handle any other demons than Bastraal, and even dealing with the demon they knew was a work in progress. Add to that, Hayden still had a lot of work to do in the ass-kicking department.

She was used to helping people, and doing her part whenever her sisters needed her, but so far she hadn't had much action. Not the fire-throwing, speed-punching, motorcycle-flying kind some of the others had experienced.

But her trial had just begun, and if her sisters' tests had taught her anything, it was don't count yourself clear until the next woman was called. Actually, not even then, because they had to stand as a united front more often than not, so she was just going to have to find her inner warrior and mix it with her ghost whispering.

Because now, it seemed she was also a demon whisperer. *Ugh.*

What would a fiend sound like? If they could even speak. If they didn't soul-suck her first.

Leaning back on the butter-soft chaise, Hayden searched for a center of calm and pushed aside the nasty imagery invading her head. She'd been more than happy to take Anna up on a girls' day at the spa.

Serial killers, irritating yet hunky cops, and now demons. She sighed. It was a lot for a witch to deal with.

As the other three women joined Anna and Hayden, the sun filtered its way through the trees outside to cast a dappled beam across the wood floor. Housed in a historic home downtown, the spa boasted ivory wainscoting with sage-green walls, hues that gave it a classic female vibe. Antique armoires in cream or dark oak held cosmetics, scented soy candles, and every luxurious bath and body product a woman could wish for. Total chick paradise.

Hayden sniffed the air as Lucia breezed through the door. "You must have had the same treatment I did."

Lucia caressed the silky skin on her golden-brown arms. "Champagne and orchid body scrub and wild orchid aromatherapy massage," she purred with her Spanish accent. "*Si.* Very nice."

"I hope you've all enjoyed today," Anna said, gazing out the window to a surprisingly sunny street below. She nodded to Lucia, and understanding the non-verbal message, Lucia shut the door behind her. Now was a time for privacy.

"Yes, and thank you," Hayden said. With one last glance at her bright pink fingernails, she sipped her water and prepared to re-enter the world of the coven.

Nine women summoned to fulfill their destiny and protect innocents from the Amara. The *deathless.* "You've heard from Quinn?" she asked, settling her gaze on the head witch.

"He called a little while ago and thinks he has a lead on a spell to reverse the branding." Anna smiled grimly. "But the ritual will require the corpse of the person marked."

The hope that had begun forming in Hayden's heart collapsed in on itself and sank like a stone. "Ronnie was buried yesterday." Holding Anna's gaze, she rubbed her thumb up and down the cool glass in her hand. "What can I do to help her now? Can we perform the spell or ritual over her grave?"

"I'm not positive, but from what Quinn said, it involves treating the skin that was painted." Anna tilted her head, empathy on her face. "I'm sorry, but he and his friend will keep working on it."

"His friend?" Kylie asked quickly before pressing her lips together and blushing a pretty color.

Remaining neutral, and wisely so, since the young girl was

trying to hide her interest in Anna's younger brother and his activities, Anna answered in a straight and even voice. "An old college friend from Harvard. A theology major who went on to specialize in demonology and the supporting folklore."

"Quinn's a Harvard man?" Claudia asked as she studied her sparkling ruby manicure. "I had no idea."

"Neither did I," Kylie added, a look of bemused wonder on her face. She and Quinn were an ever-changing puzzle, and most of the coven could see what their solution would eventually be. Even if the two stubborn witches refused to. "I guess now that we know what we're dealing with, research will move along more quickly."

"Exactly," Anna said, reaching for the pot of green tea that had been prepared for their post-massage unwinding session. "Homing in on the Droehk has narrowed the field considerably, and Quinn speaks highly of the man he's sought help from. And he trusts him, which is, as you all know, paramount, considering what we're involved with."

Hayden nodded. Quinn was a male witch with a great deal of power to go along with his sharp and voracious brain. If he was figuring out a way to release the spirits of her new ghost friends, then Hayden had absolute faith he would make it happen. And she would trust whoever he trusted.

She just had to make sure they did save the spirits, Ronnie included. She wouldn't allow the demons to find the ghosts. She couldn't let them carry out whatever malicious errand they'd been sent on.

Surely there was a way to help all of them. Could Ronnie be exhumed? Would her family even allow that? They wouldn't be the first grieving parents Hayden had ever had to convince of her skills, but then, she'd never asked any mother or father to bring their child's body back up from their resting place, either, essentially desecrating their grave.

Hayden picked her purse off the floor next to the chaise she lay on. She knew who she had to call.

Before she touched the screen of her phone to wake it up, she stared at her reflection in the shiny black rectangle. Though the image of her eyes was distorted, she could see weight and worry in the golden brown.

The eyes were windows, some said, and now more than ever before, she could see how burdened her soul was. How haunted.

No. She could handle it. She would make things right. That's what she did. She took pain and helped heal it. She gave peace to those who'd lost loved ones and helped those who were lost find safe passage to the next world.

She'd made an oath and had kept it for years. No deviation from the truth. No running or hiding. And no innocent blood on her hands.

Never again.

She paused for a moment to wonder over the guilt surrounding her. That had been happening a lot lately, and the feeling of shame always seemed to flare up when she thought of Trevor.

But Cole was also a cop, and she didn't get nervous at the thought of talking to him. Only Trevor.

So she should contact Cole, since he would probably be with his partner anyway. Then he and Trevor would hear it at the same time. Bypass the issue altogether.

She clenched her teeth. That was the coward's way. If she was being honest with herself, she knew exactly who to call. And why.

Fate might have chosen her path centuries before she'd ever existed, but right now in this moment, Hayden was making her own decision.

She opened her contacts and scrolled to R for Roch, Trevor. He hadn't achieved first name basis just yet. Instead of selecting him, she took one last breath of timidity and simply stared.

"Who are you calling?" Claudia asked, a mischievous smile

on her face. "One of those cops you never talk about?" She ran her fingers through her flaming hair and wiggled her brows.

"What do you mean? I mention them all the time." Hayden frowned, ever-amazed that despite their deathly dealings, the women in her coven could always spare a minute to talk about romance. Of course, it didn't help that so far each witch's trial had ended with love.

Hayden didn't rage against the pattern, not like Paige did, but she also wasn't willing to accept the same destiny had been set for all nine of them.

What were the odds? The purpose? Did the gods of the otherworld think true love was a fitting reward for what she and her friends would have to endure?

Trevor's angry and mysterious blue eyes suddenly floated into her daydream. Would a man like him make it all worthwhile? Fiercely protective, frighteningly intelligent, and so tenacious that a pit bull would willingly let go of a bone if Trevor were on the other end.

Maybe a man that hard was incapable of softening up, even for love.

Or maybe he would sweep her into his arms and hold all the world's suffering at bay. Apply his strength to the defense and support of one special woman. Gentle his stony exterior and smile a secret smile. For her.

"I think that faraway look says it all," Lucia said, breaking into Hayden's thoughts. Then she inclined her head to Claudia who nodded agreement. "In fact," the Spanish witch continued, "she does mention the policemen, but has never, ever said their names. Only, the Scottish cop and his partner."

"You know...you're right," Anna said, causing Hayden to blow out an exasperated breath before looking out the window and shaking her head. "In fact, she studiously avoids saying their first names." She lifted one sable brow and awaited Hayden's response.

"This isn't really the time or place," Hayden said on a huff.

"Uh, yeah." Spreading her hands to encompass the sumptuous surroundings, Kylie nodded, making her long blonde curls bounce. "We're in a day spa. Girl talk is not only encouraged, it's required."

"Fine. Fine." Squinching her eyes tight and wishing for a quick yoga session, Hayden blurted out, "All I can tell you is that both of the cops I'm working with are ridiculously good looking, and there is the slightest, most miniscule, one-in-a-gazillion chance that I have an interest in one of them."

"Right," Kylie said with a grin. "Protest. Too much."

Holding up a finger to wag at the younger woman, Hayden added, "For the record, their names are Cole Lonergan and Trevor Roch. There. And I wasn't protesting, I was just trying to maintain a professional distance."

"Looks like that plan failed. So which one is the possible?" Kylie asked, her hazel eyes dreamy. She was always a sucker for a love story.

Making a sound that was caught somewhere between a laugh and a groan, Hayden said, "The one that drives me absolutely crazy. The most infuriating, insulting, distrustful... yet, somehow the most delicious man on earth. Him." She gave a decisive nod. "That's the one."

An eruption of clear, Zen-inspiring music flowed from the phone still in Hayden's hand, the sounds of bells and rainfall.

Glancing up to glare at Kylie as if it was all her fault, she pointed the phone at her and said, "And the one, by the way..." she sighed, "who's calling me right now."

~

Maybe it was only Hayden's imagination, but Trevor's voice had practically barked at her through the phone connection. He'd told her there were new developments in the case and they needed to talk.

She'd told him she was finishing up at the day spa, and the line had gone silent before he snapped, "I'll pick you up in five minutes." Then he'd hung up without so much as another word. Arrogant, infuriating man.

And somehow Hayden had felt chastised, flooded with more guilt, just as she did now, spying his handsome scowl through the passenger side window of his car. He looked at her like a father picking up an errant teenager who was in for a good talking to.

He wasn't driving any police-issued automobile, that much was for sure. She didn't know much about cars, but this one was a classy silver with sleek but very male lines. The little bit of splash added one more dimension to Detective Trevor Roch, and Hayden found herself even more confused.

He just wasn't staying inside that grouchy, skeptical box he'd originally fit in so well.

He pushed open the door and ordered, "Get in."

Huffing but climbing into the leather seat, Hayden held her tongue. *Well, he still fits into the grouchy part just fine.*

"Have I done something wrong?" she asked, clicking her seatbelt on a little more soundly than necessary.

Easing back into traffic, he said, "Does this strike you as an appropriate time for a day at the spa?" He gunned the engine more than she thought a cop should. "And here I was beginning to believe you really cared about these cases. About these women."

"How dare you!" Hayden said, ready to blister him with a rebuttal, but he took a hard turn and forced her to cling to the door handle.

When he settled in behind a slower moving car, she said, "I have had a rough couple of days and needed to clear my head, so if I want to take some time with my friends to relax and get centered, then I will do so and without your permission."

His grunt was laden with disbelief. "Sure whatever. A rough day."

"You have no idea." Hayden thought of yesterday's meeting and all she'd learned about the Droehk, mystical writings, and the conjuration of demons. "You really have no idea."

Instead of elaborating, she chose not to give him the satisfaction. He didn't deserve answers. She'd wait until they met up with Cole and tell him what she'd learned.

"Where are we going anyway?" she asked as she dug in her purse for lip gloss. Her searching hands stilled when she realized how it might look if she applied makeup. Trevor would probably assume she was primping for him. She fumbled her small purse then, scattering its contents on his floorboard.

As he drove down Abercorn in silence, she gathered her things and reined in the bite of temper he'd caused. She felt foolish, and her face burned at the edges with embarrassment.

"Why do I make you so nervous?" Trevor asked. His eyes were still shadowed but his voice less harsh than before. "Is it because I'm a cop?" He let the question hang in the air before adding, "Or is it just me?"

If Hayden's face had been warm before, now it was flaming, burning a trail to the back of her neck. *Both!* She wanted to tell him, but her pride wouldn't survive such honesty.

She rubbed her palms down her thighs, letting the soft material of her ankle-length dress hold her attention. She'd chosen the rosy-hued garment because it was easy to slip on and off for the spa.

She felt too feminine and overdressed. Too girly. Trevor didn't take her seriously as it was, and she found herself curling her fingers under to hide the bright pink nail polish.

He did make her nervous, but she wasn't about to tell him the whole *why* of it. "Since it's so obvious, I might as well tell you that police do make me edgy." Now she tucked in her thumbs as well. "I have some history with cops, and I wasn't on the right side. But that was a long time ago."

The light at DeRenne turned green, and the silver car shot across the lanes. Trevor reached to adjust the heater, because when the sun dropped, so did the temperature. He pushed a breath out hard and said, "I know."

For a moment Hayden was confused. "What do you mean, 'you know?'" He couldn't possibly mean her past. Her hidden and deeply buried secrets. She'd been assured of confidentiality.

A freezing fire rushed over her skin at the idea of anyone finding out. Especially the cop who wanted so much to despise her.

"Your file is still sealed, since it's a juvie record," he told her in such a nonchalant way that she wanted to hit him. "But I wanted you to know I'd been checking on you."

He flicked an angry look at her, like a blue whip on her already sensitive skin. "Thought I'd give you one last chance to come clean."

"I am clean." Just like that fury blasted from her gut and flash-burned any remnants of guilt or shame. "Juvenile records are sealed for a reason. So childhood mistakes can be forgotten. If the crime is bad enough, kids might be sent up and tried as an adult. But I wasn't."

Hayden forced all of her rage into her eyes, hoping they flamed with indignation. It felt like they did. In fact, her whole body was blazing. "And since you've done such a thorough background check, you know there's nothing else to be found. No cons, no fraud complaints, no police reports. Absolutely nothing."

Reaching down for her small, brown bag she whipped out her watermelon gloss and stroked it on her lips, daring him to comment. With a hard twist she put the cap back on then shoved it into her purse before tossing it back to the floor. "Now that you've done your worst, you need to make a decision, *Detective* Roch, and stop playing games."

"I don't play at anything," he growled, eyes on the road before them.

"Bullshit," Hayden said, surprising them both. "Starting right now, this very minute, you either start accepting me at face value or leave me the hell alone." Then she went for the kill. "And no more acting like you want to kiss me."

When they cruised through the red light at White Bluff one second too late, a strobe or flash of some kind lit up in the rear view, and Trevor swore. "I'll have to deal with Mobility and Parking Services now." He sighed a deep, heavy sigh. "I'll just tell them where I was headed. Not that it matters."

"You just got a camera ticket?" Hayden smiled like her prey had been spotted. "Why Detective Roch. I'm afraid that's going on your permanent record."

"We all mess up once in a while." He slid her a look, chagrined and with less judgment. "But I guess you already know that."

She met his gaze and held it. "I do. Unfortunately, I do." She turned to face the front, hoping he would forgo any interrogation.

Trevor had to start having some faith in her or she was pulling out. She had too much to worry about without adding the conflicting emotions he stirred up in the softest, most sacred places inside her.

And wasn't it just like her to be attracted to a cop who didn't give her an ounce of respect?

Just when she thought he would go the rest of the drive without speaking, he lifted one brawny shoulder and said, "Cole and I both decided to keep you involved. For now. So he's meeting us at the morgue."

Hayden gasped. "The morgue? I thought the ME was finished with Chloe."

"She is. Chloe was released last night." He looked to the side as they passed a group of men that seemed to be arguing but who broke into laughter after one of them faked a punch. Then he spoke to the windshield and confirmed Hayden's fear. "We found another body. Yesterday."

"Yesterday." The word *whooshed* out of her throat. "Why didn't you call me?"

Trevor's hands tightened on the black steering wheel. "We were busy. We had things to do." His voice was agitated when he swung his head toward her. "And I needed to clear my head. Because I *did* want to kiss you the other night."

He glanced down her body to her brown boots then up again. "But I can't, and we both know why."

With a new energy crackling and bouncing off the interior of the car, and between the two of them, Hayden lifted her head and did her best to appear cool. Professional. Detached. *What a lie.*

"Absolutely." She coughed and threaded the fingers of both hands together. "I appreciate your honesty." Whose voice was that, all tight and proper? She was speaking the words but the sound was muffled in her head.

His hands were strong and sure as they steered the car, his thighs long and thick with muscle.

And Hayden knew she shouldn't notice these things. Not now. The mood was overcast by the reeking vibe of a sadistic killer, and once again, she wondered what demented deities had planned such a disastrous mix of passion and dread.

Thinking about Trevor's mouth at a time like this only made her feel sad. And guilty.

Hayden was sick of feeling guilty.

He turned to her and studied her face for a heartbeat. Then another. Something moved in the depths of his brilliant, blue eyes. A flash of doubt that made her believe he was struggling with the same conflict. The terrible timing of it all and the twisted, inexplicable humor fate was enjoying at their expense.

His voice rolled over her, in a deep, vibrating timbre. "I wouldn't think you could wear pink. Not with your coloring."

Hayden brushed a hand over her dress in response but didn't turn away. The car was stopped at a light, allowing Trevor to continue his scrutiny of her.

"But with the reddish-brown of your hair," he said, "and the gold of your eyes, the pink..." he trailed off and shook his head slowly. His hand lifted off the steering wheel as if he was going to reach for her, but he let it fall back instead, his fingers clenching the black leather. "You remind me of a sunrise."

Their eyes locked and silence crushed the air from the vehicle, as if the two of them were suspended in the moment. In the recognition. The acceptance.

Suddenly a horn blared behind them and Hayden jerked. Then they drove forward and veered right, in front of a hospital surrounded by towering oaks.

Though she looked straight ahead, Hayden could feel Trevor's presence beside her. Imaginary tendrils of longing seemed to reach from his body to hers. But she sat straight and ignored the pull. Trevor didn't say anything else and neither did she.

They didn't have to.

14

Several buildings stretched out before them in a line, red brick trimmed in beige cement. On the back side, pine trees hovered like tall, thin onlookers. The complex housed local offices for the Georgia Bureau of Investigation. On the far end was a section dedicated to the Investigative Division, while the center two areas included the crime lab and forensic sciences.

Hayden walked toward the far left side and the tree line, trailing behind a still quiet Trevor. Cole stood at the corner of the building waiting for them, his hand lifting in a way that told Hayden he was popping something into his mouth. Probably candy.

She couldn't help grinning. Only Cole would need something sweet before visiting the morgue.

Then the smile slipped from her face. She was here because another woman had been brutalized, and nothing could wipe out the sickening weight in her stomach when she recalled the reason for her visit.

Trevor stopped and put a hand on his partner's shoulder then moved ahead after speaking in Cole's ear. The dark-haired detective with a hint of Scottish brogue stayed put as Hayden approached. His expression was grim, but still he lifted the bag of sour chews in his hand as consolation. "Sorry to ruin your day," he said.

She shrugged and shook her head. "Not me you need to worry about, but thanks. This latest victim, do you know her name yet?"

"Nope. No identification found and so far no match with any missing persons. She appears to be in her early twenties. Maybe another student like Chloe."

He shoved the bag in his pocket with a frustrated push that made the plastic crackle. "It may take a day or so for someone to worry about her absence. Maybe a friend or boss will notice. All we can do is wait and keep searching the databases."

A cool wind kicked up as the last line of daylight clung to the horizon. While Hayden watched, the faint glow faded then disappeared completely. Dusk had arrived, but she was in no mood to enjoy the enchanting space in time called twilight.

The dark brought too many horrible things with it these days.

"Is the ME finished with the body yet?" she asked.

"Yeah. We just got her preliminary, so Trevor went ahead to get caught up." His light greyish-green eyes grew analytical. "Why?"

She stepped closer and scrunched her shoulders against the cold. "I have things to tell you and Trevor." She paused. "Incredible things. And I'm going to need your help convincing him."

Now Cole raised his dark brows. "Convincing him of what exactly?"

"There's a way we can help the women. Their...souls, I mean. Their spirits. But I'm going to ask both of you to help me with a procedure that might be a bit...unorthodox."

She continued when he remained silent. "I don't have all the details, yet, but I wanted to go ahead and pave the way, so to speak."

"And you need me to hold Trevor down while you lay the

asphalt on him."

She grimaced. "Something like that."

He nodded and took a step back, indicating she should walk with him. "I can't make any promises until I hear what you've got in mind, but I will listen." They walked up the incline to the morgue door where Cole pushed a buzzer and requested entrance via the static-filled intercom.

He told her he'd covered with the ME and the staff by saying Hayden had information regarding the case, but no one knew anything more. "And I suggest we keep it that way," he added with a no-nonsense tilt of his head toward her.

Once inside, the hallway stretched straight ahead with offices on either side. With the tan walls and warm décor, it didn't feel like any morgue Hayden had ever visited, though she hadn't seen many.

Ghosts didn't need a visitation site but could roam freely, and when they did hover near a particular place, they usually chose one with meaning. A source of nostalgia or comfort.

As soon as she peered through the glass square in the door at the end of the corridor, Hayden knew this time was different.

A young woman with long, blonde hair stood in the room beyond, shoulders hunched and shaking. She was crying and frightened, her emotions racing through the building to zero in on Hayden's paranormal receptors.

This spirit's distress was running high, and Hayden didn't have to guess why. The poor thing was in there all alone. Confused. Scared.

And staring at her own corpse.

Hayden wondered if the girl already knew she was being tracked by hell's bounty-hunters.

Before she stepped into the empty office with Cole and Trevor, she shot off a text to Anna. [**There's been a third murder. Tell Quinn we have to hurry.**]

She knew Quinn and the coven would make the preparations

as soon as they knew precisely what those preparations entailed. *Come on, Quinn.*

"I'll have her name for you soon," Hayden said, entering the room with a goal in mind. "Her spirit is in the examining room now, and she's in trouble." She didn't try to cover the urgency creeping into her voice. She needed to make them see how critical the situation was and would waste as little time as possible on the two men she believed would eventually accept her plan.

Okay, so one was a sure thing and the other would be dragged kicking and screaming.

She let her gaze drop to where Trevor sat behind the desk with an open folder in front of him. *Detective Roch, prepare to be out-persevered.* "Her soul is in danger, but there's a way we can protect her." She hoped using those words would trigger the instinct that came most naturally to Trevor. Protectiveness.

"Whoa. Hold on a minute," Cole said, drawing her surprised attention to him. He stood with both hands out, clearly not ready for her jump to light-speed. "What do you mean she's in danger? She's already, no offense, but she's already dead."

"Look. I know I'm already stretching the boundaries of your imaginations, but I have to protect these women, and the only way to do that is to tell you everything." She looked at Trevor and implored him with her eyes. "I need your help." She tucked a stray strand of hair behind her ear. "They need your help."

Opening up one hand in a go-ahead gesture, Trevor sat back in the chair and fastened those piercing blue eyes on her. She knew he would listen to what she had to say but would be judging every word with his level-headed cop mentality.

"There's so much, I don't know where to begin." She licked her lips and gave a synopsis of how she'd come to Savannah for a reason she couldn't quite explain and that she'd encountered other women who'd traveled from all over the same way. An inexplicable compulsion to move to the coastal city. To drop their lives no matter what the cost and follow an invisible yet very palpable line straight to a mysterious island.

The world's most bizarre come-as-you-are party.

They watched her with different expressions on their equally handsome faces. Cole's was completely blank, like he wasn't sure what he'd gotten himself and his partner into.

Trevor's was chiseled in stone and closed off. Not angry, necessarily, but as if he was on a precarious edge, wanting to leap over yet resentful that he might.

Then she got to the part about witches and prophecy, and Cole started waving a hand. "Wait. Wait. What does all of this have to do with these murdered women? I mean, come on, Hayden, I believe in what you do, but this takes it to a whole other level. An evil group called the Amara and a demon?" Borrowing a move from Trevor, Cole ran a hand through his dark hair and sat in a chair.

Trevor was still silent as midnight, and with sudden clarity, Hayden realized what she had to do. All this time she'd thought she needed Cole to help her convince his partner. Now she realized she had to go straight to the heart. Even if it pulsed with one-hundred-percent-pure granite.

"Trevor," she said. "The other night in the square, you believed, even if for only a split-second." She placed her hands on the desk and leaned down. "I know you did. I felt it."

He betrayed nothing of his reaction or whatever he was thinking other than to utter one flat word. "Demons."

"Yes, and there are more than just the one the Amara want to raise. Evidently there are many, and we've only just encountered them. But they are tracking the women, their ghosts, and though we don't really know why," she paused and furrowed her brow, "I just can't let them be found."

Growing warm with both tension and the need to move ahead, Hayden slipped off her jacket, glad the sleeves of her dress only came to her elbows. She needed to cool off. "There's so much to explain, and nothing is simple, but I need you to trust me."

"You want me to help you fight demons?" Trevor asked, and now the fury was there, along with what looked suspiciously like hurt. He thought she was playing him. Still?

She needed a new approach. "You were raised in a church-going family, right?" She wasn't sure but felt like she'd hit the mark.

Trevor nodded, his jaw clenching so hard she could see the muscles working along the side. "How do you choose what to believe and what not to believe?" Hayden asked.

"You aren't gonna' get anywhere that way, young lady." A new voice spoke from behind Hayden, and she swirled to see an older man, white-haired and dressed in black pants with a crisp white shirt. "He operates on proof. Evidence. Things he can't deny." The man jerked his head at Trevor. "So give him something he can't refuse."

A ghost, she realized. Another ghost. And one who'd come to help *her* for a change.

"Any suggestions?" she asked on a breath.

"Who are you talking to?" Cole asked, but she ignored him.

The old man walked straight through the desk to stand behind Trevor. His blue eyes glittered with mischief.

Hayden saw it then. The blue. The same mid-summer sky reflected there, just as it did in Trevor's eyes. "Tell him Pop said to stop dancing with the wrong girl."

"Um. Right." She pointed a finger at Trevor. "Pop said to stop dancing with the wrong girl."

Trevor exploded from the chair, sending it rolling back into the window where it crunched the blinds into disarray. "What?"

"He's here. Now. And I think he's come to help me," she told him, watching in awe as he stood to his full, intimidating height and blew out through his nose like a cartoon bull who'd just seen the red flag.

"No, I've come to help this tunnel-visioned grandson of mine open his eyes. He never was one to let go of something easily. Once he got it in his head." The old man smiled at her and winked.

"He says you've got tunnel-vision," Hayden told him, noticing as Cole stood and circled around to stand beside her.

"And sometimes you gotta' look around something instead of head-on," Pop said.

Hayden swallowed. "And sometimes you have to look around something instead of head-on," she echoed, clenching her hands together in a tight knot.

Trevor seemed to deflate in front of her eyes and crept back to sit slowly in the chair. "He always told me that when I got too hung up on the letter of the law, or couldn't make the pieces fit while solving a case." Trevor ran a hand through his hair now, and Hayden had the urge to go to him and soothe him.

No time for that now, even though she could tell he was breaking apart his very ordered world to try and make room for things he never thought existed.

Trevor was well aware that things did go bump in the night, but now she was forcing him to see that the noises weren't always made by humans.

Hayden imagined he was experiencing some of the same doubts she'd been having the last forty-eight hours. How do you fight something you know nothing about?

His grandfather didn't seem bothered at all. In fact he grinned as Trevor rubbed his hand over his mouth and jaw, working his way through mental turmoil.

"Ha. Serves him right to meet a girl like you," Pop said. "It'll do him a world of good." He laughed as only old men can then laid a ghostly hand on Trevor's shoulder. "And tell him to stop missing Sunday dinner with his family. Time is fleeting."

Hayden nodded, deciding right then and there she would leave out the part about meeting a girl like her. She would worry over that later. "Can I help you?" she asked, as he started to fade.

"No, young lady. I'm fine. I've enjoyed the ride but have to get back. It's not every day there's a good enough reason to pop back in over on this side." He smiled. "I've got to get back to my sweetheart now."

Stunned, Hayden stared until she was looking at nothing but the tan wall. Pop back in? She made a small sound of exhaustion. *Learn something new every day.*

A small bell chimed in her purse, and she glanced at Trevor before retrieving her cell phone. There was a message from Claudia. [**Quinn says they've got it. What now?**]

Cole had gone back to his seat and was sprawled into it like a man who'd just completed a marathon. His legs out in front of him and head resting on the back.

Trevor had recovered his strength, apparently, and was studying her shrewdly. He had an air about him, but she was hesitant to put a name to it. He seemed...resolved.

"My friends have found something. A method of removing the marks on the bodies," she said and saw his eyes narrow. "I'm talking about the marks that can't be seen by human eyes."

She eased closer and softened her voice. "I'll tell you everything. Answer anything, but please. Please." She gripped her phone almost painfully. "We have to save them."

His gaze fell to the phone she clasped, and she knew he understood. He blew out a sigh that almost ruffled her hair then looked to Cole who only stared back. The two had a non-verbal discussion before Trevor said, "I have a few favors to cash in."

Cole nodded. "I'll probably have to throw mine in, too."

Standing again but on more solid footing, Trevor crossed his arms over his chest and told Hayden, "There aren't any other examinations pending, so the place should be clear in about an hour."

He leaned over the desk to pull her amulet from beneath her clothing, just as he'd done before. This time he barely touched her skin, but she still felt her stomach muscles contract.

Laying the necklace on the front of her dress, he studied the colorful stones. All nine of them. And she knew he was putting together more pieces. Trying to make it all fit. "Go ahead," he said, his tone low and steely. "Tell your friends to come."

15

The hour until the GBI complex cleared out felt more like a year, and Trevor would swear he could hear the small black hand of the generic clock tick-tock-ticking an echo all the way down the hall. According to the caramel-haired woman standing in the examination room talking to the air, every second would count.

Hayden was still speaking to the ghost of the slain girl, the most recent victim of a serial killer like none he'd ever studied or read about. And he certainly hadn't encountered such brutality.

Most crimes were the average passion, rage, or money scenario, not that homicide was ever common, but this painting of the women's skin so demons—damn, he still couldn't get his brain around it—so demons could find them in the afterlife? That was seriously sadistic.

Trevor had always believed taking a person's life was the final abuse, but now he knew better. There was no safety, even in death. He'd been well and truly educated on the realm of the in-between.

By a witch with golden eyes.

So now, in addition to catching a killer, he'd been tasked with something new, something insane. If he understood

Hayden correctly, she and her friends were going to perform a ritual to remove an invisible and mystical tracking beacon from the dead girl's body. So the demons couldn't find her spirit and do...whatever demons do with captive ghosts.

He pushed his hair away from his eyes and sighed. He and Cole were in it up to their badges, letting a coven of witches— witches!—come into a federally owned building to do God knew what.

He was glad they hadn't invited the FBI in to help with the killings, yet, or he would never have been able to ensure privacy of the morgue.

The ME had left the body stored as it should have been, but what had he promptly done once she'd left for the night? He'd pulled the corpse back out and transferred it to a table with Cole's help.

If things went badly, they could both lose their jobs. Or worse. But if it came to that, he'd knock his partner unconscious if he had to. He'd protect Cole, even if it had been his fault they were mixed up in all of this in the first place.

"Hey, man." Speak of the devil. Or should he now say demon? Cole was standing beside him, following Trevor's line of vision down to the end of the hall and through the glass. To Hayden. "Having second thoughts?"

Trevor grunted and dragged his gaze to meet Cole's. "Try third or fourth." He glanced again at Hayden and shook his head. "What have you and that woman done with my good sense? Have I been hexed? Because right now, I'd believe that was possible and the only reason I'm acting like I've lost my mind."

Cole smirked. "Yeah, you've been whammied all right, but not the way you're meaning." He chewed whatever strawberry-smelling thing was in his mouth. "But don't worry, partner. I'll have your back no matter how things go down."

Cole's smile was just too bright, and considering the

circumstances, Trevor was suspicious. "Why do I get the feeling you're not talking about the trouble we could get into for what we're about to pull?"

"Trouble?" Cole asked with a laugh. "You're already in trouble, and I have to say, it gives me no small amount of pleasure to know I'm to blame."

Putting his hands on his waist, Trevor glared at his partner. "Cole, what the hell are you talking about?"

"I've seen the way she looks at you, and it might have stung a little at first, but women getting all starry-eyed around you? That's nothing new. I'm used to it." He stepped in closer and slapped a hand on Trevor's upper arm. "But seeing how you look at her?" He winked and grinned again. "That's something rare."

"You're crazy," Trevor said, but his gut burned and his heart thrashed.

Cole scoffed. "Yeah. Right. I'll just go wait for the *coven* to arrive and buzz them in." He sauntered off down the corridor. "I'm crazy, sure. Seems to be a lot of that going around tonight."

Unbelievably, Trevor could feel a smile tugging at his lips. Maybe he had lost it, had slipped all the way around the bend and then some. But damn if it didn't feel good in a way he couldn't describe.

He was absolutely sure his grandfather, or his spirit anyway, had been in the room with them before. The things Hayden had said...there was just no way she could have known. No way she could have dug up the details. The specifics. Private words his grandfather had only ever said to him.

Hayden caught his eye through the door's window, and she looked troubled. She'd told him the girl was upset, and while it was a good thing the ghost had stuck around, so they'd be able to tell if removing the tracking symbol freed her soul or not, Hayden had also explained how abnormal it was for the spirit to be so obsessed with her own death. She'd been traumatized and still was, so Hayden was trying to calm her down and gain her cooperation.

A cooperative ghost? Trevor raked his hand through his hair again, wondering if he'd make himself bald before the night was over. He was ready to get this thing started, then he was going home and having a drink.

He watched Hayden hold out her hands in a gesture meant to comfort. To console. He imagined her touch would be gentle and extra sweet.

Adding insult to injury, he thought. Not only was he giving credence to a plethora of non-living beings, but somewhere along the way he'd started falling for the con. And falling hard.

By the time this madness was over, he might need more than one drink. Maybe more than one bottle.

He couldn't even think about what would have to transpire to get the bodies of the previous two victims back in custody, or if it was at all possible within the limits of the law. Of course, he and Cole were pretty much past the boundary as it was, so why not add grave robbing to his rap sheet?

The sound of the buzzer was quickly followed by Cole's deep voice welcoming the new arrivals. Lifting a hand to hail Hayden, Trevor met his partner halfway down the corridor to get a look at this group of women who were supposed to work some magic.

A woman who stood around 5-foot-6, with a long, brown ponytail and lake blue eyes met his curious gaze with one of her own.

Then a knowing smile lifted her lips. "You must be Detective Roch," she said, and he would swear her eyes smirked. "I'm Anna St. Germaine. I'm sure you have questions, but we really should get started."

"Back here," Cole said, holding out his arm. "Hayden's waiting. She's talking to, um, the victim."

Anna fell into step as Cole led the way. "It does take some

getting used to. I know. There was a time when I thought I'd seen and heard it all, too."

"But aren't you a witch?" Trevor asked. "St. Germaine. You're the hereditary witch, according to Hayden. I know your island." He nodded. "Explains a lot," he said but didn't elaborate. When a person grew up near Savannah, they heard stories. All kinds of stories.

Until tonight, Trevor had never paid any mind to tales of haints and hauntings, but now he wondered if he would ever see his city the same way again. His orderly and explainable world had been capsized. Slowly. Surely. And he doubted he would be as quick to explain away the next strange blue streak he caught in a photo, or the glowing white orbs tourists tried so hard to capture on film.

Everything he'd thought was true was now fringed with doubt.

Trevor was the last to enter the autopsy suite and closed the door behind him as the women spread out. The walls were different here, white and clean. Sterile and austere. But how should a room like this be decorated? It felt wrong to make it more comfortable for the living, somehow inappropriate and disrespectful.

Chilled air settled on his skin like a cold, thin blanket. The room was kept colder than the rest of the building, and he forced himself not to shiver. From either the temperature or the reality of what he was trying to put faith in. Magic.

Cole eased over to him while his light green eyes scanned the collection of females. All shapes, sizes, and shades. "Do you think I can have one?" Cole asked, a wry grin on his face.

Trevor shook his head, thankful for the interruption of thought but maintaining his stoicism. "This isn't a candy store, Cole."

His friend lifted his brows and shoved his hands in the pockets of his gray pants. "The hell you say."

When Anna lifted a long, curved knife from a bag, Trevor stepped forward with his hand out. "Hold it. What are you planning to do with that? I can't let you harm the body in any way." Words like contamination, obstruction, and chain of evidence were running through his procedural mind.

Half of him wanted to rebel against this violation of the law, but the other half, the stronger side of him, was thinking about the souls of those women. They were the ones who had truly been violated, in life and now presumably in death.

So if he had to break some rules to protect their spirits, he would.

Hayden was at his side then, her hand on his arm. Her touch was like an injection of Valium, calming him instantly. "We use the athame in ritual only. We won't harm her. In any way." She shifted her eyes to the woman named Anna for confirmation.

The woman with the long, brown hair, and obviously the one who led this group, nodded with an assuring expression on her genteel face. "We will do no harm." Then as if reading his thoughts like a teleprompter, she added, "And no one will know we were here. The evidence will remain intact. I promise."

"That is forensically impossible," Trevor said but with no heat, only acceptance. "I'm only allowing this because the examination is complete. But if the ME needs to revisit this body, she *will* notice any differences."

"Then we won't leave anything behind," Anna said before turning back to the bag held by a woman with equally long hair in a ponytail. Only hers was red as fire.

Trevor took a moment to study the women as they worked in tandem to prepare a side table the younger one had rolled over. Her long, curly blonde hair wasn't what gave away her age, and all of the women had remarkably glowing skin, so that wasn't the telltale either. She had a certain innocence about her, and though she fit in with the other women, practically melded with them, there was something different about her.

Something pure.

Just the kind of goodness the man he was chasing would love to corrupt and defile. And that had to stop.

Trevor was taking this irrational and dangerous step outside his comfort zone for one reason only. To stop a killer. It was what he did. Who he was.

He just hoped his reputation and badge survived this divergence of protocol.

"Don't worry," someone said in a humorous voice near his ear. He turned his head to find an Asian woman with black glasses on his other side. "I understand your need to keep things in order, to control the facts and protect the truth." She smiled at Hayden. "But it's much easier if you just let go. Trust in the things you can't see, and in us, though I know that's asking a lot. We're here to save lives. Just like you."

Beyond her two others were studying him as he nodded. A petite woman with shorter blonde hair and kind blue eyes stood with a dark-eyed brunette who was—he thought the word was statuesque—and way too easy on the eyes. Poor Cole.

Trevor was good with faces and names, but the nine gathered here were too much to take in, especially since his brain was already packed with the stuff of creepy comic books.

When Hayden patted his shoulder and walked away, he realized all of the women were forming a circle around the table with the body. The corpse. No, that wouldn't do.

"What's her name?" he asked Hayden, tilting his head down slightly to indicate the girl, pale in death but with long, sunny hair.

Hayden's eyes warmed almost imperceptibly. "Emily," she said before moving closer to the small table that now held a variety of strange objects. Anna stood on the other side whispering to Hayden, presumably giving her the newly-acquired instructions.

Hayden nodded and Anna said to the gathering, "We're

ready. Ladies, hold your circle, and Detectives," she turned serious blues on Trevor and Cole, "please stay back. We don't want to risk any...infection."

Trevor didn't like the sound of that, nor did he appreciate the direction to keep clear, but he would watch from afar and take one huge leap of faith. Not in the strangers here tonight, but in Hayden.

He would put his trust in her and hope it didn't come back to bite.

Anna took the curved knife again and moved the blade in a tight circle over the spot Hayden pointed out. Earlier she'd told Trevor she could still see the mark on the girl's stomach, though the paint had been cleaned off.

Her description of the ribbon-like symbol had made him cringe. Alive with dark magic, the brand seemed to have a vitality, almost a life of its own, squirming as though it had trapped a roiling mass of black maggots.

So Hayden had said, and the imagery had been the final lock to snap closed on Trevor's decision. He wanted the putrid thing off that girl's body. Off of...*Emily's* soul.

Now Anna spoke aloud to explain to the room at large what would happen. As she spoke, Hayden caught the eye of the trembling ghost on the opposite side of the examination table. Emily was holding steady but barely, arms wrapped around herself for emotional support only, since her physicality no longer existed.

As she waited with the paper and pen Anna had given her, Hayden tried to ignore the two places on her back that felt hot. Twin points of energy that crackled and burned. Trevor's eyes, she could literally feel them on her. As much as she wanted to help these women and free Emily's spirit, she was filled with another driving force.

She couldn't let Trevor down. Not after he'd packed away all his misgivings and handed them to her in a pretty little box.

Now she had to make sure she cared for them properly, to let him see his confidence in her was merited.

With a shimmer of yellow and blue light, Ronnie and Chloe suddenly appeared on either side of Emily. The three ghosts hovered as a united front, a trio, with Ronnie moving in a way that suggested she'd slipped her arm around Emily's waist.

Hayden gave the three of them an encouraging smile. Three. A magical number. Hopefully that would help their cause tonight, because Hayden would take all she could get. "They're all here," she said for the others' benefit. Then she firmed her resolve and lifted the pen. "Let's get started."

As Anna had instructed, she wrote the words that had been verbally passed from the demonologist to Quinn, to Anna, and now on to her. The oral transmission of the message would serve to empower tonight's ritual.

Since the Droehk used the written word for their conjurations, speaking the spell for tonight's ritual was like a mystical slap in the face. A magical middle finger.

Inscribing the words was also too dangerous, since every time they were written they gained strength. Now however, Hayden was forced to write the words on paper. It was the only way to perform the ritual and reverse the marking on Emily's skin. The only way to free her spirit.

The only sound in the room was her pen scratching against parchment. The autopsy suite felt as if it had become a vacuum, the atmosphere sucked clean of warmth or oxygen.

Hayden scribbled on the paper. *Bind the flesh with Othala, so the jiva may be stained.* She knew jiva was the Slavic word for soul and was as close to the Thraco-Dacian languages from long ago as they could get.

For reasons she couldn't name, Hayden threw a glance over her shoulder to search out Trevor's cool, blue gaze before she began the next step in the ritual. She looked then to Anna, who lifted a mirror, ready for Hayden to hold up the inscription and read its reflection.

She would speak the words backwards and release the evil spell.

Two stones sat on the small, silver stand serving as their work table, one a smooth, polished red garnet that would repel negative energy and help reinforce Emily's aura, which followed a person into the afterlife. The other was a jagged yet beautiful gray crystal. The smoky quartz was transparent and rough and would serve as a trap, the uneven crags of its surface acting as a maze for the malicious words if they attempted to find their way back to their host. To Emily's body.

After a deep breath that seemed to scrape her lungs, Hayden focused on the mirror and read exactly what she saw there, reciting the words backwards. *"Deniats eb yam avij eht os alahto htiw hself eht dnib."*

The sounds were alien to her tongue, and her gut revolted at the formation of the guttural noise she created, as if her inner witch could actually feel the vile force being undone.

Her head snapped up as the walls vibrated. Then they stilled, and she told herself she'd only imagined it. She found Anna's stare, and was startled to see the fear there as well. "Keep going," Anna said, blue eyes snapping flames. "Don't stop." The urgency in her voice was more terrifying than the illusory earthquake.

With the words unread, Hayden took the red garnet and placed it on the corpse's stomach, a defensive measure until the spell could be completely imprisoned. As she reached for the gray quartz, she saw Ronnie throw her other arm across ghost Emily's front. "Hurry, Hayden," the spirit cried, eyes wide. "They're coming! They've found us!"

"Oh, God," Hayden whispered, her hands shaking as she opened the jar filled with salt and dry, red earth. The minerals would trap the spell and slowly siphon off its power. Then the contents of the jar would be scattered into the ocean as an extra precaution.

She grabbed the smoky quartz and shoved it into the mixture before sealing the lid as the world around her wobbled. Blinking to clear her eyes, she watched as Emily's spirit opened her mouth wide, gasping a great breath. As she exhaled, her eyes closed then opened again slowly. They were filled with peace. With freedom.

"Thank you," Emily said to Hayden as she faded from visibility, leaving this world behind and traveling to the next. The ritual had worked, and Emily's soul was gone. She was safe.

But the other two weren't. "Ronnie. Chloe," Hayden said. "Get out of here. Now!"

Just as the warning left her mouth, a blur of oily black and purple swooped through the air to brush across the examination table and Emily's body, knocking the garnet onto the floor.

Hayden didn't have to get a better look at the thing flying around the room to know what was happening. Color and form didn't matter, and neither did the putrid scent of rot and sulfur that filled her nose. She didn't need a theology degree to know what had arrived.

There was a demon in the room.

Screeching in a tone that could only be described as pure terror, Ronnie clasped hands with Chloe, and both of the ghosts disappeared.

"What is it?" Shauni called out just as Anna asked, "Did it work?" She grabbed the jar and the gray crystal it contained, clutching it to her chest protectively. "Did the ritual work? Is Emily gone?"

"Yes, it worked. She's gone." Hayden spun in a circle, trying to locate the flying monster, but the far end of the room was blackened by shadow. "But we've got a bigger problem."

"What's wrong?" Trevor asked, his face a mask of concern. He was ready-to-launch, and his hand flew to his holster as training kicked in.

Hayden hated to tell him bullets would do no good. At least, she assumed they wouldn't. The very real and appalling fact was they had no idea how to fight a demon. Not yet.

The coven had been on a learn-as-you-go program, and Quinn's demonologist friend had only offered up theories. He couldn't provide specifics based on the small amount of information Hayden had been able to provide.

The demon burst from the corner then headed straight for Anna, but Hayden got there first, knocking her to the ground. She did her best to keep the jar from falling to the hard, tile floor.

If the glass shattered, the spell could escape. Emily's spirit had already vanished, but Hayden wasn't taking any chances.

And apparently, neither was this creature. His attacks were directed at the stones, but what else could the thing do if it could make physical contact with an object?

What could it do to the humans in the room? Hayden glanced around at the people still standing, including Trevor and Cole.

Way too many targets.

"Trevor," she cried, climbing to her feet. "Get everybody out. We're too vulnerable grouped in here together."

Confusion warred with anger on his face, and she could tell he wanted to know what was going on. He burst into action, though, throwing open the door and attempting to usher the women out.

Movement and low murmurings of concern erupted from the others, a mix of questions and denials. "We're not leaving you," Paige said, marching closer to where Hayden still stood over Anna. "If we go then we all go."

Refusing to waste time arguing, Hayden said, "Fine," and bent to help Anna up, but when their hands made contact, Anna's eyes widened and she pointed to the ceiling at the far end of the room. Toward the dark. "It's there," she said, scrambling upright. "Dear Goddess, I can see it."

Rarely, rarely did any of the witches see Anna unnerved, and the fright she was experiencing now was almost Hayden's undoing. She didn't stop to ask how Anna had suddenly acquired the ability to see demons but yelled instead to Claudia as she stepped into her line of sight. "Claudia, please! Get them out!"

Claudia's river-green eyes clearly said she didn't like the idea, but her authoritative teacher's voice snapped out in a barrage of commands. "Okay, let's go. We can get outside in the open and make a plan, but for now we do what Hayden says." Then those eyes were right back on Hayden. "Because she'll be coming with us."

"Yes, I will. Hurry," she told Anna, shaking her friend in an attempt to get her eyes off of the flying menace in the corner.

With most of their group gone, only Hayden, Anna, and Paige were left, but Trevor focused on them with intent in his eye. "I don't know what the hell's going on, but let's go." He reached for Hayden, wrapping his arm around her shoulders. The warmth and security flowing from him was incredible, and for a second she leaned into it with relief.

Until she saw Ronnie materialize at the end of the table. The ghost waved for Hayden to keep going. "It wants us, so I'll distract it."

"No, you don't know what it might do to you!" Hayden cried. Fear congealed her bloodstream, freezing her life force in place.

"Neither do you!" Ronnie yelled as her eyes searched erratically for the thing that was hunting her.

"Ronnie!" Hayden screamed as the demon pushed itself from its perch on top of a tall metal cabinet and bulleted straight for the ghost with what looked like long, curved talons stretched out. Its massive body swirled with sickly colors, faster and faster as it aimed for its target.

A deafening sound roared from the fetid mass as it swept down, and Hayden clapped her hands over her ears.

Just as Ronnie vanished.

"Oh, please stay gone. Please stay gone," Hayden murmured, shock beginning to creep in on her from all sides.

The demon snarled its fury as it missed its prey before swirling around to land on Emily's lifeless body. "Get off her!" Hayden screamed and lunged before she considered her actions.

Hands grasped her from both sides, Trevor and Paige. "Move it!" Trevor barked in her ear.

But Paige stood still and cursed. "Hayden, it's huge. So big." Now she could see it, too, and her voice was terrifyingly flat with none of the usual Paige bravado.

All things considered, Hayden had to concede. She had to get away from this thing.

Then it launched itself at the three of them.

"Get down!!" Hayden cried, but instead of moving from harm's way, Paige thrust her fist straight up, punching into the beast's underbelly as it passed. As soon as she did, she screamed in pain, jerking her hand back down to hold against her stomach. She growled low in her throat. "Bastard."

With one last blast of wings that ruffled the air yet didn't disturb the contents of the room, the flying demon soared up through the ceiling and was gone. The foul smell vanished immediately.

Shaken and worried about where the thing had gone, if it was tracking Ronnie and Chloe, Hayden crumpled to the floor and sucked in a breath.

Numb all over and sick to her stomach, she didn't fully register the strong enclosure of Trevor's arms as he picked her up and carried her out.

16

The night was quiet, absent of wind, rain, or even the lonesome cry of winter birds. A strange stillness had fallen over the secluded residence where Joseph and his parents lived. An unearthly calm seemed to encompass the estate and surrounding trees.

His mother and father were safely sleeping, yet the lights still burned in the guesthouse where Joseph lived. Cool yellow on the outside, the long, sprawling garages matched the main house in both style and elegance.

As bachelor pads went, Joseph's space over one half of the building was pretty sweet. Add to that the Hawks were killing the opposing team on his flat screen TV, and the beer in his hand was still cold.

But he was unsettled. He couldn't take his eyes off the pink envelope Mrs. Lee had given him, and as far as he was concerned, his obsession with the mysterious package was answer in itself.

Time to open it.

He set aside the beer and crossed to the kitchen—kitchenette, really, since it merged with the living room—and snatched the envelope from where it was propped against a shiny silver toaster. He slid his finger under the fold and got a paper cut, swore silently and ripped it the rest of the way.

Handwriting he assumed belonged to Mrs. Lee covered the rose-bordered paper, and centered at the top was a title that brought him up short.

To Encourage Another to Contact You

Joseph choked on a small, unbelieving laugh. Sylvie's grandmother had given him some kind of spell. A hoodoo spell if he was a betting man. When he readjusted his grip, a picture fell from behind the paper along with some sort of plant sprig that had been caught between the flat objects.

Squatting to pick them up, Joseph froze as he bent, realizing the photo was of a young girl. Though there were braids on her head instead of the long, straightened style she wore as an adult, Joseph recognized the child's eyes. He'd know that unusual pale brown anywhere. He was holding a picture of a young Sylvia Marie Lee.

Her smile was bright and toothy. Her innocence radiant. Untarnished. His stomach clutched to think of what might have erased the boundless joy seen in that young face.

His original reaction to the gift from Mrs. Lee had vanished. He no longer cared how foolish it seemed, so he scanned the writing again and readied himself to follow the instructions. Now he knew why he had the photo and what had fallen out of the envelope with it. White sage. An herb he'd heard Anna speak of a thousand times.

If she only knew what he was about to do.

Shaking off the flood of self-reproach, Joseph grabbed his bottle of beer and emptied it. He would explain everything to Anna, the woman he'd essentially been raised alongside, and she would understand. She had a good heart. The best. She would understand what Joseph had taken it upon himself to do.

Just as soon as he figured out exactly what he *was* doing, so he could explain it better.

With the picture of the girl Sylvie in his hands, he began to speak, in a kind voice as the spell instructed. "Sylvia Marie, you are drawn to me. You long to hear my voice." Okay, he was starting to feel ridiculous again.

But this was important, so he repeated the words and added, "Contact me. Somehow, any way you'd like, but do it soon. Please, Sylvia Marie." He nodded to himself and added, "Sylvie."

In three strides Joseph was at his door, flinging it open with purpose. He would not give up until he gave it everything.

He spoke to the plant then, asking the sage to take his message to his intended recipient. Then he looked out onto the drive and the shadowy lawn beyond, hoping no one had seen him talking to leaves.

He lit the sage with a match and waved it around, allowing the smoke to waft up into the crisp air and carry his summons to Sylvie. He smiled at that thought. Sylvie was not a woman to answer any man's directive.

Brandishing the smoking sprig like a concert-goer with a cigarette lighter, he said the words again, three full times until the sage was completely burned. He looked over the tops of the trees to the midnight sky, hoping she'd heard him and not really sure what he would say if the spell ever worked.

With a longing for a slice of cold pizza, he went back in and opened the refrigerator, but he left the door to his apartment standing wide open. His space was cooling down considerably, but in a way the cold was refreshing, invigorating and thrilling.

While he was in the fridge, he took another beer and sat to watch the rest of the basketball game with still a quarter to go.

By the time a minute and ten seconds remained on the board, the Hawks were straight-up embarrassing the other team, and Joseph had lost all interest. He hit the remote to silence the television and heard what sounded like slow, stealthy footsteps on the wooden stairs outside.

He turned his head and there she stood. He would never mock hoodoo spells again.

"You just don't know when to heed a warning, do you?" she asked, with the sneer on her lip he always seemed to inspire. "Did you think I wouldn't feel you working a spell on me?"

With his hackles raised, like *she* always seemed to inspire, Joseph stood and cocked his head to the side. "Well, that was kind of the point, so don't go giving yourself all that undeserved credit. The way I look at things, it wasn't your talent that made you sense the summoning," he grinned like a real smartass, "but mine."

And he'd used the word summoning to see if it would get a rise out of her.

From the glitter in her eyes, he would assume the taunt had worked. She looked down at his threshold, and Joseph realized she was probably looking for brick dust. Seeing none, she stepped right in with an expression that promised he would regret toying with her.

"Don't think your tight shirt and bright smile are going to work. A boy like you wouldn't know the first thing about pleasing a woman like me, and you sure as hell can't turn me against Ronja." She let her arms hang loose, like someone waiting to jump into a fight.

Joseph looked down at his black T-shirt. He didn't think it was too tight. Swigging the third beer in his hand this night, he winked at her. "If I wouldn't know the first thing, then why are you so concerned with what I'm wearing?"

Her lips pursed as she considered her answer, and he saw the very moment she decided to change tactics. He'd made it clear her tough-girl act wasn't making a dent, so here was the sultry seduction routine.

Her hips rolled as she walked, a subtle undulation that

should be illegal. Joseph took another sip, this time to disguise the swallow he needed so badly.

When she came within arm's length, he stiffened and wondered if he should have stuck to the tactics he knew. He might be able to one-up Sylvie when it came to hostility.

But she would flatten him if she pulled out her all-natural female arsenal. She defined sexual attraction, exuding an intensity so primal he had to put the beer down to keep his eyes off her cleavage.

She wore a navy leather jacket over a white shirt, and dark jeans that showcased the artwork of her curves. Okay. So he'd wanted her to come to him, but what was he supposed to do with her?

"You think you're so special, so much better than me," Sylvie said, still with a touch of snarl. "Don't you, college boy?" She moved closer and trailed a deep violet fingernail across his chest, her mouth shifting from feral growl to seductive grin in a flash. "All that education, and you're still nothing but a servant."

Joseph let the insult slow the hammering lust inside him. "Don't let the fact that I'm employed by the St. Germaines fool you. They're family, and I stay here because I choose. No one forces me to do anything." He nailed her with his eyes. "And no one speaks badly about my family. Any of them."

"Besides," he added with a sarcastic grunt, "what are you? Ronja only sees you as a necessary object, one she'll use and destroy if need be, as long as she gets what she wants."

"You're wrong, baby," Sylvie said, her nails swirling a small circle in the center of his chest now, right where his hair formed a V. He fought the desire to lean into her palm and wondered what it would feel like to have her touch him that way, but without the shirt.

"Ronja gives me lots and lots of power, the kind you could never comprehend," she said before licking her lips as if tasting the very power she spoke of.

Joseph placed a hand over hers, and her circling fingers stilled. "But does she give you respect?" he asked, staring into eyes that reminded him of the sugar his mother used so often to cook sweets. He'd never look at the brown crystals again without thinking of this rogue of a woman.

Sylvie was such a contradiction. Sweet devilry. Joseph knew he was sinking fast and did his damnedest to ignore the teasing scent of jasmine she carried with her.

"I get all the respect I want," she told him, lips tensing just enough to tell him his dart had struck her center. Her pride. "And who are you to talk about respect? What exactly did you call me here for tonight? Out here in your private quarters? I bet what you had in mind was anything but respectable."

Moving in closer, she trailed her hands up his neck and over his shoulders. She pressed her breasts against him, making sure he felt her hardened nipples through the thin, white silk she wore. "You thinking to get yourself a piece of priestess tail?"

Need roared from a dark, secret place inside Joseph, a demand that overpowered the chivalry his parents had instilled in him. He grabbed Sylvie around the waist and held her against him, making sure she felt the evidence of his arousal, just as he did hers. "Maybe I will," he said in a low, threatening voice, his lips hovering a breath away from hers, so full and glossy with something that smelled of exotic fruit. "Be careful who you tease, little girl."

His mouth took hers then with all the fury and desire she'd accused him of. He knew his temper was riding him just as hard as the need to cover her mouth, the need to find out what she tasted like. Sweet, salty, spicy?

And like the bold woman in his arms, the kiss was all three. The flavor of her rolled across his tongue as his hands slid down the taut muscles of her back to rest on the flair of her nicely curved...

Joseph felt himself stumbling backward before he realized she'd pushed him away. The hand that had clutched at his shirt while they'd kissed had thrust against him just as violently.

And there was no mistaking what had coursed between them during the brief yet volatile kiss. A million unnamed emotions had burst inside him, and judging by the rare look of uncertainty on Sylvie's face, she'd been ambushed by them as well.

It had scared the hell out of her.

"Don't," Joseph said, his voice raw with unspent passion and the undeniable fact that he was now involved on an entirely different level. He was no longer trying to save Sylvie for her mother's sake or his, or for Mrs. Lee who worried so over her grandchild. No, Joseph was in this for only one person now. For Sylvie.

And the fact that he cared was as unnerving as it was enlightening.

"Don't what?" she spat, finding her fire again. "How about you don't put your hands on me?"

"I seem to remember your teasing hands on me first," he said, moving forward to wrap his fingers around her neck to the base of her skull. He held her still so he could kiss her again.

This time she didn't come willingly but pushed against his chest with angry fists, pounding two hard times until he let go.

He held her stare, the dark brown of his eyes locking with the softer color of hers. "You asked me why I called you here tonight."

She struggled against him, her chest rising as she gulped frustrated breaths, but Joseph kept her trapped in his brutal embrace. "I think the real question, Sylvie," he nipped her full bottom lip gently then added, "is why did you come?"

A sound remarkably close to a whimper eased from her mouth before he felt her relax against him. "I don't know," she whispered, clinging to him for support now, as if her legs had weakened.

Sylvie knew she'd somehow lost the upper hand, but she couldn't remember when or how. And with Joseph's hands on her skin and his mouth so close to hers, she really didn't care.

When was the last time she'd shown weakness to anyone, much less a man? When had she allowed any whiff of vulnerability to mar her usual badass persona?

She surrounded herself with the most evil of them all and had fully planned to help destroy civilization and everyone in it. Young, old, innocent, guilty.

Now here she was wanting nothing more than to be held. To be shielded from it all.

By Joe fucking Junior.

His grip tightened on her when she tensed, as if he'd been ready for her to change her mind again. Expecting it. And why shouldn't she? She didn't owe him anything.

No matter how good he smelled, so clean yet musky, like a man should. A combination of pure sexual energy and the kind of reliability that made most women go all dewy-eyed.

But she wasn't like most women. She was ruined. Bad to the core. And she'd die before letting anyone close enough to find out how deep the darkness in her really was. How tight a hold the hunger for greed and power actually had on her.

Sylvie felt her eyes start to burn. Her grandmother was right. She was rotting from the inside out.

"Let me go," she told Joseph, trying to turn away from him, even as he held on. "I have to get the fuck out of here."

"Stay," he pleaded with desperation and concern winding through his voice. "You don't have to go back. We can protect you. And your grandmother."

The deep timbre of his words hummed near her ear as he pressed his broad chest to her back, still refusing to let her go. "*I will* take care of you."

Sylvie clenched her eyes shut as the tears began. "Damn you! Let me go. You can't. No one can."

Suddenly she was free and without a second's pause she surged toward the door. She couldn't risk a single glance back, or she might see the kindness that was so much a part of Joseph. And she would falter. She would fall.

She ran down the stairs, practically blind from the water in her eyes, but she didn't dare stop. She didn't know if he was coming after her or not, and she squashed the tiny flair of hope in her chest that he might be. She couldn't afford to want him.

When her booted feet hit the pavement, she felt a hand encircle her arm, jerking her to a stop. Joseph kept surprising her with his strength and his unapologetic use of it, and she respected him for recognizing what it would take to get through her well-fortified walls.

His bravery mixed with gallantry was so foreign to her, so unexpected, and she couldn't deny the shiver that raced through her body every time he tried to force his will on her.

Beneath the rigid muscle and determined stare was a sweet, approachable man. And that was why he was so dangerous.

Sylvie didn't want a nice guy. She needed a man to raise his fist to her, so she could beat it back down. It's what she thrived on. What she was used to.

"Dammit, stop," Joseph growled as he swung her around to face him. He would drag her back inside and tie her up if he had to. He'd kidnap the little idiot and take her to Canada. Whatever it took and however long he had to dog her heels, he would.

She'd let her guard down now, if only a bit, and he could see his way through. But he had to keep fighting. Keep pushing. Because Sylvie was not going to give anything easily.

Her grandmother was right. The girl was still in there, maybe not as sweet as she once was, not as trusting...but surely as wounded. And just as frightened.

Sylvie, fearless, cruel, and arrogant Sylvie, was crying. And it was a moment of vulnerability Joseph intended to exploit. For her own salvation.

He let go of her arm, and instead palmed her cheek, stopping her not with strength but with a caress. "Let me help you," he said, half demand, half plea. Then he eased closer for a light, promising kiss.

Shaking her head so intensely strands of hair fell into her face, she jerked away and rubbed her cheeks to clear the evidence. "No one can help me," she said, reinforcing her denial. "And no one did."

Running hard and fast, Sylvie disappeared into the darkness before he thought to pursue her. Though he wasn't going to give up, Joseph believed he'd done all he could for now. For tonight. But he would go after her soon, and again and again until she caved.

Smashing one fist into the other palm, he jerked his head back to stare at the sky.

Then he heard a sound. The scuff of a foot on cement.

There, just outside of the open garage doors, stood the nine, all staring at him as if he'd turned into a werewolf.

The coven had returned and had seen it all. They'd seen him kiss Sylvie. A member of the Amara.

Anna lurched away from the group, her lips pressed tight and eyes filled with hurt. With betrayal. "We can have Dare come for us in the other boat," she said, her tone clipped. "He can take us out to the island." A strange blue light shone from between the fingers of her right hand before she crushed it closed and made a fist.

"No," Joseph told her, realizing there would be no more lies. No more *omissions*. The war the coven fought overshadowed any personal desires, and they couldn't move forward without the truth. Even a truth they didn't want to hear.

"I'll take you out," he said, trying not to be crushed by the loathing he saw in Anna, and a few of the others. He couldn't imagine what they must be thinking. "I should have told you before…"

"But you didn't," Anna said, hurling the accusation.

"I didn't." Leaving all the lights in his home blazing, Joseph started toward the dock, grateful he always had keys in his pocket. If he went back upstairs, they'd probably leave him behind. "But I'm telling you now," he said.

"Good idea," Hayden said suddenly, and the flash in her eyes hurt even more. Her life was the one in the most danger right now, and Joseph had to admit he'd let things with Sylvie go too far without letting anyone else know.

He'd messed up, but he would fix it. He had to, because just like he'd told Sylvie, these women were his family. So he would make things right.

Even if it took until dawn.

17

The faded jeans and white peasant blouse weren't enough to make Anna seem friendly or tame, but when flames leaped to life from the fireplace behind her, the blue-eyed witch was pretty damn scary.

Gone was Joseph's childhood friend and the woman he loved like a sister. In her place was a female tempest. A storm ready to be unleashed.

So he battened down his hatches and let her rage.

"How long has this been going on?" she asked, her calm tone belying the anger simmering in her eyes.

Thinking back, Joseph realized the timing wasn't a coincidence, but he hadn't picked up on the pattern until now. He sighed. "Since the day Hayden went to the cops for the first time."

He shuffled his eyes toward the tall, blonde man as he walked in, wondering why he had come to the island tonight. The man, Detective something, had exchanged some heated words with Hayden on the mainland dock and climbed into the boat with her.

Joseph didn't bear the guy any grudges, but he didn't really want him here. This was a conversation, or an argument, for the coven and Joseph. Before speaking another word, he stared at the cop before looking to Quinn.

Heeding the unspoken message, Quinn nodded and spoke to the man. "Detective Roch, I'll take you to a room."

The cop glanced at Hayden, who ignored him, then he acknowledged Quinn. "Thank you," was all he said.

As Quinn walked by, he thumped Joseph on the back. The male witch had been shocked to hear about Sylvie's midnight visit but had already decided he was placing some faith in his childhood friend.

Quinn's sister, however, was not as forgiving.

"And your strange *urge* to go looking for Sylvie on the very day Hayden saw the ghosts didn't strike you as odd?" Anna asked. "You knew we were afraid her trial had started."

"It wasn't like that," Joseph said, spreading his hands as he searched for the right words. "I spoke with my parents first and decided to go see Sylvie's grandmother. From there, things just started happening. I know I should have told you, but I wasn't sure where things were going. I wanted to get a handle on Sylvie first."

"Looks like you got a handle on her, all right," Paige said, her voice practically bleeding sarcasm. She stood far across the room, but Joseph could sense the barely-controlled temper in the coven's warrior. He was lucky these women all knew him so well and were at least giving him a chance to explain, but the animosity was beginning to wear on him.

"I know you're all pissed, and I understand why. I should have told you what I planned to do." He met Anna's stare. "But I am not going to apologize for trying to help Sylvie. Only for keeping it a secret."

"She could have killed you!" Anna burst out, telling Joseph the real reason behind her anger. The betrayal she felt was only fueled by her concern for him.

"I'm not a witch, and I have no magic," he said, edging closer to Anna as the fire continued to flicker behind her. "But something woke up in me that day, and not just the need to do something for the people who cared about Sylvie. It was bigger than that, an urge, as you called it, to make something happen. I don't know how to explain it, but I had to act."

Shauni sat on the green velvet couch in the middle of the room, her legs crossed. As she spoke, she stood, her body language changing from guarded to casual. "Like we felt a pull to come to Savannah in search of something we didn't recognize and couldn't explain."

She lifted her arms and let them fall again. "None of us here can question that power. When the undeniable force of magic puts something inside you, it expects you to listen."

"But we never lied to each other," Paige said, and the flames roared in the hearth.

Great, Joseph thought. He hoped the historic house didn't catch on fire because of what he'd done and witches who couldn't control themselves. His mother would want an answer for that.

"No, we didn't," Willyn said, her voice gentle and soothing, a much-needed balm to the rising tension in the air. "But we all know Joseph, and we know we can trust him." She walked over to him and smiled. "He messed up," she said over her shoulder for the others to hear. "But he's always been there for us. Looked out for us. Friends forgive each other, but especially the ones who are like family."

"Family doesn't let things go that far," Anna said, still seething. Pointing a finger at Joseph, she continued her tirade. "You brought that woman to our home, a place your parents were sleeping upstairs! What if she'd brought others with her? The Amara will kill anyone in their path, especially if they think it will hurt us. I know you invited her, Joseph, because she couldn't have gotten past the wards any other way!"

She marched over to him then, eyes shining with hurt and disbelief. "Have you forgotten what they did to Jen? How could you risk Joe and Claire that way?"

Something like a scalding fist hit Joseph's stomach. "I wouldn't...I mean, I didn't think it would come to that."

"No, you didn't think at all." Anna spun and went back to the fireside, staring into the dancing orange as if the answers could be found there.

"I had to follow my gut, and part of that was doing what Sylvie's grandmother told me to do. I'm sorry, but I have to believe it was right. Sylvie wants to change. I know she does. And she wasn't there when Jen was taken, remember?"

"That's right," Viv said suddenly, "because she was at the yellow house giving you instructions to where the Amara were going. A note that took us straight to a sacrificial altar, Jen's bloody body, and a battle we were lucky to survive."

The controlled scientist's wrath was a rare thing, and her clenched fists told Joseph just how badly he'd hurt his friends. "You're right, Viv. I'm so sorry to drag this all back up for you. And for Nick. Sylvie isn't blameless."

"Then why?" Anna cried. Pain threaded through her voice. "How could you choose her over us?"

Unable to hold himself back any longer, Joseph strode to his friend and gripped her shoulders. "It's not about you or her, Anna. It's not that simple. Something in Sylvie is wounded, and I just can't leave her alone. I'm so sorry I didn't tell you, but what I've done is meant to be. I'm sure of it. Even if I don't understand why."

"Well, I won't have any problem choosing," Anna said, snapping the words out and daring him to argue. "If it comes down to you or Sylvie, I'm saving you, even if it means destroying her."

The large room fell silent but for the crackling fire, so Hayden's whisper sounded louder than it should. "Oh, my God." She clutched her head with both hands briefly then began to pace. "Isn't it obvious?" She walked to Joseph so quickly, he wasn't sure what to expect.

But when she got to his side, she took his hand. "You had to do it, Joseph. All of it. Even the kiss."

"What the hell are you smoking?" Paige asked, raking the light, jagged bangs out of her eyes.

Hayden went on unperturbed. "You were at fate's mercy just as much as any of us were. As we still are." She hugged him and pulled back to add, "I'm still not sure how I feel about whatever is between you and Sylvie, because trusting you is one thing, turning our back to her is another."

"Might find an axe in your spine," Paige muttered.

Anna's eyes went hollow as she understood what Hayden meant. Her voice was vacant. "Sylvie is the lost one," she said. "It was her all along. Not Beth." She shook her head vigorously. "Why didn't I see it? What's wrong with me?"

Joseph took Anna's hands and held tight. "Because I had to show you."

"No. No. I don't want you doing this. It's too dangerous," Anna said, her expression bewildered and fearful.

"None of us want Joseph harmed," Shauni said gently, drawing closer to the small group near the fireplace. "I don't like it either, but his connection to Sylvie could be important. If he has to help her to fulfill the prophecy of the seven sisters, we should back him up. We all know how fate likes to get her way. Resisting will only make our lives harder." She turned to Joseph. "And his."

Anna shook her hands out of Joseph's and hurried toward the stairs. She stopped at the base, breathing heavily. She looked panicked. "This isn't your fight. It's not. No matter how close you are to it and to us. You weren't summoned to stand against the Amara, and you weren't given the powers necessary to do so. You'll be killed!"

In a flurry she rushed up the stairs, her final words anguished. "There's no reason for you to stay involved. We'll take it from here. You weren't summoned. You weren't called."

She started up the stairs.

"Anna!" Joseph said sharply, bringing her to an abrupt halt. He waited until she turned a cheek toward him. "That's the thing," he said, hoping she would listen. Praying she heard him. "I think I was."

~

Bluish-black shadows filled her bedroom along with pale white slivers of moonbeams. The cool illumination of a winter night.

Trevor sat motionless on a light-colored loveseat against one wall as he watched Hayden sleep. He was silent. Vigilant.

He'd tossed about in his borrowed bed for a couple of hours, his mind going again and again to the unexpected turn his life had taken. Finally he'd slipped in quietly, brooding over his attraction to the medium, the fact she belonged to a coven, and the threat that had come to his city. His home.

He was having a hard time fathoming the thought of witches, prophecies, and supernatural creatures. And flying demons come to pluck souls like ripe berries.

Yet something had changed in him tonight. Acceptance had snapped into his gut as if it had always belonged there. Two interlocking pieces finding each other at last. The change in his reality was disturbing.

The change in himself was catastrophic.

Who was he if not the nose-to-the-ground detective who sought hard, irrefutable proof of wrongdoing? What was he supposed to do with magic and invisible monsters?

Or a woman who gutted him with her sincerity.

Trevor couldn't explain his newfound belief in Hayden and her ability, but he was glued to her side until this madness was over. When she'd tackled the woman named Anna to the ground, he'd had no doubt she was protecting her friend from something horrible. Something dangerous.

He didn't see a damn thing. But he knew it was there.

Now all he could think about was her and that she might be injured. Or worse. Protecting citizens was what he'd been made for, but the gut-heavy feeling he had now was different. Priority one was keeping Hayden safe.

And damn his partner Cole for being right. Trevor had never looked at a woman the way he did Hayden, and all the warning signs she'd caused early on had been for an entirely different reason.

Trevor slipped up and let himself blow out a harsh breath, causing the multi-colored cat on the bed to sit up and mewl. The feline didn't hiss at him or warn him away from her human. She asked nicely, plaintively, and followed up the cooing sound with a drawn out purr that sounded like a question.

"Don't worry, cat," he said, smiling despite himself. "I'm looking out for her, too."

Hayden's hand moved to the feline's back to pet before she spoke. "Trevor?" her voice was rough with sleep, and he wondered if she'd been dreaming.

"I'm here," he said, expecting her to shoot to a sitting position and snatch the covers to her chest. Isn't that what women did when waking to a strange man in their room?

"I thought I smelled you," she said groggily. Then he sensed her freezing up, like she'd just realized what she'd said.

His laugh was a low rumble. "What do I smell like?" he asked.

Now she did sit up, straightening the top she wore to make sure she was covered. "Soap," she said then added, "Like the mountains in a clean fog."

"And you smell like citrus again. Orange blossom body spritzer?" He'd meant it as a light-hearted way to put her at ease, but again the imagery of a mist on her skin had his stomach tightening into a hard ball of want and need.

When he'd come here, his intentions had been good. Now his thoughts were anything but.

She laughed, the soft and very female sound shooting the lust in his stomach to the rest of his body. To hands that wanted to touch her, arms that wanted to hold her down as he finally took that mouth with his own, and to his heart. He wanted them both free of clothing, bare to the waist, and chest to chest.

He scraped his fingers against his thigh, reminding himself he was on duty. He was on call as far as his day job was concerned, but his drive to take care of Hayden had become a twenty-four-seven obligation. A compulsion.

If otherworldly things were attacking his city, he needed to be by her side at all times. Not only for her, but to give her some backup.

She was supposed to figure out how to save ghosts? Fine. He'd make sure she stayed alive to do it.

"Did you get any answers from your friend?" he asked, taking advantage of her wakefulness. "What's his name? Quinn?"

She threaded fingers through her ginger-colored hair to straighten it out, but he enjoyed her disheveled state. "No," she said and yawned. "He'll probably be at it all night, though. Him and the contact he has up North. A demonologist who is now ready to fly down here and jump into the fray. Quinn told him what happened in the morgue."

"And he believed it?" Trevor heard the skepticism in his tone and amended, "Sorry, but I still have a hard time with all of this." He gave her a one-sided smile. "But the upside is that your talking to spirits doesn't seem so far-fetched anymore."

"Great." She didn't sound pleased.

The cat jumped up with a quick *meeyew!* and took several steps before leaping from the bed to Trevor's lap. He jerked but instinctively brought his legs together as she circled to lie down. "Uh." He didn't know what to say.

Hayden grinned. "Daisy likes you. Guess she thinks you're a

nice person under all that bluster."

With a sardonic grunt, he said, "The same could be said for you."

Her brow wrinkled. "Me? I don't bluster. In fact, I strive to stay calm and...level-headed." She shook her head like he must be confused.

"You could have fooled me." He stroked the cat that was shaking his entire lap with her purr. "I think the word is harridan."

Now Hayden's mouth fell open, but she snapped it closed and grew thoughtful. "You've been ...difficult."

"Yes, of course. Entirely my fault." When he saw her jaw take a mutinous set, he decided to offer something in truce. "We did find something in the bushes at the bed and breakfast. We still don't know if it means anything. There were no prints."

He readjusted on the sofa, careful not to disturb the orange and black ball in his lap. He found the cat's soft motor oddly comforting.

Hayden sat silently, so he continued. "A wrapper from a stick of gum. Cinnamon flavored. It might not mean anything, but you never can tell." Trevor paused, hoping his willingness to share would help Hayden understand what he couldn't bring himself to say outright. That he was relinquishing a part of himself. Exchanging cynicism for confidence. In her.

"Do you think he's done this before?" Hayden asked, her face eerily pale in the moonlight.

"I have no doubt. His MO is too clean. He's had practice."

"And that's how you'll catch him, right? The way he's finding or assaulting the women? His MO?" Now she did clutch the blanket in her hands but held it at waist-level.

"No, that's probably changed over time. The MO is simply how he goes about doing the things needed to capture and kill." He winced at the distant, clinical sound of voice and eased down his tone. "For example, he uses a Taser now. Maybe he used to do something else to incapacitate his victims, but he learned a better way. So, while his MO may change, his signature won't. Whatever it is he gets from the rape or murder. Or both."

"And if you can figure out his signature, you might discover his motivation. Why he does it could lead you to what kind of person he is."

"And narrow the field." He gave her a grin. "Not bad for a civilian. I'm not exactly a profiler myself, but I've picked up a few of the basics along the way."

Hayden didn't return the smile. "I need to find out who's giving the killer the *ayjehr*."

"The what? Oh, the spell you and Anna were talking about?"

"The writing itself," she said. She studied him seriously for a moment, like she was considering how much he could take in one night. "The language has power when written down, and the symbol being used by the murderer is not his. Someone's let him borrow it."

"So we can either find the person who gave him the symbol then follow him or her to the killer..."

Hayden picked up where he trailed off. "Or we catch the killer to find the Droehk. The owner of the enchanted language."

Trevor stayed where he was as Hayden climbed from beneath the covers and stood next to the bed. He lifted a brow as she stretched her arms out to her sides.

"Looks like we've got a tentative partnership going on," he said then stiffened when she bent at the waist and lowered her head to the floor. "You do your part with the magic, and I'll do mine with the police work."

She let out a groan and Trevor almost unseated the cat. "What are you doing?" he asked, as unsettled as he was fascinated.

Hayden stood back up, her eyes closed. He scanned her lithe form and noticed she wasn't wearing a bra with the T-shirt and pajama bottoms.

Of course not. He'd caught her in bed.

"This conversation is unpleasant and stressing me out," she said. "I'm just stretching to ease my nerves." She opened a lid and accused him with one golden eye. "You could stand a little yoga yourself. It does wonders for..." She paused. "What's the male word for harridan?" Then with a bubbly laugh she stretched her hands high above, lifting the hem of the shirt to expose her belly button.

Determined to behave, and because the cat was now giving him a suspicious look, Trevor leaned back into the loveseat and relaxed. "I'm not really into yoga. Just not my thing."

Her T-shirt pulled across her chest. "But don't let me stop you." He smiled in the shadows. "I'll just watch."

18

"I have to get back to work," Trevor said, snapping his phone closed with unnecessary force. His handsome face was a picture of discontent. "If you get dressed now, we can make good time."

Hayden frowned right back as the kitchen came to life around them. An expectant thrill was in the air this morning, so everyone was up early. And there was no way to miss the bright fuchsia lilies on the center of the island or the other pink flowers gracing every corner of the mansion.

Yes. Hayden's challenge was in full swing.

"Trevor, I can't stay with you every minute. It's not practical." She sipped water in preparation for her yoga routine. It was well past time for her to get back on schedule. "Besides, what happened to you doing your part and me doing mine?"

Sliding his phone into a pocket in his black jacket, Trevor glanced grimly around the room. "I guess you'll be safe if you stay here." He narrowed in on her and said, "If you stay with your friends. You said this place was...warded?"

Hayden nodded and smiled. She wasn't about to tell him the coven had no idea how to fend off demons yet. Trevor had to go be a detective if the man raping and killing women was ever going to be caught, and he couldn't, no, he *wouldn't*, do that if he was worried about her.

She dismissed the warm fuzzy in her chest and the rampant rush of heated blood through her veins. He was still obstinate and overbearing, but there was something about a powerful man coming to her defense. Sure it was old-fashioned and would seriously disappoint Gloria Steinem, but that didn't change the truth of it.

Trevor Roch was raw sexuality, and having his complete attention and concern made her toes curl.

She had to shake herself and remember he was a cop, though his badge and hardened scowl weren't what caused her anxiety now. Instead it was the blue of his eyes and the way he ran his hand through that thick, blonde hair. The stubble he had this morning was the kicker.

She loved seeing an unruly side of the straight-laced law enforcer.

"Would you like some coffee before you go?" she asked him, trying to look at anything besides his mouth.

A discordant whir exploded and drew Trevor's attention. He gestured to Paige as she stopped the blender to add another raw egg. "I'll have whatever she's making," he said with a jerky nod for the blonde bruiser.

Paige gave a wide smile of pure smartass to Claudia who was sitting at the island. "Finally. Somebody who gets it."

Decked out in her usual to-the-nines, Claudia shrugged and glanced at Trevor. "One look from him and salmonella will run screaming." She grinned. "So I guess he's safe."

"Thanks," Trevor said. "I think."

Hayden laughed and touched Trevor on the elbow before throwing her bottle into the trash. "Now we've both been labeled as aggressive."

Paige stopped in the middle of dumping a powdered substance into her concoction. "Hayden? Aggressive? Who called her that?"

Trevor made a sound in his throat. "You mean she's not that

way with everybody?"

From the opposite end of the sprawling kitchen, Kylie looked up from her magazine. "Hayden isn't meek or mild when she's standing up for others." The younger woman's hazel eyes were thoughtful. "Only for herself."

No one spoke for a moment, but then Claudia shook her spoon in Kylie's direction. "Freakishly astute, that one is. And when least expected."

The cacophony of coffee machine, blender, and female chatter resumed, and Hayden allowed a small smile to pass over her lips. She loved these women. They were her sisters. And she silently echoed Paige's sentiment. *Finally. Somebody who got it.*

After receiving a plastic cup of Paige's special sludge, Trevor thanked her but refrained from drinking. He caught Hayden's eye and pulled his head to the side. "Walk me out?"

"Sure." She fell into step beside him and wondered why her stomach jangled with nerves.

Once they'd made it to the large foyer, Trevor set the cup on a side table and turned to take Hayden's hands in his.

Then he slowly reeled her in, stopping only when he had her close, hands on her back and head bent toward hers. "I can't put this off any longer," he said, "so if you want to stop me, make it quick."

Breath rushed from her lungs, but she raised herself up to meet him, too afraid to answer. She couldn't pinpoint the specific moment Trevor had shifted from adversary to anticipation, but all she wanted now was an answer. How would it feel to be kissed by him?

Then she knew. A soft brush of lips gliding toward a more insistent pressure. Warm and wet, his intoxicating scent engulfing her as he claimed her. Clean yet salty. Hayden couldn't keep track of all the wonderful things his moving lips made her feel, allowed her to taste, but she clung to his thick biceps and let him give all he wanted.

She felt his fingers curl into her skin as if he struggled to keep his hands in acceptable territory. Then he jerked back and focused on her, still holding on, but loosely. "How the hell did this happen?" he asked, voice husky and deep.

Sun sparkled through the stained glass on both sides of the massive front door, bathing them in a rainbow of colors.

"I don't know," she whispered, easing back to the floor and glancing at his mouth one last time. She met his unreadable stare and asked, "Are you sorry?"

His hand was on her neck then, moving down to her shoulder and lower to her arm, as if he was learning every curve. "Sorry? No." He shook his head.

"Then what?"

Lowering his forehead to hers, he squeezed her tight then withdrew. "I'll talk to you soon."

Hayden guessed he wasn't ready to commit to an answer. Maybe he had misgivings after all. Did he still see her as a fraud?

No, she was sure he didn't. If it was one thing she knew about Trevor, he didn't prevaricate. He said what he felt and meant it, even if his words carried insult. So she couldn't be self-conscious if he wasn't ready to admit his feelings.

Because once he did, there would be no going back. That's just the way he was made.

"Stay with someone at all times," he told her in his policeman voice. "And let me know if you learn anything on your end. I'll do the same."

Hayden worked up the best smile she could and nodded.

With a look that could only be described at disgruntled, Trevor leaned in and gave her a peck on the lips. "Be safe," he said before grabbing his drink, opening the wooden door, and disappearing on the other side.

She stood there gingerly running her fingertips over her

mouth, marveling at the way it still tingled. She licked her lips and tasted him again. And her toes curled.

"Hey," Kylie said from behind her, making Hayden whirl around like she'd been caught doing what she'd been imagining. And the fantasy included Trevor. "What?" she asked, feeling ridiculously indecent.

"We're meeting with Quinn in the dining room...err, I mean the magic room. Whatever. Where we make potions." She bounced on her toes. "Get ready for Demon Self-defense 101."

"Oh. Good." Hayden pulled a band out of her pocket and twisted her hair into a tail. "I'll be right there." *Just as soon as I get all my wits back where they belong.* She blamed Trevor for her scattered mind. The man certainly knew how to kiss.

As she started toward the doorway, Ronnie materialized in front of her. Then Chloe followed in a blur of yellow and blue. "When you're finished, we need you to come with us," Ronnie told her without preamble. "We found someone you should talk to."

"Who?" Hayden asked, a hundred thoughts fighting for position in her head. So much was happening at once.

"Someone who knows the murderer." Ronnie paused to glance at the other ghost before telling Hayden, "His first victim."

~

Armed with her brand new demon-fighting kit, Hayden strolled down the street as if she was on her way to dinner with a friend, an evening soiree, or simply home after a hard day's work. Her demeanor wasn't that of a woman on her way to a darkened graveyard. Or one headed to meet with a tortured spirit.

With the bag of "weapons" stashed in her purse, Hayden walked with a sense of purpose and duty. She'd told the coven she was going to see Trevor, which was the only reason they let her go alone.

And she did plan to speak with him. *After* she'd talked to the ghost to find out what she knew about the serial killer. Then she'd have something he could use in the investigation.

And it wouldn't seem like she just wanted to see him again. Though she did.

Regardless of how concerned Trevor and her friends were, dealing with supernatural entities was Hayden's job. Her calling.

She'd tried to run away from her responsibilities once before, in her youth, when handling it all had been too much for a naïve and selfish girl. When she'd resented the intrusion into her life. Begrudged the deceased who disturbed her every waking hour. And the sleeping ones, too.

Hayden shrugged her purse strap higher on her shoulder and clutched the bag to her side. Yes, she'd run from her power, her gift, and the consequences had been… She lifted her head, refusing to be dragged back down the tunnel of shame.

There had been consequences. That was all.

Instead she let her thoughts wander to the contents of her large bag and the lessons Quinn had shared with them earlier. His friend the demonologist was preparing to come to Savannah, bringing knowledge and experience with him. But until he knew exactly what they were dealing with, the man who studied the lore of fiends had only been able to share the most basic of protection methods.

In other words they would be fending off monsters with a variety of materials and hoping one or some of them worked. Kind of a broad-spectrum antibiotic technique. Except for demons.

Hayden went over the list of items in her mind again. Cemetery dirt for confusion. Evidently the smell of soil infused with death was like catnip to the creatures, but Hayden didn't want to think too long on that.

Then there was old reliable, as she thought of it, holy water, which Claire had happily commandeered from the Catholic Church she attended. Joseph's mother was an intriguing woman and a mix of cultures. No wonder her son was such an open-minded yet principled man.

Hayden frowned to herself, hoping Joseph's faith would guide him through his current problem, because Sylvie was nothing if not trouble.

A cold wind swept around the corner, and she was glad she'd worn the long, cable-knit sweater with jeans. The outfit was the perfect combination of warmth and flexibility, in case she needed to run.

Stopping at the rough-hewn granite archway to survey the wrought-iron fence on each side, she said a silent incantation that she would be able to get back out in a hurry. If she were in danger. The graveyard was locked up at night, but her spirit friends would help her if she stayed too long. Hayden didn't plan to find herself trapped in a cemetery at night.

Even mediums had their limits.

With twilight fading to navy, no tourists were left milling around the historic site. The girl she'd come to find had been buried here due to a family plot purchased long ago, so her body had been laid to rest next to civil war soldiers and yellow fever casualties.

Steeling herself, Hayden strode through the archway and followed the path of the sea shell material she now recognized as tabby. She would do her part to stop the maniac using black magic as he raped and murdered, even if it meant battling unknown forces. Trevor would be angry, but eventually he'd come around. He'd understand.

This was Hayden's way to protect and serve.

The coven had administered a collective blessing before she'd left the island, since according to Quinn, the focused will of a magical group could interfere with a demon's power. However, the practice was often used to combat demons who'd possessed human bodies. No one really knew how it would work on those flying around freely.

As Hayden passed an old, cement crypt, she spied Ronnie and Chloe. And others. Bodies were interred both under and above the ground here, and as she opened herself up to let psychic vision take over, she realized many ghosts were present.

And they were all staring at her.

Focusing on the headstone that Ronnie and Chloe were flanking, Hayden kept her eyes forward and her steps true. So far so good. The two spirits seemed calm, so no airborne hunters were in the vicinity.

She assumed.

A chilling mist settled over the area, shrouding the moss-heavy trees in a gray fog. Tendrils of the haze skirted around edges of grave markers and tombs, and something about its directed movement raised the bumps on her arms.

Unnatural forces were at work here tonight, whether gathered to observe or to interfere, she wasn't sure, but until she actually saw an enemy, she was driving on.

She told herself the spectator ghosts weren't sliding closer. That they weren't giving her an undue amount of scrutiny.

Coming to a halt at what she guessed was the foot of the grave, Hayden indicated the glossy, gray headstone. "Is this the one?" Simple and classy, the marker displayed the name Melanie Lynn Thomas and a short epitaph. *Beloved Daughter and Sister.*

Combined with the girl's age of death, the brief inscription wrenched Hayden's heart. Melanie had been sixteen years old.

"I knew him in school," a soft, sad voice said, causing Hayden to jerk her eyes up to the newly-emerged ghost. A teenage girl with black curls stood behind her own gravestone. Melanie had made an appearance. "I didn't know him well, though. He was weird."

"Hello, Melanie," Hayden said, hoping she could serve dual purpose here tonight. Finding the man who'd hurt these women and taken their lives would be a step toward releasing the souls of Ronnie and Chloe.

But she also intended to help Melanie pass over. Hayden knew a spirit who'd lingered too long when she saw one, and the brutalized teenager clearly had. The area under her eyes looked bruised, her cheeks sunken, as if she'd been starved for years.

In essence she had been. Starved of peace. Of freedom. Of rest.

The girl's gaze was locked on the grass covering her grave like a sad, sparse blanket. She didn't speak again.

"What was his name?" Hayden asked, going straight to the key piece she needed. Melanie's grasp on her reality, such as it was, seemed fragile. The spirit could waver out of touch any second.

"Everybody called him Dover, but it wasn't his real name. I can't remember why he was called that, but it wasn't something he liked." If a ghost could be pensive, Melanie was. Her eyes moved to the side as she thought back, to life and childhood days. The only kind she would ever know. "Dover Briggs. That was it."

A gust of icy wind burst from behind Melanie then, and her eyes bugged from their hollow depths. "I don't want to talk about him anymore!"

The gathered ghosts murmured and moaned, as if they all felt the young girl's pain. A collective consciousness of loneliness and loss.

Ronnie floated to Melanie's side and comforted her somehow without speaking. Even Hayden wasn't privy to all the abilities of those stuck in between.

Melanie brushed her black hair away from her face, giving

Hayden full view of the misery etched there. "He was a freak. That's all I know. He was always alone, hair long and greasy with his Walkman on. If you got too close, you could hear hard, acid rock of some kind blasting."

Melanie slumped and stared back at the ground. "He was always chewing gum. You could smell it in class. Cinnamon."

Hayden had to stop herself from reacting too strongly, but the spirit's description gave her a jolt. Cinnamon gum. A definite connection.

Now she had a name, even if only a nickname, Trevor could find out where Melanie had gone to high school. How hard could it be to figure out who Dover Briggs really was?

"I know you've waited a long time, Melanie, but I'm going to help you. I promise." Hayden met Ronnie's brown eyes and nodded firmly.

"Help me," Melanie said in a whispy voice, and Hayden wasn't sure if it was a plea or just a repetition of her own words. Melanie was fading now, and desolate sobs rang out as the girl vanished.

Trauma in life was causing torment in death for the teenager, and Hayden was more than ready to track down the sadistic man who'd caused Melanie's suffering. And the others. Ronnie, Chloe, Emily. How many more?

She shivered in the cold, realizing dusk had passed, and full night had fallen. Purplish-blue light coated everything in the cemetery, as if she'd stepped into another world.

"We're getting closer," Hayden told Ronnie, feeling a fire in her chest that burned with hope. For the first time she knew what to do next and was optimistic about helping the ghosts pass over to where they belonged. Far from the evils of mankind, the Amara, and wicked Droehk magic that could imprison their souls.

"Just hang in there a little bit longer," she said with a smile of encouragement. "Just keep moving and stay hidden."

Ronnie opened her mouth to respond.

And that's when the demons came.

19

The scent of decay rushed through the air seconds ahead of the reeking monster. The flying demon almost had Ronnie, but she vaporized just in time. This time the thing didn't waste its breath—if it had such—on crying out its anger but curved high overhead to make another diving pass.

All of the ghosts who'd been loitering in the park winked out of existence one by one. Escaping the threat.

Straight ahead of Hayden stood a memorial with four columns, reminiscent of a Greek construction, but the beauty of the marble structure isn't what held her stare. Something was crawling on the underside of the roof, defying gravity as it curled talons from beneath the overhang. The creature shoved its gaping jaw into the moonlight then, revealing sharp, jagged teeth that bore no resemblance to man or animal.

Eyes of firelight zeroed in on Hayden, and she hardened herself, trying to hide in her own skin. She stood completely still, terrified to move. Shock made it impossible to respond as creatures emerged from the shadows.

Hayden struggled to think, to rationalize what was happening, so she could defend herself. *How many are there? How many?* Her eyes darted back and forth until she counted three. The black one flying overhead, another creeping around the base of a winter-bare crepe myrtle, and the one in front of her. Glaring at Hayden like she was its worst enemy.

Or its prey.

The winged demon from the morgue had been beaten before, deprived of its prize, so this time it had come prepared for human interference. It had brought backup.

A gurgling scream echoed through the park, and Hayden looked to find Chloe still standing near the headstone. Why hadn't she left? Disappeared with Ronnie? Maybe she'd been too terrified to act, like Hayden still was.

But none of that mattered anymore. Hayden's stomach tightened with revulsion, and what she saw made her want to scream in tune with the ghost. To purge the horror of what was being done.

A long, curling tentacle protruded from Chloe's abdomen, from the very spot the ayjehr symbol had been painted on her living body. Black as pitch, the tongue-like appendage wrapped itself into a knot like a sewing thread, and the realization of what that meant rocked Hayden's reality.

With its hook firmly anchored inside of Chloe, the huge, oily demon starting pulling her in. It hovered a few feet behind the spirit and just above her head, its black body swirling with bruised purples and yellows. The wide, thin-skinned wings ruffled as if riding a maelstrom, and a huge black void formed in the place the head might be.

Sensing what was coming, Chloe stretched out one arm to Hayden. A cry of despair flowed from her open mouth. Too late Hayden leaped into action and stumbled forward, but in a fraction of time, Chloe was sucked into the whirling mouth. Gone.

Now the beast did bellow, but the scream was one of victory instead of rage as it shot over Hayden's head and into the sky. Wide wings flapped once before it vanished.

Furious, sad, and frightened all at once, Hayden jerked her

head back to check on the roof-hanging monster and the one under the tree, then she turned back to the sky. But the demon and Chloe were lost in the black.

The horror of what she'd witnessed froze Hayden into place again. Her pulse pounded in her ears and breathing was a harsh, painful act, like dragging sand into parched lungs.

A sloppy, wet noise sounded from behind her, so she spun in a tight circle. The demon had emerged from the shadow of the tree and was snuffling the air like a pig rooting out truffles. Skin the color of phlegm shivered as it raised its head and howled, a call to announce it had located its quarry.

The demon had scented Hayden and was leaning forward, ready to charge.

Fumbling in her bag, she closed her hand over the first bottle she felt and wrenched her arm free. Uncorking the lid with a pop, she stood and waited, brandishing the holy water in front of her like a crucifix.

A crucifix. *Why hadn't she thought to get one of those?*

The attack came from her left instead, catching her off guard so she toppled the bottle and spilled some of the precious liquid. Jumping from the Greek-styled structure, the demon with the massive jaws and serrated teeth lumbered after her, snarling at the smaller monster, warning it to back off.

Hayden didn't know if that was necessarily a good thing. As the beast approached, her palm started to burn, maybe from her grip on the small glass bottle? Where was that blue light coming from?

She didn't have time to think about it. The monster was closing in fast, so Hayden gripped tight on the bottle to still her shaking hand. She only had two chances to slow or stop these things. Then she would have to run.

Whooshing air from its mouth and spewing greenish saliva, the larger demon lowered its head and charged. Closer and closer. Ten feet. Five. *Now!*

With a squeak she was thankful no one was around to hear, Hayden swept her arm out and pelted the demon in the face with holy water. As it screamed, she spun in the grass and sprinted, not bothering to stick around to gauge the damage done. If she wanted to live she had to get out of the isolated graveyard and back to moving, breathing population.

She just hoped the creatures wouldn't follow her and make a feast of any innocent pedestrians.

Footsteps pounding, she veered around markers and through trees, making it to the last row before hurtling herself to the ground behind a crypt. She could barely breathe, choked by a combination of exertion and terror.

Fear had her huddling against the brick and cement, but could a person even hide from demons?

Multiple voices broke through her anxiety, bawdy sounds of joking and laughter. She spied a group of four or five men on the sidewalk through the black iron bars.

Should she make a break for the archway and for safety? Or would her flight only endanger other people? She might be leading a hungry demon to its meal.

Will it actually eat us or just rip us to pieces?

The stink of rotten meat forced her to her feet, and she jogged toward the gate. Checking over her shoulder as she went and holding the Ziploc bag of graveyard dirt to her chest. Just in case. She saw the hulking demon on top of the very crypt she'd sheltered under, and her heart stuttered to a frigid halt before regaining strength to pump.

No wonder she'd smelled it. The thing had been right on top of her.

And those men had probably saved her life.

For whatever reason the demon stayed where it was, glaring after her with promise in its flaming eyes.

Paying no heed to the stoplights, Hayden continued across the street, coming to a stop in front of the fire station. More people would be inside. She prayed crowds were demon-deterrents.

Hayden fumbled for her cell phone, panting rapidly, and dialed Trevor's number.

He picked up on the second ring, but she didn't give him a chance to speak. "Trevor, I'm at the graveyard, no, now I'm at the fire station. The one near The Barracks. Please come get me." The words rambled out in one long stream of fear.

"Colonial Park?" he asked, but she could hear him walking and keys jangling. "I'm on my way. Don't move." She heard a door slam. "Go inside and wait. Tell them I'm coming. They know me."

"Okay," she said, gulping as her body began to crash from the adrenaline rush she'd been riding. Trevor was coming for her. He knew where she was.

Her thoughts came in short bursts, incoherent and dazed. She moved like a person drunk on liquor, but didn't go into the building. What would she say to the fire fighters? They'd think she was crazy.

Besides, Trevor was coming. He'd be there soon.

A siren wailed a few blocks down, and relief burst somewhere deep inside Hayden. That was him. She knew it.

With regret pouring into her, Hayden slid down the bricks and sat on the sidewalk. She had failed. Horribly. She'd let Chloe be taken from right in front of her. Stolen by a winged demon from hell.

She had no idea where to look for the poor, young girl's spirit. Or how to save her soul.

~

An hour later and Hayden's lips had finally stopped quivering. Her stomach had settled and was free of the nausea. Her skin was warm once again.

All thanks to Trevor, who'd literally ridden to her rescue before taking her back to his apartment. He'd insisted she have a hot bath and something to eat after she'd babbled incoherently on the short ride to where he lived. Trevor had taken complete control of the situation.

Thank Buddha. Because for a woman who'd been talking to ghosts since she was a little girl, Hayden had fractured.

Feeling both safe and shy in Trevor's overly large T-shirt, she came out of the bathroom with her folded clothing in her arms like a security blanket. "Hey," she said to Trevor who was sitting at the desk in his room and staring at a computer monitor. He'd left her alone to soak in the bath and nibble on the snack of toast, cheese, and fruit. But he hadn't gone far.

He was worried about her. Physically and mentally.

Wearing only blue exercise pants and a white shirt, the same as he'd dressed her in, Trevor looked more casual than she'd ever seen him. Relaxed. Like the boy next door. A tall, muscular, serious boy next door, but still, he was trying to put her at ease.

The gesture touched her. Instead of grilling her about what had happened tonight, he'd guided her home like a lost child and allowed her to tell him what she could in bits and snatches. The gradual purge had been exactly what she needed, and he never once looked at her like she was crazy.

He turned around in his chair and leveled her with those vibrant blue eyes. His hair was damp and recently combed, so he must have showered elsewhere. "How do you feel?" The question held a million possible doors, and he was letting her choose the ones she wanted to open.

"Better. Thanks." She wouldn't say "fine," because that just wasn't true.

"It's late," he told her, "so you're welcome to stay the night. You take the bed, and I can sleep on the couch." He grinned. "It's much bigger than the one in your room. More my size."

Lacking the energy to do anything but crawl into his dark gray sheets, Hayden nodded and laid her clothes on a nearby chair. The sheets smelled clean and were cool on her skin. Smiling, she curled up and enjoyed the sensation. The comfort.

Trevor shut down the computer, clicked off a desk lamp, and crossed the room to the door. A nightlight in the hallway spilled softly through the opening. "Get some sleep," he said in a low, easy voice.

Hayden didn't want him to go. "Wait," she said, pushing up on one elbow. "Will you stay here? Sleep with me?"

"Uh...I thought you might want some space."

"I know, and I appreciate your concern." She was glad the dark hid most of their faces. "I would feel better if you stayed." She took a deep breath. "I want you beside me."

Trevor stepped back in but left the door ajar. He started to pull his shirt off but paused. "I didn't mean..."

"It's okay. Take it off." She grinned. "This is your home, and you should be comfortable." And she imagined the scent of him in the night would help chase away any nightmares. Or memories.

He slid in next to her, and they came together naturally, as if they'd been coordinating the move their entire lives. She lifted to let his arm sweep around her shoulders before nestling into the curve of his body. They were a fit.

"This is nice," she said, then blushed at the simple statement.

His hand rubbing her back erased the embarrassment, and she burrowed in when he said, "Yes. It is."

Hayden enjoyed the intimacy for a few minutes, both of them silent and thoughtful. She eventually tapped her hand on his hard, flat stomach. She couldn't stall forever. "I'm not sure how clear I was earlier tonight. I know I was mixed up."

"I know. And your state of mind is the only reason I didn't chew your ass for going out alone. And to a graveyard." He shifted one leg, still apparently upset over what she'd done.

"I would have deserved it, and I'm sure my friends will do some chewing of their own when I tell them, but the important thing is what I found out." She flattened her hand against his stomach, fascinated by the ridges of muscle. "I have the killer's name, or at least part of it. And where he went to high school."

She'd expected him to jump up and start questioning her, but he only asked, "Did a ghost give it to you?" His legs had stopped moving, and his breathing was even.

"Yes. She was the first girl he ever raped and killed. She knew him."

"It's common for serial killers to start in their comfort zone, and lucky for us, the act can also give them away. If we make the connection." He lifted his hand to stroke her arm. "Good work. Cole and I will follow up, but I have to tell you, whatever we find might not get us a warrant. I can't produce the witness who gave us the tip."

"That is a problem." She closed her eyes and savored his warm touch. "But you'll look into it?"

"Of course." He kissed the top of her head, surprising her. "Maybe if we find this guy, he'll be able to tell us how to save Chloe."

A heavy warmth centered in Hayden's chest. Trevor was ready to continue battling against creatures he couldn't see, hear, or smell. Accepting a lead that was not only hearsay but had originated from a spirit.

He believed in her, and despite witches, monsters, and ghosts, he wasn't running away or pushing her aside. He was standing up for the murdered women, for the life they'd been robbed of. And the afterlife they sought.

What a man.

And now, more than ever, she would need his support. "I know you'll work as fast as you can, but we're running out of time. Honestly, for Chloe it may be too late. I just don't know." Hayden knew what had to be done, and her skin prickled and chilled with the knowledge. "Regardless, I don't think we can wait that long."

Trevor felt Hayden stiffen in his arms. Her tone had gone flat. "What do you mean?" he asked. "You have another idea?"

"Yes." She sighed against his chest. "And you aren't going to like it." When he tried to sit up she held him down but lifted her head to meet his eyes. The gold of hers was intense, worried maybe, but determined. "Quinn said something this morning, about a gathering of magical people and what their power could do."

"And your coven will get behind you on this?" He didn't like the way she lay limp against him, resigned instead of optimistic. "If you think whatever you can do will work, why are you so apprehensive?"

"I'm not going to lie to you."

"Good," he said quickly.

"We need to get some answers. Some real answers from the source." She was suddenly interested in his forearm, his wrist, then his hand as she entwined her fingers with his. Trevor knew avoidance tactics when he saw them.

Hayden curled her fingers tightly with his and said, "There will be risk."

"Then I'll be there." He held onto those fingers and willed himself to tamp down on the fear clogging his throat.

"No. I'll have my coven to protect me." She kissed his neck.

"This isn't a debate," Trevor said. "You've thrown a lot of crazy shit at me the last few days, and now that we've established a working relationship, you're not just going to cut me out when you feel like it."

He cupped her chin to end her argument before it began. "I need those answers, too, don't forget."

Hugging her close to balance the harshness of his words, he lowered his head to kiss her, gently, with no hint of passion. Only affection. "When and where?" he asked with an authority that told her he wouldn't tolerate evasion.

Hayden placed her hand over his heart and waited, her palm absorbing his steady beat. She was connected to him. One body. One purpose.

"Tomorrow on the island," she said finally. "The great room where we hold rituals. It's sacred, and very, very old." She snuggled against his chest again and whispered against his bare skin. "The coven is strongest there."

Now the worry in his throat spread to his mind, his lungs, his gut, stinging and scraping his insides with dread. "What are you going to do, Hayden?"

Her fingers went limp in his. "Summon a demon."

20

"Yes, I've got everything we need, and the ritual should work." Quinn dropped a plastic box on the dais in the great room. Crossing his arms over his broad chest, he scowled at his sister before giving the same look to Hayden. "But I wish I'd kept my mouth shut. I don't think we should do this."

"You won't be doing this," Anna said, nudging her younger brother aside to look into the box. "I want you to go to the mainland like the others."

Hayden shot a worried glance to Paige, but she only shrugged and let the two siblings fight it out. After putting forth her plan to the coven, they'd unanimously agreed the possible intel they might get from a demon would be worth the risk of inviting him in for a chat.

That hadn't kept them from shipping Mr. and Mrs. Attinger off to spend the night at the yellow house with Joe, Claire, and Joseph. No one was taking chances with the older couple, in spite of the assurances from the old book Quinn was holding in his hand.

Despite the ancient text on summoning dark forces that promised a strong enough circle would keep an evil entity in check, Anna wasn't satisfied. "That means you, too," she said, pointing a finger at Trevor.

"Sorry, but if Hayden insists on throwing herself into the line of fire, I'm staying." He crossed his arms over his chest just as Quinn had done. Both men were immovable.

Anna hiked a brow and looked to Hayden in question. "Well?"

"As long as you don't interfere," Hayden said to Trevor. "We've had unimaginable pressure and responsibility heaped on our shoulders. A prophecy, an immortal witch, fiends from hell." She stepped in line with Paige and Viv to form a united front. "We can handle this. We're destined to."

Kylie grinned at Quinn and sauntered over to stand with Shauni and Willyn.

"I'll drink to that," Paige said, winking at Hayden for a speech well done.

"Good. Then it's settled." Trevor met eyes with Quinn and the two males exchanged decisive nods, as if they'd been the ones to lay down the law.

"Blessed Buddha," Hayden murmured.

"Oh, give them a break," Shauni said with a mischievous grin. "Truth be told, Michael had a fit when I filled him in. He had a surgery scheduled and was none too happy that I waited until the last minute to tell him." She pursed her lips. "We agreed to be honest. We never said anything about sneaky."

"Right," Viv agreed. "I told Nick I'd call him after the dinner rush." She spread her hands. "Can I help it if we'll already be done by then?"

"What about you, Willyn?" Hayden asked.

"Oh, Dare knows all about it, but he gave me a kiss and wished me luck. Then he made waves to the mainland with Tadd." Her eyes softened. "He knows I'll be more focused if my baby's in his capable hands."

Viv and Shauni exchanged guilty looks. "I think I'll go call Nick now instead of later," Viv said.

"Yeah," Shauni heaved a great sigh. "Guess I'd better prepare one huge apology."

"What for?" Paige asked with a wrinkle between her light blonde brows. "This is our fight. We shouldn't feel guilty about making our own decisions."

"I know," Shauni said, "but my making sure Michael wouldn't show up and endanger himself is just as bad as his trying to stop me for the same reason."

Paige threw up her hands. "Love. *Pffft*." She went to join Anna who was inspecting the contents of the box, leaving Shauni a chance to sidle up to Hayden. "Just thought I'd let you know," she said, green eyes twinkling. "Michael had all good things to say about Trevor. Well, about his aura anyway."

The vet Shauni had fallen for was also an empath. He could read people's colors like neon signs. "He said Trevor is a good strong blue. Defiant but honorable."

Hayden laughed. "That sounds exactly right." And how had she not seen that all along? Maybe because he'd sniped at her constantly. Until he hadn't. Until he'd stopped her from falling on the square that night.

In fact, he'd caught her more than once. Always with sturdy and stubborn arms that refused to let her get hurt. And here he was again, having his way. Protecting her, even if he had to brow beat her to get it done.

Defiant. But honorable.

Hayden felt something *ping* inside her heart then release with a sweet sigh. Trevor chose that moment to return her gaze and hold it. His blue eyes locked with hers, promising he wouldn't leave. No matter how hard she tried to make him go.

"Right. That's everything," Anna said, standing and dusting off her hands. Some of the items in the box had come from the tower, a place that hadn't been put to use for years. "This list of demons has been compiled over centuries, but it's hardly a complete account." Anna regarded the women of her coven as they drew closer to the platform to listen.

The dais was at the far end of the great room and had been

built over a hundred years earlier. And even it was younger than the room itself. Overhead, wooden beams intersected to form a pentacle and iron light fixtures held candles for lighting.

The effect was one of solemnity and reverence, for all great spirits of the earth, gods, and goddesses. Heritage and mysticism seemed to emanate from the stone walls, ensuring the room served its purpose. To feed and justify the coven's magic.

"To be honest, I never gave much thought to any demon other than Bastraal," Anna said, flashing a quick smile. "The devil I knew, I guess." Her face grew somber again. "But the instructions in Quinn's book say it's best if we know the kind of demon we wish to speak with. Since we're seeking answers, I suggest we call a Scietta demon. Their name is derived from the word *scientia*."

Viv spoke out. "That's Latin. It means knowledge."

Quinn stepped up to stand beside Anna on the stage. "Exactly. Sciettas specialize in secrets and history. They trade knowledge and are generally," here he paused and shifted his eyes to Trevor, "they are *usually* less hostile than some other demons."

"But not exactly friendly?" Trevor asked, the words thick with sarcasm.

"I'm guessing there aren't any friendly demons," Lucia said, edging in to stand next to Claudia, her chocolate brown hair contrasting with the history professor's red. "I still have reservations, too," Lucia continued in her Spanish lilt, speaking to Trevor, "but if anyone can hold a circle and control a fiend, it's us."

She said it matter-of-factly, without pride or boast, and her honesty seemed to give Trevor the final nudge he needed. He spread his legs and notched up his chin. "I believe that. But I'd still like to stay."

"What else do you have there?" Hayden asked as Quinn

lifted an intricate brass bowl from the plastic container. He dusted it with a rag before pulling a small bag from his pocket and jumping off the dais. "The offering vessel. Since you'll be heading up the ceremony, I'm giving these to you."

She hefted the small, blue velvet bag he handed her in one hand while accepting the bowl with the other. "Stones?" she asked, testing the weight of the sack.

"Close," Quinn said. "Crystals." He quirked his mouth to the side. "Scietta demons don't work for free." Then he chucked her under the chin. "No worries. You've got this one."

As if an unspoken direction had been given, Quinn and Trevor moved to one side of the spacious chamber to stand near an antiquated hearth roaring with fire. The fireplace was big enough to hold a table for eight, so the flames went a long way toward lighting the great room.

The coven circled around the center altar, as they had in previous rituals. The amulets they'd all received in this room shimmered in the natural light, proudly declaring the owner's signature color.

The women had all worn black tonight, pants and tops alike. The unity and might flowing from their gathering was potent, and Hayden reveled in the vibration their link caused. She let the vibe of their joined magic hum through her veins and bolster her courage.

She was surrounded by her sisters. Ready to battle the monsters of the netherworld.

And that was exactly what she might have to do.

Placing her hand over her own necklace and the pink stone in its center, she met the gaze of each woman. As she did, they covered their stones in turn. A salute to the witch facing her trial. And a pledge to their friend.

She wouldn't face the darkness alone.

Anna was the first. With her sable hair free and flowing, the head witch palmed her sapphire gem. Then Lucia touched her vibrant red, the color of passion, as befitted the brave explorer. Next Willyn enveloped her amulet and smiled, as pure and clear as her stone.

Kylie was the color of the sun, bright yellow like her hair. Emerald for Shauni, reflecting the depth of her green eyes. And Paige gave a cocky wink as she placed her hand over an aqua blue stone.

Finally Viv caressed her necklace, dominated by a violet hue, and Claudia was the last. A coral gem for a red-headed witch.

Hayden breathed deep and channeled a healthy Zen. She was ready.

With measured steps she approached the white marble altar and set the brass bowl in the center. Pouring out the crystals with great care, she filled the vessel then gasped at such beauty. Polished and gleaming, the crystals reflected their colors, decorating the room with a million points of light.

Suddenly the coven stood inside a giant kaleidoscope. Much too pretty for what they had planned.

Easing back into her designated spot, Hayden joined hands with Anna on her right and Claudia on her left. Once all of the witches were connected, Hayden licked her lips as she remembered the guidelines from Quinn's worn book.

When the words formed in her mind, she spoke in a clear voice. "We call to the bearers of wisdom and knowledge. Scietta, hear our plea. We offer a bounty in return for knowledge. Scietta, you are welcome here."

Nothing happened, but after a quick glance to Quinn who nodded encouragement, Hayden resumed. "We open our circle to you, Scietta. We offer payment for truth. Hear our..." The air in front of the altar shimmered. Then again. "Hear our plea. Accept our gift."

"It is no gift when offered in exchange." A voice rolled from the middle of their circle, undulating as if riding on waves.

"I heard that," Claudia whispered, her lids at half-mast as she tried to contain her excitement, but her fingers squeezed Hayden's. Judging by the expressions on the other witches' faces, they'd heard the voice as well.

The guidelines specified honesty and directness when calling forth a demon, so Hayden acknowledged their unseen guest's statement. "Yes. We offer you payment for information. Scietta, you are welcome here."

Atmospheric shifts fluttered again, and this time a figure shimmered into full visibility. Though her friends didn't gasp or cry out, their faces made it clear they saw the demon, too. Just like in the morgue, whenever Hayden touched another witch, that woman could also see the monster.

The Scietta was tall yet doubled over, a hunchback with dull brown clothing that hung like multiple tattered robes. His face was more human than any of the others she'd seen yet, but its nose was large and curved. Given his olive coloring and rounded features, he called to mind a tortoise-human hybrid.

"What is it you seek?" the hunchback asked, one white eye open and staring at Hayden. She couldn't tell if the orb was filmy or absent an iris. Either way, the affect was creepy.

"We are dealing with a Droehk and her magic."

"We?" the thing asked with a leering smile.

Hayden cleared her throat. Be honest. Be direct. "*I* am dealing with a Droehk and her *ayjehr*. She has allowed a human to use her mystical writing to mark other humans. The mark allows great, flying demons to find the spirits of the branded women." Direct felt more like callous, but Hayden needed to know.

"Why do you tell me instead of ask?" The demon smiled again, thoroughly enjoying Hayden's inexperience with this particular type of exchange. The creature did know everything, so why was Hayden explaining the situation?

"Where do the demons take a captured spirit and why? How

can the ghosts be saved?" She shot her questions like a Tommy gun.

"I do not know the first or the last, but I can tell you *whyyyy*." The demon dragged the last word out and shuffled a step closer to Hayden. Then it opened its other milky eye and beckoned her to come near.

"Don't break the circle," Willyn called out suddenly, her brow furrowed with concern.

Trevor and Quinn had remained silent, but after Willyn's outburst, Trevor lurched forward. "What's going on?" he demanded, but he was stopped short when Quinn grabbed his upper arm.

"Just wait," the male witch told Trevor.

Ignoring both men, the demon crooked its finger again and asked Hayden, "How much is the knowledge worth to you?"

She dropped Claudia's hand then Anna's and walked slowly forward. "Careful," Claudia warned her. Hayden nodded in return.

"We've still got him," Paige said as she and the other women all broke their links with each other. "I can still see you," the blonde soldier told the thing in the middle of the room, her tone fierce.

"So can I," Kylie called out. Golden lightning skittered over her skin in warning.

The Scietta only had eyes—filmy, egg-white eyes—for Hayden, no matter what else went on around them. "Ask *meeeee*," it said, voice thin as a midnight gale.

Hayden stopped a mere two feet from the olive-green creature. "Why is the Droehk sending demons after the ghosts?"

"The Droehk gathers them for her master. The souls are fuel."

"Fuel for whom? Or what?"

The Scietta widened its eyes as if calling Hayden a dense fool. "For the master."

"For Ronja?" Hayden asked, struggling to keep her questions simple and afraid she would be cut off any moment. How much could she get for the bowl full of crystals?

The demon cackled a wet, phlegmy laugh. "Your minds are so limited. You are only capable of grasping the simple. The basic." Its white eyes brightened as if lit from inside. "That is why you will lose."

"How can we save the souls? How can we get them back?" She was out of time. The Scietta was shaking its head now. It threw one arm back toward the altar, and the crystals flew through the air in a rapid-fire of color, straight to a weathered pouch hanging on the monster's hip...or rather, its hip-like area.

With its prize confiscated, the thing scrambled closer to her, causing a few of the women to cry out. "Heed me, witch. The doors are open. If you dare taste of the underworld," the Scietta licked its lips, "the underworld might take a taste of you."

Without warning it flicked a long thin tongue out to slap Hayden's cheek before holding up stubby arms and gasping out a dry, crackling laugh. Then the demon puffed into nothingness as if it had never been there at all.

Hayden lifted her hand to wipe the wetness on her face, but before she could, her body seized. Her throat closed.

A convulsion snapped her torso backward until she was staring at the pentacle above. Her limbs wouldn't respond, their muscles spasming and completely out of her control.

"Hayden!" She heard Trevor's roar echo, but her eyes couldn't see through the shield around her. Other voices joined his, yelling to Anna and Quinn, asking what to do.

She heard Viv's cry above the others. "What's all around her?"

Straining, Hayden tried to focus her eyes, but everything was hazy and blue. Was she dying? Having some sort of reaction to the demon's saliva? Had she been poisoned?

"Control it, Hayden!" Anna cried then. "It's your magic. It belongs to you!"

"Get her out of there!" Trevor's voice again. He sounded muffled, like he was struggling against someone or something. Trying to get to her.

Whatever was happening, she couldn't allow him to get too close. He could be hurt. Or worse. After all, despite all his strength, he was only human. He wasn't equipped to siphon magic this strong into himself and master it.

But Hayden was.

The blue sizzled around her and under her skin, no clear design or pattern. Chaotic.

Forcing herself to breathe deeply and find the calm, she opened herself up to the energy. She let it flow into her center, inviting it in just as she had the Scietta. Into her inner circle, where she could take control.

Her solar plexus burned like freezing fire, but again she sucked in the cleansing air and channeled the magic to her limbs, to her hands, her palms. Where it belonged.

She recognized the pale blue as the illumination she'd seen in the graveyard. She'd been too terrified of the massive demon charging her to realize the light was hers. That it had come from her palm.

Anna was right. This was her magic, and the demon's lick to her face had triggered an immediate and very violent response.

The new gift eased off slowly, a tide flowing back out before rushing inland once again. Only each time the waves broke over her they were softer. Kinder. Until she felt her feet lose their painful arch and flatten against the floor again.

Gathering the power into her hands, she closed her fingers into fists and snuffed it out.

It wasn't until the hum left her ears that she heard Trevor's voice behind her. That she felt his hands on her waist.

She turned into his arms and gripped his shoulders. "I'm

not going to fall," she said, working up a tired smile. "I've got it now. I'm fine."

"You don't look it," he snapped. "Your eyes are glassy, and you're still panting."

Hayden was seriously worried about herself, because she was beginning to love it when he chastised her. The big, tough cop's way of showing that he cared.

"I thought your spine was going to snap in two," he said, shaking her once then wrapping her in his arms. His breath was hot against her ear, his tone low and filled with concern. "I don't want you to ever do that again. Never. I couldn't see what you were talking to, but I saw you have the mother of all seizures."

He drew back, angry again. "Promise me." His voice grew hoarse. "You have to stay away from demons, ghosts, or whatever the hell else doesn't belong in this world."

His blue eyes looked pained when he ground out, "I don't know how to fight these things."

Sliding her hands around to the back of his neck and into his silky hair, she held him still and met his worried gaze. "But I do, and I'm getting stronger all the time." She tilted her head to indicate her friends. "And so are they." She kissed him, sweet but firm. "It's what I'm meant to do."

"No. You said you talk to ghosts. Not monsters."

"Trevor, you more than anyone should understand."

The look he gave her was puzzled. "What do you mean?"

She lifted one shoulder. "Helping lost spirits, and now especially this killer's victims. I have to put myself out there, no matter how scary things get. This is my fate." She considered what to say. How to get through to him. "It's my duty."

He lowered his forehead to hers and sighed. "I get it. I do. But how far do you have to go? What are the limits?" He stroked her back. "Because you run head-first into insanity without ever thinking of the risk you take. You seem hell bent on sacrificing yourself, and I know there's more to it than fate or prophecies."

Slipping a hand under her chin, he held her in place with eyes blazing blue. "When will it be enough, Hayden? What are you trying to make up for?"

"What?" She drew back and tried to pull away.

"Save it," he said, his cop voice like the slam of a cell door. "I've seen the flashes of guilt, heard the evasions. Doing your duty is one thing, but you act like you're punishing yourself. And I want to know why."

"So do I," Paige said then, reminding Hayden she and Trevor weren't alone.

When Quinn and her coven all looked at her, she realized she'd finally hit the wall. Nowhere left to run. Or to hide.

Her past was the very reason she'd become the woman, the witch, she was today. And what good was her trial if she couldn't come clean with her new family? With Trevor?

"If it's all the same to you, let's take this somewhere more comfortable. I'd like to sit down." She took Trevor's hand but looked at Anna. "And I only want to tell this story once."

21

"I didn't always want to be this way," Hayden said before pulling the blanket tighter around her. She was sitting in the middle of the green velvet couch in the grand hall with her friends and Trevor. Despite assurances that the demon was long gone, lights burned brightly throughout the house.

No one trusted the shadows just yet.

"It's still hard for me to admit, but there was a time when I was very resentful of the spirits invading my life. I railed against my gift, shunned ghosts in need, and spent most of my days angry." The words tumbled out before her mind could come up with a reason to stop the flow. To censor the truth she was about to share.

She paused and pressed her lips together, giving strength to the things she should say. Her voice and back would both need to stiffen up. Her skin would have to be tough, because as much as she trusted both the coven and the man at her side, she was still ashamed. Bone deep and gut sick. Ashamed.

She drew a deep shaky breath and said, "I lived in two perpetual states. Pissed at the world or too high to care."

A few of the women responded with perplexed looks or tilted heads, but Kylie's question cleared the confusion. "You mean high as in stoned? On drugs?" There was no censure in the younger witch's voice, just amazement.

Hayden had expected this reaction, because the woman she was today, the person she'd carved from a tumultuous youth, was a far scream from the screwed up kid who'd made her single mother's life miserable.

She nodded and looked to Trevor next, searching the depths of his blue eyes for disgust or distance. She saw neither, and the softening of his gaze drilled so deep into her heart that she stuttered. "I..." His large hand slid over to encapsulate hers, and anxiety flowed from her like a young and optimistic river finally bursting through a dam.

Her breath was shaky as she inhaled. Steadier when she spoke again. "I found a way to avoid the ghosts, to make them fuzzy and hard to hear. At first it was an accident, a rebellious and reckless attempt to have some fun."

She smiled but knew by the tug on her cheeks it had failed. She was too sad to fake it. "In fact, a ghost was there at the party, telling me not to do it. He'd been hounding me for a couple of weeks to get a message to his wife. Something about their son."

Tossing the blanket off her shoulders, Hayden swallowed regret. "You see? I don't even remember what he wanted. And after that night, he stopped trying to talk to me." She shrugged. "I guess he found another medium." Her voice dropped. "I hope so."

"How long did it last?" Trevor asked. His thumb was circling the back of her hand, a small but telling action. He'd dealt with plenty of addicts, she was sure, and didn't shy away from the touchy subject.

Hayden appreciated his directness. "About a year. I started small, I guess you could say. Pot was the first and did a great job, but my mom got wise to that pretty quickly, always sniffing my clothes and things in my room." She looked to Willyn then, the only parent in the group. "Funny. My mother had been a shaky wreck from the day I started seeing ghosts, and I'd held that against her. I felt abandoned. But when I started using, she changed into a bloodhound. Always after me, poking into my business."

"I imagine the kind of trouble you were in was something she could get a handle on," Willyn told her. "I've had days when I didn't know what to tell Tadd about his magic and the things he can do. At least there's a system in place for drug abuse."

Hayden nodded, grateful for the objectivity. She should have known she could tell them anything, but like Anna was always saying, everything in its time.

"I came to that myself," Hayden said. "After I'd matured and could step away and look from a distance. Despite how things turned out, that year brought my mother and me closer than we'd ever been. So at least one good thing came out of it."

Everyone was standing so still, listening so intently that Hayden suddenly became shy and her skin grew clammy. She pulled the blanket back up around her shoulders, feeling exposed. Unworthy. And as usual, guilty.

Trevor stopped rubbing her hand and squeezed it instead. "What was the bad that came of it, Hayden? You can tell us. All of us."

"I had a friend I spent most of my time with. We tore through blurry days and wild nights. By then I'd gotten into trading prescriptions with other kids, but my mom stopped keeping meds at home, so I did some coke."

She cringed as the word *coke* echoed in the elegant grand hall. It felt sinful to talk about such things in the presence of beautiful artwork and rich, dark wainscoting. Like she was dirtying the air.

"I didn't really enjoy the cocaine high, and I was scared by what I saw in other users. Nosebleeds freaked me out. The idea of corroding inner membranes and sensitive tissue." She swallowed against nausea. "But it kept the ghosts away, and by then I couldn't tell if the drugs or my hostility was what kept them at bay. I just didn't care and wasn't going to trade the never ending party for the life I'd known before."

"You see," she continued, "when I hit puberty, it was like a call went out to every spirit in the state of California. I was bombarded by them, all hours of the night. I couldn't sleep or bathe in privacy. They were always there pounding at me!" Even now the memories upset and angered her.

"It wasn't fair," Shauni said, empathy filling the animal-whisperer's emerald eyes. Like most of the women gathered here, she knew what it meant to feel like a freak. An outcast with talents she couldn't explain. Shauni had been happy to talk to animals, but some of the people she'd told about her gift had hurt her with their responses.

"No, it wasn't fair," Anna agreed. "And your mother couldn't help you. No one could." She sighed and shook her head. "That age can be a time bomb for those with supernatural powers. Like the hormones in your body, your mystical chemistry, so to speak, goes bonkers at the same time."

Every female in the room made a sound of agreement.

"Yes, but that's no excuse," Hayden said with more bite than intended. "You can get over typical bad behavior. Yelling at your parents or siblings. Being sulky and belligerent. Those things are almost a rite of passage for teenagers. Some even get into trouble with alcohol or drugs, but I didn't just need those things, I demanded them. Escape was my number one goal, and I truly didn't care if I hurt anyone along the way."

She clamped a trembling hand to her mouth. "And I did. I hurt someone." She wanted to cry to let it all out, but that would only reduce her to a hysterical mess. Crying would be a kind of protection, and she wouldn't allow herself to take that easy out. Not now.

"My friend and I were out looking for the next party, the next thrill. The sun had barely set, and we were already smashed. It was that time of late afternoon when everything is orange and rusty. So pretty over the ocean." She was the one who gripped Trevor's hand now but did her best to keep her nails from gouging his skin.

"We didn't see the car pulling out from where it had been parked on the side of the road. We were driving too fast and cresting a hill. You know those hills in San Fran."

She stared into the fire, refusing to meet anyone's eyes. She couldn't look at them now. She just couldn't. "We were at full speed when we hit them. On the driver's side and the back seat. Then the whole world became a distant reality of sirens and screams." She thumped a fist against her thigh. "Just like I'd made sure it would be."

Scalding tears finally forced their way from her eyes, and the fire became nothing more than a big, yellow distortion. Movement surrounded Hayden, but she couldn't tell what it was.

She had to keep talking. "I didn't even know what had happened until the middle of the night, when I sobered up and found myself in the hospital. Handcuffed to the bed."

"Were you driving?" Trevor asked gently. He knew it was better to get all the poison out at once. So it wouldn't fester.

But the infection of what she'd done had ravaged Hayden's body and psyche for so many years, she doubted she would ever fully recover. "No. I wasn't driving, but I could have been. It was dumb luck that my friend climbed behind the wheel instead of me. I got less time in juvie than she did, for what we had on us, but the time served wasn't enough. Nothing was. Not even the ghosts who flooded me in lock down. I was clean and couldn't fend them off any longer."

"Was the driver of the other car hurt?" The soft voice came from Hayden's left. Paige. She was kneeling next to Hayden. All of the women had come closer, surrounding her during her confession. Providing a cocoon of love and support.

She didn't deserve it, though, and would lose their concern when she told it all. "No. The woman driving was fine. Physically." Hayden clutched her stomach as pain stabbed dead center. "But the toddler in the back. He was in a car seat. He should have been safe, but our car hit theirs so hard. The impact was too strong and direct. Small bodies like that aren't meant to be rattled around with such force."

She heard Willyn make a sound of pain, and a few others gasped. Shock, despair, or revulsion, Hayden couldn't say. And she dreaded finding out.

"He died that night. In the same hospital I was in." She tore her hand from Trevor's and locked her arms around herself. "The cop sitting with me told me everything. How they couldn't save the baby. How the mother cried. He hated me. I could see it and hear it. He thought I was scum. And I was."

"You were partly responsible, but not completely guilty, Hayden." Claudia stood nearby, her voice cool and logical. "Yes, you could have been driving the car, and if you had, things might have gone differently. Maybe you would have taken a different route, driven faster or slower, missed the car entirely."

Hayden threw up her hands. "There's no way to know that. And I was in the car. I knew she was probably too high or sleep-deprived. I knew she shouldn't be driving, but I let her. It's my fault as much as hers."

"That's my point. There was no way to tell what would happen, and while you should have behaved more responsibly, I know you never intended for anyone to get hurt," Claudia said. "You served your time, as you should have."

"Claudia!" Shauni said on a gasp, but Claudia held up her hand, standing tall and straight. "I'm sorry, but accident or not, I believe we should pay for our crimes." Her voice softened. "And you did, Hayden. You were locked up and got yourself clean. And I have a suspicion you started helping those spirits as soon as you were able."

Hayden took the tissues Lucia brought to her and wiped her eyes and nose. "Yes. I almost drove myself into the ground when I got out. There were just so many, and I'd neglected them for too long."

"How old were you when the accident happened?" Trevor asked, taking her hand back and daring her with a look to refuse his offer of comfort.

"Sixteen."

"How old when you were released from juvie and jumped into life as a round-the-clock medium?" he pushed.

"Seventeen. I only did a year, then another in community service. It wasn't enough," Hayden said again. She would never forgive herself, and didn't think she should.

She helped ghosts because they needed her. She punished herself because she was the only one who could.

"That's a hell of a lot to take on your shoulders at seventeen," Trevor told her. "And I know from your file you've been helping ever since."

"Her file?" Anna asked with a frown.

Trevor sighed. "I looked into her past. And I won't apologize, because I didn't believe she was what she claimed when she came to the station poking around our homicide case. I thought she was a con artist."

"Well, you don't know Hayden very well," Paige snapped, hands going to her hips. A sign that usually meant trouble. Despite the tension, a spark of gratitude flared to life in Hayden. After what she'd heard, the coven's warrior was still ready to defend her sisters. All of them.

"Easy," Trevor said, lifting one blonde brow. "You're right. I didn't know her at all." He touched Hayden's cheek, in front of everyone. "But I do now. And what happened in your past explains a lot," he told her. "You're driven to come to the rescue of anyone who needs it, especially your ghosts. You're no longer the kid who made such bad choices. Horrible mistakes, without a doubt."

His eyes were tender when he continued. "The woman I know has a pure heart and would never hurt anyone. I also know you carry the pain of that child's death with you and will never be rid of it."

"I don't want to be. I can never let myself forget." Rolling her shoulders, Hayden looked around the room to her sisters, Quinn, and finally Trevor.

She coughed to cover her sob. "Poetic justice, I guess. The only ghost I never saw, never spoke to," her voice broke, forcing her to clear the emotion clogging her throat, "is the one that will always haunt me."

The group fell silent then, fire hissing in the background. Nothing more could be said. No help for the raw wound Hayden had shown them all.

With a pat on Hayden's knee, Anna rose from the sofa and padded quietly across the stone floor. Soon sounds came from the kitchen, and the others slipped out as well, leaving Hayden alone with Trevor.

Taking advantage of his sturdy shoulder, she let the grief pour out, sobbing as quietly as she could and lacking the energy to go anywhere more private. He didn't offer empty words, but sat and let her lean on him.

Hayden considered herself lucky to still have the backing of the coven. That they chose to see her, like Trevor did, for the person they knew now instead of the delinquent she'd once been.

But despite their acceptance, she sat staring into the searing flames, wishing for the thousandth time that her gift had been different. That she had the power to do more than speak to the dead. As futile as it was, she relived the memory of screeching tires and grinding metal.

And wished she could go back in time.

~

The late dinner preparations were somber and grave, as one by one the women pulled Hayden aside for a private word. They each gave encouragement and assurances they viewed her no differently. As the space filled with the smells of cooking, and conversation turned to lighter topics, Hayden began to relax.

Her stomach growled when a deep dish of beef stroganoff was set on the kitchen island, along with olive bread and steamed vegetables. She was starving and emotionally drained but somehow still buzzing from the summoning they'd performed.

Or maybe it was from the strange new power that had coursed through her.

Kylie wrapped her arms around Hayden and whispered in her ear before they sat to eat. "None of us are perfect, and we all have secrets. Good ones or bad ones, it doesn't matter. Just things we don't want others to know. Or to judge."

Resting her cheek against the young blonde's, Hayden grasped Kylie's forearm in thanks then let her scoot off to grab a stool.

By the time they got to the raspberry cheesecake—prepared by Mrs. Attinger before she'd been forced to evacuate the island—Hayden and her friends were all wearing smiles. Trevor and Quinn were deep in discussion over beers, and as the dishes were cleared by Paige and Viv, the conversation turned to coven business.

She'd become accustomed to the duality and paid it no mind, but Trevor tossed a look at the women as they blithely discussed immortal witches and centuries-old prophecies over dessert and coffee.

Shauni stood up from her chair and waved her tea glass around to encompass the group. "I think the gods or whoever set this whole thing into motion knew what they were doing by bringing us all together. The nine of us balance each other out.

Give each other strength."

"Right," Paige agreed. "Just one more way of making sure we're able to make it to the end." A faraway look settled on her face. "I've seen my share of war and know the importance of teamwork. Of knowing someone's always got your back." Her eyes cleared, and she tapped her beer mug to Shauni's tea. "We've got that in spades."

"Speaking of being strong enough." Viv stepped away from Kylie to stride across the room to where Hayden sat. "What's with the blue light?" she asked. "During my trial, magic from the three sisters of the prophecy burned a similar blue, but not quite the same."

Turning her liquid, silver eyes on Anna, Viv cocked her hip. "And you told Hayden the magic was hers. What did you mean?"

"It was more instinct than certainty," Anna said, holding out her hand palm-side up, opening and closing her fingers as if testing their strength. "I felt something the night we caught Sylvie and Joseph together. When I saw her on my property, with him, my defenses kicked into high gear. My palm grew warm and lit up with a blue light, but I didn't know what was happening and clamped down on it instead of letting it out."

Still staring at her hand, Anna frowned. "It hasn't come back, and I was beginning to think I'd imagined it."

"Until tonight," Hayden said. "When you saw it in me."

"In you, hell," Paige grumbled, pacing around the crescent-shaped counter like a caged tiger. "In you, under you, all around you. I really thought you were about to be zapped to an alternate universe. Or fried to a crisp."

Willyn abruptly came over and hugged Hayden. "So did I, and I was so scared."

Placing her hand over Willyn's, Hayden shared a mutual smile with her sweet friend. "I know. I remember the night you came home, beaten and so..." She broke off. "I was terrified then, but you came through. Just like I did. And if I'm right, I've discovered a new power. If I've got it and Anna's got it, we all do. We just have to figure out where it comes from."

"I hope we can learn fast, because your challenge isn't over, yet," Shauni said. "And what the Scietta demon told you was more disturbing than helpful." Her brilliant green eyes sparkled with a fearful curiosity. "It said 'the doors are open.' What doors?"

Stretching her back and grimacing, Hayden realized she was sore from the forced contraction of her muscles. The unsummoned magic had been strong, and she would have to learn to rule it. Or it would rule her. "I only know of one place that might have one of these doors, if the demon was speaking literally, but I dread going back to check it out."

"That bar," Willyn said and shuddered. "The vamp bar."

Trevor groaned. "Bedlam? Nothing good ever happens at that place." He shot a scowl at Hayden. "If you intend to go there..." He faltered. "Well, I don't really have to say it, do I?"

Infused with a thrilling warmth that stole her breath, Hayden smiled at him. "If I go, you go. Does that about sum it up, Detective?"

He only grunted, but the answer was clear. Hayden had shaken him once, but he wasn't letting her out of his sight again. And the notion pleased her. While they still had work to do, and puzzles to complete, she liked the idea of having him close.

Trevor was like looking in a rougher, tougher mirror, a stubborn and more masculine version of herself, but his intensity was appreciated. So sure, she'd let him stay the night.

And in the dark, they could protect each other.

22

Hayden came out of her bathroom fresh from a shower to find Trevor standing in the doorway. He scanned her bedroom and seemed unsure what to do.

When his gaze landed on the loveseat he'd slept on once before, she walked over and tugged him inside, closing the door behind him. "I want you to stay with me again," she said, putting the matter to rest.

She wore a babydoll slip of white cotton beneath a longer robe, and was glad of her recent mani-pedi. She felt polished and feminine. As indecision played on Trevor's rugged face, she ran a finger over his stubbled jaw and licked her lips.

He didn't miss the female gestures, eyes darkening with desire and breath stopping short before drawing deep again. "You want me to sleep in your bed again. Like the other night." There was a question behind the simple statements.

"No. Not like the other night." She ran her hands over his shoulders, down his deliciously hard back, and under the edge of his black polo-style shirt. "I said I want you to stay with me, but I'm too wired to sleep."

"Hayden," his hands hung straight at his sides, as if he was forcing them to stay off her, but that was the opposite of what she wanted. "You've been through an ordeal, and I will sleep in your room, even in your bed, but…"

She trailed her fingers up his heated skin in a light, sensuous tease. When she rimmed the waist of his jeans, he sucked in a breath. "Hayden," he said, but the tone had less threat to it.

Stepping away from him, she undid the belt of her robe and let it drop to the floor. Granted, cotton wasn't the sexiest material, but it was more her style. So she went with it.

And judging by the way Trevor's eyes traveled up and down her figure and bare legs, he thoroughly approved.

"I didn't like you at all when we first met," she told him, causing his brilliant blue eyes to jerk back to her face. A grin blossomed over her lips. "But I do now."

His mouth lifted on one side. "I didn't much like you either."

Unfazed, she edged closer. "But I understand why you were so rude." When he would have objected, she held up a finger. "I know who you are now and how important the safety of your city is."

She dared one more step. "You're a strong man and not just in the physical sense. Defense of your people is priority, and you would stand against the devil himself to protect them."

Now her expression grew serious. "You're a good man, Trevor, and I'm almost ready to believe I deserve you."

He shook his head. "Don't ever doubt yourself. If it's one thing I'm well-versed in, it's bad guys, the cruel and the selfish. But I was wrong about you. You're not one of them." The smile that broke over his face was devastating, and Hayden put a hand to her stomach to still the effect he had on her.

"In fact," he said, "I think we're a lot alike, and that's probably why we clashed. I have to look out for those who can't take care of themselves or get abused by others, but you do the same thing." He pulled his shirt off, and Hayden nearly swooned.

His voice was gruff with emotion. "And I'm almost ready to believe I deserve you, too."

Hayden studied the unbreakable man standing in front of her. A cop, half naked and in her bedroom, telling her he admired her. That he wanted her. How much stranger could her life get?

The answer was...*very.* Because she wanted him just as much, handcuffs, patrol cars, and all. She'd trusted him with her worst fear and greatest shame. Now her heart was lighter than it had been in years.

They came to each other on even ground. Angry cop to secretive ghost-whisperer. A man who guarded citizens and a woman who guided souls. Partners turned lovers.

When Hayden reached for him, the scent of citrus flowers came with her. Trevor's brain went foggy, aware of nothing but the seductive witch in his arms as she wrapped around him and pressed closer.

Needing no further prompting he slanted his mouth over hers, moving lip to lip before he probed deeper and slid his tongue against hers. She was sweet. And mysterious. Layers and layers to be discovered, he thought, tasting her with a wildness he'd never known.

He heard a growl and Hayden wrenched away, her eyes burning gold and heavy-lidded. "You want me," she said. Trevor made the noise again, a deep rumble he could no longer keep down.

He'd never thought to have a woman of his own, given his occupation and the relentless workload. The demanding hours spent in the office or pounding the streets.

Now he knew different. Every obligation in his life paled to the driving need to keep Hayden safe. The very person he'd tried so hard to rid himself of was the one he couldn't live without.

Let the prophecy bring demons to his door. He'd find a way to travel to hell and back if he had to, ripping those cursed mother fuckers to pieces as he went. But nothing, witch, immortal, or spawn from Hades, was going to touch his woman.

He lifted her and held her tight, arms circling her waist as her legs folded around him. Her heat was burning through the clothing they still wore, transforming the controlled cop into a mindless beast. He rocked against her core until she cried out and gripped his hair. Not gently either. His timid little medium had a rough side.

So he'd do his best to match her, stroke for stroke. Easy or desperate, he'd be right there with her. Her mouth found his neck then, and she nipped his flesh before suckling in the hollow below his jaw. "Damn, Hayden." His gruff voice told her how much he liked what she was doing, and she moaned in response.

"You've got to get this off," he said, tugging on her slip and turning to the bed to deposit her against the silk sheets. The soft pink surrounded her like a halo, making her hair seem almost as rich as her eyes, amber and gold.

His very own sunrise.

Slowly now he put his hands on the outside of her ankles, holding her in place when she would have moved. "What are you..." she began, but Trevor shook his head and grinned.

Her skin was satin as he felt his way up the curve of her calves then dipped to the back side of her thighs. The bottom of her short gown had caught on his wrist and rose with his arms as he continued his exploration.

When he made it to the sides of her breasts, she gasped and let her head loll to the side. Eyes closed, lips parted. He teased her there for a moment before continuing up and lifting her arms with his hands under them, caressing and cherishing until the material was free of her hands and tossed to the loveseat across the room.

All that remained was a triangle of cotton, rosy like her lips. The comparison made him throb harder in his pants, but Hayden would soon relieve him of that particular ache. She licked her lips and stared at him, then lower, as if she was imagining the same thing he was.

He flicked the button on his jeans, and she made a low noise in her throat, squirming farther onto the bed until she had room to sit up. She seized the denim and yanked, pulling him toward her and declaring her intent at the same time.

While the thought of making her ask nicely might be fun some other time, he couldn't wait another second to have all of his skin touching every single inch of hers. When they kissed again, the world became a blur. Hot and frantic, straining bodies blended with whispered promises.

Stroking a hand over her hip, Trevor grabbed the back of her thigh and hiked her leg up. He settled himself between her legs and Hayden thrust her chest against his.

She couldn't think straight. And she didn't care.

All she could feel, see, or smell was Trevor. Clean yet masculine, the muscles in his shoulders and back were like an aphrodisiac. Fascinated by his strength and how easily he lifted and positioned her, Hayden broke away from his roaming lips—the man could really, seriously kiss—and dragged a breath into her lungs.

She was dizzy and overrun with desire, but she wanted to see his eyes when he took her. When they became one for the first time, she wanted to drown in the blue of his eyes, be completely aware of the powerful man who had her in his arms. And would never let her fall.

When he ran a thumb over her bottom lip and said her name, Hayden knew he understood. He locked onto her with those eyes, waiting for her to lead the way. To tell him what she wanted.

One of her hands gripped his dark blonde hair while the other curled around his strong arm. When she offered him a devilish smile and lifted her body, he answered her by driving deep, touching her and filling her as only a true lover could.

Trevor held himself still and rasped out a breath before moving within her, long slow strokes that sped up as their passion grew out of control. Hayden was crazy with need, every time he came back to her was another piercing thrill of pleasure.

Every nerve in her body was tingling and pulsing. Her hips lifted and her head fell back, allowing him to capture the sensitive skin on her neck with his mouth before he dragged himself up to her lips again.

He trailed the scalding heat over her skin, awakening magic each time he kissed her, until the whirling forces inside raged toward her center. She could hear Trevor whispering but couldn't make out the words.

Shimmering lights filled Hayden's head as waves and waves of pure pleasure broke over her and through her. The climax was staggering, but beyond she heard Trevor's roar as he met the same end.

Reveling in the airy feel of her own skin, Hayden gradually floated back to reality to find Trevor facing her. At some point they had rolled onto their sides. His arm was beneath her head, and his dazed eyes were on her face.

She licked her lips and blew out a breath. Lights still lit the room, since neither one of them had been able to break free and turn them off. He reached out to capture her cheek then brush her hair back from her face.

"I hate to ask," he said, "but no one is here, right?" At her puzzled look he added, "No ghosts?"

A short laugh burst from Hayden, and she took the opportunity to run her hand over his amazing abs. "No. No one's watching." She lifted smiling eyes back to him, biting her bottom lip as she studied the wide, firm mouth that had covered almost every bit of her skin. Almost. "There are rules, you know. Boundaries to be respected."

"Good," he told her before easing on top of her and rising up to his knees. When his hand reached around her to grasp her hip and roll her over, lust curled into a liquid pool in her belly.

Wearing a carnal grin, Trevor pulled her up and placed her exactly where he wanted her. He leaned down and kissed her ear before whispering, "Because we wouldn't want to shock anyone."

A curious feline *meewl* came from underneath the bed, and Hayden had to stifle a laugh. "Um. I think we already have."

~

Sylvie was in the foyer when Searenn walked through the front door of Ronja's plantation home. Her black hood was pulled forward to shadow her face, but Sylvie could sense the tension of the woman who manipulated evil entities. Who summoned and controlled demons.

As soon as Searenn cleared the door, Sylvie saw why the Droehk woman was uneasy. A man in a long, black coat came in behind her. He also wore a hooded sweatshirt, but his head was uncovered, hood hanging down his back. This was the guy recruited to murder women and brand them, so their spirits could be found in the afterlife.

His presence along with Searenn's agitation was a bad sign. The two were responsible for gathering those souls, and based on the man's darting eyes, he hadn't completed his task.

Ronja would not be happy.

Another thought rode on the tail of that assumption and cheered Sylvie. Searenn's ass was on the line, too, since she'd promised her demons would find and bag the souls as soon as they'd flown from their dead human bodies.

The last count was one out of three. Not good odds for the Droehk and her accomplice.

Sylvie sniffed to show her disdain when the man edged by her and down the hallway. He was also a rapist, and despite her affiliation with the Amara, some things just turned her stomach.

She frowned when she recognized her anger for what it was. Empathy for other women who'd had their bodies ravaged. Against their will and without invitation. Upset over her own abuse as a child was one thing, but she had no business feeling sorry for anyone else.

She'd almost blown it with the bartender, avoiding the kidnapping to deliver the note to the coven instead. She'd been lucky the others in her group had mistaken her cowardice for an act of bravery. Taking a message straight to the lion's den, as Ronja had proclaimed.

But it was a lie. Maybe something inside her had known she'd be safe, even if caught in the act. Had she suspected the woman who'd known her mother would give her a pass? Honor old allegiances?

Whatever her subconscious had been whispering, the fact remained that Sylvie had been careless. She'd moved too slowly and made too much noise. Had she been testing the waters even then? Because she'd let herself get busted. By Joseph.

Sylvie closed her eyes and willed the images of his stern face to erase themselves from her mind. She told herself the kisses they'd shared hadn't broken her heart wide open and invited him in. That she hadn't wanted to take his hand the first time he'd offered.

Biting the inside of her cheek, she shoved pain and rage to the forefront, the things she specialized in. She'd only endanger herself if she kept thinking of Joseph and his soulful eyes, firm lips, and tender touch. Wishing things could be different was a waste of her time and talents.

There was no way he would ever come over to the merciless side. And she could never learn to be kind.

That way would only lead to her death, her punishment. Two things she had sworn to avoid, even if she had to destroy others for her own benefit.

Sylvie had been promised unimaginable power and immortality, life eternal at the top of a very bloody food chain. And all in exchange for a few brief years of servitude and brutality. Was that really such a bad deal?

The only reason she'd been able to hold her head up the last several years was because of the Amara. They'd accepted her as she was. Broken and wrathful. They'd embraced her fury and helped her build on that violent emotion.

She'd learned to harden herself against the poor and the pitiful. To convince herself that they weren't really innocent or deserving of pity.

So why was she so conflicted now?

Damn that man! How had he managed what Sylvie's grandmother never could? Gran had been prying into Sylvie's personal life for a while now, begging her to come clean about what she was doing with the new people she'd "taken up with." Pleading with her to remember her mother and the things she'd wanted for her little girl.

Her grandmother had suspected, but all her insistence had done little to crack Sylvie's mean and hard-earned armor. Though Gran had known horrible things were controlling her granddaughter, she'd never stopped trying to save her.

Neither had Joseph, and he knew a great deal more about what Sylvie was involved in. He knew about the attack on those witches that night in the street. That Sylvie had known Jen would be abducted, even if she hadn't been sure she would be killed.

Sylvie actually shuddered as the screams came back to her.

She was guilty by association, all right. More than that, she could have acted, done something to warn the bartender and maybe saved her life. She was culpable, and telling herself she hadn't known what R.J. would do was bullshit.

"What's the matter with you, Princess?" Sylvie had forgotten

Searenn was still there, but the bitter question brought her head up with a snap.

"Just wondering when you and your boy are going to get it together and do what you promised. Or was all that talk about your magic just that?" Sylvie sneered. "All talk." She flipped her hair then to prod the grotesque woman even further. *Princess my ass.*

"Aww. Is someone feeling defensive?" Searenn asked.

Sylvie tried for an expression of dismissal, telling herself she couldn't show an ounce of fear. Not to this one. "I'm not the one who's about to have her guts twisted on a pulley. Ronja can't be pleased by your lack of..." she picked the next word carefully, "expertise."

Searenn lifted her chin and glared at Sylvie with her disturbing eyes, the light blue and inky black never failed to send a shiver down her spine. "I'll be standing beside Ronja long after you've been put into the ground."

Freezing her features and her lungs in place, Sylvie did her best to conceal her reaction to the threat. The sinister woman's prediction was way too close to what she'd been thinking to herself only seconds before.

"Don't think I haven't noticed the change in you lately," Searenn said, knowing when to push forward on an attack. She adjusted her hood and mocked Sylvie with one raised brow. "Don't think R.J. hasn't noticed, because he has. Consider yourself real lucky that Ronja's been too involved in my work with that human leech to notice the disaster waiting to happen in her own clan. You, Sylvie." She lifted a gray-painted claw and pointed. "You're the one fucking up here."

Sylvie crossed her arms and looked down her nose at Searenn, more bothered by her gravelly voice than ever. "You don't know what you're talking about and should stick to the things you're good at. Like hiding in the shadows and whispering to monsters." She made a scoffing sound. "Those dregs are probably the only friends someone like you will ever have."

"Someone like me has got what it takes to finish the job and reap the rewards. I plan to sit beside Bastraal and serve losers like you to him on a silver platter. I'll lick up the blood that falls from his fangs and give it back to him through a kiss." Searenn waggled her tongue at Sylvie and made a slurping noise.

"You talk big, *Princess*," she put emphasis on the title, because she knew Sylvie hated it, "but you're weak where it counts. Where it's needed."

Searenn thumped her own chest with a fist then slammed her open palm onto Sylvie's, just above her heart. "Your ruthlessness," the Droehk sneered, "needs work."

Sylvie thrust the other woman's arm away. No one invaded her space or touched her without permission. No one since her dear old stepdad. "Don't fuck with me, Searenn." Finally she'd found her spine and meant the words.

"There you go." Searenn's one blue eye gleamed. "That's a little better, but still such a pretty face to go with that ugly mouth." She trailed a finger over one of the tattoo swirls on the side of her neck. "Maybe I should call something up to even them out. A Vesco demon would just love to steal some of that beauty from you. Maybe even leave a scar. Hmm? Maybe I could take you more seriously that way."

Sylvie quivered, muscles bunched and ready to strike. "Don't threaten me!" Then she reined in her temper and smiled cruelly. "Just because you're so damn ugly." Sylvie knew the barb struck home when Searenn's pierced lip curled.

The hooded Droehk leaned closer. "I can smell what's going on between your legs and in your mind. I can smell your lust and your need, but that's not what bothers me."

Sylvie remained silent, terrified Searenn really could sense what she claimed, worse, if she knew who Sylvie had those feelings for. *Joseph.*

Sylvie would be staked out and stripped of skin. Joseph would be hunted.

"What bothers me," Searenn continued, "is why you haven't taken care of those delicious sexual cravings. If you see something you want, take it. If you want to fuck somebody, then throw them down and straddle their ass. And if you feel the need to rip his throat out when he comes, don't pause. Don't think." She leaned in until their noses almost touched. "Just fucking do it."

Licking her lips so the silver loops there glistened, Searenn narrowed her mismatched eyes. "Remember, pretty girl, the Amara is nothing but a pack." She turned to stalk away, her raised voice carrying back to Sylvie with warning. "Weakness will get you killed."

23

Hayden and her friends may have spent the day arming themselves with knowledge, but on the foggy, nighttime streets of Savannah, Trevor still preferred the Glock 17 at his hip.

The black, customized grip screamed for him to hold it, to have it at the ready, but he could only hope the tingle in his palm was just an active imagination. Not premonition.

Who could blame him for the extra-heightened awareness considering the lessons he'd been given today? Hayden and her coven had poured over Quinn's array of books, some so old the male witch had insisted gloves be worn, protecting the pages like a combatant librarian. They'd learned as much as they could about the Droehk tribes and thoroughly dissected any mention of ghosts or sprits in relation to demons.

What they'd discovered had made Hayden's face turn to chalk, but she'd kept it together and forced herself to keep studying, keep looking for a way to locate and save the ghosts. Before their energy was consumed by the master.

Bastraal. That was the conclusion the witches had come to. That the Droehk, whoever that might be, only wrangled her demons at the demand of an even greater entity. That she and the serial killer were working together to claim souls for some unnamed yet dominant being.

One of the books had in fact mentioned ghosts in its text, a very detailed description of what had once been known as *Jiva Victimare*. Soul sacrifice. A practice some Droehks had employed to increase the strength of certain entities, especially when those beings desired transformation.

In other words, the spirits of Chloe and Ronnie had been captured for Bastraal, the Amara's mighty demon, so he could become powerful enough for his conversion. His jump to a human body.

Not a possession, because those were often weaker connections and easily broken. No, Bastraal wanted something permanent, the complete ownership of a corporeal form.

Trevor didn't want to imagine what happened to the unlucky person chosen as receptacle.

All day he'd felt like a tightly strung wire, practically shaking with unspent and undirected energy, so it felt good to finally be doing something active. Even if the something was reconnaissance of a bar. A supposed vampire bar that may or may not contain a gate to the netherworld.

He ran a hand through his hair. Lord, how the world had changed.

Skimming his gaze over the moderately busy street before settling on Hayden's unbound and windblown hair—he was crazy about all that caramel—Trevor considered other transformations. Not only had Hayden gone from possible suspect to trusted partner, his primary concerns had shifted. Reprioritized themselves without his say so.

He was accompanying Hayden, along with Dare and Willyn, to the aptly named Bedlam to make headway on the homicide case he still had to solve. But more than that, he didn't want Hayden coming here without him.

Where before her acquaintance was part and parcel of working the murders, all of that had been reversed. He wanted to catch the killer and help the anguished souls of the victims for a whole new set of reasons.

Because it would help Hayden and give her peace as well as the murdered women.

Especially now, because Ronnie hadn't been heard from since the night in the graveyard. Hayden wanted to believe the spirit had made good on her escape, but as hours passed with no communication, anxiety escalated.

First Chloe had been taken and now Ronnie was MIA. Trevor's palm itched again.

Things were not looking good.

"There," Hayden said, pointing out the massive door decorated like an evil gate. Trevor knew exactly where Bedlam was located, but he could sense the strife in the woman he'd come to care about and let her lead the way.

Surely that was the extent of his feelings. He cared about her. Sure. Okay. Nothing too out of the ordinary. People often experienced intense emotion when thrown into a crisis.

So why did his heart feel like a quivering mass when he saw her barge toward the night club and possible danger? "Wait," he barked, scowling when she stopped and swung around to give him an impatient look. "You don't know who or what is in there. They might be expecting you."

He blew out a breath and eased his growling tone. "Or they might *not* be expecting you, and believe me, the element of surprise doesn't always have great results."

Pursing her lips in an obvious pique, she nodded and looked at Willyn, but Trevor didn't miss the eye-roll that clearly conveyed her opinion of overbearing men. To Willyn's credit she only returned a serene smile.

Then she winked at Trevor when Hayden's back was turned. For some reason, the gentle woman's encouragement made him grin. She knew Hayden well and saw the strain her friend was under, having experienced the awful uncertainty herself not too long ago. The gentle blonde was telling Trevor in her own way to hang tight.

That he was appreciated, and more importantly, he was needed.

Willyn's husband, Dare, sidled up to Trevor and put his hands on his hips. "Tough to stand by and watch the woman you love rush head first into the devil's den. Believe me, I know."

Now Trevor felt his face turn to chalk. "What? No. Hayden and I...we aren't like that. I'm just doing my job, and of course, I don't want to see her get hurt either. It's just..."

Slapping him on the shoulder, Dare cut him off. "Sure, buddy. Whatever you need to tell yourself to get through. But these witches?" He lifted his head with a proud expression on his face. He was staring at Willyn. "They really are something else, and if one of them opens her heart to you? You'd be wise to take a long, hard look at what's being offered."

Then just as quickly, the dark-haired man's expression became a storm cloud. "Damn. They slipped in without us. Stubborn females."

"You were saying?" Trevor joked as the two of them cut off a group of newcomers and caught up with Hayden and Willyn. They were getting their hands stamped by a goth woman when the men moved in behind them.

"I can feel a weird vibration already," Hayden said to Trevor over her shoulder. He noticed the hand she placed to her stomach.

Looking aside to Willyn, he saw that she also seemed ill, wan and shaky. Dare had his hand in the center of her back, the two of them forming a tight unit. Her light against his dark. A formidable pair.

Hayden slipped her fingers through Trevor's and pulled him along as she headed toward another set of doors. He tried not to notice how much he liked her small hand sheltered by his larger, or that he suddenly burned hotter and brighter in his chest.

Hayden wasn't too proud to lean on him, just as she wasn't too shy to tell him off when she thought he deserved it. So no matter how things turned out on this night or the next, Trevor was sure of one thing.

Hayden belonged with him.

The music hit his eardrums like angry machinery. Screaming drills and thudding hammers. How the hell did anyone listen to this stuff?

The lights on the dance floor were blood red, making the writhing bodies seem sinister. Faux skeletons were imbedded in the walls, and medieval style torches glowed with electricity instead of flame.

Bedlam was not intended to soothe but to encourage debauchery. Of any kind.

Several strides into the large room but before she reached the edge of the dance floor, Hayden stopped and looked up to the balcony. Her eyes were wide with shock, but he didn't think it was because of the half-naked girl twirling around a pole.

Her mouth moved, but he had to lean closer to hear what she said. "It's active," she yelled before glancing at Willyn. The other woman nodded, her face stricken as well. Whatever the two of them were looking at terrified them both.

Trevor saw Hayden start to lift a hand and point, but she caught herself, glancing around to see if anyone had noticed. If any of the patrons or staff at this bar knew what they were partying with, they might not appreciate the presence of these particular witches.

Judging by her reaction, Trevor assumed the sight Hayden had given her coven when they'd linked in the great room was still in effect. He couldn't see anything out of the ordinary, but Willyn could.

"Oh, my God, Hayden," Willyn cried, huddling closer to her friend. "What's going on? What is that?"

"What do you see?" Dare asked his wife, shooting a worried look to Trevor. The message was loud and clear. Any shit starts going down and we're out of here. Whether the ladies like it or not.

Hayden leaned into Trevor, for support and to be near his ear to avoid shouting. "A body of some kind is pressing itself through the door, or portal, whatever you want to call it. I can make out a head and an arm, but it seems to be struggling."

She shook her head as if unable to believe what she was seeing. "The door is round but uneven, and it's shifting. The material looks...sticky, maybe gelatinous. It's as if..." She stalled and closed her eyes.

"Tell me," Trevor said.

She made a sound of distress. "It's almost as if it's being born. Pushing its way into this world."

Somebody plowed into them from behind, and Trevor whirled around, ready to fight.

"Sorry, sorry," an exceptionally drunk man said as he laid a hand on Trevor's shoulder for stability and barreled on through the crowd.

Trevor drew in an aching breath and nodded to Dare. "Have you seen enough?" Trevor asked Hayden.

Nodding rapidly, she moved with him toward the door, checking over her shoulder to make sure the other couple was coming with them. She made an unexpected turn, gasping as she looked again to the upper deck. Then she spun more slowly, surveying the club in its entirety.

Willyn grabbed Hayden's shoulders and shook her lightly. "I know. I know. But we need to get out of here first. Keep moving."

The no-nonsense tone from the mild woman made her words that much more alarming.

Like a fullback protecting his runner, Trevor pushed through the mass until he had Hayden outside in cooler, cleaner air.

And not a moment too soon, as she looked like she was going to pass out.

"My God. How many? How many, Hayden?" Willyn was beside her friend asking the questions, though she appeared shaken and stunned.

"How many what?" Trevor asked, but he was afraid he already knew the answer.

Hayden swallowed like she had a grapefruit in her throat. "There were more demons inside. I didn't see them at first. They were hidden." She looked to Willyn. "The woman dancing on the pole upstairs. Did you see?"

"Yes. And the male bartender, big with the blonde ponytail. He looked the same way." Willyn leaned back against Dare's chest when he closed in behind her.

Meeting Trevor's quizzical stare, Hayden explained, "Their faces, if you look long enough, their faces...I don't know. They flickered between looking normal and then transparent. Horrible Halloween masks of monsters I can't begin to describe."

She pressed both hands together, fingers threaded and clenched. "They were either demons disguised as humans..."

"Or people possessed by demons," Willyn finished.

Shoving aside the shock their theories caused, Trevor said, "Neither option is all that good, but at least we have a better idea of what we're dealing with."

"Forewarned is forearmed?" Dare asked wryly.

"Something like that." A piece of cardboard rustled down the street on a strong breeze, and all of them cringed before identifying the source of the noise. "It's all we've got for now," Trevor said. "But I hope that friend of Quinn's gets here soon. Hard to come up with a strategy when you don't know anything about your enemy."

"Right," Hayden said, pressing her lips into a white line. "And we already have one battle to win. Why invite more trouble until we know what we should do?"

"But what if those people are possessed?" Willyn asked, brow furrowed.

"Sweetheart." Dare touched his wife's arm. "We can't help until we know how. Rushing in blindly might get them hurt. Or us."

"My head hears you, but my gut is all twisted up. What if it happens to one of us? Or to Tadd?"

"Stop." Dare's command brooked no objection. "That's not going to happen."

Hearing the approach of male voices, Trevor glanced around and spoke to Dare in a low but level tone. "We should go somewhere more private."

"Agreed," Dare said as Willyn and Hayden both nodded.

But halfway down the block they came face to face with two burly men, and Hayden jolted.

Taking her by the elbow, Trevor tried to step around the men. "Excuse us," he said, meeting the larger of the two in the eye. He sensed Dare moving to stand a step in front of the women.

Then, of course, the damsels in distress moved right up in line with him and Dare. So much for protecting them.

"Something got your attention?" the hulking one asked. His mean, dark eyes were trained on Hayden. His bald head gleamed under the street lamp. "You look like you might have seen...something."

Trevor didn't need confirmation to know this one was probably flickering. A demon himself or demon-controlled.

"We were just leaving," Trevor said.

The man's glare lifted back to him. His upper lip curled. "Naw. You weren't."

The other guy laughed and sounded like a lifetime smoker. He took a step to the side, but Trevor had a bad feeling it wasn't because he was leaving but getting out of the bigger man's way.

"What are you?" Hayden demanded, and she too was putting

distance between her and Trevor. Her move forced the stranger to split his attention between the two of them.

Soon Dare and Willyn took up similar positions, and Trevor had to hand it to them. His newfound friends might quibble over who did what, but when trouble found them, they functioned like a well-orchestrated fight club.

"Something tells me you already know what I am," the gruff man told her, breathing more heavily. "I've never tried one like you on for size," he snarled. "Ready to have me inside you, bitch?" He smiled with teeth like gravel. "And I mean inside you in every possible way."

A hazy film slid over Trevor's vision, and his muscles gathered to leap at the bastard. The right hook was already forming when a sharp female voice bit into the confrontation. "What are you doing? Is this how you keep a low profile?"

The two thugs jerked their heads and sniffed the wind before leveling Hayden and Trevor with one last murderous glare each before heading toward the club. They made snuffling sounds as they went, like pit bulls who'd been pulled off their kill.

Trevor still wanted to take the big guy down, but he was more concerned about whoever had the authority to make them back off.

His face went slack, probably looking as surprised as his friends did. The woman sauntering down the street and into the fall of lamplight was the black woman from the other night. When the coven had respectfully asked Trevor to go upstairs and leave them to their "conversation" with Joseph.

Sylvie of Amara infamy was walking straight for them. "Take that as a favor and get the hell out of here," she said before any of them had a chance to speak. "And since I've helped you stay alive, you can take a message to Joseph for me."

"Leave Joseph out of this," Hayden said, squaring off with Sylvie.

"That's exactly what I'm trying to do." A wave of what

might have been agony washed over Sylvie's features before she hardened into one-hundred-percent-evil bitch again. "To be clear, I don't give a shit what any of you think of me. But Joseph has been...decent to me, even though you and yours don't want that."

"Joseph makes his own decisions," Willyn said, somehow reminding them of the common ground they shared. That they all cared about Joseph.

"Well this time I'm asking you to help him make one." Sylvie took two booted steps closer. "I don't want him hurt, and one of us is bound to be just that if we keep on doing like we have. So you go back to your coven and make damn sure he stays away from me."

Hayden crinkled her brows. "You're not just using him? Trying to find a way to turn him and somehow get to us?"

The toffee-skinned woman laughed. "Honey, Joseph came to me, not the other way around." She shook a finger at Hayden. "Now I'm trying to do the right thing. Just this once, because his mama and mine were friends. So you tell him..." Her voice broke then she tried again. "You tell him to stay away. Just. Stay. Away."

She brushed past them to march in the direction of Bedlam but stopped short to issue one last directive. "And he better not try working any more spells on me. He doesn't know what he's doing or what might come the next time he calls." Her voice lowered to a conspiratorial whisper. "Savannah's not the place it used to be."

Her head jerked up, and her pale brown eyes went wide. She pointed to power lines and said, "The crows are perching." As she rasped the warning out, she rubbed a pendant hanging around her neck. "Someone's going to die this night."

Without another word she bolted for the metal-gated doors and disappeared inside.

The four of them stared after her, dumbfounded, until the

silence was shattered by Trevor's cell phone.

"Roch," he barked into the device then listened intently. "How long ago?" A pause before Trevor reached into a pocket and retrieved a small pad with a pen. "I'm ready. Give me the address."

He heaved a great sigh before adding, "Cole, man. You don't need to lose your job over this. I might be in too deep, but you're not. Besides," he joked, "we might still need someone on the force when all this is done."

Hayden and the others listened quietly to Trevor's end of the conversation.

"How much time can you give us?" he asked. "Fine. Give me as much of a heads up as you can. I won't be alone." He bowed his head and said, "Thanks, Partner. I owe you."

"Bad and good news," he told Hayden when he hung up. "Looks like our man grabbed another woman."

Hayden closed her eyes and put a fist to her stomach. Willyn and Dare simply stood still and silent.

"But he's gotten sloppy. A witness got a plate, so we have a name and address." He told Hayden, "Looks like he's been living under an alias. That's why your lead about his high school name didn't go very far."

He ran a hand through his hair and started walking, gesturing for them to follow. "We don't have much time, though. Cole's getting the warrant and a team together, but with a woman in danger, there's really no excuse for him to wait before going in. I want to take a look at this bastard's place before the team gets there."

"I want to look, too," Hayden said, jogging to keep up. "And we're going to need some help, a very special kind of search team that the cops just don't have."

Trevor clicked a button to unlock his doors as they ran toward the silver car. "Who?" he asked.

Willyn and Dare climbed in back, and the blonde witch was

nodding as her blue eyes clashed with Hayden's gold. "We need to get Lucia and Claudia."

24

The apartment reeked. That was the first thing Hayden noticed when Trevor worked the lock and opened the door with a cop's caution. He made her wait in the hall with Claudia while he cleared the rooms to make sure no one was inside.

Capturing the man who'd murdered Ronnie and Chloe, and even now had kidnapped a third woman would be a coup, possibly ending the Amara's plan to feed souls to their demon master. But if the man held more magic than painting charmed symbols, the situation could get ugly and quick.

Trevor poked his head back out and motioned for her and Claudia to come in. He'd shut the door behind them and scanned the foul living space. "It looks like he vacated the place several days ago, at least."

Claudia edged up to a round table at the end of a beat-up sofa and pointed at a newspaper. "Someone's been here as recently as yesterday," she said and rubbed her arms as if fending off the funk of the apartment. Open pizza boxes were in various stages of decay, and viewing the mushrooms on one ensured Hayden would never eat fungi again.

"He must be insane, a completely disgusting individual, or so focused on his task that he didn't notice the squalor he was living in." Trevor wrinkled his nose as he looked at a bowl of cereal on the floor. The contents were lumpy and partially desiccated. Then he glanced up at Hayden. "But we have to move fast. The second Cole calls to say he and the others are on their way, we have to leave. No matter what we're in the middle of."

He lifted an arm to indicate what was probably a bedroom. "There's a work station in there. Pictures, books, and other things I didn't spend much time looking over." He handed Hayden and Claudia the same blue, medical gloves he was wearing. No talcum. They needed to leave the scene as pristine as possible.

Willyn, Dare, and Lucia waited outside in Lucia's car for the same reason. The fewer people, the less disturbance. And a cleaner getaway if required.

Hayden hoped it wouldn't come to that, and when she brushed closer to Trevor in the bedroom doorway, she nudged him with her elbow. "I can't tell you how much this means to me. I know it goes against everything you've been trained to do."

A semi-grin lifted his lips. "I swore to protect and defend the citizens of this city, and I'd rather break a few rules and save lives than stick to the letter and let innocent people suffer." He tilted his head, indicating she should go in.

He followed closely but veered off to investigate the closet while Claudia looked over the desk and the disarray of papers. "I just need to decide what he held most often or was most important. Meaningful items will hold more memory."

"We could get a call any time," Trevor said from the closet as he rifled through clothing.

Claudia spread her hands. "Okay, okay." She picked up an empty box with a large, square indentation. Hayden caught the words *Wood Burning Set* as Claudia lifted it. "I'm not sure I'll get anything through these gloves," she said, but as soon as she got the words out of her mouth her tone changed.

Hayden knew that tone. "Trevor. Toss me your note pad." She caught the small yellow pad and pen and jotted down everything Claudia said as she channeled the history of the box and verbalized anything she picked up on.

"He really liked this set and wanted to keep it, but *SHE* needs it more and he can't make her angry." Claudia babbled the words so quickly Hayden was afraid she wouldn't be able to read her own writing later. "But they've promised him so much, so much, so much more. *POWER* and as many women as he wants when they win." Claudia gasped and clutched the box until her knuckles went white. "*SHE* has to trap three."

With a brief cry, Claudia slammed the box onto the desk and panted. "Holy shit. That was intense." She looked to Trevor. "You were right on two counts. He's totally focused on his mission." She wiped her brow where perspiration darkened the red of her hairline. "And he is absolutely bat-shit bonkers."

"Are you okay?" Hayden asked. "I've never seen you like that. Is it too much?"

Still trying to catch her breath Claudia nodded. "Oh, yeah. It's too much." She winked at Hayden. "But then again, I'm too much, too. And we're going to get this sick son of a bitch."

Hayden smiled. "Why, Professor. What a potty mouth you have."

"When times call," Claudia muttered before drawing a deep breath and picking up a map with no markings of any kind. But if the killer had used it, touched it, or sweated over it, Claudia would nail that sick SOB to the wall with his own twisted thoughts.

She started again. "*HER* monsters missed one! I did my part. I did my part. Now I'll have to find another, and this time there will be no interference." Claudia bore a hole in the wall with her stare, gripping the wrinkled map delicately. She shook so hard Hayden had to hold herself back. She wanted to wrench that revolting paper away from her friend.

Claudia's tempo increased and her voice scratched. "We will bind them all and take them to a place powered by misery where the evil can be called. So many forgotten ones. So many unnamed souls. *BELMONT!*" With a guttural sound of pain, she threw the map on the desk and stumbled back, tripping over her own feet and falling on her backside.

"Claudia." Hayden kneeled on the floor beside her friend and held her shoulders. "Are you all right? What happened? Are you hurt?"

"I hope no one heard that downstairs," Trevor said, his frown heavy as he went to the front room, presumably to listen for anyone who might come to check on the noise. If the neighbors had ever run into the freak who lived here, though, Hayden doubted they'd give the loud bump a second thought.

In fact, they'd probably stay very clear.

"Whew," Claudia said on a heaving breath. "That was awful. The son of a bitch came at me." She ran her hand over her throat. "No. That's wrong. I was just seeing the memory. The remnants of how angry he was. He didn't like it when we saved Emily at the morgue."

Claudia wrapped her long, pretty fingers around Hayden's wrist. "His eyes did glow. Oh, Hayden. There's something more in him, other than the Droehk's borrowed magic or his own insanity." She lifted fearful, river-green eyes to Hayden. "He's got something much worse living inside, and I'm not even sure he knows it."

Looking up to the desk again, Claudia scrambled to her feet. "He had to get a third victim for a magical number. If he kills this woman tonight, and we don't get there in time, they'll summon Bastraal. They'll let him come get the ghosts. All three of them."

They heard Trevor's phone ring out, and a heartbeat later his boots thudded over the floor. "That's it, ladies," he said from the door. "We have to move."

~

"Where should we go now?" Hayden asked Trevor as soon as they piled into his car. Claudia and Lucia were in the back seat with Willyn and Dare following in the other vehicle.

Claudia had taken an old Polaroid off the killer's desk in his apartment. A young boy, possibly the infamous Dover Briggs, or whatever he was calling himself these days. The child's face had been scratched out, so the picture must be important to the man they were chasing.

Claudia gave the Polaroid to Lucia. "Will this help you get a bead on him?" she asked the Spanish witch who was famous for her ability to find things. Human or object, Lucia could locate anything that was lost.

"*Si.* I believe so." She pressed the photo between flat palms and shut her eyes to focus. Meanwhile, Trevor was dialing a phone number on the screen of his dashboard as Hayden relayed the digits. The conversation would be heard over the car's speakers, essentially making it a conference call.

Anna answered on the other end. She and the rest of the coven were gathered at the yellow house on the mainland with everyone else, including Tadd, the Attingers, Joseph, and his parents. With demons running unfettered and already having been to the island home, no one was to be left alone.

"What did you find?" Anna asked, the echo on the line telling Hayden they were on speakerphone as well.

"The killer had to get three souls before he could give them to Bastraal." Hayden told her in a hurry. "We have to find him before he kills this woman, not only to save her life but to keep Chloe and Ronnie from being...consumed."

She gulped at the awful imagery before continuing. "Lucia's working on tracking the man now. Claudia got some details, but none of it makes any sense."

"Tell us," Anna said, the clip of her tone conveyed the urgency they all felt.

Outside the darkened streets of Savannah whizzed past the windows. Trevor was driving down Abercorn, the central artery of the widespread city. "We think he's taking the woman to a place where he can kill her then summon Bastraal. The only clues we have are these."

Hayden flipped a page of the small notepad to review her scribbles. "Okay. A place powered by misery. Many forgotten ones. Many unnamed souls." Hayden blew out an exasperated breath. "The last thing Claudia said was a single word. Belmont."

She looked up at the digital screen as if she would see her friends' faces. "Trevor knows Savannah as well as anyone, but he doesn't recognize the name. Claudia's searching on her phone for any mention online, but so far we've got nothing."

"Stay straight on this street," Lucia said suddenly from the back seat. "He's somewhere southeast of here. I'll let you know when we need to change direction."

"Roger that," Trevor said, bearing down on the gas to increase his speed.

Over the speakers, Joseph's voice was deep and serious. "Did you say Belmont? And what were the other words you used, nameless souls?"

"Unnamed, but yeah," Claudia said over Hayden's shoulder. "Think you got something?" They could hear Joseph speaking to someone in the background. It sounded like his father, Joe.

Joseph's voice was animated when he came back on the line. "Belmont Cemetery."

Hayden made a face. "Another graveyard. Of course."

Joseph said, "My dad took me there once when I was a teenager. The place is unique, because it's the burial ground for bodies that were uncovered when they did construction out at Hunter Army Airfield."

"Bodies they couldn't identify?" Hayden asked.

"Exactly," Joseph said. "Forgotten ones, unnamed souls, and Belmont. That's got to be the place." Shuffling noises filtered through the speakers. "We'll meet you there," Joseph said.

"No!" Hayden answered more sharply than she'd meant to. "No one else needs to put themselves in danger. Let's face it. We don't know what we're doing or if this Dover Briggs will be the only one out there."

"Exactly why you need more of us to come," Paige said on the line. Hayden could almost see her angry stance and determined face.

"There are five witches and one cop heading there now." Hayden met Trevor's grim stare in the dashboard light. "We shouldn't spread ourselves too thin in any one place. All of you should stay there and protect each other." She hardened herself and said, "Guys, these demons could be anywhere."

"We aren't far if you need us," Anna said, and Joseph's swift denial was muffled in the background. "Keep us informed."

The line went dead and classic rock streamed from the speakers in its place until Trevor switched off the radio. "We'll be going onto federal property," he said. "Does everyone have identification on them?"

Affirmative answers came from the back then Lucia said, "I'll call Willyn and Dare."

"I'm not flashing my badge," Trevor said. "That will just raise the question of whether or not I have my gun on me, and we don't have time for all that. It's bad enough we'll have to stop and get a pass." He met Lucia's eyes in the rearview mirror. "Tell Dare to say the same thing as us. We're meeting friends at the bowling alley."

Lucia nodded and repeated the instructions, as Hayden slid her hand over to Trevor's thigh. "I just keep pulling you in deeper and deeper. I'm so sorry, and I hope you don't get in any trouble."

His blue eyes swung over to her. "Get one thing straight, Hayden. You didn't do any of this. It's not your fault." He wrapped strong fingers around her hand and kept it pressed to his leg. "No matter what happens, you didn't cause this and have done everything in your power to save those spirits. And the latest victim."

She let her gaze drop until a squeeze on her hand brought it back to Trevor. "You can't blame yourself forever," he said. "You've done more than your fair share to make up for the past. You're fighting for humanity, for God's sake."

Old fears and recriminations tried to surface, but Hayden pressed them back down. "I know. I try, but sometimes, it's so hard."

He lifted her hand now and kissed it. "And I'll be there when it's too tough to face alone."

Hayden felt Claudia's hand on her shoulder. "Same goes."

A light shimmered its way into Hayden's bloodstream, filled with hope and the possibility of self-forgiveness. Trevor was right, she would have to make peace with the death of that child someday, or the guilt would slowly destroy her.

For over ten years she'd tried to do good, to help others in an attempt to balance the scales, but it took a whole lot of decency to weigh as heavily as a mother's loss. A baby's death.

Hayden didn't know if she could ever do enough, or if good deeds were the right way to salvage herself. All she could do was keep her eyes up and her loved ones close. They gave her strength, and with the war that was coming, she would need to be stronger than ever.

"There's the gate," Trevor said, shaking her out of the trance. He lifted his chin to Hayden in question. "Do you have what you need?" he asked.

She rubbed her amulet through her shirt and looked in the rearview mirror at her friends. Then she met the blue eyes of the man who not only held her heart but guarded it. "Almost," she said, reaching out to stroke his face. "Almost."

25

Lightning flashed in the distance as Trevor carefully kept the car to the posted thirty miles per hour. They were on a military base now, and MPs didn't mess around. "Can you take us to this cemetery?" he asked Lucia.

She firmed her lips and looked unhappy. "I can tell you the direction. We'll have to rely on Joe's instructions about which roads to take."

Hayden gestured as they eased around a traffic circle. "Look, there's the water tower on the left he mentioned. We need to take a right at the stop sign then follow it to the end and go left. That should be the perimeter road. A few minutes down we should see something."

After they made both turns and were riding in tandem with railroad tracks on the outside of a tall chain link fence, Claudia spoke into the anxious silence. "I can see another reason this Dover Briggs guy chose this place. It's desolate."

"Not much traffic," Lucia added. "Let's hope that's a good thing."

"The fewer witnesses to whatever goes on out there the better," Trevor said. "I still haven't figured out how I'm going to cover all this up."

Hayden rubbed his arm. "We'll help. Anna has some

impressive tricks at her disposal."

They would have driven right past the cemetery if Lucia hadn't patted Trevor on the shoulder and said, "There. Right there." She pointed out the right window.

"I don't see anything," Claudia said. "There are no lights."

"I'm telling you this man, this Briggs is there." Lucia tapped the glass emphatically.

"Hey, I believe you," Claudia said, holding up her hands. "But I still can't see in the dark."

Easing into a grassy area across the road, Trevor turned off the headlights but not before they'd highlighted a plain brown sign with the words *Belmont Cemetery*.

Lucia made a satisfied *hmm* sound in the back seat.

High wind rustled dead leaves and whistled over yellowed grasses as they exited the vehicles. Hayden could tell the area was wide open, but darkness stretched before them. She could barely make out a tree line against the equally blackened sky.

Lightning did them the favor of heating up long enough for Hayden to make out a flagpole and memorial marker. Another strike revealed hundreds of small American flags placed next to as many cement squares. "The unnamed souls," she whispered, so heartbroken her chest ached. "I hope they were remembered by someone."

She noticed the absence of ghosts then. Regardless of history, location, or even relocation, every graveyard had at least one ghost. Usually several. The complete lack of paranormal activity twisted Hayden's instinctual warning system into a tight, vibrating knot.

Very little in this world or the next could scare off a bunch of ghosts, but Hayden knew of one thing that might. "There's a demonic presence here," she said, squinting in an attempt to make sense of the inky shadows.

The moon peeked out from the stormy clouds and turned on a pale, gray nightlight.

"I see them," Trevor said. "Looks like," he paused then added, "five of them. I can't tell male or female."

"They already know we're here," Dare said as he and Willyn joined the group. "Can't you feel that?" he asked.

"Yes, but I'm surprised you can. No offense," Willyn added, taking her husband's hand. "Someone, rather, some *thing* is looking at us. It feels like the other night with the Scietta demon, only weaker."

"It must be Briggs," Hayden said, steeling herself for the confrontation. "Claudia said he had something in him."

"Do you think the Droehk is out there, too?" Lucia sidled up to Hayden. "At least we'll know who she is from now on."

"I don't know. She's kept herself hidden so far." Hayden turned to Trevor. "There's only one way to find out."

"I'm ready," he said, and started across the field.

Hayden kept pace with him but was swamped by guilt as she stepped on various stones. She tried to avoid the act of disrespect, but tonight her primary concern was for the living. And for the souls that could very well be damned if she didn't act fast.

"I'm going to throw a cloaking spell," Dare told Willyn before kissing her and squeezing her hands. "Save one of the bad guys for me." With a wink to Hayden and the others, the dark-haired witch went back to make sure the activities in the cemetery stayed private. If a car did pass by, they wouldn't see a thing.

As they drew closer, Hayden could make out the Amara members. The moon had gone back in, but a strange light glowed in the far corner of the field. She sniffed the winter air. "I smell cinnamon."

"Scarlett," Lucia said, and no word had ever been filled with such contempt. Thunder boomed in agreement. The red witch was brutal and enjoyed making others suffer.

The ever-so-sweet Willyn snarled as they approached the umber illumination. "And I still owe her one."

A round orb floated several feet off the ground, casting yellow-brown light on dead grass, leaves, and pine needles. Their enemies were actually backed into a corner with trees lining their chosen site on two sides.

Scarlett whirled when she heard their footsteps. She rolled her eyes and made an ugly face. "You have got to be kidding me," she said with a flip of her crimson curls. "R.J., tell that idiot human to get it done. We've just run out of time."

Instead of leaving Scarlett alone, R.J. turned and yelled. "Just mark her and kill her! We've got company."

A woman in a dark gray sweatshirt with the hood pulled up walked into the brighter light. Her face was hidden, but menace sparked off of her so violently the evil energy was almost palpable. She didn't say anything, only stared from beneath her hood.

The sound of crunching leaves and soft curses made Hayden search out the source. First she saw Sylvie standing several yards away from the rest of the Amara. With arms crossed over her chest and legs spread wide, the woman they'd just seen outside Bedlam appeared resentful of everyone around her, including Scarlett and R.J.

But the loathing on her face was directed toward the person on the ground. Correction. There were two people, one on top of the other, and they were struggling.

"Let the woman go," Hayden told Scarlett in a flat tone. She sounded calm, but the softness of her voice belied the fury simmering beneath.

"You think you can take her from us?" Scarlett asked. The elegantly-dressed witch started glittering, and around her the air became a mist, the same ruby red as her hair. "Just try. You know I'm stronger than all of you combined."

"I'm not sure that's true any longer," Claudia said, sending a fierce gust of wind that dispersed Scarlett's glow.

The red witch laughed. "Good. Good. I might finally have

some decent combat." She quirked a brow in disdain. "If all of you come at me at once."

Lucia grabbed Claudia's arm to still her response, but Hayden took three resolute steps forward to take up a fighting position. "You're not going to hurt her." Hayden realized they still didn't know the kidnapped woman's name.

"Do it!" R.J. yelled, but this time the man on the ground argued. "Not until I'm done," he said before threatening the woman underneath him. "Stop struggling."

No doubt remained that the bastard on the ground was Dover Briggs. The man who'd raped Chloe, Ronnie, and Emily before strangling them to death.

"We don't have time for that anymore, asshole. So either do her now, or I'll slit your fucking throat," R.J. told him before turning back to Hayden. He looked past her to Lucia and Claudia. "We'll keep them off you long enough to get it done," he yelled to Briggs.

With curly brown hair and blue eyes, R.J. was deceptively kind looking, but when he invaded a person's mind, he could make them see, do, or feel anything he wanted. "Searenn!" he shouted suddenly. "Get it done!"

The hooded woman jerked into action. So now they knew her name, and Hayden felt sure she was also the Droehk. The Amara female Anna hadn't been able to sense.

Searenn tried to wrench the man off of the woman, but with a snap of his jaws he lunged up at her and shoved her back. "I get what I want first."

He fell onto the woman again as she screamed madly. He clamped a hand over her mouth and ripped her shirt. "Shut up, bitch. You'll take it."

Willyn shouted and ran toward the man as he continued to tear at the woman's clothes and force her down. A stench similar to cinnamon but much more foul wafted from Scarlett as she channeled her magic for an attack. Just as quickly

Claudia and Lucia pummeled her with balls and streaks of fire, forcing her to focus on them instead of Willyn.

Hearing Willyn's swift approach, Searenn surged forward and tackled her to the ground. From across the field, Dare's enraged voice called his wife's name.

Trevor fired his gun, and a tuft of grass jumped near Searenn's foot.

Her hooded head whipped toward Trevor, and Hayden swore she heard an animal-like growl come from the woman.

"Get off of her!" The scream came from Sylvie just before she launched herself at Briggs. She kicked him soundly in the side of his face and stood over him as he clutched his cheek. The hoodoo priestess towered over the injured man. Her chest rose and fell with erratic, harsh breaths.

The unexpected clash within their own camp had all of the other Amara brutes staring at Sylvie in shock.

"What's your fucking problem, Sylvie?" R.J. demanded, his eyes wide. Beside him, even Scarlett looked dumbfounded.

In a sharp and blindingly-fast move, Sylvie pulled a knife from her belt and shook it at R.J. "You shouldn't have done it. You went too far." She edged back and stood straddling the woman on the ground who had been struck silent by the commotion and her altered situation.

Briggs crawled to his knees, but as soon as he spit blood from his mangled lips Sylvie leaped over to him and kicked him in the ribs. She bent to grab the woman's arm then dragged her to her feet. Holding the poor woman in front of her body like a shield, Sylvie put the knife to her captive's throat.

"Wait!" Searenn shouted. "It's too soon!"

"Shut up!" Sylvie screeched. "Just shut up and let me think. I need to think." Her light brown eyes were frantic as she staggered back toward the trees with her hostage.

Glancing around her, Hayden saw the Amara were concerned about what was happening. In fact, they looked more afraid now than when Claudia and Lucia had pelted them with flames.

"Don't kill her!" Briggs screamed from where he still sat on the ground. Bloody spittle flew when he added, "She hasn't been marked. You'll ruin everything!"

So that was it. Hayden clenched her fists and focused on Sylvie. She was obviously having a quarrel with her conscience. Maybe the coven was right and Sylvie had been the lost one from the seven sisters prophecy all along.

If so, that meant Sylvie was destined to betray the Amara. She already had, because she couldn't turn back now and give the woman to Briggs. The Amara, more specifically Ronja, would never forget how Sylvie had rebelled tonight. How she'd interfered with Ronja's will. Her dictates.

So here was Hayden's opportunity. She could see Sylvie was confused and on the precipice of treachery. The Amara would kill her if she turned against them, but judging by the angst in the hoodoo woman's eyes, she might not be able to live with herself if she didn't.

But to get through to Sylvie, Hayden would have to believe every word she spoke. She would have to place faith in their truth if she was going to convince Sylvie to do what she needed her to. To release the woman she held against her will.

Sylvie struggled for her own answer, but Hayden was sure she wouldn't get there alone. She needed a push, encouragement, support. And it had to come from someone who understood. Someone who'd moved past her own mistakes to embrace the possibility of a future.

The words would never get through to Sylvie if they weren't heartfelt. So before she spoke, Hayden searched her own mind.

Could she have a life with someone as worthy as Trevor? Would she ever allow herself a reprieve? Would she ever forget the pain she'd caused by her own action or lack thereof?

No. She would never, never forget, because that would mean losing the horrible life lesson she'd learned as well. An experience, no matter how hurtful, that had helped shape who she was today. A person who cared and often put the welfare of others above her own.

Was she perfect? Not even close. But she tried, and working on being a better person had value in itself. *She* had value. And there was no shame in that.

She would never forget what she'd done as a foolish teenage girl. But maybe she could finally forgive.

Hayden felt a pinch in her heart as the toddler's innocent, lifeless face flashed in her mind. Then she let the memory fly free, just as she was sure his angelic spirit had done long ago.

The pink stone in her amulet sang out in sweet release, but Hayden's voice drowned out the melody when she cried, "Sylvie! You have to let her go!"

The hoodoo woman turned bewildered eyes on Hayden before clenching them tight and shaking her head wildly. Her knuckles worked on the hilt of the knife as she loosened and tightened her grip.

"You have to do it, Sylvie. Now!" Hayden reached deep into her own agonized past to find empathy. Her trial might be over but her duty wasn't. It never would be.

She'd been tasked by the gods and goddesses to help injured spirits cross over, and if any soul was ever in need, it was the conflicted woman with a knife in her hand.

Sylvie needed to cross over.

Hayden raised her voice above the thunderous clouds moving in. "Sylvie, second chances aren't meant to be given! They should be *taken*! Because you are the only one who can decide what your life will be worth!"

Shooting a worried glance to the other Amara as they watched Sylvie, Hayden walked closer. Her voice was lower but just as earnest. "I know you care about Joseph. And I know you don't want to hurt this woman. She's done nothing wrong."

Hayden licked her lips and surged forward as angry winds

lashed her hair against her face. "No one would go against the Amara to warn Joseph or save a woman from rape if they were all bad. You have good in you, Sylvie. Now grab onto it and make it yours! Let the woman go and save yourself, before it's too late."

Sylvie's face went slack, almost too calm. She seemed to look right through Hayden as she approached.

Holding out both hands, Hayden pleaded, "Take your second chance, please. It belongs to you. Only you."

A bellow of rage and pain tore from Sylvie's throat. She screamed again and lifted the knife high. Hayden choked on fear, terrified she'd pushed too hard and too fast.

Gathering fire in her palm, Hayden held it at the ready, prepared to shoot it at Sylvie if she had to. Just as she screamed, "Don't!" Sylvie brought the knife down to her side and shoved the woman away.

Flinging her arm out straight, Sylvie pointed the knife at Dover Briggs. "Kill him! You have to kill him!" Her light brown eyes met Hayden's. Her chest heaved as she switched sides and risked her life. "He has to die or the spirits he branded will never be free."

"Sylvie, no!" R.J. yelled, pounding his fist against his chest.

"What?" Hayden asked as she panicked. She would have to commit murder to save souls? Briggs was evil incarnate, hell, he was probably demon incarnate, too, but that didn't change the fact that he was still a human being.

One Hayden would be forced to kill.

By now the woman had stumbled over to Willyn who used her witch's magic to heal and her Christian heart to soothe. R.J., Searenn, Scarlett, and Dover Briggs stood apart from each other but seemed to have one common goal. Based on their expressions of hatred, they all wanted Sylvie's blood.

Willyn told the woman to hide in the trees and wait. Then she hurried over to flank Hayden from the right. Lucia and

Claudia closed in from the opposite side, and behind them was Dare. He'd left the cloaking spell running on residual energy, and knowing him like she did, Hayden was sure he would fight to the death.

For his wife, for Hayden's victory, the coven, and to protect the innocent woman in the woods.

That left only one.

Hayden heard solid footsteps behind her. Trevor had her back, both literally and figuratively.

Sylvie held her ground, but there was no returning from the choice she'd made. She was now pitted against the Amara as surely as Hayden was, and the odds were stacked in their favor. Seven to four.

Even if Sylvie did nothing. Even with Scarlett's putrid yet very powerful magic, those who played for team righteous were well in the lead.

"You've lost this one, Scarlett," Hayden yelled out to the highest-ranking of the opposing group. "I've already succeeded in my trial, and we're taking the woman with us. To safety."

"Dover Briggs!" Trevor called out. "Don't move. Don't speak." He aimed his black pistol. "Or I'll put a bullet through your skull."

"Don't talk to them!" the woman called Searenn shouted, lifting her face enough for Hayden to see she had mismatched eyes. The pale blue against black was eerie. Disturbing. "This is my show, and no coven bitch is going to tell me when I'm defeated." She ripped the hooded sweatshirt over her head, leaving only a skimpy tank top that had been sheared off below the breasts.

Her flesh was covered in black, purple, and navy tattoos, a mysterious and mystical language used only by the reviled Droehk clan. *Her ayjehr.*

Storm clouds thundered overhead, roiling a sinister mix of sooty black and molten lead.

"Then I'll tell you," Hayden said. "You might as well give it up, because the murder of innocents and torture of spirits ends tonight." She lifted her arm, and fire erupted in her hand to back up the threat. "You're outnumbered."

But Searenn only laughed before licking her own bare shoulder, swirling her pierced tongue over the patterned ink. With her head still tilted to the side, she sent Hayden a devious smile and said, "Not for long."

26

The Droehk lifted both arms, palms up, but instead of looking to the sky, her stare drilled into the earth, through every fiery level of hell. A foreign language rolled from her tongue, its hard consonants an offense to Hayden's ears.

She would likely be more than offended if she understood what Searenn was saying. She caught a few random words that sounded like *vatama, gide,* then the ink-covered woman ended with a loud *darimah!*

For a moment the atmosphere stood still, and so did the diverse gathering of people, waiting, a few holding their breath and some exhaling tension.

A feather-soft particle landed on Hayden's cheek and then her eyelashes. She wiped at the tiny flakes on her face and studied her fingers. *Where did snow come from?*

More of the fine material dusted the ground and danced on the turbulent winds before Hayden noticed the color. Then the stench. Not snow but *ash*.

Her eyes ripped to Searenn as that one nodded. "Oh, yes." The Droehk clapped her hands and laughed. "Here they come." She lowered her head like a bull considering a charge. "And they will melt the skin from your bones."

Hayden knew what was coming a moment before she heard

the wicked shriek. A flurry of heavy wings behind her should have been warning enough, but instead of ducking she twisted to face her assailant. The great flying demon who'd taken Chloe from the graveyard was back.

With about twenty friends.

From every direction demons stalked toward Hayden and the others in her group, circling around them and closing off any escape route. Even the woman from the woods sensed evil and came tearing back into the clearing. She fell at Willyn's feet.

The monsters moving in all looked similar, with brown, leathery skin and grisly faces. Their brows were wrinkled and fell heavy over red eyes. Though walking upright like humans, the beasts' similarity to people ended there. Each of the predators had two sets of arms, enabling them to hold giant weapons with ease.

Stunned by the army of unnatural beasts bearing down on them, Hayden had forgotten the winged soul-stealer still circling the field. A shout from Lucia told her that had been a mistake.

Hayden felt a push of air as the demon dove straight for her. She turned just in time for its outstretched claws to rake her neck and shoulder, splitting the skin down to muscle.

What happened next was a blur of pain and confusion. She thought she'd fallen, but couldn't be sure. All of her concentration was on the burning in her neck and the warm flood she felt pumping there.

With one hand fluttering at her leaking neck, Hayden's line of sight skimmed over the top of the grass. When she saw a pair of feet running to her, she knew she'd gone down.

"Oh, Jesus! Hayden!" Trevor's anguished voice covered her as his strong hands fell to her shoulder to press. Then he switched back to her neck, the more serious injury.

"Move! Move!" Willyn's voice, as pure as crystal but stretched thin with alarm. Fire erupted in the sky above. Hayden's eyes rolled to see.

Nothing made sense. Were there dragons now? Their flames spurted in beautiful flowing ribbons, and ash fell in her open mouth. Were the fire-breathers destroying the world?

"They're real," Hayden said. Or had she only thought the words? The earth was spinning so slowly. Streaky, like watercolors...and numb.

The pain was draining away with her lifeblood, into the cold, dead grass of winter. "So pretty," she whispered as a single gray flake fell toward her eye. Before her lid closed.

"No. No." Huge arms gripped her and shook her weakened body. A man. A very strong man who smelled good and clean.

Next came a burning sensation, only the flames were cool as they licked over her skin, into her veins, and traveled to explode inside her heart. The sweet voice of crystal was still talking, telling someone to hang on. To come back.

A loud sound like all the oxygen being sucked from a room in a millisecond filled Hayden's mind. *Sfffffft!*

And her eyes popped open. "Where are the dragons?" she asked while two agonized faces looked down at her. Willyn laughed through tears and Trevor cussed like a sailor. "Those aren't dragons, they're the women you call your sisters, and they're fighting alone."

He shook her again, fear bleeding through the anger he was forcing into his stern voice. "So get your ass up, Hayden, and this time, keep an eye on the goddamn sky."

Then he hugged her so tightly she heard bones creak. "I can't see them, Hayden, but I saw what they did to you." He kissed her and pulled her up. Then he spun, putting his back to hers. "Want to add your fire to the arsenal?"

Taking in the chaos, Hayden slapped her hand to her neck then her shoulder. Her clothes were still torn and bloody, but her skin was like new. Willyn and her handy gift.

Her sister's healing power was better than adrenaline, and by the time Hayden spread her legs in a fighting stance, her eyes and brain had cleared. She saw the chaos erupting around her as the witches clashed with brown-skinned devils.

Lucia and Claudia continued to throw flames as the fiends stalked closer and closer, but it only kept the demons at bay. The hulking beasts didn't like fire, but neither did they fear it.

Willyn was throwing other elements, trying wind or water, experimenting to see which worked best. But none did.

Sylvie and R.J. were nose to nose now, screaming at each other and pushing. R.J. hadn't taken his partner's defection well at all.

Then a movement behind Sylvie caught Hayden's eye. Briggs was moving in and had the knife in his hand.

After playing a part in Sylvie's decision, Hayden couldn't stand by and let Briggs hurt her. She tossed a fireball at the serial killer and took no small amount of pleasure in his surprised yell. He batted his burning coat, long and black, just as Ronnie had described, and waved his hands when they blistered.

Hearing the commotion, Sylvie fell on the knife where Briggs had dropped it, but slipped it back in her belt instead of brandishing it at R.J. The two of them still seemed hesitant to do real damage to one another.

Groaning in pain, Briggs ran to Searenn's side like the coward he was.

"Nothing's working," Claudia called to Hayden. "And they're getting closer." With her attention split between the battle and Hayden for even a second, Claudia missed the demon rushing toward her back.

The thing moved so fast and was on her before anyone could throw fire. Besides it was too close to Claudia. If they burned him they would burn their friend.

The monster wrapped all four of its appendages around the

red-haired witch when her back was turned. When the demon's flesh met hers, she screamed in a way that made Hayden's heart twist inside her chest.

"It burns!" Claudia cried, writhing in pain as she tried to untangle herself from arms that were clamped tight and sizzling through her shirt like acid.

Lucia jumped to her friend's defense but only seared her own skin when she tried to pry the things off. "*Mi dios!* It's burning her! It's hurting her!"

A familiar urge to resist flowed from Hayden's subconscious. The bastards from hell were for the nine to deal with. Their vile touch could be a catalyst, opening channels to a new and specialized magic.

But Claudia was in too much agony to find her way to it.

Hayden breathed deep and found calm in the middle of anarchy. This was still her challenge and still her duty.

So she opened the gates.

Magic roared down Hayden's arms like a tidal wave until it crashed into her palms, shining a glorious blue. Here was the mysterious light that had surrounded her after her encounter with the Scietta demon.

She didn't know the power's origin or if she could master it, but the sizzling energy only showed itself when she faced danger. Specifically danger of the demon variety.

And with her friend, her sister, screaming in pain, Hayden would damn well find a way to use it.

"Claudia!" she shouted before blasting a stream of her newfound power at the monster. The magic was coven-made and wouldn't harm one of its own.

But the many-armed beast that held her friend let out a high-pitched whine as it shuddered and shifted. Parts of it bulged then shrank before the entire thing burst into a million tiny pieces of black dust.

"Willyn, hurry!" Lucia cried while Claudia, in too much pain to be ashamed, let tears run freely down her cheeks as she, too said the healer's name over and over. The burn of her corroded flesh had to be incredible.

The beasts surrounding them all stopped as their comrade blew away on the mighty wind. They hadn't expected their enemy to have a real weapon. One that could annihilate even those summoned from the depths of the abyss.

With the other two women caring for Claudia and Dare standing guard over the kidnapped woman, Hayden and Trevor stood shoulder to shoulder to face off with Scarlett and Searenn.

"Well. Look at that, Searenn," Hayden said with a malicious grin. "I know how to make ash, too."

Then in a move of pure arrogance, Hayden thrust both hands into the air and aimed everything she had at the flying monster who'd stolen Chloe. And possibly Ronnie. Twin blue beams shot into the beast's underbelly. The sound that came from the black, oily creature was one of wrath instead of misery, but that didn't stop him from dissolving into dust.

R.J. and Sylvie had stopped arguing, and Briggs stayed far in the background. Scarlett looked severely pissed, but her mocking tone was for Searenn. "Go ahead," she told the Droehk, sarcasm drenching her words. "After all. You said this was *your show*."

By now Claudia had regained her footing and her fury. With the same ease as she'd mastered fire, the tall, flame-haired woman pulled blue magic from her depths and shot two more demons to oblivion.

"You think you're going to make a difference?" Searenn asked, scoffing again but with less confidence than before. "The underworld is brimming with fiends that will make you cower and beg for mercy." She flung her arm out to indicate the demon horde. "These are mere foot soldiers, the only ones I can call at will."

"I'll admit I wasn't prepared for you tonight," the Droehk woman said, nodding to herself. Then she smiled and rubbed spread fingers over her tattooed stomach. "But so many more await my command. It doesn't matter how many you destroy. For every one you take out, another ten will come through the doors, stronger than the ones before." She wiped her face and ash smeared. "The walls are getting very, very thin, and Bastraal will have his day."

Hayden held out her palms and let the light flicker there in warning. "But not this day, Searenn. Not this day."

With a cry of anger, the Droehk woman began muttering her strange words again, and to prove herself, she did make another ten entities appear. More of the hulking fiends who looked as if their only purpose in hell was to wage war.

Like the others still standing and waiting, these demons held weapons with their four arms. One a giant sledgehammer, another a mace, and of course, just so no one would sleep tonight, another had a sickle.

Behind the battalion of evil soldiers the storm was churning in a frenzy. Black clouds slashed by lightning portended a terrible fate.

Searenn pointed at Hayden and bared her teeth. "Just when you think you've won, there will always be more of us."

Thunder boomed like a god's base drum. "Just as there will always be more of our kind, Droehk!" A new voice pierced the rising winds. Hayden jerked around to see Anna marching through the cemetery with Joseph at her side.

Hayden grinned, grateful they had ignored her request to stay away. "Right," she said, motioning for Dare and the shell-shocked woman to come over to where she stood. "Trevor, you, Dare, and Joseph have to stay together and take care of her."

He furrowed his brow. "What are you going to do?"

"We," she said, indicating herself and the other witches, "are going to circle the proverbial wagons around those of you who can't see these beasts."

Raindrops started pelting the ground, their clothes, faces, and hair, washing away some of the ash. As Anna and the others took up defensive positions, Trevor growled and pulled Hayden in for a brief, heated kiss. "I guess if anyone's going to take care of me for a change," he grinned, "I'd want it to be you."

A shower of warmth rained down inside Hayden to counteract the chilling wetness on her skin. "You might actually like it," she said before whipping around to face whichever thing was bellowing behind her.

As Trevor watched Hayden race through the rain like a Celtic warrior, hand raised in lieu of a sword, he felt a clutching pain behind his sternum. Then, when he accepted the fact that he'd crashed hard and wasn't going to recover, the pain lightened and grew to a steady pulse.

What a woman he'd found. Sweet enough to temper his heat but tough enough to hold her own. Even against him.

And now she was off fighting demons.

Invisible to his eyes or not, Trevor had no doubt the creatures were real. And when Lucia went flying through the air to land near the center of the circle, he wished for magic bullets to stop the damn things in their tracks.

Before he could ask if she was all right, the Spanish woman was on her feet and throwing blue firestorms like nobody's business.

He'd been crushed to realize the kind of evil that had Savannah in its sights. Demons, shape-shifters, and immortals? How could humanity survive? Would they even stand a chance?

Now as he watched Hayden spin in a flurry of wet, caramel-hued hair, vengeance and justice strengthening her every move, Trevor not only believed the coven would win, he expected the slaves of Hades to run with their forked tails tucked between their legs.

Scarlett was leaving now with long, angry strides, retreating for the night like a pissed-off prom queen. The bloodthirsty Searenn stood and watched the ongoing battle, while Briggs hunkered low to the ground near the trees.

"Sylvie." Joseph rasped out the woman's name on a breath. He was next to Trevor, but his deep brown eyes were fixated on the fight. R.J. and Sylvie had squared off again. But this time they were serious.

The two Amara members circled each other, taking turns punching and grappling. Trevor felt Joseph prepare to jump, but before he could say anything, R.J. knocked Sylvie a solid blow to the face and she went reeling, landing on the rain-drenched ground.

Then Joseph was off the mark.

Darting through God knows what kind of monsters, Joseph made his way past the skirmish to tackle R.J. The two men rolled and fought, dirty punches to kidneys, throats, and worse. Trevor was torn between wading in to help and staying with the woman.

She was on her knees, staring blindly into the void. The trauma she'd been put through had washed away any hint of lucidity, but he wondered if that might not be for the best. As long as she recovered once this was over.

Looking over to Dare, Trevor could tell the male witch was also wavering, but the two of them had to stay.

If Sylvie cared for Joseph half as much as he apparently did her, she might step in to help. Regardless, neither Trevor nor Dare could desert the helpless woman.

Trevor had no way of telling if the battle was waning or if the foes were being defeated. The women, powerful witches or not, were tiring.

Willyn slipped and went down hard, causing Dare to nearly jerk from his skin. "Get up. Get up," he said as his wife rolled over. Flat on her back, the blonde woman threw up both hands, giving the impression something was coming down on top of her. "Willyn," Dare whispered.

With an unearthly scream, she sent a blue, hissing stream straight up. Whatever had been closing in on her was gone. She made it to her knees then stood, lifting a hand to Dare. After a tired smile for her husband, she looked around and nodded.

"It's almost over," Dare said aside to Trevor. Then he kneeled down to the woman and put his hands on her head. "It's almost over," he said in a low, even cadence. Then he told her to block it all out. That she was looking at a blank wall.

Given the odd phrasing and the way the words were delivered, Trevor found himself wondering if the dark-haired witch had his own abilities. He hoped so.

Sylvie's screech shook the tree limbs with its torment. "Stop it, R.J. You're killing him!" She was standing but stumbled as if dizzy.

She held her left hand out, trying to steady herself as she walked slowly toward Joseph. He was on the ground, arms and legs splayed in four directions. His head was back and bouncing against the ground.

"Anna." Willyn raised her voice across the circle. "R.J.'s got Joseph. He's drilling into his mind!"

Anna blasted another stream of magic at some unseen demon then pivoted to run toward her friend and the man who was scraping the insides of his skull.

Judging Anna's pace, Trevor knew she wouldn't make it. Blood was leaking from Joseph's mouth. Willyn was sprinting now as well, ready to heal Joseph's battered mind. If there was anything left to mend.

Trevor pulled his gun from the holster, sure he could make the shot but worried about the witches as they leaped into his way.

The battle wasn't over, and he prayed no one stepped into his line of fire. He raised the pistol and found his target, holding true through the pounding rain and swirling ash.

But Sylvie got there first. With a heavy grunt she flung herself at R.J., burying the knife in his chest as she landed. Together they toppled, with Sylvie's grasp still on the handle. She pulled the blade out and shoved it home again. "You won't heal from this," she yelled into R.J.'s face.

His hand scratched through the leaves and pine needles but found no purchase. "You Satan's son. You won't heal from this." Again she extracted the thick shard of steel and plunged, until R.J.'s blue eyes grew flat and lifeless.

Finally convinced he was dead, Sylvie eased off R.J.'s body and made her way to Joseph's side. Willyn was still working hard on him, and Anna sent a suspicious look to the approaching hoodoo priestess. But when Sylvie clung to Joseph's hand and cried, Anna frowned and simply studied the woman who'd just saved her friend's life.

Then she stepped away, allowing the two to have their moment when Joseph opened his eyes. A soft moan escaped his lips, and Anna clamped a hand to her mouth, dropping to the ground next to Willyn.

Reaching across Joseph's stomach, Anna laid her hand over Sylvie's, and when the woman lifted her head in response, Anna said the only thing she could say. Two of the most profound and powerful words in any language.

"Thank you." The acknowledgement was half sob, half whisper. The leader of their coven showed gratitude to an enemy, and offered safe passage to the seventh sister.

The lost one had been found.

"It's over," a bedraggled Hayden said as she walked over to Trevor. "That's the last of them." She tossed a glance to the fuming Searenn who'd retrieved her hoodie and was putting it on. "At least I think so."

"You look drained," he told her, running gentle hands over a scrape on her cheek and a gash on her leg. She was bleeding through her jeans. "Is it my turn yet?" he asked, rubbing wet strands of her hair between his fingers.

When she only lifted her eyebrows, he added, "To take care of you. I might not have blue flashlights embedded in my palms, but I make a mean beef stew. And," he held up a finger, "I've always been curious about those hot baths women like to take."

"I'll be more than happy to let you test one out. As long as I get to be there, too." Hayden lifted on her toes to meet Trevor's lips, and love blew straight through him. Her arms circled his neck as a sweet sound murmured from her lips.

An angry growl sounded next to them, and they ripped apart. Trevor went for his gun and Hayden lifted her hand.

The man known only as Dover Briggs stood about fifteen feet away, and his glowing eyes were homed in on the still-kneeling woman. Dare had gone to his wife's side once the all-clear sign had been given, so nothing stood between the serial killer and his victim.

"His eyes," Trevor said, turning to put Hayden behind him.

"I know. What is he?" she asked through trembling lips.

Frankly, Trevor didn't care what the bastard was. He could see him, and that was all that mattered.

With his left hand he pushed Hayden slowly to the side. His cop instincts were kicking in, and he could almost smell the killer's next move.

"She's mine," Briggs said in two different voices. The growl had intensified, and his arms were spread wide, ready to swoop in and make his kill. With a final snarl, Briggs took a step forward.

And Trevor took aim. The loud retort blasted through the rainy night as a hole appeared in the middle of Briggs' forehead. Like a severed tree, Savannah's murderer of women fell to the ground. And stayed there.

"I'll tell you what he is," Trevor said, walking over to nudge the still body with his boot. Once satisfied the killer wouldn't be getting back up, he slid his Glock into its holster. "He's nothing more than a very bad man."

Then Trevor met Hayden's eyes. "With a bullet through his skull."

27

Slapping a hand to her chest with sudden dread, Hayden rushed past Trevor as he stood over the body of Dover Briggs. With his death and Searenn's disappearance after the battle, there was only one person who might know about Ronnie and Chloe.

Had they been sent to Bastraal to suffer? Was it too late? Had they crossed over with the death of the man who'd branded them before raping and killing them?

Sylvie was standing by quietly since Willyn had declared Joseph would be fine. The toffee-skinned woman looked uncomfortable with the presence of coven members, now that the crisis had passed.

Was she used to such duplicity? Did she think they would all turn on her after she'd saved Joseph's life?

"Are they free?" Hayden asked, skidding to a stop in the sodden mix of leaves and grass. She took Sylvie by the shoulders, but gently, so as not to seem a threat. "The spirits. You said they would be freed if Briggs was killed."

"Briggs?" Sylvie looked confused. "Oh. You mean him," she said jerking her chin to point out the fallen rapist. "He's gone by many names. Yes, killing him was the only way to break the tracking symbol that marked them, but that's only part of it."

Then in a panic, Sylvie swung around, her eyes scanning the corner of the field where the Amara had originally grouped together. She heaved a sigh of relief. "She left them here. Searenn, she left the binding tablets here."

A malicious gleam entered Sylvie's eyes when she added, "I guess blowing up her demons rattled her psychotic cage."

"Not a fan?" Hayden asked, sharing a quiet moment of camaraderie with one of the last people on earth she'd expected to like. Even the tiniest bit.

Dropping her eyes with an expression Hayden knew all too well, shame, Sylvie whispered, "Turns out I didn't agree with a lot of what my so-called allies did."

"I won't tell you we'll all forget the things you were a part of." Hayden's mind flashed back to Jen's carefree smile. "Or the things you could have stopped but didn't."

When Sylvie crossed her arms, Hayden touched her shoulder lightly. "But I can promise you that I understand regret, and the only way to move past mistakes, even the worst ones, is to make a better life. Touch as many people as you can with kindness."

Eyes still on the ground, Sylvie said, "I won't ever have a chance to undo things."

"No, but you can ease the pain. All that matters now are the choices at hand. How you go on from here." Hayden sighed. "And now's the perfect time to make your first decision."

Hayden looked to Joseph then to the woman on the ground that Dare and Trevor were still tending to. "Actually, this will be your third good choice." She offered a smile. "Looks like you're already on your way."

Sylvie looked up but frowned. "I don't know how to handle you people being nice to me. It freaks me out."

"Freaks us out, too," Hayden said in the same frank tone. "Now. Please help me do whatever needs to be done for Ronnie and Chloe to pass over. They deserve at least that much."

Sylvie nodded emphatically. "On that we can agree." Trodding over the wet ground and wiping the still falling drops from her eyes, Sylvie pulled the lid off a wooden box.

Inside were three tablets of what looked like pine, light in color and grainy. Two were inscribed with symbols. The third was still blank, and Hayden would bet money it had been intended for the woman Briggs had kidnapped.

"Found the wood burner," Hayden said more to herself than anyone. The tools were also in the box.

"Searenn said something about etching with fire on wood. More powerful binding spells." She held up the wood pieces. "These have to be destroyed. They are the last thing tethering those women to this world."

"That's it?"

Sylvie handed them to Hayden. "Fire would work, but whatever means you use, they have to be all gone."

"I have an idea," Hayden said as Claudia and Lucia strolled over to join her and Sylvie. The two witches gave cautious nods to the hoodoo woman gone rogue. Rogue to the Amara, anyway.

Setting the tablets down in a secluded area and away from the other people, Hayden backed up several feet and aimed her hands at the wooden prisons. "Let's see what else our new weapon can do."

The pale blue radiance sparkled to life and covered the tablets before they dissolved and sunk into the grass as piles of ash. The rain gentled then, as if sensing its righteous duty, and washed the remaining powder into the earth.

Moonlight outlined two shapes in silver as the spirits formed before Hayden. Ronnie and Chloe were with her again, and for the first time, their faces and eyes bore no signs of stress or sorrow. Finally, the two women were at peace.

"We couldn't leave without taking advantage of our own personal medium," Ronnie said with a grin. It continued to surprise Hayden how much spirits retained of their human personalities. She had a feeling she and Ronnie could have been friends. If things had been different.

"Thank you so much, Hayden. I wish I could give you a hug." Chloe held out transparent hands and shrugged. Hayden had seen all kinds of outfits from her years of helping spirits pass over, but she would always remember the spunky redhead and her polka dot tights.

Hayden shook her head. "I'm just relieved you're both free now. I'll miss seeing you but will sleep better knowing you're in a safe place."

"So will we," Ronnie said on a laugh. "Or whatever form sleep takes where we're going." Her brown eyes grew solemn. "Hayden. Please take a message to my parents. Tell them I love them and will be waiting for them." She winked. "But they better not come anytime soon."

"I will. Of course I will." Hayden firmed her lips and struggled to stop the familiar tickle in her chest that could soon turn to tears. Her spirit friends had seen more than their fair share of anguish, and she wouldn't give them any more to carry with them.

"And my sister." Now Chloe was the one trying not to cry. "She raised me after our parents died. Tell her I was happy and that I had a great...no, I had a *wonderful* life, and she has to promise to have one, too. She deserves to be happy."

Tilting her head and marveling at the human heart's capacity for love, Hayden smiled at the art student whose talented life had been cut short. "I will. On that you have *my* promise."

"Thank you." Chloe let her hands fall to her sides. "Well. I guess that's it. Ready for the next adventure?" she asked Ronnie.

"Yes," the tall brunette said before meeting Hayden's gaze once again and lifting a hand to wave. Her expression was both tranquil and sad. "Goodbye. And thank you." Ronnie blew a kiss as the two spirits faded. "Thank you."

Sniffling and wiping at her eye, Hayden turned to find the others watching her. "They're gone," she said, expelling a bittersweet breath. "They're safe."

Trevor had left the woman with Dare and Willyn and was walking toward Hayden. Without a word of question or sympathy, he wrapped his arms around her and kissed the top of her head.

He continued to hold her when Anna and the others started repairing the divots and gouges in the cemetery lawn. Most of the battle had occurred on the most distant part of the graveyard, but out of respect for the unnamed people who rested here, the coven would do what they could to return the area to normal.

With their magic, the cemetery would be left unscathed.

Finally pulling away, Hayden gave Trevor a grateful smile and asked, "What will you do with her?" She indicated the woman. "Will she remember anything?"

"I'll call Cole and work something out." He put his arm around her waist as they walked, and Hayden basked in the comfort of such a simple yet meaningful gesture. "I think she'll be fine, emotionally. Dare seems to have some sort of power to affect a person's mind?" Trevor's expression was a cross between concern and relief.

"That's right." She squeezed his hip where her hand rested. "Don't worry. Dare will be gentle, and with his help, she'll probably come out of this with very little damage."

Trevor nodded but looked grim. "Good. That only leaves the two bodies and the fact that a slug from my registered weapon is out here somewhere."

"I'll ask Lucia to help with that," Hayden said. "If she can't find it, no one else will."

As if in answer to Trevor's other problem, Sylvie cut across the clearing to intercept them. "I'll take care of them," she said, pointing to the killer's body then R.J.'s. "I still have plenty of debt to repay." She looked to Hayden. "Don't want to break my streak of good choices."

Hayden glanced to Joseph as he moved up behind Sylvie and with all confidence she said, "I don't think you will."

When Sylvie and Joseph left to speak in private, Trevor turned to Hayden. "I need to get the woman somewhere warm and dry. I'll take her and call Cole." He lifted a golden eyebrow. "Do you think Willyn will let me borrow her husband to take care of any lingering memories of this place and what went on?"

"I think she'll insist and will want to come with you." Overcome by shyness and acute insecurity, Hayden bit her bottom lip. "And once you're finished, will I see you again? Now that the killer's been caught?"

He lowered his tawny head to hers and placed the lightest of kisses on her lips. "Just try and stop me."

~

The black satin of Ronja's robes dragged across the dungeon floors as she glided through the underground chambers. The onyx color was a favorite and made her fair skin and golden hair even more becoming, but tonight she didn't wear it for vanity.

Black was the symbol for death and bereavement. Loss and despair. The only appropriate color for the punishment she would receive.

When she reached the far wall, Ronja waved her hand and spoke ancient words to open the charmed entryway. An arched door formed in the stone wall, wavering at the edges, as it was not of this world.

She stepped through and followed rough, stone steps farther down into the earth, into a large room, a pit really, that had been gouged from the rocky Georgian soil. Here was where she came to commune with the greatest power she'd ever known.

Bastraal. The demon who'd granted her immortality over a millennium ago in exchange for her vow. She'd sworn to navigate the human realm until the energies of the universe aligned, and he could take corporeal form.

She'd also agreed to do as he ordered. To make the necessary arrangements for his ascension. Battle his enemies and find him a vessel when the time came.

Three centuries ago she'd done her part and had succeeded in raising the demon from the darkest depths, so he could reign in the southern sunlight. The blame for his defeat and banishment at the hands of the original three witches—those cursed sisters—couldn't be laid at Ronja's feet.

But tonight's failure could be.

Four times she and her Amara had come up against this new coven. *The nine.* And four times they had failed. Ronja ruled with a tight and thorny fist, so if her underlings, the soldiers in her personally chosen army were defeated, then she was defeated.

The painful throb in her chest tonight had alerted her before Scarlett had even returned. By the time her closest female friend, and favorite female lover, had told her of the lost battle, lost spirits, and the coven's new and formidable magic, Ronja had already known she was due a reprimand.

Though Bastraal could love her like his own progeny— as much as any demon *could* love, she supposed—his disappointment was to be avoided. And now, her master was far beyond disappointment.

The connection to the demon had been forged long ago, and as surely as she held his ascension in her hands, he held her life in his.

The primitive structure in the center of the cold, dark room had been made several centuries before. She'd created it with her own hands, inscribing the most powerful of runes. Made of brick, mortar, and other minerals, the chest-level altar was cylindrical and resembled early mosaic styles.

The various crystals, teeth, and pieces of bone gave it charm, she thought, as well as blood magic to strengthen the conduit, the link...the connection to Bastraal.

The lava stones inside were almost as old as Ronja, though not half as ancient as the demon she planned to summon. Though in reality, he had called for her. The pain she'd felt in her chest before had been fleeting, but a message nonetheless.

Now as she laid her hands on the stones and whispered the words of submission, agony that would shred the sanity of a lesser witch rushed up her arms and into her head. The blood in her brain boiled with Bastraal's fury. Her internal organs twisted into tight coils, binding and pulling until she almost begged for death.

When the pain decreased enough for her to think again, Ronja spoke in a broken and ragged voice. "Yes. Yes. *Tilgi meg.* Forgive me." She held on to the stones though they burned her palms and radiated fire into her muscles. "Never again. *Nei, ikke igjen.*"

Her forehead, middle back, and armpits were soaked with sweat by the time Bastraal finally ended the punishment. She panted as she begged again for forgiveness. As she apologized and promised in multiple languages.

Ronja took the torture without complaint, because she knew she deserved it.

She shook her head to keep the perspiration from running into her eyes. She deserved punishment, yes, but so did that hoodoo bitch. The betrayer. The seventh fucking sister.

The prophecy had never been about Beth, that meek little runt. It had always been Sylvie. And wasn't that a rip of the guts?

As Bastraal's grating and angry voice faded from her mind, Ronja let go of the rocks and kneeled. The action wasn't to show reverence, she'd already done that when she'd let her master rape her brain and body with fire. She dropped to the cool, dirt floor, because she was too damn exhausted to stand.

But that never stopped Ronja from doing what had to be done.

Pulling the smart phone from her robe pocket, she paused for a few deep breaths then dialed Dalton Morne, her lawyer and one of the few full-blooded humans whose depravity she admired.

"The recruit is dead, and so is R.J.," she said when he answered. She coughed to clear the rasp from her throat.

"Find me another. Immediately." As her own anger flew through her veins, so did a renewed strength, and an even firmer resolve to reap vengeance on Anna and her bastardized band of women. They found victory in the rescue of a few pathetic ghosts?

Then Ronja would just have to give them a greater challenge. "No," she barked. "Bring me as many as you can find. Searenn will take the ones you deem worthy and train them."

She smiled in the dank darkness of the pit. "We'll feed this entire wretched city to the demons. Bastraal will be so full from his meals he'll vomit out their souls."

"Find me more. Rapists. Murderers. We'll fill them with strength and send them out." She laughed at the awful imagery her twisted mind had conjured. "Do it, Dalton. Do it now."

Tossing her phone to the ground and curling her fingers into the soil, Ronja sat in the underground blackness. Reeking of her own charred flesh, she laughed. Laughed like the mad, vengeful witch that she was.

~

Sylvie turned out to be as valuable as any spy who'd switched sides. The more she'd spilled about the Amara's camp, the faster she spoke and the lighter the look on her face.

But when they'd arrived at the yellow house, there'd been a very tense moment as Joseph's parents walked out to take a look at the daughter of Claire's childhood friend.

The now fully grown woman who'd been on the wrong side of right and wrong for years and had captured Joseph's attention. Maybe more.

When Joseph pulled Sylvie forward to introduce her to his parents, Claire's lips trembled before she said, "You look like your mother."

The two women hugged, both remembering Regina Lee and how she'd touched their lives.

"Come have some tea," Claire said, cupping Sylvie's chin, "and I'll tell you some stories about her." Then she smiled a real smile. "Stories your grandmother never knew."

The decision had been made for Sylvie to stay on the mainland until her grandmother could be notified. Joseph had stayed with her. Neither of the hoodoo women would be safe now that Sylvie had betrayed the Amara.

Relocation was imperative, and Anna would help. The coven's own witness protection program.

Now Hayden stared into the fireplace of the grand hall, comforted by the snaps and crackles as much as the warmth. A number of problems had been dealt with tonight, yet plenty still remained.

Savannah was being infiltrated by demons, and most people weren't built to handle the monsters. A frozen snake crawled down her back as she remembered the flickering faces at the night club. How many more were out there, and would that number continue to grow?

"Here you go," Shauni said, suddenly at Hayden's side with a tall coffee mug in her hand. The hot drink had an exotic scent and was garnished with sliced carrot. "I made you some canjee." The raven-haired woman gave a half-smile. "Seemed appropriate."

"You remembered," Hayden said, flashing back to the first night in the yellow house when she'd met Shauni and the other women. "I haven't had this since I came to the island."

Shauni tugged gently on Hayden's still damp hair. "I know, but I think you've earned it." Then she whispered in a theatrical voice. "Demon-ass-kicker-extraordinaire." She laughed. "Or so I'm told."

"Yeah. About that," Paige said, bounding down the wide staircase to join them. She stopped to turn on a lamp. "Everybody around here always wants to be in the dark," she grumbled before getting back to her original complaint. "How is it that our very first battle with the underworld gets to be led by our mild-mannered, no offense, yoga-bending, Zen girl?"

"Not to worry, Paige," Hayden said tilting her head and lifting her eyebrows. "You're the one who theorized that every challenge will be harder than the last. Maybe you'll get lucky and be number nine."

Nodding and wiping the shag of white-blonde hair from her eyes, the ex-soldier smiled and said, "There is that. Maybe I'll get the big guy himself." Then she rubbed her arm. "Wonder if he'll be made of acid like his brethren."

"Don't remind me," Claudia said. Now she and the rest of the crew were filing in. "Let me tell you those things hurt like hell, and forget our special blue firepower when they've got you locked in their clutches." She shivered. "I don't think I even knew my own name. I just wanted the pain to stop."

She sent a soft grateful glance to Willyn. "Too bad we can't clone you, sunshine."

Dare brushed Willyn's blonde hair aside and kissed her cheek. "Now there's an idea," he said with a lecherous grin.

"Uh." Willyn tried to sound affronted, but the gleam in her eye gave her away.

Anna was in her favorite royal blue robe, and like Hayden

and the others who'd been fighting in the rain, her long sable hair wasn't quite dry. She held a short glass with some dark-colored liquor on ice. "At least we have a full roster on the Amara now," she said, lifting the tumbler. "Thanks to Sylvie the turncoat."

"You don't sound very happy about that," Lucia said, her long legs stretched across the green sofa.

Anna swirled the liquor in her hand. "I'm getting used to it, but there won't be anywhere she can hide if she turns on Joseph."

"I don't think she will," Viv put in. She and Nick had been fairly quiet. The news of R.J.'s death had been unexpected, and while they were glad to have Jen's murderer punished, the emotional news still churned them up inside. "I think she's falling for our Joseph. Maybe she already has." Nick took her hand, and Viv leaned into him.

"Do you think Joseph loves her?" Kylie asked, crowding close to the fire with Hayden and Shauni.

Anna sighed. "I asked him that. He said he cares for her but is still all jumbled up about everything. I don't think he'll be going with her and Mrs. Lee, but I expect he'll visit occasionally. Or at least keep in touch." She tossed back her drink. "They both want to let things settle for now, and Sylvie has a conscience that needs a good scrubbing."

"At least she's making wise decisions," Hayden said. "The old Sylvie would have snatched Joseph right up and damn the consequences or damages."

Anna smiled. "You're a softie."

Sipping her canjee and shrugging, Hayden leaned against the side of the hearth. "Nah, just a sucker for lost causes."

Hoisting her glass, Anna toasted, "Here's to second chances." Then she noticed the dry ice. "Oh. I'm out." She swept across the room like the lady of the manor to a liquor cabinet.

Hayden knew Anna still worried about Joseph's relationship

with Sylvie, but all any of them could do was wait and see.

A knock on the front door had a few glances shooting toward the parlor, but the sound made Hayden's heart bang against her ribcage. "That should be Trevor," she said, unsure why her nerves tingled and her breaths came in short, quick draws.

"Girl, you've got it bad," Shauni said, winking at Hayden before she sauntered over to Michael. The tall, blonde vet was kneeling to pet Shauni's dog, Skid. "And I should know," the black-haired witch called over her shoulder.

When she got to her boyfriend, Shauni leaned to whisper in his ear before straightening again and giving the fakest imitation of a yawn Hayden had ever seen. "I think we're turning in."

Michael stood, pushing his glasses up firmly before coughing and saying, "Yeah. Early day tomorrow." He grinned and ran to catch up with Shauni.

"Then don't keep each other up too late," Claudia called after them with a Cheshire grin.

"Jealous much?" Paige said, also standing to head up to bed. "I know I am. Hayden's caught herself one fine looking piece of..."

"Paige!" Claudia said, but laughed just the same.

"Hey, I said I'm not interested in romance." Paige lifted her hands as if she really shouldn't have to explain such things. "One has nothing to do with the other."

Then she held up a high-five for Hayden as she passed. "Good job, Swami. Looks like you were a warrior all along."

Hayden slapped the waiting palm. Her face felt warm and glowed from the praise.

"But don't think that gets you out of morning sessions," the sparring instructor for the coven said. "Well, maybe just tomorrow." Paige passed Trevor as he came from the foyer, and turned right after to make a butt-grabbing sign to Hayden.

"And here I was thinking I was done protecting you," Hayden

told Trevor as she waved off her friend and laughed.

"Huh?" he asked, frowning.

"Never mind. I'm glad you could make it back..." Her words were cut in half when Trevor scooped her up and pressed his mouth to hers.

By the time he set her down, her head was spinning and they were alone in the huge room.

"Me, too," he said, escorting her closer to the fireplace. "Your hair's still damp. You'll get cold."

"Oh, boy." She ran her fingers through her hair to test the level of dryness. "You know, I have managed to make it twenty-seven years without your supervision." She quirked her mouth to one side. "Are you always going to be bossy?"

He furrowed his forehead. "Not exactly. Guess I still have too many protective urges where you're concerned." He touched her hair to see for himself. "I'll work on it, but don't look for me to be a completely hands-off kind of boyfriend."

"Boyfriend?" Terrified elation bubbled in her chest. "Were you going to consult me on this decision?"

He lifted one muscular shoulder. "Like my grandfather always said, sometimes you need to go around a problem." He kept rubbing her hair as if mesmerized. "Especially when it's important."

Hayden's lungs absolutely stopped pumping. "Is this?" she asked in a low, hesitant voice. "Important?"

He lowered his head so that warm, minty breath brushed her lips when he said, "Yes. You are." Then kissed her long and deep. The fire flamed higher, but the blazing logs couldn't compare to Trevor's heat.

His hands circled her waist, burning through her shirt, straight to her skin. And she didn't care about wet hair anymore, or whether or not her domineering *boyfriend* wanted her to warm up. He provided all the warmth she could ever need.

When she was on her tiptoes and pressed too firmly against him for modesty, Hayden eased back and put a hand on his chest. "You sleeping on the couch tonight?"

His possessive growl was answer enough.

"Good," she said, and took his hand to pull him with her as she moved.

Even with the slight distance between them, Trevor could still smell orange blossoms. He would have to make sure Hayden never wore anything else. He'd buy out the company who made the body-spritzer stuff if he had to.

No, he wouldn't be too demanding of the sweet, golden-eyed woman who'd stolen his heart, but a few things were non-negotiable.

He let her lead him up to her bedroom, the girliest place in the world, all pink and creamy. He'd never tell a soul that he actually kind of liked it. Then she left him to turn on a small, discreet lamp.

Her cat sat still as a statue in the middle of the bed. Two giant yellow eyes amidst a patchwork of black and gold. The feline cooed at him like a dove and disappeared under the bed.

Hayden laughed as she took both of his hands to pull him toward the bed. "You're back on Daisy's short list. She's a sweet girl, but has a suspicious nature."

He laughed low. "A cat after my own heart."

"I'm just glad *I'm* not a suspect anymore," Hayden told him, lifting his shirt over his head without giving him much of a choice. Not that he minded. "You were a pretty unlikable guy when you thought I was a con."

Trevor returned the favor by taking off her shirt and leaving her in a lacy bra. He loved her lingerie.

"Yeah, well, I didn't like you much either." He nipped her bottom lip and ran his palms down her arms. "When I thought you were a con."

"Now you know better." She unsnapped his pants, and

Trevor's stomach clenched from the promised pleasure of her touch. She kissed the hollow over his collar bone and laughed. "I still can't believe I'm with a cop."

Picking her up and carrying her to the bed, Trevor tossed her down and removed the pajama bottoms in one quick tug. As she lay there in all her splendor, Trevor gave silent thanks to his grandfather. *Going around.*

And then to Cole, who'd brought this irritating and amazing woman into Trevor's life. A life he hadn't even realized was missing something. Something soft and sweet, with caramel hair and silky skin.

Oh, and the ability to send blue light out of her hands to blow up demons. There was that.

"And I can't believe I'm with a..." Trevor stopped and faked a confused look. "Where do I even begin?"

Gazing up into piercing blue eyes, Hayden marveled at her luck. She would never have expected the man of her dreams to come with a badge, a gun, and an authoritarian attitude.

But the strong, stubble-roughened jaw, and abs she couldn't keep her hands off of? All in all, they helped make Detective Trevor Roch a pretty sweet deal.

Then there was the way he looked at her, with passion, admiration, and intrigue. She saw all these things in his eyes, but when his gaze went all dreamy, when he focused on nothing else but her, like he was right now?

That's when she saw deeper. That's when she saw beyond the blue.

"You know," she said with a hitch in her voice. "I think I'm almost ready to let you fall in love with me."

Trevor covered her body with his, one finger running up under her chin then down the side of her cheek. "Do I seem like the kind of man who waits for permission?" He took her mouth swiftly and thoroughly to make his point.

Hayden sighed inside. She didn't need a man to stand for

her or to guard her from the evil in the world, but it was a really nice feeling to have one do it anyway.

Trevor lifted his head and put his hand in the juncture of his shoulder and neck. He kneaded his muscle and grimaced. "You know. All of this has been stressful. I think what I really need right now is some yoga."

Hayden drew back, surprised. "You want to do yoga? Now?"

He grinned and put his finger to her lips. "I didn't say I wanted to bend over backwards." He circled the same finger around her belly button. "But I wouldn't mind watching."

A hot ribbon of lust curled in Hayden's lower belly. She used yoga for different reasons, but this was a brand new motivation.

When Trevor's rough jaw scraped her neck, his tongue following after, Hayden lifted her hips involuntarily. She was done in when his hand slipped down her thigh.

"You know the one about the tree?" he asked. "When you lift your arms up and bend a knee?" Her big, tough detective kissed her soundly and grinned. "That one's my favorite."

Suza Kates writes both paranormal romance and romantic suspense. She lives in Savannah, Georgia with her family and three ridiculously spoiled cats.

For more on Suza and her books visit

www.suzakates.com